LARRY BOND'S

FIRST TEAM

LARRY BOND'S

FIRST TEAM

LARRY BOND AND JIM DEFELICE

A TOM DOHERTY ASSOCIATES BOOK

NEW YORK

LARRY BOND'S FIRST TEAM

Copyright © 2004 by Larry Bond and Jim DeFelice

This book is printed on acid-free paper.

A Forge Book
Published by Tom Doherty Associates, LLC
175 Fifth Avenue
New York, NY 10010

www.tor.com

Forge® is a registered trademark of Tom Doherty Associates, LLC.

Library of Congress Cataloging-in-Publication Data

Bond, Larry.
    Larry Bond's First team / Larry Bond and Jim DeFelice.—1st ed.
        p. cm.
    "A Tom Doherty Associates book."
    ISBN 0-765-30711-1 (alk. paper)
    EAN 978-0765-30711-8
    1. Radioactive wastes—Transportation—Fiction. 2. Terrorism—Prevention—Fiction. 3. Intelligence officers—Fiction. 4. Military intelligence—Fiction. 5. Honolulu (Hawaii)—Fiction. I. Title: First team. II. DeFelice, James. III. Title.

    PS3552.O59725F57 2004
    813'.54—dc22

                                                        2004040356

First Edition: May 2004

Printed in the United States of America

0 9 8 7 6 5 4 3 2 1

To those who go into darkness to keep us safe

AUTHORS' NOTE

The Team—and the Joint Services Special Demands Project Office—is an entirely fictional creation. While Special Forces units and the CIA work together on a variety of unique and difficult missions, their operations are conducted within a framework and chain of command that provide for extensive review of their actions. In no case do real-life personnel or their units operate beyond the limits of U.S. law. Nor would such operations be authorized or condoned by counsel in the employ of the president of the United States, much less the president himself.

The nuclear waste, storage, and dumping facilities, transportation arrangements, and processing operation described in this book are fiction. The threat, however, is not.

ACT I

So from that spring whence comfort seemed to come,
Discomfort swells.

—Shakespeare, *Macbeth*, 1.2.27–8

1

OVER CHECHNYA

The wind blew without mercy. The man preparing to enter it was a man of great faith, but at twenty thousand feet in the pitch-black night, even faith had its limits.

Samman Bin Saqr took a breath, then uttered a prayer of praise and trust he had learned as a boy. He edged his feet forward, poised at the lip of the apparatus that would help free him from the aircraft's slipstream. The plane held to its course, guided by the hand of an automated pilot, which was also being tested on this flight. The copilot—human—called from the seat a few feet away that they were approaching the target area.

Samman Bin Saqr went by many names in the West. To some, he was Ibn Yaman, the mastermind of the attack on the British embassy in Beijing. To others, he was Umar Umar, who had shown the Australians that Sydney was not immune to suicide attacks. To the Americans, he was either Abu Akil, whose plot to blow up Independence Hall in Philadelphia had been foiled only by a dead car battery the morning of the planned attack, or Kalil Kadir Hassan, whose genius had turned an IRS tax center in Massachusetts into a fireball.

The latest of those attacks, the one that had consumed the devil's tax collectors, had occurred five years before. Because he had not struck since then, Samman Bin Saqr was presumed by many to be dead, or worse, to have lost his nerve. But in fact he had spent the entire time planning and building his next operation.

The idea for it had come to him one evening in Karachi, Pakistan, where he had gone to meet some associates in the Bin Laden group to discuss funding. He happened to pick up a Western magazine and saw a picture of Honolulu. And from that moment, he knew what he would do.

It was a momentous decision. It had stretched his skills beyond belief. It meant locating in a place—Chechnya—he was unfamiliar with. It meant learning a great deal about a wide range of subjects and risking his life in ways the infidels could never imagine.

But more importantly, it meant doing nothing against the enemies of his faith for five long years. Samman Bin Saqr was a man of belief whose whole life had consisted of sacrifice, but even he was not immune to the temptations of glory. It had proven impossible at first to obtain the materials he wanted, and several times he had nearly changed direction to execute a lesser plan.

But he had not. Obstacle after obstacle had been pushed away. Allah had overseen and blessed all, in the end supplying the most coveted ingredients through the greed of the French and the idiocy of the Russians.

After five years of labor, Samman Bin Saqr was nearly ready. But as the project drew close to fruition, he had begun to consider its consequences on a deeper level. From the start, the plan had called for his demise; it seemed fitting and fair that he should reach paradise as a reward for his struggles. But his death would necessarily bring the end of his organization and the scattering of its abilities.

Was he not being selfish, he wondered, to choose this moment to die?

To reach heaven would truly be wonderful—yet even he realized that his blow would not end the struggle with the West. On the contrary, as Bin Laden himself had taught, it would only provoke them. It would take many such provocations until the final war began; at that point, and at that point only, would Allah assure victory. Did Samman Bin Saqr, whose plan would prove his greatness as an agent of the true Lord, not have a duty to see the battle further?

After much prayer and thought, he had realized that the answer was yes. And after further consideration, work, and prayer, a solution had been found. He had now only to test it.

Assuming that he could overcome his fear. Samman Bin Saqr had jumped from airplanes five times before, but never from this height in the darkness of the night. Nor had he had to pass through such a tricky and potentially deadly slipstream.

His engineers had solved the problem of the howling, wrathful wind by building what amounted to an extendible tube or funnel that could expel him past the fuselage. It had been tested twice, and it worked, but Samman Bin Saqr reserved the final test to himself—it was necessary, he felt, so that he would not be surprised when the time came.

He felt the plane vibrating, then saw his hand shake. To calm himself, he thought of his place in paradise.

Then, still waiting for his copilot to give the signal, he pictured the American paradise covered with radioactive dust, a ghost town filled with the walking corpses, rendered unusable and unlivable for centuries to come. He heard the cries of his enemies, felt their anguish, and was at peace.

"Now," said the copilot.

In the hushed howl as the wind kicked through the apparatus, the word sounded as if it came from God Himself. Samman Bin Saqr pushed the lever and left the plane, plunging through the whirling vortex into the dark night.

2

KYRGYZSTAN

 Bob Ferguson liked to think of himself as a reasonable man, so when the two rather large fellows confronted him in the restroom of the Samovar Cafe, he smiled benignly and asked in Russian what they wanted. When the man on the left called him a dirty foreigner, Ferguson wholeheartedly agreed—he hadn't, after all, had a chance to shower for nearly forty-eight hours. And when the one on the right asked how much money he had, the American answered truthfully, "not much."

But when the second man took a knife from his pocket and slashed the air in front of him, Ferguson sighed and started to reach into his pocket. As he did so, however, the first lurched toward him, and Ferguson found it expedient to duck forward, at the same time swinging his hand into the man's windpipe so sharply that he cracked the man's Adam's apple with the flat part of his palm. The momentum added speed to his right leg as it swept up and landed in the other man's groin.

"How much money do you want?" Ferguson asked, as the men rolled on the floor.

The man he'd kicked in the groin blubbered something in what was probably Kirghiz, the native language.

"Sorry, didn't catch that," said Ferguson. He bent and propped the man up against the wall—probably a little too quickly, as the man's skull smacked against the wall, knocking him unconscious. Ferguson decided whatever he'd been saying wasn't particularly important and let him slump to the floor next to his dozing partner.

"I admire people who can fall asleep anywhere," said Ferguson. He stepped over to the sink, washing his hands, then running them through his hair, which had a tendency to get mussed up when he did a snap kick. Satisfied that he was looking his best, Ferguson stepped over the local toughs and left the restroom, walking up the steps and through the long narrow hallway to the cafe's dining room.

Punctuality was not highly prized in Kyrgyzstan, but as he'd been waiting for nearly two hours, Ferguson decided that the man he'd come to meet probably wasn't going to show at all. And so, rather than returning to his table, he merely waved at the proprietor and slid a few bills out on the counter to pay his tab. Besides a few son for his tea, Ferguson left fifty dollars euro to cover the mess in the restroom.

A dark, inky haze hung over the street, spread by the incinerator smokestacks that clustered around the city like trees the developers had forgotten to clear away. Tall and thin, built of bricks that were once bright yellow but were now black almost to the bottom, the brick forest vented the smoke from the region's only moneymaking industry—waste disposal. The furnaces beneath the stacks handled refuse from all over Europe; encouraged by the former Soviet Republic's lax environmental standards and even laxer bureaucracy, the waste industry had made this corner of the landlocked country a cosmopolitan capital of refuse. The countryside around it was a repository for everything from onion skins and spoiled lettuce to spent nuclear waste. Located twenty miles south of Talas near a new railroad spur, the city had been a ramshackle collection of one-story hovels and played-out mine shafts ten years before. Now it boasted wide, macadam streets and new town houses, three movie theaters and a Western-style grocery that outshone anything in Bishkek, the capital far to the northeast.

For many of the inhabitants the fine layer of soot that covered everything was a small price to pay for relief from grinding poverty; others had never known the city without it. Anything that could be burned was burned here, and many things that couldn't be burned often found their way to the furnaces as well. The waste dumps were located on the other side of the railroad spur beyond the incinerator forest. The largest dumps were for ash and chemical refuse, but there were smaller, deeper facilities for more toxic materials as well. On a good day, the wind slashed through the sweet, terrible odor, leaving the city with a merely nauseous smell; on bad days, it formed an impenetrable barrier to the outside world.

Today was a good day. Ferguson jabbed his hands into his pockets, practically bouncing as he walked briskly past the local police station, head tilted slightly as if to increase his forward momentum. Though dressed in clothes almost identical to what the two thugs he'd met in the restroom were wearing—dirty black jeans, a plain brown shirt over two thick T's, a black leather jacket—there was no question that he was a foreigner, and most of the natives who saw him would undoubtedly think he was some sort of spy—CIA, probably, because that's what every foreigner was considered in Kyrgyzstan. Russians from Moscow, French nuclear waste engineers, the Spanish interior commissioner who had concluded a deal just yesterday to bury waste near here—all were perceived to be spies in the employ of the American Central Intelligence Agency. Most visitors welcomed this perception, if for no other reason that spying was a considerably more glamorous profession than garbage, though at their heart their concerns were exactly the same.

It happened that Ferguson—or Ferg as he was more often called—was in fact in the employ of the CIA, though in the Agency's parlance he was an operations "officer" as opposed to an agent, "agent" generally meaning someone of foreign extraction persuaded to supply information. Ferguson had a cover—he was in the country as the American representative of a small firm that manufactured gas nozzles used in waste combustion apparatus. The CIA officer was so thoroughly "covered" that he actually was authorized to make a sale on behalf of the firm, though if it came to that he would not be entitled to the sizable commission—60 percent—independent sales representatives for the company normally took.

Ferguson turned the corner to Yeliseev Street, making his way to the office of the man he had come to the city to meet, Alex Sheremetev. His appearance there would undoubtedly throw the eminently corruptible official into something approaching a panic. But in Ferg's view panic was a healthy thing; he quickened his pace as he turned the corner and crossed the dusty street, ducking between ten-year-old Ladas and even more ancient Hondas, which here were considered symbols of wealth.

Sheremetev—though Russian, he was no relation to the family that gave Moscow its famous garden—worked on the second floor of the Municipal Order Building #2. In a cramped room overlooking a dusty alley, Sheremetev processed permits for a number of waste projects. One in particular interested Ferguson—a French-Russian project to contain and dispose of experimental nuclear reactors built in Russia during the 1980s. Spent fuel, reactor rods, and assorted machinery from the devices were processed at a site south of Buzuluk on the Samara River. From there, special casks of the material were shipped by train in special cars south to Kazakhstan and then into Kyrgyzstan, where they were buried in a deep-earth facility. The material was transported under heavy guard and carefully accounted for. But two months before, the CIA had detected a discrepancy between the radiation count taken by an American monitoring station near the Kazakhstan border and the one officially recorded at the waste facility.

Ferguson had been sent to Kyrgyzstan to account for the discrepancy by the Joint Services Special Demands Project Office—a CIA–Special Forces unit that answered directly and only to the deputy director of operations at the CIA. Generally referred to either as the "First Team" or simply "the Team," Ferguson worked with a Joint Special Operations Forces (SOF) unit headed by Colonel Charles Van Buren, who not only had a battalion of Army Special Forces soldiers under his command but controlled a range of resources to support them as well. The Team had been created to address unconventional threats in an unconventional way, without interference from the bureaucracy of either the intelligence or military establishments. The arrangement made Ferguson and the SF troopers who worked with him essentially free agents, and Ferg was a free agent par excellence.

Ferguson had never been in the municipal building before, but he had studied its floor plan earlier, thus knew to go in through the side entrance, avoiding the security officer in the lobby. A quick turn to the left, a jog up the steps, and the caffeine rush from all the tea he'd drunk earlier was almost entirely dissipated.

Sheremetev's secretary momentarily revived it, her short skirt riding up on her hips as she hunched over a filing cabinet behind the desk. She wore a tight sweater despite the fact that it was spring and comparatively warm outside; Ferguson smiled at the fit, then asked in Kirghiz for her boss.

The secretary frowned and replied in Russian that he wasn't there. Ferguson apologized for his accent, then asked where she thought he might be. She said in Kirghiz that she had no idea, and repeated the information in Russian.

Under other circumstances, Ferguson might have lingered a bit to refine his accent and admire the scenery, but he knew that the two SF soldiers who comprised his trail team were probably getting antsy. So he left a business card and brochure on the desk and trudged back down the steps, carrying the slight glow a pair of smooth legs always left him with.

Out on the street, a black Lada whipped toward him. Ferg kept one eye on it as it barreled past, noting that there were three men crammed into the backseat. He resisted the impulse to throw himself to the ground; when the back of his head wasn't ripped by bullets, he congratulated himself on his good judgment and told himself that he was being much too paranoid. Continuing down the block, Ferg smiled at an old lady pulling a two-wheeled folding shopping cart, then cut through the gas station—a special deal on A92 petrol today and every day—turning down a street lined with apartment houses that looked as if they'd been built by Stalin in the fifties, though in fact they were only a year old. Beyond the apartments were industrial warehouses waiting to be demolished for more housing. Sheremetev's apartment was on the other side of the buildings in a row of town houses that marked the outskirts of the affluent neighborhood.

Three boys were playing soccer in a field near the end of the block. The ball bounded away and rolled toward him; Ferguson ran to it, dribbling back and forth, then passing off to one of the kids on the left. The boy fumbled badly, sliding as he went to kick it; his friends started to goad him. Always one for the underdog, Ferguson swept back and dribbled the loose ball toward the goal, marked by upside-down water buckets. The others gave chase belatedly. He bounded back and took them on, ducking left and right, then launching a bullet that smacked one of the buckets so hard it left a dent. Laughing, he caught the ball on the rebound and headed it skyward.

The kids started jabbering in Kirghiz that he should play. Ferguson laughed and told them thanks, eying the black Lada moving slowly along the nearby road. It looked exactly like the car he'd seen earlier—but then that might be said of any black Lada, which came in dozens of varieties and had been made for decades.

Ferg reached into his pocket for a few coins, tossing them to the kids. Then he launched the ball in the direction opposite to the vehicle. Two men were just getting out; Ferguson made like he was running with the boys after the ball before veering off to the left, crossing the road, and running toward a pair of squat factory-type buildings. He bolted over the chain-link fence, hustling to the right and back around, running the whole way though he didn't think the men in the car had given chase.

It took a good ten minutes to work his way back around to the street where Sheremetev lived, and he waited another ten minutes against the alley of a garage to see if the Lada reappeared. Finally, he went to Sheremetev's door, knocking discreetly at first, then pounding to make sure he was heard. When no one answered, Ferg decided to play tourist—he reached into the pocket of his coat and took out a set of picklocks so he could sightsee inside.

The dead bolt at the front was about as secure as any tumbler lock in the West, which meant it took him nearly five seconds to open.

"Sheremetev," said Ferguson, closing the door behind him. "Yo!"

Middle-class opulence in Kyrgyzstan was still a work in progress and, like most other city residents, Sheremetev hadn't quite gotten the hang of it. His front room looked like a combination bedroom, den, and storage area. A small TV sat on a pile of books perched between two bookcases on the right. A daybed with tangled sheets sat opposite it. There were some paintings on the wall—Kandinsky as drawn by a five-year-old. Tall piles of newspapers and magazines sat against the rear wall; one of them had a lamp on it.

Ferguson walked toward the open doorway at the back, stepping over a pair of pajama bottoms on the floor.

The next room was a kitchen. Sheremetev sat with his back to him, head slumping over his chest as if he were dozing.

"What the hell, Sheremetev, sleeping off a drunk?" said Ferguson, stepping into the room.

It was only then he realized there was a pool of blood on the floor. Sheremetev had been shot once in the back of the head, slightly off center.

"Shit," said Ferguson.

He might have said more but there was a knock on the door.

Hugh Conners and Stephen Rankin sat in the front seat of the van, Conners sipping tea from his thermos and Rankin sliding his thumb obsessively back and forth against the trigger housing of his Uzi pistol. They'd lost track of the CIA officer after he started playing with the kids and had circled around to Sheremetev's apartment just in time to see a black Vax-21063 Zhighuli—better known as a Lada— pull up in front. Two men had gotten out and gone to the front door.

"Got a walkie-talkie," said Rankin, pointing out the man waiting at the front door. "Think they're cops or mafiya?"

Before Conners could answer, the man at the door knocked, then stepped back and drew a Makarova from a holster beneath his coat. Then he shot through the lock and rammed inside the apartment.

"Shit," said Rankin.

Conners grabbed him before he could jump out.

"He's out already," said Conners, pointing at the small LED screen propped on the transmission hump. "Relax."

Conners flicked the key and started the truck.

"Siren," said Rankin.

"Yup," said Conners.

"He fucking likes to cut it close."

"That he does."

As the siren grew louder, Conners reached down next to the seat and located his Beretta. He was just about to suggest they get out and take a look when something in the mirror caught his eye. In the next moment the back of the truck flew open.

"About fuckin' time," said Rankin.

"Relax, Skip," Ferguson told him, closing the door behind him and coming forward in the open van. "Dad, get us the hell out of here."

"Good idea," said Conners, putting the car in gear. He saw a flashing light behind him as he pulled out; one of the men from the Lada jumped into the roadway, his hand out to halt him.

Conners stomped on the gas pedal. The man in the road was obviously rather thickheaded, for he blinked several times before ducking off to the side, barely missing getting run over. Conners wheeled the van down a narrow street to the left, then screeched his wheels on the hard pavement of the main drag. There was a knot of traffic ahead, so he slapped the van down a side street, taking out a clothesline but emerging on the cross street otherwise intact. He took a right and managed to get two more blocks before running into a dead end and having to turn around.

"We're going back the way we came," Ferguson told him calmly as he turned.

"That'll confuse the shit out of them," said Rankin.

"Let's just drive to the Fiat," said Ferguson.

"You really think that's necessary?" said Rankin. He hated the little car.

"Yeah."

"Cops," said Conners, as a car with the light and siren passed on the street. Its driver immediately hit the brakes and pulled into a 180, slamming against a car that had been following.

"Guess you're right," said Conners. He started to turn down the next block, then saw that there was an intersection with a traffic light ahead; he feinted right, then went straight through, barely missing two cars in the intersection.

"They're coming for us. Gonna have to clip 'em," said Rankin, looking back.

"Hate to do that," said Ferguson.

"Gonna have to."

"We won't make the Fiat, Ferg," said Conners.

"All right, the dump then," Ferguson said.

"Place smells like hell," said Conners.

"The rest of the town doesn't?"

They took a corner a little too tightly, making one of the leaning telephone poles lean a little farther. Conners pushed the van left down a long dirt road, dust whipping behind them. The entrance to one of the waste areas was ahead, but they'd noticed yesterday that there was no fence and no attendants farther down the road. Inside the waste area they took a sharp turn past a stack of boulders, zigzagging down a hill constructed of treated ash from the furnaces. The police siren had begun to fade, though all three men assumed it was still in pursuit.

The road led down to the main area of the dump, where a pair of forklifts were heaving masses of compacted waste from one pile to another. Behind them, smoke curled from a ribbon of smoldering flames. A large orange dump truck blocked their path, spreading ash either to extend the road or smother the fire.

"This is where we get out," said Ferguson, at the back door.

Conners grabbed his gun and the ruck holding their small laptop computer as Rankin and Ferg jumped out the other side with their own gear. Someone shouted something, but they didn't stop to listen, running toward the front of the dump truck. Conners, called "Dad" because at thirty-five he was the oldest of the group, fell in at the tail end of the formation as they climbed across a pile of trash. His stomach turned over three or four times with the stench before they reached the far side.

A flock of birds—they looked like vultures, only uglier—swirled a few feet over the surface. Garbage stretched halfway up the ravine on the left, but to the right was an administrative building and then an abandoned factory shed, which was where they had put their second hideaway vehicle, a 1986 Honda Accord.

A large excavator threw its claw around the base of the refuse heap so close that Conners ducked to the right. He immediately lost his balance, tumbling into the decomposed household waste. Choking, he felt himself lifted up and for a moment thought the claw had him—but it was only Ferguson, pulling him from the muck.

"Not the time for a swim." The CIA officer pushed him upright, steering toward the administration building.

Two workers stopped and stared at them as they ran. Undoubtedly others had noticed them—it was, after all, the middle of the day, and they didn't particularly look like they belonged. But no one bothered them, either out of sheer surprise or because Rankin and Conners both had their guns in their hands.

The shed had looked abandoned yesterday, but that was because they had come there early in the morning. Now it was late afternoon, and a crowd of men had gathered there to drink. Three or four men were leaning against the Honda, which was parked at the front of the shed.

As Rankin raised his gun to threaten them, Ferguson grabbed his arm.

"Not necessary," he said.

The CIA officer had a wad of twenty-dollar bills in his other hand. With a flick of his wrist the money scattered across the gravel; by the time the first bill had been recovered, Conners was pulling open the door on the driver's side of the car.

"No offense, Dad, but I'll drive," said Ferguson, already behind the wheel. "You already raised our insurance premium far enough today."

3

Six hours and several long showers later, Ferg and the two Special Forces soldiers sat down in a hotel room in Talas, trying to figure out who had killed Sheremetev. They were examining the digital photos Ferg had taken, which he'd loaded onto their laptop. Copies had already been uploaded to the CIA for analysis.

"Professional job," said Rankin, who had two towels on his head and a third around his shoulders. He'd stayed in the hot shower long enough for his toes to wrinkle. "Nothing to do with us."

"Awful convenient timing," said Ferguson.

"Guy was taking all sorts of bribes for signing his papers," said Rankin. "Maybe he asked for too much. Boof, they take him out."

"Boof, Skip?" Ferguson smirked. Rankin had worked with him on an assignment in Russia two months before. Ferguson had specifically asked for the weapons sergeant to be assigned to him on the mission, but Rankin nonetheless tended to irritate him. He was a middle linebacker type; Ferg had played quarterback in prep school and college. Defense and offense rarely mixed well.

"You don't know boof?" said Rankin. "I thought that was one of those Harvard words."

"Fergie graduated Yale," said Conners. "Bitter enemies."

"Summa cum laude," said Ferguson.

"What's that mean?" said Rankin.

"He screwed everybody in sight," said Conners.

"Just the girls and the sheep," said Ferguson.

There was a knock on the door. Ferguson took his P7 H&K pistol out and asked in Kirghiz what they wanted.

"Shit, don't screw with me. I'm paranoid as it is," said the man outside in English.

The others laughed. Ferg swung open the door and pulled Jack "Guns" Young inside the room. A Marine who'd been recruited by Ferguson primarily for his language skills, Guns had come to Joint Demands via Marine Force Recon. Though the unit was thought of by many as the Marine equivalent of Special Forces, its emphasis was actually very different; Recon lacked such traditional Army SF missions as foreign internal defense and wasn't a career specialty like SF was in the Army. He felt a bit out of synch with the others, who bore a typical Army prejudice toward members of the more enlightened military brotherhood—namely, the Corps.

Guns carried two large canvas bags, which contained bread, several large paper-wrapped parcels, a jug of water, and two bottles of vodka.

"Party time," said Rankin, handing the liquor to Conners.

"How'd we do, Guns?" Ferguson asked.

Guns—Young was a Marine sergeant who had achieved the E-7 rank, commonly known as "gunnery sergeant," hence the nickname—shrugged. His accent might be perfect in five languages, but he wasn't particularly adept at bargaining or currency conversion, and only the inherent honesty of the Kyrgyz shopkeepers had kept him from getting ripped off too badly.

The room rapidly filled up with the scent of the food. Ferg took a hunk of the *lipioshka*, a thick, unleavened bread that tasted a little like Italian peasant bread left in a cupboard with turnips for a few days. He ripped open one of the parcels, which contained charcoaled mutton, called *shahlyk*, and made himself a sandwich.

"*Plov*," said Rankin, scooping up a bunch of the fried rice mixture with his bread. "Good for what ails you."

"Yeah, if what ails you is your colon," said Ferg.

"What's this?" asked Conners, ripping open the last parcel. "Some sort of mcat?"

It looked like a stew with a thick sauce. Guns told him the word quickly. Conners picked up a piece and plopped it in his mouth. "What's that in English?" he asked.

"Horse meat," said Guns, and Conners promptly spit it back into the pile.

"Horse is good for you," Ferguson told Conners. "Plenty of protein."

"You eat it then."

Ferg got up and opened one of the vodka bottles. There were no glasses; he took a long pull, then set the bottle down. "How'd it look outside?" he asked Guns.

"Same as always." The Marine had stayed behind in Talas the last two days, arranging for transport and poking around. He'd also met with a local police official who was on the CIA payroll, though there was some question as to the value of his information.

Ferguson glanced at his watch. He was supposed to call home for an update in five minutes.

"All right. Opinions," said Ferg. "This is what I think—Sheremetev got bumped off because he knew what happened to the shipment, and he was going to tell us," said Ferguson. "Police are involved somehow."

"Why police?" asked Conners.

"Because the mafiya doesn't drive Ladas," said Ferguson.

"You're a foreigner, and you beat the shit out of two guys in the restroom. One of them might've woken up and called them," said Rankin.

"Those guys are probably still sleeping," said Ferguson.

"Bottom line," said Rankin, "we still don't know shit, one way or the other."

"Well duh, Skip."

"Hey, if you don't really want our fuckin' opinions, don't ask for them," said Rankin.

"Sheremetev's still our best bet," said Conners. "We ought to concentrate on him, check him out, who he knew, who he didn't know."

Ferguson took out his phone. Each man carried one of the high-tech devices; though the size of cell phones, they connected to a dedicated and secure satellite communications system. The only giveaway was a tubular antenna at the side about the size of a fountain pen, which had to be extended to communicate. The phone included a GPS locator chip and a distress mode, which if activated would allow the folks back home to find the phone to within a tenth of a meter. It could also act as a modem for the laptop, and had two silent modes—a vibration alert and a blinking light, as well as associated voice mail.

Ferg keyed in the combination for the special operations center in Virginia known as the Cube, where a mission coordinator—the title sounded more dignified than "gofer"—was on duty twenty-four/seven while the Team was deployed. Unlike a traditional case officer or control arrangement, the coordinator was subordinate to the head of the operation, which was always the officer in the field. The desk handled support, which could literally mean anything; most often it came down to sifting through intelligence and making sure money and cover stories were in place.

Technically, orders for the SF units backing up the Team passed through the desk to the DDO, who then issued them to Van Buren, the head of the SOF group supporting the field operation. In reality, Ferguson and Van Buren generally short-circuited the procedure by speaking directly. While the Team was deployed, an SF unit—generally though not always two ODAs, commonly known as A teams—along with supporting assets—were standing by to bail them out if things got nasty.

"What?" asked Jack Corrigan as the connection snapped through.

"What yourself, Sunshine," Ferg said.

"It's fuckin' two o'clock in the morning," said Corrigan. "You want cheerful, call back in twelve hours."

"You got anything for me?" asked Ferg.

"Yeah, you're off the hook—bullet was definitely a .22 or thereabouts." Corrigan had had the photos analyzed by an FBI lab.

"Well thank God, because I thought I was a murderer," Ferguson said. "Who killed him?"

"You're going to find this hard to believe, but I haven't a clue."

"We're counting on you, Jack." Ferg reached over and took a swig from the vodka, which burned slightly as it went down his throat. "You think the police down there know?"

"NSA intercepts say they're looking for you guys as primary suspects. Driving a van, right?"

"Yup."

"Ran through a garbage dump?"

"Rankin got homesick."

Corrigan snorted. "They have some sort of Russian investigator coming down to their office."

"Yeah?" Ferg sat down on the edge of the bed, then lay back. "What's it all about?"

"Damned if I know. But he's not police. FSB."

FSB—the *Federal'naya Sluzhba Bezopasnosti* or Federal Security Service—was one of the successor agencies to the KGB.

"What division?"

"Antiterrorism. Rock your socks?"

"Right off. So the murder had to do with the waste?"

"Maybe, maybe not. Your guy was into everything. Mafiya might just have gotten tired of paying him off."

"Maybe we can liaison some information out of them."

"Oh yeah, right after we turn you over to be arrested," said Corrigan.

Ferg rolled off the bed. "I can bug the police station down here. Maybe the Russians know more than we do."

"Set up a tap on the line," said Corrigan. "Easier."

"Yeah, but the conversations inside the office are going to be the real thing. He there yet?"

"Not until tomorrow night."

"Great. Can you work it out with the NSA?"

Corrigan didn't say anything, but Ferg could picture him leaning back in his black vinyl armchair away from the computer screens and looking up toward the ceiling. "Working it out with the NSA" meant setting up a special channel to capture and analyze the links, and even under the best circumstances it could be a bureaucratic nightmare. These wouldn't be the best circumstances, either—there were very few Kirghiz language specialists at the NSA. In fact, Ferg knew of only one—a rather curvaceous beauty with too much overbite but a darling accent.

"I guess," said Corrigan finally.

"Talk to you when it's done."

"Look, Ferg, this is probably just another wild-goose chase of yours. The DDO has been asking—"

Corrigan probably said something else, but Ferguson had slapped off the phone before he could hear it.

4

It was Conners who started the singing.

They were on the road from Talas, driving in two cars—a car and a truck actually, the first another Honda Accord, the other a Zil, a large truck that had once belonged to the Soviet army. Roughly equivalent to an American 6×6, it easily held the Team's gear as well as extra gas. Since many were owned either by mafiya members or ex-soldiers with heavy connections, it was a relatively safe vehicle to drive. The only problem for Guns, who was at the wheel, was the clutch. It caught only at the very bottom of the floor when it decided to work at all, and he ground the gears on every second or third shift. Rankin groused every time he did, but didn't take up the offer to change places.

In the Accord, Conners slumped against the door and after an hour or so of driving began to hum. After a while, Ferguson recognized the tune.

"Whiskey you're my darlin' drunk or sober," he sang out, when Conners hit the chorus.

"You know that one, Ferg?"

"My uncle used to sing it all the time," said Ferguson. "He was the black sheep of the family."

"Poor drunk Irishman?"

"Drunk and definitely Irish, but not poor," said Ferg.

His family had made a fortune in the construction industry—probably thanks to a good deal of graft—by the turn of the twentieth century. Conners, by contrast, had been born and raised in suburban New Jersey, nowhere near rich but not by his sights poor, either. His father had been a union carpenter in New York City.

"You know this one?" asked Ferguson, changing the subject by starting "Finnegan's Wake."

The two men traded verses of the old Irish folksong about a painter who'd fallen down from a ladder dead. Finnegan was revived by whiskey at his wake.

"What the hell's going on up there?" asked Rankin over the radio. Conners had inadvertently hit the mike feed on his belt, regaling the others with their singing.

"Old Irish drinking songs," Conners explained.

"Yeah, well, lay off the vodka," griped Rankin.

"You can join in if you want," suggested Ferguson. "You, too, Guns."

"I'm not much of a singer," said Guns in the background.

"Neither are they," said Rankin. "And if you start singing, too, I'm taking the Uzi out."

Ferguson and Conners both laughed. Conners spent the next hour teaching the CIA officer the words to "A Jug of Punch."

Guns hadn't been in the town yet, so Ferguson chose him to go inside the police station and plant the flies, miniature microphones with transmitting devices about the size of a large freckle. Foreigners were required to report in anyway, and they figured it wouldn't be particularly difficult to come up with an excuse to get back into the detective area—all he had to do was claim that he'd been robbed on the way into town.

"You think they'll ask me a lot of questions and try and trip me up?"

"Nah, they're not going to be interested at all," said Ferguson. "They'll pretend to fill out the paperwork. You slide the fly in under the desk, and we're good to go. Leave one in the men's room, and another out near the front desk. Easy as shit. There's only three rooms in the whole place—front, back, and the restroom off the hall. Bing-bang-boing, you're done."

Though not entirely convinced it was going to be half that easy, the Marine nodded. They were now all in the back of the Zil, parked at the side of the gas station near the center of town. It was 05:45 local; if Guns timed it right, he could go in, be given a seat and told to wait out the shift change, plant his devices, then say he'd come back.

"In and out," said Ferg.

Guns had joined the Marine Force Reconnaissance for a variety of reasons, including the fact that his older brother had gone through the program. The training was a blast, rigorous but a blast, and he'd proven an adept free-fall jumper. His first assignment had been to the Persian Gulf, where among other gigs he'd infiltrated an oil rig and taken down a two-man suicide boat operation. Everything after that had been rather boring. He was forced—he used that word, though in fact the school was voluntary and his superiors had merely suggested it—into enrolling in a number of language courses run for the military by a company that did a lot of work for the CIA; it was through them that he'd come to Ferg's attention.

Ferg had made the Team sound as if it was direct action twenty-four/seven. But so far it had been all spy bullshit—talking to people mostly, along with a fair share of sitting around in hotel rooms and driving places. Maybe the Army guys got off on this, but Guns was already thinking he'd join the stinking SEALs before signing up for another round.

"Hey, you going IBM on me?" Ferg asked, noticing Guns wasn't paying attention.

"What's that, sir?"

"You're not thinking, are you?" Ferg frowned at him. "Don't think. Just do. If you think, you're going to get sweaty."

"Yes, sir."

"Screw the sir shit, right? Makes me think I'm my old man. And he's dead."

"Yes, sir."

Ferguson smiled at him, then playfully pushed the Marine toward the back of the truck. As he reached the tailgate, he stopped and twirled him around.

"You can't go with this," said Ferguson, holding up Guns's Makarova pistol.

He'd managed to grab it out of his belt without Guns feeling him take it. The Marine was torn between belting him and asking him how he'd managed to get it away so smoothly.

"I'm going in there unarmed?"

"We're here for you, Guns," said Ferg. "Just walk in there, do it like we rehearsed. You can seem nervous, that's fine. Be nervous."

"I ain't nervous."

"Yeah, right," said Rankin. "Give us your fuckin' phone, too."

Guns scowled at him but handed it over. He ducked out the back of the truck.

Rankin had climbed up a telephone pole down the street from the station an hour ago, sliding a thick rubber sleeve containing the bugging mechanism over the wires; it was already uploading stolen data to an NSA eavesdropping satellite. Once the flies were in place, Ferg would activate the booster transmitter nearby, and they could split.

"All right children. Be ready. I'll take the walk," Ferg told the others, getting out to cover Guns into the station.

"Long as Conners don't sing, I'm fine," said Rankin, picking up his Uzi.

Ferg cocked the beak of his cap down over his head. If the others had argued that he'd been seen too much to shadow Guns—a fair argument—he'd have told them their Russian sucked too bad for them to get out of trouble. But he'd have gone no matter what; he was a little worried about the Marine.

The police inspector's right and left eyes didn't work together, and Guns had a hard time not staring at them as he gave him the basic information for his report. The man looked to be about fifty; his fingertips were stained brown from cigarettes. He asked his questions in Russian though Guns had started out in Kirghiz.

The story Guns told of being robbed was common enough—a roadblock on a dark road after making a wrong turn. The policeman could probably have copied it from a dozen reports in his computer. Instead, he hunt and pecked it in, using a keyboard so old half the letters were worn away.

"Occupation?"

"Sales representative," said Guns. He was a Belgian working for an Italian firm interested in shipping medical waste. There was in fact an appointment at one of the furnaces that the inspector could check if he wished.

The phone rang. The inspector reached over to answer, continuing to type with one finger. His bored expression didn't change, though his left eye rotated a little.

Guns got up from the chair, making as if he were stretching his legs. He'd planted the first fly near the front desk when he came in, but had waited to find a good spot for the second. Ferg had told him he could put it under the lip of a desk or under a chair if all else failed, but it would be better if it were higher. It was so small that it could sit out in the open and not attract attention.

According to Ferg anyway.

A nude calendar hung on the wall. Guns inspected it, pausing over Miss MaPT (March). As he did, he pressed his hand against the wall, sliding the fly beneath the calendar.

As he backed away, he watched it slip to the floor.

He froze. As nonchalantly as he could, he stepped back, glancing toward the detective. The man was still hunting and pecking with one hand, holding the phone up with another. Every so often he grunted. He didn't seem to be watching Guns at all, though it was hard to tell with those eyes.

Guns took a few steps as if stretching, then bent to tie his shoes.

Which were loafers.

He slid the fly onto his thumb, got up. As he did he lost his balance, banging against the waste can and falling against the wall. Once more he pushed the bugging device in—this time sticky side against the paint.

If the detective had noticed his display of coordination and lust, he didn't let on. The man finished his conversation and looked at Guns with skewed eyes, asking where he was staying. Guns gave the name of one of the city's hotels, noting that he hadn't had a chance to get over there and check in yet, though he had a reservation.

More hunting and pecking followed.

"We will contact you if anything comes of it," said the inspector finally. His tone of voice pretty much admitted that there was no possibility of this ever happening. "Would you like advice?"

"Sure," said Guns.

"Next time, fight back. It's legal."

Given the circumstances Guns had described—two men with shotguns approaching the car in the dark—fighting back would have been suicidal. But Guns thanked the inspector as if he had given him the soundest advice in the world.

He stopped in the restroom on the way out and got rid of the last fly. Two officers in the front were joking about how fat they were getting as Guns passed. He pretended not to hear and started for the front door.

"You're an American, aren't you?"

In a perfect world, Guns would not have reacted to the question. But the sharp tone, and more importantly the fact that the words were in an almost unaccented English, took him by surprise. He turned to the right and saw a man in a rumpled yellow jacket staring at him from a metal chair at the side of the room near the door, his legs sprawled forward on the floor and his head propped up by two fingers stuck against his nose.

"No, I'm Belgian," Guns answered in English. He gave it a slight French accent, or at least what he hoped would sound like a French accent. He reached into his pocket and took out a business card to give to the man, though a voice inside his head was screaming at him to get the hell out of there.

The man reached his hand up and flicked the card away.

"Arrest him," he told the police officers who had been joking together. "He's an American spy."

Before Guns could protest, another policeman came through the front door, blocking any possibility of escape.

5

Ferguson, sitting at a cafe next to the police station, glanced at his watch. Guns had been inside for over two hours.

The wait wasn't particularly long by Kyrgyzstan standards, but Ferguson didn't like it. Several men had gone inside since Ferg had gone into the restaurant, and while most were clearly policeman, he guessed that the man from the FSB had been among them.

Ferguson leaned back in his seat, hiding his face behind a newspaper. He had an earbud in his left ear, which was facing the wall. He lifted his hand to his face, pretending to scratch his nose.

"Rankin, Conners, what do you guys think?"

"I think I got to take a leak," said Rankin.

"That's helpful," said Ferg.

"Can we use your boom to listen in?" asked Conners.

The boom was a long-distance microphone with several modes, including one that could pick up vibrations off windows. But it was rather bulky and could be easily spotted.

"Better to switch on the flies," said Ferg. He'd hesitated doing so because there was a theoretical possibility that they could be detected.

"I say do it," offered Rankin.

"Yeah, all right. I'll go hit the transmitter. You know the routine, Dad."

"Take a minute," said Conners in the truck.

The flies transmitted to a receiver they'd placed in a sewer a short distance away, and from there would upload to the same satellite system the phone tap used. Corrigan could access the line from the Cube and relay it back via the secure sat phones.

Conners would call and arrange for the relay while Ferg slipped out to activate the transmitter.

He was just getting up when the door opened at the front of the police station. Two policemen emerged, shouldering Guns between them to a police car down the block. A short man in a yellow sports coat followed outside, casting his eye up and down the block before getting into his own car.

"Shit," muttered Ferg.

"I see it," said Rankin.

"Meet me at the sewer."

"Story of your life," said Rankin.

By the time Ferg was close enough for his phone to turn on the transmitter, the car had a good head start. He jumped into the Zil as Rankin hit the gas.

"We lost 'em," said Conners, sitting between them.

"Fuck," said Rankin.

"All right, let's not get a speeding ticket," said Ferg. "Rankin, slow down and take that left. I think I know where they're going."

Ferguson guessed that they were taking Guns to the detention facility in the basement of the old Soviet building at the end of town—a logical guess borne out by the fact that the car, or one that looked just like it, was double-parked in the street as they passed.

"Let's hit 'em now," said Rankin.

"Relax, Skippy," said Ferg, who knew the sergeant hated the nickname. "Let's reconnoiter first."

"We can't leave Guns in there," said Conners.

"We're not going to," said Ferg. "But we don't want to be guests ourselves, right?"

Rankin turned the truck down a broad but empty street just past the building, going as slowly as he dared while looking out the side window. The building looked solid, and while there were no soldiers or guards outside, getting Guns out wasn't going to be easy.

To Ferguson, Guns's arrest represented a break, but it was difficult to explain to the others that the longer he remained in the Kyrgyz custody, the more information they were likely to gather. That was the downside of working with the SF people—they were bodacious in firefights and quick on their feet, but they tended to want to reduce everything to bangs and bigger bangs. Sometimes you had to put a little sweat in.

"What are we doing, Ferg?" asked Rankin as he took a second turn around the block.

"I think I have a spot where we can put the boom up, see what we get. Park the truck as close as you can get. Dad, did you set up the bug relay?"

"Didn't have a chance."

"Go for it as soon as you park. Let me out here."

"Why?" asked Rankin.

"All that chay made me have to pee," said Ferg.

"Fuckin' officer material," said Rankin, unleashing his worst slur as he stopped the truck.

Why are you interested in the Chechen?"

Guns gave the man in the yellow jacket a quizzical look. It wasn't difficult—he had no clue what the SOB was talking about.

The man frowned. He'd told Guns that his name was Sergiv Kruknokov, that he was Russian, attached to the Federal Security Service or FSB, and that he had no jurisdiction here.

Then he urged him to cooperate.

Guns stuck to the story about being Belgian and working for an Italian waste company. He even rattled off a few words in Italian.

"The police won't torture you," said Sergiv. "But they will complicate your plans, whatever they are. Should we call your embassy?"

Guns didn't know whether there was a Belgian embassy in Kyrgyzstan or not, so he shrugged and again insisted that he was who he said he was.

The Russian shook his head, took a cigarette from his pocket, and left him in the basement room alone. Guns sat back in the chair, looking at the walls. Any second, he figured, Ferguson and the others would come in guns blazing and rescue him.

It figures, he thought to himself. There's finally going to be a little action, and I'm not in on it.

Ferguson walked up the steps, his weave just this side of sober. He reached for the door handle and pressed it open, pulling it open and starting inside.

He took about half a step before he found his way blocked by two rather large soldiers.

"*Vinavat*," he said in Russian, starting to apologize. "I need to use the can."

The soldier pushed him back. "Not here, asshole."

"Where's Misha?"

"Get the hell out," insisted the soldier, and the door was slammed shut.

"You were lucky, Ferg," said Conners, coming up behind him.

"What are you doing out of the truck?" asked Ferguson.

"I figured you were up to something stupid."

"Just looking for a place to pee."

"You like to push it to the edge, don't you?"

"Always," said Ferguson.

———————

Rankin was getting antsy in the truck. He had the Uzi in his lap, trying to look nonchalant but so tense that when Conners pulled open the passenger-side door he nearly blasted him.

"What's the story?" he asked.

"They don't have any bathrooms," said Ferg, climbing in behind Conners. "Bad sign."

He pulled the door shut. "Let's go someplace and get something to eat, take a breather."

"A breather?" Rankin nearly slammed the machine gun against the dashboard. "Are you out of your fuckin' mind?"

"They have soldiers inside. We have to get the layout before we can go in."

"Fuck that," said Rankin.

Ferg leaned across Conners to look at the SF sergeant. "When you'd get to be such an asshole, Rankin?"

"I'm not an asshole. I don't want my guy getting killed."

"Makes two of us," said Ferg.

"Three," said Conners. He hadn't talked to Corrigan yet; he took out his sat phone to do so.

"See if Corrigan can get us a map of the place from the library," Ferguson told him.

The CIA had an extensive database stocked with information about foreign buildings, kept for just such emergencies.

"We'll see what the bugs tell us, what else is going on. We'll get him," Ferguson told Rankin.

"When?"

"Sooner or later, Skippy."

"Don't fuckin' call me Skippy."

"Then don't be such an asshole."

"Hey, Ferg, Corrigan wants to talk to you," said Conners, handing him his phone. "They already have information from the phone tap. They're charging Guns with Sheremetev's murder."

6

KYRGYZSTAN, MIDNIGHT THE SAME DAY

 Their rules of engagement dictated a nonlethal takedown, which made the whole thing much more dangerous and a bigger pain in the ass than it would have been.

Not that it wouldn't have been a big pain in the ass anyway.

While Rankin set some M118 C4 block charges at the front of the building, Ferg and Conklin put their knives to the rubber of all the vehicles in the area, preventing anyone from following them when they were done.

From what they could tell with their infrared sensors, there were no more than six men in the building, not counting Guns, who was being kept in one of the basement rooms along the west side. Two and sometimes three guards worked the hallway; another sat in a guardroom near the stairs. The others were up on the first floor, which only connected to the basement from the front stairwell.

Ferg crouched on his haunches, checking his watch. In his hand was a Mossburg twelve-gauge shotgun loaded with solid lead shot, its sole purpose to blow out the hinges on the door. As soon as the door was gone, he'd reach down and grab his MP-5—his was the only lethal assault weapon on the team, a necessary backup in case things somehow got out of hand. He also had an M79 grenade launcher loaded with a special canister of tear gas to cover their exit, as well as a sawed-off Remington loaded with M1012 twelve-gauge nonlethal point target cartridges for any odd contingencies.

Conners and Rankin had Jackhammers—combat shotguns that contained ten-round cylinders or "cassettes" loaded with rubber-bullet cartridges. The twelve-gauge cartridges contained plastic-wrapped rubber cylinders that would bruise and perhaps break bones, but were not likely to kill the guards. Rankin's gun was slung over his shoulder; in his right hand he had an M79 grenade launcher, loaded with an M1029 40

mm crowd dispersal round. Though designed to disperse a crowd, the forty-eight cartridges in the launcher would take down anyone within thirty meters. Conners also
had a flash-bang—officially, an M84 stun grenade, which they would pop in as soon as
the door came off to disorient the guard or guards in the hall.

All three men were wearing respirator masks with NODs; the charges would
take out the electricity and lights, along with the telephone. Conners and Rankin had
AN/PVS-14s, lightweight monocles that were preferred by most SF troops because of
their weight and the ease of switching over to regular light. (Unlike the older
AN/PVS-7, only one was strapped into the device.) Ferguson had a pair of Air-Force-
issue Panoramic Night-Vision goggles, which gave him a hundred-degree field of vision. The wide angle would be more useful in the alley and leading the way out. The
gear was somewhat bulkier than the others'. They were also wearing lightweight
Kevlar vests.

"Ready, boys?" asked Ferg over the com system, staring at his watch.

"None of us are boys, Ferg," said Rankin.

"Girls, excuse me. Sixty seconds."

The charge at the front right side of the building—activated by a timer—blew
about five seconds sooner than they'd planned. Ferg stepped up and took out the door
hinges; as he pulled it away Conners pitched the flash-bang. A second later Rankin
leapt into the hallway and unleashed the M1029.

There had been three men the hall; all were taken down by the exploding canister of rubber balls. Rankin, breathing heavily in his respirator, kicked their weapons
away, moving down the hall, expecting others to burst in at any second. He pulled the
CS grenade off his vest; as soon as he was close enough to get an angle on the guardroom, he tossed it inside.

Conners meanwhile was trussing the Russian guards with plastic hand restraints
while Ferg pounded on the doors, yelling for Young with the aid of a loudspeaker device that fit inside his hood. He heard something at the second door, shouted at the
Marine to stand clear, then brought up his submachine gun and fired out the lock. It
took two kicks to get the door open. Ferg waited half a beat, then threw himself across
the frame, sweeping his gun around.

The room was empty.

At the far end of the hallway in the guardroom, Rankin pumped a shell into a
coughing, writhing figure on the floor in front of the bunk beds, then pulled the door
to the room closed, sealing in the incapacitating gas. As he jumped back outside, something clattered down the steps at the front of the building.

Rankin hit the first man down square in the stomach, bowling him over with a
shell. Bullets ricocheted down the stairwell—real bullets, which sent chips of masonry
from the walls splattering into Rankin's bulletproof vest.

"Let's move it," he yelled into his mike. "Get that fuckin' Marine the hell out of
bed and let's go."

Ferg went to the next door in the hallway, shot it open, and leapt inside.

Through his viewer he saw someone coughing on the floor. He grabbed at the man's arm, pulling him outside.

"Guns?" he asked. The man was wearing different clothes—military-style khakis—but he was the right size and shape, and he didn't have a weapon or a belt. "Guns?"

The man coughed in reply. Ferg had to stare a moment at his profile to make sure it was his man, then began dragging him backward just as a fresh burst of automatic fire ripped down the stairwell at the front of the hall.

"Let's go, let's go, let's go," said Rankin. He waited for the gunfire to stop—whoever was firing had burned the whole clip—and tossed another tear gas grenade up the stairwell. His ears felt like they'd been hit with large rocks.

This would have been a hell of a lot easier if we could just kill the bastards, Rankin thought to himself.

One of the guards on the ground near him started to move. Rankin cursed and threw himself across the hall, kicking the bastard in the head. A fresh round of bullets stuttered down the stairwell.

"Ferg? Conners? What the fuck?" he yelled.

"Yeah, I got him," said Ferg. He left Conners to help Guns out and ran to the exit to make sure they were clear. "Time to go, boys."

"We ain't fuckin' boys," said Rankin. As soon as the rounds from above stopped, he leaned the Jackhammer around the corner and leaned on the trigger, sending three rounds of the rubber balls ricocheting upward. Then he began retreating backward.

Ferguson slammed his canister of tear gas down the hall, but it didn't explode properly. Cursing, he grabbed a smoke grenade from his pocket and thumbed away the tape he'd applied to keep them from accidentally going off. Smoke from the cartridge began whispering out as Conners emerged from the building. When Rankin didn't appear immediately behind him, Ferg put his hand on Conners's side and pushed him toward the alley. Rankin was about ten feet from the exit. A shadow moved at the far end.

"Duck," said Ferguson. He'd grabbed the Remington, and now he pumped it twice, the shells and shadow disappearing in the smoky interior. An AK-47 barked; Ferg fired two more shots and started to run. As he cleared the alley he tripped the two small M5 MCCM bangers set near the doorway—pseudoclaymore mines, they unleashed a hail of plastic balls with a good loud boom and fierce flash, stalling any pursuit.

Firing the Remington conjured a bit of unwelcome nostalgia—he was nine, learning to shoot clay pigeons with his father at a range in Connecticut. Ferg pushed the memory away from his mind, but it was impossible to banish it from his hands, which caressed the stock even as he ran for the Honda, which they'd parked two blocks away. By the time he reached it, he'd pulled off his gas mask and night goggles. They weren't being followed, at least not as far as he could tell, and the charge that had taken down the electric lines seemed also to have knocked out power to that part of the city.

"Blow the truck," he said as he pulled open the rear door. "Hit it, Rankin."

The truck was in a lot near the building, back two blocks away. They couldn't hear the explosion.

"Did it go?" Ferg asked, as Conners slapped the car into gear.

"It went," said Rankin.

"You sure?"

"Fuck you."

Ferg turned and looked at Guns for the first time. He had his face in a wet towel and the window rolled down.

"Hey, you all right, Guns?"

The Marine coughed and shook his head in a way that seemed to mean yes.

"Turn left," Ferguson told Conners.

"Where the hell are we going?" demanded Rankin.

"We have to make sure the truck blew," Ferg told him.

"I set the fuckin' charge," insisted Rankin.

"Don't take it personally."

"Screw you, don't take it personally. You didn't want a big goddamn explosion, right? So now you think I screwed up."

Ferguson had the shotgun between his legs, the barrel pointed downward into the floorboards. He caught another whiff of nostalgia—his father instructing him on gun safety. "Keep the gun cracked in the car," was the way he always put it.

His first shotgun, a real grown-up gun. Not a toy, said his father.

"Something's burning," said Conners, pointing to the red glow in the distance. It was beyond the ministry building they'd hit, about where the truck had been.

"Good," said Ferg. "Hit the road."

"This all would have been easier if we could've just killed the bastards," said Rankin.

"Would've been easier with a whole A team," offered Conners.

"Hey, next time we'll call Delta," said Ferg. "They would've done it with bare hands and sticks."

Conners laughed, but Rankin, still angry, said nothing. In his opinion, Ferg had made the takedown too risky by insisting they not use lethal force. The CIA officer had the authority to override that directive if the situation warranted.

In the back of the car, Guns's eyes felt like they were going to fall out of his skull. His throat felt as if it were made of rug that a dog had used to sleep on. His nose was stuffed with oily rags. The towel Conners had given him wasn't helping his eyes any; more likely it was rubbing the irritant into them.

"You used fucking tear gas?" he said finally.

"You're welcome, Jarhead," said Rankin up front.

Ferguson reached to the floor and brought up a squeeze bottle. "Irrigate 'em. I'm sorry about the gas."

The car veered hard left, then settled back onto the roadway. Conners had lost the pavement in the dark. They'd mapped out a route to the main highway over dirt roads, but it had looked a hell of a lot easier in the daylight.

"Rankin, I need you to get out the map," Conners said.

"Yeah, I thought so," said Rankin, reaching for it.

Guns recounted what had happened, starting with the man with the yellow sports coat.

"Some sort of Russian," he told Ferguson. "FSB."

"What sort of questions?"

"Nothing really. Asked if I'd cooperate. When I played dumb, he split."

"No other questions?"

"Asked me about some Chechen."

"Which Chechen?"

"Jesus, I don't know. Some sort of guerrilla. Muslim, maybe."

"If I get Corrigan to say a bunch of names to you, you think you could pick it out?"

" 'Kiro,' he said."

"Kiro. We can check that," said Ferg. "What else did they ask?"

Guns pushed his eyes into the towel, re-creating the interrogation. There had only been one with an FSB man. The others were with a local inspector, who asked over and over why he had killed Sheremetev.

"What'd you say?" asked Ferg.

"I said I didn't."

"That's all they asked?" said Ferg.

"That's it."

"Where'd you get the duds?"

Guns laughed, then told him about the examination in front of the doctor and his nurse.

"Fuckin' guy checked me over good. I'm standing there thinking I want to pork his nurse—Mr. Young starts coming to attention, I swear—and he does a hernia check."

"Shit. Stop the fuckin' car," said Ferguson. "Shit."

"Huh?" asked Conners.

"Pull off the road."

"But—"

"Now!"

As the car skidded to a stop, Ferg threw open the door. He reached back and pulled Guns out, dragging him around the back of the car to the side of the road. A row of darkened buildings sat a few feet away.

"Take off your clothes," Ferg told him.

"Huh?"

"Take off your clothes," said Ferguson, and he grabbed Guns's waistband and helped. As the Marine started to undress, Ferguson reached into his pocket for his flashlight, then pulled down Guns's underpants.

"Hey!"

"Shit." Ferg put his fingernails on the Marine's leg next to his scrotum and pulled off a small black disk. He held it up in front of Guns's face just to prove that he wasn't a pervert, then threw it toward the abandoned buildings. He took a small bug detector from his inside jacket pocket and ran it over Guns's body, cursing himself for not taking such an obvious precaution earlier.

When Guns, completely naked without shoes or anything, got back in the car, Ferguson told Conners to get onto the highway and floor it.

"I'll give Yellow Jacket one thing," said Ferguson, pulling off his vest so he could give his shirt to Guns to wear. "He's no dummy."

7

 Ferguson unscrewed the cap on the bottled water and poured it into the tall glass. He leaned back on the balcony of the hotel, glancing down toward Conners, who was watching the street. They'd split into twos at the Kyrgyzstan border, unsure whether or not Yellow Jacket was still tracking them here. Guns and Rankin were about a half hour late.

Conners looked over and shook his head, then went back to staring at the street. After Kyrgyzstan, Cel'abinsk felt not only huge but almost luxurious. The air was clean; the weather pleasantly warm and dry. Ferg loosened his jacket and took out his phone; if he waited too long to call home, Corrigan would get nervous.

"How we doin', Jack?" he said, leaning back against the chair.

"How are *you* doing?" said Corrigan. There was a funny note in his voice.

"What's the problem?"

"Hold on."

Ferg realized what was up as the phone line clicked. The next thing he heard was the melodious baritone of his boss, the deputy director of operations at the CIA.

Only his voice was melodious.

"You shot up a police station?" demanded Daniel Slott, by way of a greeting.

"Actually, Dan, it wasn't a police station. And knowing what your reaction would be, we used nonlethal weapons."

"Tell that to the ambassador."

"Give me his number."

"The secretary of state is wondering what the hell is going on," said Slott, in a way that implied he actually cared what the secretary of state thought—which Ferg knew wasn't true. "He asked the director in front of the president what we're doing tear gassing police officers in Kyrgyzstan."

"How is the General, anyway?" Ferg asked, referring to Thomas Parnelles, who headed the CIA. Parnelles was an old CIA hand and a good friend of Ferguson's deceased father; they'd done time together during the good ol' bad days of the Cold War. General was a nickname from an operation where Parnelles impersonated a Jordanian officer.

Only a captain, actually. But Ferg's dad had been a private, and to hear the story not a very convincing one.

"Don't change the subject on me, Ferguson," said Slott. "You used tear gas in a police station?"

"I can definitively say we did not use tear gas in a police station."

"Then what did you do?"

"I recovered a member of my team who was being held under false pretenses." He yawned. "I'm a little tired."

"You're a little reckless. More and more."

"More and more?" asked Ferguson. "I wasn't reckless before? I thought that was a job requirement."

Slott made a grinding noise with his teeth. Recognizing that he would get no real details from Ferguson—and admitting to himself that he probably didn't want any—he changed the subject. "Have you found out what's going on?"

"Working on it."

"Did they take uranium or what?"

"I don't think so. The way it looks, the most likely accounting for the discrepancy is two casks of the control rods," said Ferg. "But that's only that one trip. I'm not really sure."

"When will you know?"

"Not sure. We're working on it."

"Well work faster."

"Aye-aye, Captain Bligh." Ferg leaned forward and took hold of his glass. "If you're through busting my chops, I'd appreciate talking to Corrigan again."

There was a click. Corrigan came on the line with an apology.

"Yeah, yeah," Ferguson told him. "You run through the satellite photos?"

"We have it narrowed down to six possible spurs," said Corrigan.

"Just six?" said Ferg. "Not twelve?"

"Actually, it is more like twelve. But I had them arbitrarily lop off some."

"Who the fuck is doing the analysis for you, Corrigan? Monkeys?"

"Monkeys would be faster," said the deskman. "We've been screwed since Nancy left. I need someone who can coordinate this stuff for me."

Special Demands was essentially a client to the analytic side of the Agency, which could supply a variety of intelligence reports, processed or unprocessed. The staffer who had worked to coordinate the reports—and had the more difficult job of assessing them—had gone on maternity leave two weeks before, and had not yet been replaced.

"You've been moaning about this for days, Corrigan. Get somebody."

"Easy for you to say. Just finding a warm body that has something approaching the background and clearances—"

"Man, you're a whiner." Ferg glanced at his watch. "We'll look at them all."

Having lost their source in Kyrgyzstan, they were back to grunt work—looking at all of the places where something might have been taken from the containment cars. It seemed logical that it had happened at a siding, and there were twelve between the last sensor and the border. The Team had extremely sensitive radiation meters—detectors based on gallium-arsenic chips that were as sensitive as gas-tube Geiger counters but fit in the palm of the hand—that would detect trace radioactivity. Unfortunately, this was likely to find something only if the material had been handled or some stray waste had attached to the train and been deposited accidentally.

"So tell me who Sergiv Kruknokov is," Ferguson said, sliding around in the seat. "You've had enough time to write the guy's biography."

"I keep telling you, I need someone to handle real-time intelligence. I literally got this as your call came through."

"Whine, whine, whine," Ferguson told him. "You have it or not?"

"Yes."

"So?"

Conners gave him a thumbs-up from the side; the others had finally come in. Ferg waved to him, and Conners left to make sure the others had no problem getting settled.

"Antiterrorism division of the Federal Security Bureau. High-level guy," said Corrigan, who was scanning a paper report.

"I didn't think he handled shoplifting."

"Yeah, well, listen to this. He was involved in a case in 1996 involving a plot to explode a dirty bomb in Moscow."

"Whoa, no shit. Give me the details."

"Chechens wanted to blow up a dirty bomb in Moscow. They broke it before the bomb went off."

"Dirty bomb. What kind of waste?"

"Um, that was cesium, I think. Medical stuff. Nowhere near as dangerous as spent uranium or the control rods you're after."

"Nasty stuff though?"

"You saw the science reports—depends who you're talking to. You have enough of it, and it's a problem."

Ferguson sat back, thinking about what they had: a discrepancy in a waste shipment, a Russian investigator with expertise in dirty-bomb investigations, a question about someone named Kiro who apparently operated in Chechnya, and an attempt to explode a dirty bomb nearly a decade before in Moscow.

Shit.

"Was this 'Kiro' involved?"

"We haven't ID'd Kiro yet. All the known conspirators are dead or in jail."

"Those spurs connect to Chechnya?" Ferguson asked Corrigan.

"Uh, hold on, let me get the map up. Remember, Ferg, the satellites showed all the cars made it. Hell, if they had a car missing, that would have set off all sorts of alarms. This may all be a wild-goose chase."

A waiter poked his head out from the doorway. Ferguson pointed to the bottle of water and asked for another, just to get rid of him.

"Ferg? You with me?"

"Just a distraction," Ferguson said.

"You could get there by train, but it's awful convoluted and far."

"Truck?"

"Sure. Same thing."

"Where's Sergiv been lately?"

"The Russian?"

"No, my brother-in-law."

"Don't have a good line on it."

"Find out. Because if it's in Chechnya, that's where I'm going next. And run down Kiro, okay?"

"I've been trying. Listen, Ferg, that's not as easy as you think. If Nancy were still here—"

Ferguson smiled as Corrigan gave him his usual song of woe. Any second now it would segue into the terrible time he had had in Egypt during the Gulf War—Corrigan had been in PsyOp as part of USSOCOM during the conflict. His main claim to fame before coming to work for the Company had been placing anti-Saddam dialogue in Egyptian soap operas.

"Yeah, well listen, dude, I have to get rolling here," said Ferg, cutting the performance short. "And listen, tell VB I may need an equipment drop."

"Where?"

"Well let's think this through, Corrigan. I just asked you to track down where a Russian FSB agent was in Chechnya, and to get information on a guy we think is a Chechen. Now do you think it's possible that I might be going in that direction?"

"Yeah, OK. I get it now."

Ferg clicked off the phone and sipped his water, waiting for the second bottle to arrive. He signed the bill, finished his glass, then took both bottles up with him to the room. The others had already gathered inside.

"Skip, Guns—how was the trip?"

"Brutal," said Rankin. "Fuckin' Marines drive like they screw—all over the place."

"Sounds like a compliment to me," said Conners.

Guns shrugged. "We got some stares, but as far as I could tell, nobody tagged along."

Ferguson pulled out the laptop from beneath the bed and powered it up. Turning it on after leaving it alone a few hours was always an adventure—if someone had fiddled with it, the machine was hardwired to eat the hard drive. The bright double beep indicated it was all right; Ferguson entered his passwords and opened the file with the area map.

"There were twelve spurs where the train could have pulled off the main line after the last measurement, before it got down to Kadagac."

"That's it?" said Rankin. He wasn't being sarcastic; he imagined that there would be many more sidings in the fifty-mile-or-so stretch.

"Yup," said Ferguson.

"You sure it happened on a siding?" asked Guns.

"At this point, I'm not sure of anything," said Ferg. "Corrigan got some NSA geeks into the computer system that our murder victim used in Kyrgyzstan, but they didn't find anything except a lot of URLs for porn sites."

"My kind of guy," said Conners.

"So maybe he knew something and maybe he didn't. We're watching the investigation and trying to play connect the dots. In the meantime, we do a little slug work and run the meters around in case they got sloppy."

Ferguson clicked two keys on the laptop, and a satellite image filtered in.

"It stopped along this siding for the night. Guards front and back. You could get a truck right here," Ferg said, pointing.

"So let's say we get some hits on the counters," said Rankin. "What then?"

"Then we follow those hits," said Ferg.

"And if we get nothing?" asked Guns.

"Then we go to Chechnya."

"Chechnya?" said Rankin. "Fuck."

"Probably not. They're pretty religious there."

8

 As they'd expected, they found no particularly interesting radiation hot spots at any of the spurs, although there were slightly higher than normal background hits at three sites. None of the buildings near the railroad sidings were housing waste-processing operations. If alpha- and high-gamma-level waste had been handled at any of the spots, it had been done expertly.

But back home, Corrigan had discovered that the FSB was working with Kyrgyzstan police on Sheremetev's murder, looking for a pair of Chechens described as extremists, though the bulletin describing them made them sound more like killers for hire. Even more interestingly, Corrigan had tracked Sergiv Kruknokov's movements. They had arrested a man in Chechnya who had visited a prisoner in a high-security prison outside the capital. Not just any prisoner: one of the men who had been involved in the plot to explode the radiation bomb in Moscow more than a decade before.

The Russians thought that the visitor was acting on behalf of a guerrilla leader they called "Kiro." Corrigan was still tracking down Kiro's identity—it wasn't clear whether the name was merely a pseudonym for someone else, a mistaken identity, or the nom de guerre of a heretofore unknown troublemaker. He did not appear to be one of the major leaders of the separatist movement. Over the past few years, radicals of all stripes and allegiances had moved into the Chechen hills, using the lawless territory for various purposes. Tracking them was a difficult task, even for the Russians, who had more than a hundred men assigned to the job.

This one was clearly worth finding. The Russians had clearly not put everything together yet, but the fact that they were nosing around told Ferg they were worried, very worried.

The ability to go where his gut told him to go was one of the most important aspects of the Special Demands setup, but even Ferguson knew driving into Chechnya without hard evidence of a link to the waste he was looking for was unlikely to yield results. Team missions weren't always this open-ended; the idea of having so much firepower at his fingertips was to find a good place to use it. But he didn't hand out the assignments, Slott did. His job was to play them out as far as they would go.

And so the Team had driven to central Chechnya, passing through miles and miles of burned farmland and bulldozed villages, arriving at a town called Irktan south of Urus-Martan. Irktan was located in the center of Chechnya, just at the foothills of the rugged southern mountains. At present, it was not particularly close to the front lines of the conflict, which was concentrated farther west. Russian troops patrolled the streets, but things were relaxed by Chechen standards; there were armored vehicles but no tanks manning the checkpoints into town. Ferguson sent Conners and Guns in to nose around while he and Rankin looked for a place to set up shop. Rankin for once didn't bitch—he tended to be happier, or at least less cranky, when he had the more dangerous job.

T wo Russian soldiers flagged Guns and Conners down as they were entering town. Guns translated the nearly five minutes' worth of conversation into a single sentence: "We better get guns if we plan on staying."

Their papers said they were part of a Mormon charity group running a clinic at the far end of town. The soldiers knew all about the clinic and pointed out the building, a red-roofed one-story at the end of the main street. The walls had last been painted white; the outer coat was chipped away in a dozen places, each revealing a different shade. Two Russian soldiers with a dog were standing outside the clinic, eying them warily as they drove by.

"Explosives dog," Conners said.

"Yeah."

They drove along to the end of the block, then turned left. The buildings abruptly disappeared; on both sides the lots were covered with rubble that seemed to run all the way back to the mountains in the distance. They got out and grabbed two suitcases packed with medicine, along with smaller bags. Conners holstered the Makarova in plain view—a fifty-ruble note would take care of the "fine" assessed to foreigners who broke the law against possessing weapons.

Assuming the guards weren't in a bad mood.

They didn't seem to be, and in fact didn't mention the pistol. The dog sniffed them and stood back, waiting while the soldiers looked through the bag of medicines; they took a bottle of Tylenol but nothing else.

Cleared inside, they found Sister Mariah Baxter, the director of the clinic. She pulled a stray strand of her long black hair back behind her ears as she inspected their gifts, eying the wares suspiciously but taking them nonetheless. A forty-year-old missionary from Utah, Sister Baxter knew how the game was played; she called over one of the nurses and told her to take the two men to Mr. T, who served as the clinic's unofficial security officer.

Conners was surprised to find that Mr. T was barely twenty and skinnier than a rake handle. The Chechen nodded when Guns told him they needed information.

"We want to find out about a man named Kiro, who operates around here," Guns told him in Russian.

Mr. T shook his head and clamped his teeth tightly together, his face flushing as Guns switched to Chechen and tried cajoling him with the few words he knew well. Conners took a step backward, his gaze drifting through the door back out into the large open room of the clinic. Half the room was a waiting area; the rest looked like triage stations where nurses tried to determine what was wrong with the patients. There were some slings for broken arms and bandages that might cover deep flesh wounds, but for the most part the people had less-visible ailments, probably a lot of the same stuff that people went to the doctor for in New Jersey—headaches and viruses and walking pneumonia, pregnancies, ear infections, coughs that wouldn't go away. The difference was that here, with sanitary conditions for shit, food scarce, and medicine difficult to obtain, even a cold might be fatal.

Guns, meanwhile, fumbled with the words as he tried to get information from Mr. T. He had listened to Chechen language files for the past two days on the MP3 player, refreshing his memory, but it was difficult to get into the rhythm of the language. Mr. T wasn't helping either, though obviously he knew who Kiro was.

"Think I should pound him?" he finally asked Conners.

The question caught Conners by surprise. "What good's that going to do?"

"Scare him so he'll talk."

"He's already pissing his pants," said Connors. "If Kiro is that scary, odds are Sister Baxter knows who he is."

Mr. T started to move past Guns to leave the room. Instinctively, the Marine threw his hand out to bar his way. The Chechen glared, but moved back and sat down.

"Don't hit him until I come back," said Conners.

He found Sister Baxter cleaning a scabbed knee on a nine-year-old girl. Conners watched her fingers daub the wound. They were a man's hands, rough and worn, too big for the slender body they belonged to. Sister Baxter's long hair was tied back with a piece of household string. She wore plain black pants and a blue denim shirt, and Connors realized as he approached that she was pretty despite her age, or maybe because of it. He didn't understand the kind of religious devotion that would lead a woman here, though as a young boy going to Catholic school he had seen enough of it. Back home his grandmother and her friends still went to church every weekday at 6:00 A.M., sitting in the front pews and mumbling the rosary, repenting sins they only dimly recalled.

Sister Baxter straightened, smiled at him, then picked up a roll of gauze bandage. "She was playing in a field with barbed wire. It could have been a mine. Maybe next time."

Connors wasn't sure how he was supposed to react to that—her tone implied that he had put the barbed wire there himself, and maybe even planted the mine.

"What do you want?" she said, cutting the wrap after several winds. Her fingers moved gently despite their size, and though the girl looked at her apprehensively, she seemed calm.

"We have to talk to a certain man. A rebel."

Sister Baxter's lip curled in a way that suggested a sarcastic smile, yet Connors saw there was something else there, too.

Fatigue? Weariness? Sorrow?

"Mr. T is not being particularly helpful, and it's important," said Connors. "I don't want to hurt him. Or anyone else."

"Are you threatening us?"

"The opposite. The man we're looking for is going to hurt a lot more kids like her," he said, thumbing toward the little girl.

In another place, under other circumstances, Sister Baxter's eyes as she looked into his would have made him fall in love. Even here they made him reluctant to continue, as if a simple question might hurt her somehow.

"The man's name is Kiro," said Connors.

The sarcastic smile again. "Why don't you ask the Russians where he is?" she said.

"If I thought they would help me, I would."

She got up and gestured to the row of people sitting in the chairs, adding something in what Connors thought was Chechen. One of the women came forward, talking excitedly. The two women conversed for a while; they seemed to be arguing.

"She thinks you're a doctor," explained Sister Baxter finally.

"I, uh, well, I have some medic training," said Connors. *Some* was correct.

"Yes, well, how are you at gynecology?"

Connors could feel his face starting to burn.

"I need to do a pap smear," said Sister Baxter. "Her symptoms sound like cervical cancer. But she wants a doctor, not a nurse. I'll do the real work, but I'll tell her you're the doctor."

"OK," said Connors.

"I'll get the speculum."

Connors watched her move across the room as the patient began talking to him nonstop. He nodded and smiled in a way he hoped suggested he had been to medical school.

"We're going to do this here?" he asked, when Sister Baxter returned and rolled out a fresh rug.

"You have a better place?"

"Don't you have an examining room?"

"This is it. The other two rooms we have are filled with patients. One is for people who are missing limbs. The other is for operations."

Connors nodded. Sister Baxter, meanwhile, had the patient lie down.

"Don't be shy," she told him.

He got down on his knees and took the instrument. But that was just for show—as he smiled as reassuringly as possible for the patient, Sister Baxter took the actual sample.

"You did all right for an American," she told him after she had logged the information on the sample and told the woman when to return.

"Thanks."

"Kiro has a small group outside of the town," she told him.

"Near here?"

"Near enough."

"Why don't the Russians attack him?"

"There is the philosophy of live and let live," she said. "And there is also the fact that this is a very poor place for a commander to be posted."

Conners assumed that she was hinting that Kiro bribed the local commander, something that was not unheard of though obviously not condoned by the central authorities. While a bribe might not even be necessary—if the guerrilla wasn't going out of his way to make trouble, he might not be attacked—it would explain why the FSB people hadn't been able to obtain a lot of information about him—and why the CIA hadn't then been able to steal it.

"I have a person who can guide you, but it will cost you money," added Sister Baxter.

"How much do you need?"

"We need a lot. But the money's not for us. One hundred dollars, as soon as it's dark in front of the gas station going out of town."

9

 Ferguson pushed another wad of gum into his mouth, continuing to chew furiously as he watched Guns approaching the rendezvous at the gas station. He had the NOD's magnifier on max, but he still had trouble seeing in the distance beyond the corner. Conners was tagging along behind Guns, his MP-5 hanging down at his side. They'd decided the heavy weapons were necessary after dark, and Guns had his under his coat.

"Don't see nobody," said Guns, still walking.

"He'll be watching you," Ferguson told them. "Just keep going. Dad, you're going to have to go in there with him so it doesn't look like you're waiting to ambush them. Tuck the gun beneath your coat. It should show a little, just don't make it too obvious."

"You gonna fuckin' blow their noses for them, too?" said Rankin. He was sitting next to Ferguson in the passenger seat, his Uzi in hand. He had a grenade launcher and a dozen 40 mm rounds on the floor. Both men were wearing their vests.

"I will if I have to," said Ferg. "What color snot you figure is in Guns's nose?"

Rankin gave a little laugh. Ferguson pushed against the steering wheel, noticing something moving in the station.

"Okay, Guns, your man is in the station looking at a magazine. Look menacing."

"Shoulda sent Rankin for that," said Dad.

Ferg swung the NOD around, looking through the back window. The Russians tended to stay put once it got dark—they weren't dumb—but there was always the possibility of a patrol.

Anyone else on the street could be assumed to be a rebel or a member of the local black-market gangs, or both.

Inside the gas station, Guns went to the clerk behind the counter and asked if he could buy some cigarettes. The clerk pushed a pack toward him on the counter. It said Marlboro on it, but instead of red the label was a sickish orange, an obvious counterfeit.

The price was a hundred rubles.

Without saying anything, Guns reached into his pocket for the money.

Connors, standing by the door, eyed the other man. He was about five-four, and his rib cage seemed to have been shifted permanently, as if his chest were twisted on his body. He had a scar at the base of his chin and a blank look in his eyes, as if he were staring at a spot far in the distance.

Guns dropped the bill on the counter, took the cigarettes, and went outside. Conners followed; the informant came out last.

They walked to the side of the building. The man held up his hands, seeming to anticipate a pat-down. Conners didn't disappoint him, pushing his legs apart as he slid the muzzle of his submachine gun in the man's back. He wasn't wearing a bulletproof vest, and he didn't have a weapon. That worried Conners, because it implied that he was being watched by a bodyguard, even though they hadn't seen one.

Ferg told him he was worrying too much.

"And you're worrying too little," said Guns.

"Nah, we're cool," said Ferg.

"Five-mile hike," Guns said. "Up that road near the creek, then off the trail for another two miles."

"What happens then?" Ferg asked.

"Won't say. He'll show us up the road, then that's it."

"Probably an ambush," said Rankin.

"If it were, he'd have a vest," said Ferg. "Go for it," he told Guns. He watched with the NOD as they crossed the street, the Chechen in the lead. The man walked with a limp.

"I wouldn't trust that fuck as far as I could throw him," said Rankin as they watched them cross the street.

"You have a better plan?"

"Let him point it out on the map, we check it out tomorrow night."

"Which only gives them more time to set up the ambush, or to shake information out of our guy," said Ferguson. He waited a few minutes, then put the car in gear as Conners began to hum "A Jug of Punch" over the radio.

"You do 'Danny Boy,' and we're not backing you up," Ferguson threatened, parking the car. The two American soldiers and the Chechen source were behind them now; Ferg could see them in the rearview mirror.

"Hey, I like 'Danny Boy,' " protested Conners.

Ferguson and Rankin waited for the others to pass before getting out of the truck. Carrying rucksacks with gear as well as weapons—Ferg had his shotgun and Rankin the Uzi—they gave the others a good start, then began trailing them. The truck would have been too obvious and an easy target besides.

The road twisted and turned as it climbed into the mountains. It took a little more than an hour to reach the turnoff that allegedly led to the guerrilla stronghold. Connors walked off the road about ten yards and promptly lost the trail in the rocks.

"He's going to have to do better than this," he told Guns.

Guns started to explain that the Chechen would have to accompany them farther. They weren't going into the camp, but they wanted a better idea where it was.

The Chechen started to back away.

Ferg and Rankin had steadily closed the distance, and by then were only a hundred yards behind. As Guns continued to argue, Ferguson came up and put his Remington 870 against the back of the Chechen's head. Then he reached into his pocket and pulled out five one-hundred-dollar bills, pressing them into the man's hand.

"Five more when we see it. We won't cause trouble," he said in Russian. "But you have to earn your money."

The guerrilla camp was bigger than they'd expected, and housed enough men to spare six guards on the perimeter that faced the road and town below. Rankin saw at least one ready but unmanned gun emplacement, and the configuration of the hills suggested there would be any number of weapons trained on the approach. He also thought there was also a minefield across a valley that flanked a large rock outcropping commanding the approach.

"No way we're sneaking in the front door," said Rankin when he returned to the copse off the road where the others were waiting. "And the way the ridge runs off to the right and left, I don't know if we can get in at all."

"We'll have to rethink this," admitted Ferguson. He pulled a hundred-dollar bill from his pocket and gave it to Guns, then pointed to their informant. "Tell our friend this is just extra rent—he's our houseguest for the evening."

"He's not going to be pleased," said the Marine. "Claims he has to get back to his wife."

"Tell 'em we'll kill the person she's sleeping with for no charge when we're done."

It took them more than an hour to get back to the car and drive the five miles to the abandoned building Ferguson and Rankin had found earlier. The ramshackle farmhouse had a few small holes in the roof but was otherwise intact. The road to it was another story—pockmarked by bomb craters and two rubble barriers, it was so bad they had to leave the car about a mile from the house. They slipped it in under some trees, obscuring it from the Russian helicopter patrols; as a precaution against thieves Rankin pulled the wire from the coil and took it with him.

Conners gazed at the stars as they walked, trying to orient the unfamiliar sky against his faded memory of an astronomy course he'd taken in high school a million years before. There was a time when knowing the stars would have been a critical talent on a deep insertion like this; compass, sextant, and a clear sky would help you work out where you were. But GPS gear had made the math obsolete; now the stars were just pretty things to look at.

When they were a little less than a half mile from the farm building, they spread out into the field, approaching slowly to make sure they weren't walking into an ambush. Guns told the Chechen to stay with him—and to stay nearby. He didn't bother threatening the man with his submachine gun; their informant wasn't happy but had already proven he was the sort of man who would stick around as long as the hundred-dollar bills kept appearing.

Even when the infrared glasses told them the building was empty, they moved in cautiously, looking for booby traps and signs that someone had been there. They found neither. Ferg divided them into two shifts—him and Conners, Guns and Rankin—and told them they'd catch some Zs, Guns and Rankin first. Their guest took a sleeping bag and curled up in the corner of the basement; Guns and Rankin tied his hands and feet together, then positioned themselves so he'd have to step on one of them to sneak out.

Upstairs, Ferguson swung the antenna up on the sat phone and called home.

"Ferg?" asked a female voice on the other end.

"Actually it's Joe Stalin," he told Lauren DiCapri, Corrigan's relief on the desk. "If I sound a little faint, it's because it's damn hot down here in hell, even with the air conditioners cranked."

"You're real late checking in. Major Corrigan was worried. I'm supposed to call him at home."

"Major's not an honorary title," Ferguson told her. "You don't keep it after they kick you out, especially on a dishonorable discharge."

"How are things going?"

"Shitty. I have some GPS coordinates on a guerrilla camp near here where our source is. I need satellite snaps ASAP. Not just library stuff—I need an 8X," he added, requesting an up-to-date and detailed satellite image of the target area.

"This is where you think Kiro is?"

"Yeah."

"I have more information on him."

"Let me read you the coordinates first," said Ferg. He actually didn't "read" them—he'd recorded them using the phone's GPS gear earlier and merely had to hit a key combination to send them over to her.

"Got 'em," she said, as the transmission went through.

"So how come the camp wasn't in our brief?" he said.

He could hear her checking back through their files to see.

"Um, you'd have to ask Corrigan," she said. "The notes here are that there was activity and probably a base."

"Cross out 'probably.'"

"It's possible that the Russians don't know."

"Right."

"FSB doesn't."

"That I believe."

"Let me tell you about Kiro," said Lauren.

"Make it dirty."

"Is that supposed to be funny?"

"It's late over here."

"Kiro is on the FBI wanted list. He's gotten al-Qaida funding and blew up the Carousel Mall in Syracuse, New York, more than a year ago. We want him. Slott's already approved an extraction."

"I think we just got hit with a sunspot," Ferguson said. "I'm in Chechnya, but you just said something about New York."

More patiently than Corrigan would have, Lauren explained that Kiro was believed to be Muhammad al Aberrchmof, an Islamic militant thought to have escaped from Afghanistan during the American action there in 2002. He had gone to Pakistan, where he was responsible for a bombing in a Karachi nightclub. Then he had managed to slip into the United States through Canada, masterminding a suicide attack on a Syracuse shopping mall. Following that, he had been spotted in Georgia—the one next to Russia, not Florida—and was now believed to be leading some of the Chechens.

"His friends are even worse. He seems to have met with Allah's Fist, the people who tried to blow up Independence Hall and got the IRS center in Massachusetts," said Lauren. "Nasty bunch."

"How associated?" asked Ferg.

"Not sure. Allah's Fist hasn't done anything since the attack on the IRS center. The leader, Samman Bin Saqr, disappeared right after that attack, just fell off the map. He might be dead. In any event, you have a green light to bring Kiro out. They want this guy, Ferg. They want to put him on trial for murder."

"I can't clip him?" said Ferg.

The term, taken from the American mafia, was slang for an assassination. It had to be approved by Slott and the CIA director, either from a list of high-level terrorists or on the president's direct command. An extraction generally applied to a lower level of terrorist or enemy prisoner of war, though there were exceptions.

Three people had been killed in the mall attack, and dozens wounded. Ferguson shook his head—that ought to be enough to have the bastard's heart cut out, no questions asked.

Five hundred people had been killed or wounded in the IRS attack. Was that what it took?

"They really want him, Ferg. They want a scalp. We don't have a positive connection," Lauren added. "But the people at the NSA have a voice match that we think is good, and there's one photo. We'll upload them."

"The Russians know who he is?" Ferguson asked.

"Not as far as we know."

"We're going to tell them?"

"Not until you bring him home. Slott has been on Corrigan's back since we made the connection. He wanted to call you right away. Corrigan held him off."

Ferg held the phone down and took a few steps along the front of the building, scanning in the distance of the road. The team was getting a little ragged; they'd been out in the field for about two weeks.

If Kiro really was Aberrchmof, he ought to be grabbed.

Then castrated, burned, and pissed on.

He put the phone back to his ear.

"Ferg?"

"Yeah, I'm here, Beautiful."

"Colonel Van Buren has already been alerted."

"OK," said Ferg, even though he knew an all-out assault on the fortress would be out of the question, even if they were absolutely sure Kiro was there. Too many Russian troops were nearby, ready to gum up the works. They'd either have to get the Russians in on the game or find a way to finesse it. "I'll get with him," he told her.

"You need anything else?"

"Well my inflatable doll sprang a leak last night."

"Very funny." She killed the connection.

10

IRKTAN, CHECHNYA—TWELVE HOURS LATER

 Rankin spotted it, staring at the images upside down.

"They run out that tunnel, then pick up the vehicle there," he said, pointing at the laptop screen. "You can see the wheel in the hide."

Everybody squinted over the screen.

"So we knock on the front door, they run out the back?" said Ferguson.

Rankin snorted. "Yeah, right. They could take two companies on before they felt the heat. Even then, you don't have armor, you're not getting in."

"What do you think, Dad?" Ferg asked Conners.

"Got to figure they have at least one guy inside the cave at all times," he said, pointing at the escape route. "I have to tell you, I don't quite see the cave, let alone the tire or even the hide Skip's talking about."

"It's there," said Rankin.

"I'm not arguing with you. I just have older eyes." Conners smiled at him. Rankin reminded him of a racehorse that had been shot up with amphetamines for a race, always jittery, sensitive to the touch. Great in the race, but hell before and after. "Be booby traps, probably twists and turns. You'd never get in that way."

"I don't see us getting in at all," said Rankin.

"Yeah, Skip's right on that. We're going to have to make him come out," said Ferguson. He got up and started pacing around, thinking over the situation. It was now almost noon. Every hour they stayed there increased the chances they would be found by either the Russians or the Chechen rebels, or both. They still had their informer, but even holding on to him was not without risk.

The Russians had two companies in Irktan. That was probably the reason they didn't attack the camp; they figured it wasn't worth the effort.

That would have to be changed.

"Rankin, you see any guard posts on that back end there?" Ferguson asked.

"They have people on this road way the hell over here," he said, pointing at a highway nearly two miles from the rear of the fortress area. "The thing is, there's no way in from the roads. So if they're dealing with the Russians, they probably figure they don't have to guard along this area here. Terrain's for shit, and the Russians never go anywhere without either a caravan of armor or helicopters, or both. If you're in the fortress, you don't need to be anywhere else."

"And this?" Ferguson pointed to a ravine that ran out the back of the fortress.

"The escape route," said Rankin, repeating what he had told Ferguson earlier. "Got a bike right there."

The hide for the bike was visible on an earlier photo; the area was not quite as sharp in the most recent shot. But Ferguson decided it must still be there.

"Why only one bike?" asked Guns.

"Only one person is important enough to escape," said Ferg.

"Only one's chicken enough," said Rankin.

"Maybe it's for a messenger," said Conners.

"Could be," said Ferguson. One of the briefs on the rebel organization that Lauren had posted with the satellite data emphasized that the leaders looked at the war as a long-term affair—survival was important. In his opinion, the bike was Kiro's parachute, nothing else.

"We might be able to sneak in that way, take them by surprise," said Rankin.

"We don't know what's beyond that opening," said Conners. "Assuming it is an opening."

"Got to be," said Rankin.

"Yeah, OK. Listen, I gotta talk to Van," said Ferguson, standing up. "In the meantime—Rankin, that mortar we have in the kit—"

"The English piece of shit?"

"The same," said Ferguson. "You think you could rig it so some of the shells it fires don't explode?"

"What do you mean?"

"I mean they fire and land somewhere, but don't go boom."

"I could do that," said Conners.

"Yeah, I could figure it out," said Rankin quickly.

"Good. Only a couple. Don't blow yourselves up, guys," said Ferguson. As he jogged up the basement steps, the plan began to form in his mind.

11

 Rankin finished setting the charge, waiting beneath the car behind the army headquarters building. He could hear Guns haranguing the guards a few feet away, asking about the clinic—demanding to know in very loud and seemingly drunk Russian why foreigners were allowed to poison people there.

The guards were getting impatient. Rankin heard one of them shove Guns and rolled away from the car. They started kicking the Marine, who'd fallen to the ground as part of his diversion.

It took Rankin all his self-control not to jump up and run to help his companion. Instead, he got up slowly, walking toward the battered Accord, where Conners was waiting with their Chechen informer.

A woman was walking near the road. Rankin looked at her for a moment, worried that she would stop and say something to him. But she hurried on.

The sergeant looked back in time to see one of the men give Guns a kick in the ribs, leaving him in a heap against the wall. He waited for him to make it to the corner and start across the street. Then Rankin opened the car door and pulled the Chechen informer out.

"In two days," he said, repeating the Chechen words Guns had told him. "Go to Sister. You'll be paid."

The Chechen's eyes were glued on the hundred-dollar bill in Rankin's hand.

"Two days. Understand?"

The man nodded.

"Now run."

The Chechen understood that. He shook his head and put up his hands.

Rankin took the pistol from under his jacket. "Run," he said. "Run."

He had to bring the gun up almost to the man's face before he started.

The soldiers didn't see him until he was a good distance down the block. One began yelling; the other knelt to aim at him. As he prepared to fire, Rankin pushed the button on the radio detonator, blowing up the car.

When Ferguson heard the explosion, he dropped the round into the L16, involuntarily ducking back as the 81 mm projectile whipped upward from the small mortar. In quick succession, he loaded and fired five more rounds from the British-made weapon, raining a half dozen shots on the Russian headquarters. Had these been normal rounds, they would have done considerable damage; the bombs weighed a bit over nine pounds, much of it explosive. Rankin had fiddled with them, essentially turning them into duds. Still, it was very possible that the attack would injure someone, and while Ferguson had no particular love for the Russians or locals, his own people and the Mormons were down in the village. He finished with the dud rounds and moved the mortar to bomb out the road; these rounds sounded the same as they left the tube but their booms were potent cracks that shook the air even where he was positioned, roughly two thousand meters away.

Ferguson kicked over the mortar, then kicked dirt all around to make it seem as if there had been more people there. Grabbing his gear, he hiked up the ridge he'd scouted earlier, tracking down, then across the hills to a point north of the Chechen stronghold, where he was supposed to meet Rankin and Guns. Conners was already watching at the rear of the fortress; if Kiro tried to escape before the rest of the team got there, Ferg had told him to blow him away. Authorized or not, the death would not be lamented in Washington.

It took nearly an hour for Ferguson to reach the rendezvous point. As he reached it, he heard an airplane approaching and worried that perhaps the plan had succeeded a little too well—perhaps the Russians were so angry they'd pound the guerrillas so severely that they wouldn't have a chance to escape.

The jet was too high and too fast for Ferguson to see. It circled twice over the camp, which was between two and three miles away. On its second orbit the steady hush of the jet seemed to stutter. Then it roared louder than before. Ferguson instinctively ducked; a few seconds later he heard the muffled thud of two medium-sized bombs exploding near the fortress.

As the plane zoomed away, the CIA officer climbed up the rock with his MP-5 and Remington over his shoulder, looking in the direction of camp. White smoke curled into the sky from beyond the rocks, but he couldn't see the fort itself from where he was.

"That bomb get you, Dad?" he asked Conners.

"Thought we were on silent com," grumbled the SF soldier.

"Just checking."

Ferguson went back to the ledge and stowed his gear, then took his binoculars and scouted the approach, adjusting his com set to make sure he'd hear the team when they got into range. He sat down cross-legged, shotgun in his lap, submachine gun at his side, and made himself as comfortable as possible to do the thing in the world he hated the most—wait.

Guns had been beaten pretty badly, but he was able to walk, and when the car exploded, Rankin ran around the block and met him as they'd arranged. The mortar shells began falling in the field short of the center of town; the timers on the other charges he'd set around town began going off. Rankin applied the coup de grace to the attack by igniting the charge on their Accord; a fireball shot straight up from the gas tank, a spectacular show that would have rated a ten at a fireworks display.

They took a quick left turn off the main drag and jumped in a truck they'd stolen earlier. Guns slumped against the door as Rankin drove around to the road that led to the rendezvous point.

"Fuckin' Russkies don't have a clue," he told the Marine, who merely groaned in response. "They're little rabbits, cowering in their holes. Assholes had any sense, they'd have their knives out—cream us just as soon as look at us."

In Rankin's opinion, the Russians' entire posture had invited attack—he would have had a better perimeter force, better sweeps, checkpoints—he wouldn't have let a couple of foreigners, one of them a gimp, waltz right out of town under his nose. A machine gun would have commanded the top of the ridge beyond the road, wiping them out as they drove.

"You complaining?" Guns asked him, as they stopped to get rid of the truck just beyond the ridge.

"I'm just saying they're awful lazy."

"They kick pretty good."

"You all right?"

"Yeah."

"I was worried they were going to arrest you."

"Ferg said they wouldn't."

"Yeah, well, Ferg's not always right."

"Think they broke my rib."

"Bastards. We shoulda killed every one of them," said Rankin.

He climbed on top of the truck and turned his field glasses back toward the town. Two BMPs, armored personnel carriers mounting a light cannon, had taken up a position at the nearest end of town.

"They coming for us?" Guns asked.

"Not yet. They better get their act together, or we're back to square one."

"You don't think blowing up the commander's car will piss them off?"

Rankin spun around so quickly he nearly fell off the truck. "What the hell are you doing here?" he asked. "You're lucky I didn't shoot you."

"With what? Your binoculars?" Ferguson looked at Guns, who was hunched over the front of the truck. "You all right, Marine?"

"I'm fuckin' fine."

"That's what I like to hear. Come on, boys; we got a long walk to catch up to Dad, or he's going to have all the fun."

12

IRKTAN, CHECHNYA

 After more than two hours in the woods, they were still a good mile and a half from the back of the fortress. With the sun starting to set, Ferguson decided they'd have to split up. He was worried that the rebels would decide to sneak out of the fortress as soon as it was dark.

"Conners'll just blast 'em," argued Rankin.

"If he has to, that's OK. But he also might get his ass handed to him," said Ferg. "You help Guns come up as fast as you can."

"I can make it by myself," said Guns. "Both of you guys go."

"I don't know, Guns," said Ferguson.

"Go on."

"I don't need no Marine Corps macho bullshit," said Ferg. "I need you in one piece."

"Fuck yourself, I am."

"He can make it," said Rankin.

Ferguson debated with himself. If there was a firefight behind the fortress, Rankin would be extremely useful. On the other hand, Guns wasn't likely to go too much faster with Rankin helping him.

"You sure you can make it?" he said to the Marine.

"Yeah, I can do it," said Guns.

"I'm counting on you. I got to keep these Army guys in line. One Marine, two Army—about right."

"You need five grunts for a jarhead," said Guns, wincing through his smile.

"Yeah, that's about right," said Ferg. "You use the radio if you get stuck. You got me?"

"Yes, sir."

T hey had to stop after a mile and put on their night goggles. The quickest way to the ravine over the cave exit was across a sheer rock wall. It would be impossible in the dark—Ferguson had mapped a route below, which would have brought them almost opposite the vehicle hide—but if they got across it they'd be almost on top of the exit, in perfect position to control it. From there, one man could cover the other as he went across to the left down to the spot where Conners was waiting near the vehicle, which he'd already incapacitated.

"You're out of your mind," said Rankin, looking at it through his goggles. "No way."

"Leave the pack if it's too heavy," said Ferg. "Come on. I've gone across rock quarries that were tougher."

"At night?"

"Oh shit yeah," said Ferguson, examining the wall. "There's plenty of hand-holds, couple of ledges. Won't be a problem."

"You're crazy man. I'm not doing that."

"Your call," said Ferguson, starting out.

"Fuck," said Rankin, snugging his ruck tighter and following.

Ferg found a ledge about chest high and climbed up onto it. It was about eight inches wide, and he didn't have to lean too much to keep his balance as he went. He stopped after a few feet to tighten the shotgun; the MP-5 was in its Velcro rig. There was a guard post about a hundred yards farther up the ridge to the left, but to see down here the lookout would have to crawl out and peer over the rocks, extremely unlikely as long as they were quiet.

The ridge ended twenty feet out. A hundred and fifty yards of nearly sheer wall separated Ferguson from a pile of rocks that would be easy to scramble across. The drop was at least two hundred feet.

Rankin really didn't want to know how far down it was. He could feel the sweat swimming down his fingers. He watched Ferguson begin climbing the wall, working his way across. Fucker probably wants me to fall, Rankin thought to himself, pushing his fingers into a rock and kicking for something to put his foot into.

Ferguson was about ten feet from the rocks when he ran out of places to put his hands and feet. At first he thought it was just because of the darkness and eye fatigue—the goggles tended to make his eyes blurry after a while—but gradually he realized it was a real problem. He climbed up a few feet, only to find his way barred in that direction as well. He stared and stared, trying to find a hold, and was still staring at it when Rankin finally reached him.

"Now what?" whispered Rankin. He was breathing hard, probably hyperventi-
lating.

"I don't know," said Ferguson. "The rock's so smooth I can't find a hold anywhere. No cracks. Nothing."

"Well you better find one. I'm getting tired."

"We could turn around," said Ferguson.

"I'm not going back."

"Just wanted to give you the option. I'm going to push off and jump."

"You're out of your mind."

"Better keep your voice down," said Ferguson. He went back to studying the
wall. If he were wearing climbing shoes, he might take a risk on a nub just out of his
reach; the face sloped ever so slightly, and he thought—knew—he could get his finger
there before his balance got too unwieldy.

Nah. Too far. He had to jump.

"Hold my gun," he told Rankin, sliding the shotgun off his shoulder. He took
one last look with the night goggles, then took them off and worked them into his
ruck, figuring—hoping, really—they'd be safer there.

"Shit," said Rankin.

"Dude, you got a ledge there, you ain't fallin'."

"It's three inches wide."

"Suck it up."

"Fuck you."

Ferguson took his gun back. "When I get on the rocks and get the NOD back
on, you can toss me your gear."

"You're nuts."

"Well, jump with it if you want. And be quiet. The guard post isn't that far away.
If you curse when you land, do it quietly."

"Shit."

Ferguson shifted right, shifted again, got his left leg in place, and sprang to the
rocks.

His belly caught the side, but he held on without slipping. He got up, unsteady
but intact, then put his NOD back on. He waved at Rankin, waiting.

Rankin tossed the MP-5 to him. Ferg caught it with one hand, a stinking circus
catch.

What a hot dog, the SF soldier thought as he eased himself out of his ruck. He
waited until his head stopped spinning, then tossed it out to Ferguson, who used two
hands this time.

"Your NOD," said Ferguson in a loud whisper.

Rankin had already decided he was keeping it on. He shook his head, then
waited as Ferguson began moving toward the edge of the rocks, positioning himself so
he could grab Rankin if he fell short.

Rankin waited a second more, then jumped. Heavier than Ferguson and without the experience of midnight daredevil sessions in college, he came down short of his mark but still on the rocks, bowling Ferguson over as he fell.

"Serves you right," he groaned, getting up.

"You got to lose weight, Skip."

Conners watched them come down the rocks, picking their way down the right side of the ravine.

"You took your time," he told Ferguson, as the CIA officer made it to the base of the hill.

"You're still here? I thought the Chechens would have asked you inside for a little training."

"There's two motorcycles," he told Ferguson. "I moved them. I figured they might come in handy."

"Good thinking, Dad."

"Guns hasn't checked in, has he?" asked Conners.

"Would've been with you. We weren't in line of sight coming down the hill. He'd only use the sat phone if there were a problem."

"Unless he couldn't."

"You worry too much, Dad." Ferguson laid out the terrain for the others, showing how the escape route was lined up. The crevice that opened below the mouth of the cave made an offset Z as it descended toward the woods where the bikes had been hidden; Conners guessed that there would be booby traps or mines to further narrow the route. Ferg doubted that—the route had to be secret and usable in haste, and mines would pose a danger to the escapees as well as be potentially detectable.

They moved back behind the rocks near where the bikes had been hidden and waited.

"You sure the Russians are going to come?" asked Rankin.

"If I blew up your car, wouldn't you want to punch me out?" said Ferg.

"I want to punch you out anyway."

Between his roundabout route and bum leg, it took four hours for Guns to make it to the ambush. By then the cold had seeped beneath Rankin's skin, turning his bones into rods of ice. He worked back and forth in his spot near the mouth of the cave, the motion more to keep him awake than warm.

"Anybody else, I'd think you were doing some Buddhist meditation," Ferguson said to him.

"Maybe I am," said Rankin.

They showed Guns the layout and told him the plan. Once Kiro was out of the cave, they'd close off pursuit by dumping grenades in and detonating the charges Conners had set along the ravine. The explosives hadn't been placed close enough to seal the mouth of the cave—that would have risked tipping off any guard inside—but Rankin pointed to a spot about fifty feet above the cave entrance and slightly to the left.

"After you put the grenades in and set off the charges, put another grenade on those rocks. That oughta start an avalanche."

"And run like hell," Ferguson added, eying the hill.

"All right," said Guns, though he didn't feel much like running. His ribs were pounding, and his ears were swollen; he thought he looked like Mickey Mouse. "You sure you can tell who Kiro is?" he asked Ferg.

Corrigan had given them a series of FBI sketches and one blurry photograph, along with some physical descriptions from Russian FSB files. Kiro had a scar on his cheek and stood only five-four, but it was a fair question.

"Shit yeah," said Ferguson.

Rankin sniggered. "We oughta just kill 'em all and be done with it."

"We may," said Ferguson.

Rankin moved back near the hide, taking Conners's position. He had the grenade launcher, which was armed with a ponderously long charge that protruded from the mouth of the weapon like a rectangular lollipop. The tube contained a large Teflon net and a stun charge. The net would cover a twenty-foot-round area when it exploded; though the netting was strong, its effect was probably more disorienting than anything else. The charge that fired it was roughly the equivalent of a flash-bang grenade, generally not harmful unless it happened to land exactly in your face.

Which of course would be where he'd aim it.

Ferguson walked back and forth between the positions, his body racing with adrenaline. He had reloaded the shotgun with nonlethal shot and slung it over his shoulder with the submachine gun, both weapons ready. Conners took the safety position, deep in the backfield. He had a Minimi M249 machine gun with a two-hundred round belt—anyone who made it past the others wasn't staying alive very long. While small for a machine gun, the weapon weighed fifteen pounds empty and without its scope, and having lugged it this far, Conners would just as soon use it.

The men used various ploys to stay awake, biting lips, rocking, thinking about how cold they were. Ferguson was mostly worried about Guns and kept checking on him, but the Marine had endured worse in boot camp, or at least was thoroughly convinced that he had. The memory of getting through that—along with the fear that he might let his friends down or, even worse, disgrace the Corps—was more than enough to keep him alert.

A little past five, they heard a helicopter in the distance. Each man stretched his arms and legs, then fell into position—Guns propping himself against a tree, Conners and Rankin on one knee, Ferg standing and watching. The sound grew, but then faded.

The hills remained silent for another half hour. This time the low drone came from trucks and tanks, a column moving along a road.

"Five of 'em," said Conners over the com set. "Two tanks at least. Trucks, personnel carriers."

"What'd they have for breakfast?" asked Ferg.

Conners was still trying to think of a smart-alecky comeback when the heavy whomp of helicopter gunships began shaking the ground. They were flying in from the northwest, crossing from the team's left, almost over their shoulders.

It was still dark, but with his night goggles Ferg watched the six smudges in double echelon roar toward the fortress. They were Ka-50s, single-seat attack birds powered by a pair of counterrotating rotors and armed with rockets and a monster cannon. They swung into an attack on the other side of the hill, launching rockets at the east and west sides of the encampment. One of the first rounds caught something flammable, and a series of secondary explosions began shaking the ground.

"Be ready," said Ferg.

The onslaught moved to the front door of the fortress, rockets and cannons blasting the rocks and caves that looked down in the direction of the town. As one of the helicopters started away, a shrill zip sounded from the other side of the hill; a shoulder-launched missile veered upward and caught it on the side. Its fellows moved in for revenge, and at roughly the same time the tanks began to pound the caves, firing point-blank into the mountain.

"Be ready," said Ferg again.

But nothing happened on their side of the fort. An hour after the attack had begun, the gunfire began to ease off. It was impossible to know what was going on from where they were, but it seemed unlikely that the Russians had made much of a dent in the rocks. A half hour later, two jets appeared; one of their bombs struck near the top of the hill over the cave, sending dirt far enough to dust Guns's face.

"Fucking bastards. We're going to have to go in there and get him ourselves," said Rankin.

Ferguson's real fear was that the Russians would try flanking the cave network and stumble across the Americans. Van Buren had raised the possibility earlier, pointing out that he didn't have a large enough force to protect the flanks, but had reluctantly agreed when Ferg said bringing more men in—and waiting the day or two it would take to do so—presented other problems. It had been Ferguson's call in the end, and he'd opted for surprise and quickness.

"Movement," said Guns.

Everybody pushed forward a half step, weapons ready.

"Two, three men. First has a gun, the third," said Guns.

"Guy in the middle," said Rankin, who could see them from about twenty yards. "He's short."

"No, they're all scouts," said Ferg. "Hold on."

"Going for the hide," said Rankin.

"Hang tight."

"Something else," said Guns. "More people in the cave."

"I got these three guys covered," said Rankin.

Two more men came from the entrance to the cave. One was very much shorter than the other, stooped a little.

"The midget in the second group," said Ferg. "Rankin?"

"Yup." He shifted to his left—he didn't have a shot on the target group, and the first trio was almost at the hide.

"Guns, get the grenade ready," said Ferguson, seeing the two men now below them.

One of the trio that had come out first started shouting. A moment later someone in the cave began firing an automatic rifle toward Rankin. Guns fired the grenade into the cave, then tripped the charges. As the hillside shook, he put a grenade into the pile of rocks Rankin had pointed out. Dust and dirt flew everywhere. He launched another, then lost his balance as the rocks clattered down the hill in a roar.

Rankin still couldn't see the target pair. He dashed down the hill toward the crevice, trying to get close enough to fire the net grenade. Bullets ricocheted all around him, the air humming with automatic weapons fire. Losing his balance, he slid down, falling on a direct line to the mouth of the cave, which was obscured behind a cloud of dust and rocks. He steadied the launcher but couldn't find a target.

Ferguson pushed his submachine gun up and emptied the clip into the three figures who had come out first. By the time the last of the three men fell to the ground, rocks were sliding down the hillside.

Rankin cursed into the com set—he couldn't find Kiro.

Ferguson pulled up the Remington, realizing that the terrorist had somehow managed to get beyond Rankin, possibly by climbing up the embankment. As he started to move toward the shallow ravine, he lost his footing. The slide saved him— one of the Chechen guerrillas had popped up on the slope directly across from him and begun firing. Ferguson scraped his fingers to hell as he fired back, the rubber slug slapping his target with a thud.

Ferg jumped to his feet and fired twice more, crazy with adrenaline now. He took a few hard shots to his chest before he had a target; he saw legs and fired the shotgun point-blank at the man's face. His target howled and fell down. Ferg reached to grab him, then saw the other man climbing the rocks at his left to get away. He raised his gun and fired but either missed or didn't do enough damage to stop him. Ferg fired again, then started after him, running and shooting until his gun was empty. He threw down the weapon and kept going, closing the distance to five yards before the man whirled.

He had a pistol in his hand. Part of Ferg's brain saw the weapon and tried to tell his body to duck away; the rest missed it entirely. One of the bullets landed hard against the top of his body armor, but Ferg didn't feel it—he'd already launched himself into the man's midsection, tackling him against the stones. His right hand fished for the man's neck and found a knife blade instead. Ferguson swung around, pinning his opponent and smacking his head back at the same time.

There was a flash, and Ferguson felt his head slammed to the side. Rankin had caught up and nailed them both with the net.

Ferguson, his back caught in the netting, saw the shadow of his assailant in front of him. He punched at it; the knife clattered away, and the Chechen, already stunned by the flash-bang, fell senseless. Ferguson stood up, pushing against the Teflon material of the net.

"Looks like you caught dinner," he said to Rankin, who had his Uzi practically in Ferg's face.

"This better be him."

"There was one back on the lip of the ravine," said Ferguson.

"I got him," said Guns. He'd had to put a burst from the MP-5 into the man's head when the bastard reached for his gun.

Conners and Rankin helped Ferguson out of the netting, then pulled the other man out and trussed him with handcuffs that looked like twists for Hefty garbage bags.

"Kiro," said Conners, shining a flashlight in his face. "Yeah, that's the bastard."

"Take his picture so we can upload it to Corrigan and make sure," said Ferg, handing the small digital camera to Rankin. As he ran back and grabbed his shotgun, something exploded at the top of the hill; Ferguson heard the heavy thump of the helicopters and started shouting to the others.

"Go, let's go! Go!" he repeated, over and over.

Conners carried the Chechen over his back like a sack of potatoes. He started to slide him onto the seat of one of the bikes behind Guns, but Ferg stopped him. The CIA officer jabbed two syringes of Demerol into the terrorist's rear, counting on the synthetic narcotic to keep him dazed for a while. Then he pushed him onto the bike, holding it while Conners got on at the rear. It was a tight squeeze, but it beat walking.

The helicopters were taking turns pounding the front of the fort and circling nearby. There was a chance they would see the bikes as they headed into the forest, but once they were in the trees, the choppers would have a hard time pursuing them.

"Do it," said Ferguson over the com set.

Guns stalled the bike, then kicked three times before it started again. This time they jerked forward, nearly falling over but finally gaining their balance.

Something exploded behind them. Conners heard the roar of the helicopter and leaned his head into his prisoner's shoulder, waiting for the cannon shells to tear them apart. They were nearly a mile away before he realized they were going to make it.

13

The prisoner's moans weren't enough to match his voiceprints, but Ferg decided they'd keep the bastard incapacitated with the Demerol rather than trying to get him to say something coherent over the sat phone. The visual image was a match at least, and as far as he was concerned, that was good enough. According to Corrigan, the Russians were telling headquarters that they had completely obliterated the guerrilla stronghold. Sixteen Chechens had been killed. The attackers had suffered three fatalities and five wounded.

The skies overhead were filled with Russian aircraft, complicating the team's escape plans. They were about fifteen miles southwest of the cave complex, holed up in rocks with a good view of the valley to the west, all the way to the east–west train line to Georgia. There was an airstrip about three miles to the south where they had originally planned their pickup, but Van Buren had put the operation temporarily on hold. The Russians had put some Hinds there, along with supporting troops.

"Shouldn't have pissed them off, huh?" Ferguson told him.

"Guess not."

"It was an old car. Could have used a wash and wax."

"So you saved him money."

"Yeah."

"We're working on finding a better site," the SF colonel told Ferguson. "But the Russians are watching the main airports pretty closely. We may end up going to a backup plan, maybe getting a pair of helicopters."

"We're not particular," said Ferg. "Just get us the hell out of here."

"It's safer for you to sit and wait. Only be a few days."

"I don't like waiting around, VB."

"Neither do I." Van Buren sighed on the other end of the line. "Corrigan says there's a car for you at Narzan. Some CIA ops drove it down from Moscow in case you needed it. Fully fueled and everything."

"Yeah, he already told me. But that's seventy-five kilometers away. We might just as well walk to Georgia."

"Your call."

Ferguson snapped off the phone without saying anything else.

"Maybe we can take the bikes and swing up to the train line west of Groznyy," said Conners, who'd been listening nearby. "Ride it all the way to Moscow."

"There's an idea," said Rankin sarcastically.

"I'm serious," said Conners. "Once we're in the car, we can get pretty far. I've been looking at the maps, Ferg. Turn on the laptop."

Ferguson humored him, though he realized it would be far safer to wait there than try and hop a freight. A train line did run north out of Chechnya, and Conners showed Ferg from sat photos that it wasn't well guarded beyond Groznyy heading north.

"We need two spots to get on," said Conners. "Nice grade with a curve would be perfect. Two guys get on, blow a lock off a boxcar, climb in, dump out shit, get the door open, make it easy to throw raghead over there in."

"What, you saw this in a dream?" asked Ferguson, impressed.

"We used to hop trains all the time when I was a kid. Rode one up from Jersey to Ramapo up in New York once, caught another back. Be like old times."

"Patrol," warned Guns, who had the lookout. "Trucks, a BMP."

Ferguson went to the edge of the mountainside overlooking the road. He could see the Russians moving in a small caravan southward. Suddenly a white cloud appeared near the lead vehicle.

"Great," said Ferguson. "Just what we need."

They watched as a group of Chechen rebels picked off the Russian patrol from a hillside about a mile and a half away. By the time a pair of helicopter gunships arrived to assist the ground troops, it was too late; three of their trucks had been destroyed, probably by radio charges planted in the road though the rebels had also used rockets and possibly grenades.

"Nice little operation," said Rankin, genuinely admiring it.

"That'll take the heat off," said Guns.

"All right boys, saddle up," said Ferg. "Narzan's about fifty miles away. We have a car waiting for us. We walk fast, we can make it in two nights."

I t was in fact less than fifty miles to the Chechen city, which sat west of Groznyy on the main east–west highway in central Chechnya, but they couldn't travel in a straight line. They took turns carrying their prisoner on a makeshift stretcher, trekking over trails that roughly paralleled what passed for the main road west.

After about three hours of walking, they came to a small settlement at the intersection of three different mountains. They'd gone about five miles at that point—fantastic time considering the terrain—but the village stopped them cold. There were a dozen buildings scattered along the main road, which was more a trail than a highway. Rankin and Ferguson scouted the approach and saw two sentries in sandbagged positions next to barricades that blocked the way. They were Chechen guerrillas.

Given the topography, there were dozens if not hundreds of spots where reinforcements might be lurking. If not for their prisoner, they might have been able to work a deal with the rebels. Instead, they had to find a way to skirt the tiny village; it was nearly light before they managed to get beyond it by crossing a field to the east and climbing a fifty-foot sheer wall. They pulled Kiro up by a rope, slipping and sliding, until they found their way to a cave about two miles southeast of the hamlet.

They were so tired that they all actually slept.

The first two miles the next night were not only uphill, but were very uphill—they climbed five hundred meters within a half mile on a remarkably wide path. From the satellite photos, they knew that there was a farm in a high valley on the other side of the ridge; when they arrived there they found a small cart with rickety wheels parked next to a shed. Ferguson's conscience pricked at him when he stole it, and he left an assortment of small bills in its place. The money might be a fortune to the poor farmer—or it might be completely useless in this isolated spot, sure to raise questions if he dared spend it.

The cart made it possible to go much faster on the road. Within an hour they had come to another farm, this one obviously belonging to someone much more prosperous—there was a truck next to a shed near the barn.

"I say we steal it," said Rankin.

"You think you can hot-wire it?" Ferguson asked him.

"I can," said Conners. "If it's old enough."

They sneaked into the yard, Guns and Rankin standing guard between the house and shed as Conners worked open the hood. The truck was an old Zil based on a Western European design that probably dated to the fifties. Conners lifted the hood and hunted for the ignition coil and starting solenoid, trying to get a feel for the wiring. He had just found the coil when the engine rumbled. Startled, he jerked his head up and smacked it against the hood.

"Keys are in it," said Ferg.

A light came on in the house as they were backing out. Rankin fired a burst from the Uzi at the side of the building, and the warning was enough to slow down whoever was inside.

Ferguson changed plans, and with the help of the satellite photos they were able to get within sight of Gora Tebulsikva on the border with Georgia several hours before dawn. They left the truck outside the town, continuing by foot to the southwest, where the hills were rutted with paths. The Russians had fenced the border with two rows of razor-wire fence and a series of guard posts, but Ferguson figured it shouldn't be too difficult to find a passage.

He took out his phone and sat down to call Corrigan, whom he'd promised to update every hour when they were on the move.

As he was talking, Kiro woke and began struggling against his restraints. They were out of Demerol. Guns tried talking to him in Russian, but he pretended not to understand. The Marine offered him food, but Kiro refused, continuing to struggle though he must have realized it was useless. Rankin put his Uzi in his face; Kiro smiled but continued to struggle until a hard smack on the side of the head with the short but hard metal stock rendered him senseless.

As they rolled him over to make sure his restraints were still snug, Conners noticed that the prisoner's pants were soiled. He felt a twinge of sympathy for the bastard, but it quickly passed.

"The good news is, the helicopter will meet us in the pass five miles on the other side," Ferguson told them, snapping off his phone. "The bad news is the asshole they set up to pick us up ran off with a better-paying customer, and they're not coming until tomorrow night."

"Fuck," said Rankin. "Why isn't this an SF operation?"

"We don't need all that fuss," said Ferguson, who had turned down Van's offer to send in an evac team. In the CIA op's opinion, that would draw way too much attention and was only a last-resort option. "You worried, Skip?"

"We can't stay here. We're too damn exposed."

Ferguson rubbed his face. He was tired, but if he fell asleep now he wouldn't wake up for hours and hours. He figured the same must be true of the others.

"Let's get across the border now," he said, pulling his ruck back on. "We should be able to find someplace to sleep on the other side of that hill there, in those woods."

They found a well-worn passage underneath the fence about a half mile farther south. Ferguson and Guns scouted along the fence line until they came to another somewhat less worn. Worried that despite Corrigan's intelligence to the contrary there were high-tech sensors between the fence, Ferguson sent Guns through. By the time he made it back, it was nearly dawn.

Conners and Rankin carried Kiro between them as they approached the fence, then dragged him under like a trussed pig. Meanwhile, Guns and Ferguson scouted the area for a place to hole up. About a half mile into Georgia they spotted a military post manned by six guards, who had a jeeplike vehicle mounting a machine gun near the post. The shoulder of the road dropped off a good eight feet as it passed, but to get by without being seen they'd have to crawl along it—impossible to do with Kiro. They trekked back up the hill, moving along the valley and actually crossing back into Chechnya before coming around through another pass, this one unguarded.

It was nearly midmorning before they finally found a secure place to camp, throwing themselves down against the rocks as if they were down-filled pillows. Ferguson started talking about the plan for tomorrow; he had them climbing aboard the helicopter before realizing not one of the others was awake.

14

 In the early stages of the war against terrorism, the U.S. had sent ten UH-1 Hueys to Georgia to help fight against Islamic rebels. Ferguson thought one of the Hueys would be coming for them now, so when the helicopter descended low enough for him to see clearly with his NOD that it wasn't a Huey, he hesitated before blinking his flashlight. The chopper descending toward the patch of dirt across from the mountain stream had large struts extending from its cabin to giant wheels at the side. Its massive engines groaned and wheezed as the seventy-foot rotor above lowered it precariously close to the streambed.

A crewman jumped out and blinked a flashlight several times. Ferguson blinked his in response.

"Corrigan sent us," yelled the crewman.

Actually, the words sounded more like "Car came sent blues."

"And us," said Ferguson, stepping forward.

"Fregunski?" said the crewman.

"Close enough," Ferg told him. He waved the others forward from the copse where they'd been hiding.

"Quickly," said the crewman. "It's not safe. The rebels are everywhere."

The man turned out to be the pilot, and the only man aboard. Ferg slipped into the unoccupied copilot's seat. The pilot smiled, then concentrated on getting the helicopter launched. The old Mi-8 shuddered, then groaned upward, passing so close to the cliff at the left that Ferguson closed his eyes.

"Ten minute," said the pilot cheerfully.

"Ten minutes to where?" asked Ferguson. The airport at the capital was close to a half hour away, if not longer given their plodding pace.

"Pandori," he said, practically signing the name of the mountain village.

"We're going to Tbilisi," said Ferg.

The pilot turned toward him. "*Nynah,*" he said, drawing out the no.

"Tbilisi, yeah," said Ferguson.

The man began speaking in Georgian. Ferguson told him in English and then in Russian that he couldn't speak Georgian, but that didn't stop the tirade.

"We need to go to Tbilisi," Ferg told him. He put his hand on the man's right arm.

The helicopter pitched forward sharply. Ferguson, who hadn't belted himself in, slammed against the dashboard. He threw himself around and took out his gun.

"No more of that," he told the pilot.

"Tbilisi, no," said the pilot.

"What's going on?" asked Guns, poking his head between them.

"Our friend doesn't want to go to the capital," said Ferg. "How's your Georgian?"

Guns shook his head, but between them they puzzled out some information. The pilot had been challenged at the airport before taking off and had been buzzed by a Russian fighter just before finding them. He was afraid of being arrested if he returned to the capital. The closest he would take them was Micheta, a town about five miles north of Tbilisi.

Ferguson called Corrigan and told him to get a car up there.

"That's not as easy as you think," said the desk man.

"We're not walking," said Ferguson. "Why the hell didn't you get us a real helicopter?"

"It is a real helicopter."

"Corrigan, you and I are going to have a serious talk when I get back. You're supposed to facilitate my mission, not make it harder."

"I'm sorry. The embassy made the arrangements."

"They know we're on the same side, right?"

"Hold on the line while I talk to them," said Corrigan.

"Good idea."

"The embassy'll send a car," Corrigan told Ferguson finally. "It's on the way now. Plainclothes Marines."

"Guns'll be overjoyed," said Ferguson, snapping off the phone.

T he pilot had apparently been to the small town before, barely hesitating as he angled in between a set of power lines to land in a small field behind a school building. He stayed in his seat, with the rotors moving.

"It's been real," Ferg told the pilot in English.

The man gave him a thumbs-up and a wide smile, as if they'd had the time of their lives. Ferguson barely got the door up and closed before the helicopter whipped back upward.

"Starting to rain," said Guns.

"Figures," said Rankin.

"We have to move up to the road," said Ferguson, checking his watch. The Marines were due in ten minutes.

" 'All the money that ever I spent, I spent it in good company,' " started Conners, singing an Irish folk tune, as he picked up Kiro and slung him over his back. The prisoner groaned; Conners sang louder.

"*All the comrades that ever I had, they're sorry for my going away,*" he sang. "*All the sweethearts that I once had, they wish me one more day to stay. But since it falls unto my lot, for me to rise and them to not, I'll gently rise and softly call, good night and joy be with you all.*"

"See, the guy's dying," Conners explained to the others. "It's that kind of song."

"Yeah, no shit," said Rankin.

"You got a good voice, Dad," said Guns.

"And you're fuckin' crazy," said Rankin.

"And the rest of you aren't?" said Conners, spotting a pair of headlights approaching.

T he Marines took them to a house in the southeast quadrant of the capital, bringing them in through an alley, which made Kiro a little less obvious. Fully conscious, the prisoner had either reconciled himself to the fact that he wasn't going to escape or had decided to conserve his energy. He meekly allowed himself to be carried from the car into the house.

Ferg left the others to work out shifts for showering and sleeping while he went over to the embassy. He was met not by one of the resident CIA spooks he'd expected but the *chargé d'affaires*—a young woman in a black silk miniskirt who could have stepped out of any one of two dozen wet dreams he'd had as teenager.

And any number of others since.

"You need a shower," said the *chargé*. Two buttons of her mauve shirt were unbuttoned, giving a hint of lace beneath.

"I need a plane," said Ferguson.

"We're working on it." She brushed back her curly blond hair. Obviously she'd been woken up a short while before—Ferguson wondered what she'd look like if she had time to prepare.

"You really do need a shower," she said.

She must be right, he reasoned. Despite all of his innate animal magnetism and the powerful ESP messages he was beaming into her brain, she remained across the room.

"First I need to talk to the, uh, consul security coordinator," said Ferguson, using a euphemism for the CIA chief.

"I'm her. Really, Mr. Ferguson—you need a big-time shower."

"Really?"

"If I had a fire hose, I'd hose you down myself."

Ferguson spread his arms. "Take me, I'm yours."

"Up the steps, to the right."

"You really are getting me a plane, right?"

"We're working on it. We were told that you were to be picked up by your own people in Chechnya in a few days." She looked at him accusingly, as if he'd been boogied out of a date.

"Didn't make too much sense to hang around there," Ferguson said. "Russians were beefing up their patrols, and the Chechens were kicking them in the face."

"I'll find you some clothes."

"Why don't you help me in the shower instead?"

"I doubt I'd make it without passing out."

"I have first-aid training."

"I'll bet."

Ferguson used half the hot water in Tbilisi washing Chechnya out of his skin. He found a fresh set of clothes—but no *chargé*—in the room outside the shower.

The outfit included polyester boxers—not his style, but at least his size. The rest of the outfit was so preppy it came complete with tasseled loafers.

Miss Miniskirt was waiting downstairs.

"You missed a great shower," he told her.

"Sounded like it. You were singing."

"If I'd known you were close, I would have taken requests."

"I heard you down here." She held out her hand. "I'm Amanda Scott."

"Pretty name," said Ferg. "Goes with your eyes."

"I think you've been on assignment too long."

"Ain't that the truth," said Ferguson. "You going to offer me a drink?"

He followed her into a reception room, then through a side panel to a smaller, book-lined study.

"What are you drinking?" she asked.

"Whiskey. Pour yourself one."

"No thank you."

Ferg watched her pour out two fingers into the tumbler. He touched her hand as he took the glass; it was warm, as if her internal thermostat was set several degrees higher than his.

"So I hate to ask—Why the hell didn't you get us a real helicopter up to make the pickup?" he asked after a sip.

"We tried. It was sabotaged."

"By who?"

"Take your pick—drug runners, arms smugglers, Muslim crazies, Russians. Place is out of control."

She gave a weak shrug. Her breasts heaved up in a way that made it difficult to question her further.

"We'll have an airplane ready no later than tomorrow afternoon," she told him. "The Marines will stay with you until then."

"I could stay here."

"I'm afraid the ambassador wouldn't approve."

"I'll go to your place then."

"My boyfriend wouldn't approve."

"He's an idiot anyway," said Ferguson.

"True," said the woman. "But since he's standing out in the hall with a gun, maybe we'd better not talk too loud. He's the Marine who drove you here."

15

Colonel Charles Van Buren tried rubbing the fatigue out of his eyes as he powered up his laptop, waiting to hear from Washington that his people were not needed to grab the team and its prisoner. He'd received unofficial word already—from Ferguson himself—which had allowed him to order most of the men and equipment tagged for the operation to bed. Van Buren sympathized with the complaints as they'd disembarked from their MC-130—to a man his volunteers preferred action to sleep—but nonetheless he'd been sincere when he offered them a job well-done.

The colonel felt strongly that it was the outcome that mattered. If the team had gotten out without needing them, then the mission had been accomplished as surely as if Van Buren's two planeloads of paratroopers and Special Forces A teams had gone into action. Indeed, the military people on the Team had been drawn from Van Buren's own force, and he felt nearly as paternal toward them as he did toward his own son, James.

Ferguson was a different story—more brother and friend than son, though he was nearly young enough to be one. Van Buren admired the CIA officer a great deal; though they'd worked together for only a short time, they were good friends. On a professional level, they were a good match, Van Buren's caution and ability to plan balancing Ferg's tendency to work by the seat of his pants.

Still waiting for the official order to stand down—it had to come through the Pentagon—Van Buren pulled out his laptop to compose an e-mail home to his wife and son. Since taking the appointment as the commander of the 777th Special Forces Joint Task Group six months before, Van Buren had communicated with his family almost exclusively through e-mail. It had its advantages—it was certainly quicker than writing a letter, nor did he have to worry about time zone differences. But it surely wasn't the same as seeing them in person.

Van Buren brought up the most recent e-mail from his son, James. It was typical James, a terse account of his Babe Ruth League baseball game:

Dad—2 hrs., trip.; won 7–2.—james

Two home runs and a triple—Van Buren wondered if his son might have the makings of a pro ballplayer. He'd always thought of James as athletic and brilliant, but now that his boy was fifteen he wondered how brilliant and intelligent and athletic he *really* was. He had a ninety-five average at school and had started on the varsity football and baseball teams since freshman year. But the school was in a small rural community, and there was no way of knowing how it really compared to the rest of the world.

Van Buren selected the text of the message and hit reply. Then he began to type.

James:
Great game, son.

He backed up the cursor, erasing "son." It sounded too stiff.

Van Buren hunched over the laptop, searching for something else to say. His writer's block was interrupted by the phone. He grabbed the handset.

"Yo, Van Buren, who the hell do you think you're fooling, playing with snake eaters?"

The voice caught him off guard, but just for a second.

"Dalton, what the hell are you doing calling Dehrain?"

"Oh is that where I'm calling?"

"How'd you track me down?"

"Friends."

"Look, it's 2300 here, and—"

"What, you keep banker's hours now that I'm not around to kick your butt?"

"Yeah, that'll be the day."

"Listen, I can't really go into much detail on the phone, not this phone anyway, but I have something I want to talk to you about the next time you're in Washington."

Van Buren leaned back in his seat. Like Van Buren, Dalton had served as a captain with Army Special Forces, bringing home a Purple Heart from Central America. He'd gone on to hold several important posts with USSOCOM, before retiring a year ago to join the private sector.

Dalton joked about his medal, claiming it was certified proof that he was an asshole, but the fact of the matter was that he had earned it rescuing two civilian DEA agents from a guerrilla ambush, and had humped one of his own men to safety besides. Few officers, even in Special Forces, could make such a claim; in Van Buren's opinion, the military had lost a good man when he separated from the service.

"So?" asked Dalton.

"I'm going to be in Washington pretty soon," said Van Buren. Assuming the Team's assignment wrapped up without a problem, he'd be returning to debrief with Ferguson.

"Good. When?"

"Soon." Van Buren wouldn't elaborate even if he knew, not even for an old friend.

"Need to know, huh?" Dalton laughed after a few moments of silence.

"My schedule's not really my own."

"When you're here, I want you to drop by and talk about career opportunities. Give me a call at home. Just leave a message where I can get you. Don't worry about the time."

Van Buren laughed. "What, you have an inside track for general?"

"Something better, VB. Much, much better."

And with that, Dalton hung up.

16

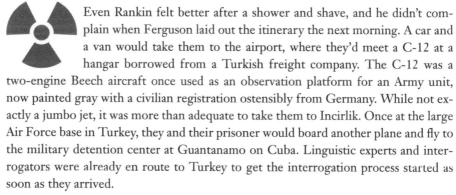Even Rankin felt better after a shower and shave, and he didn't complain when Ferguson laid out the itinerary the next morning. A car and a van would take them to the airport, where they'd meet a C-12 at a hangar borrowed from a Turkish freight company. The C-12 was a two-engine Beech aircraft once used as an observation platform for an Army unit, now painted gray with a civilian registration ostensibly from Germany. While not exactly a jumbo jet, it was more than adequate to take them to Incirlik. Once at the large Air Force base in Turkey, they and their prisoner would board another plane and fly to the military detention center at Guantanamo on Cuba. Linguistic experts and interrogators were already en route to Turkey to get the interrogation process started as soon as they arrived.

Thanks to the Kiro lead, analysts at the CIA were eying Chechnya as the nexus for a large operation aimed at stealing nuclear waste. Presumably Kiro would tell them something once they got him to Guantanamo; in the meantime more than two dozen people were poring through intercepts, studying satellite photos, and rummaging through mountains of data looking for hints of an operation that had thus far remained hidden.

Ferguson hadn't forgotten that the shipment of waste that had started all of this hadn't been tracked down, nor was he necessarily impressed by the analysts' efforts thus far. He would have liked to talk to the imprisoned Chechen who knew about making dirty bombs. But he was ready to go home and take a few days off.

Tbilisi sat in the center of ancient trade routes connecting Europe and Asia, and was a prized possession and sometime victim for Persians, Byzantines, Arabs, Mongols, Tartars, and Turks, all of whom had occupied and occasionally mugged it for centuries after it was founded in A.D. 455. The Russians came to the city in 1801; Georgians tried rebelling but were ultimately crushed in 1905, their revolt a little premature. When the successful revolt came, Georgia remained in the empire.

Under the Soviets, life had been constrained and drab. Deep in the heart of the Caucasus, the city had a European feel to it; the buildings and bridges over the Kura reminded visitors of Austria or eastern Czechoslovakia, as the Czech Republic was then known. An industrial center with a population over a million, the city boasted a major university as well as important research facilities and a lively theater. But years of civil war and failed economic reform since the end of the Soviet Union had helped transform the country into a kingdom of gloom. Tbilisi now was the forlorn capital of chaos, ruled by crime lords, corrupt politicians, drug runners, and committed madmen. Armed escorts did not draw a raised eyebrow here, and when the Marines—dressed in plainclothes though even a casual passerby would know they were Americans—blocked off the street in front of the safe house, no one even bothered to glance their way.

The Marines brought three vehicles—two Mercedes sedans borrowed from the embassy and a van that carried the bulk of the security team. Ferg put Kiro in the backseat of the second Mercedes between Conners and Rankin. They'd changed his clothes and handcuffed him, nudging him into a compliant haze with a shot of Demerol; he also had a hood so he couldn't see where he'd been or where he was going. Guns, sitting in the front with his MP-5 and three clips on the floor, had a syringe with another double dose of Demerol in his pocket in case the prisoner began acting up.

Ferguson got in the front of the van, which was trailing immediately behind the sedan with the bulk of the security team. The first Mercedes started out as they locked up; it would run ahead to make sure there were no problems with traffic.

They were just crossing the river when Ferg spotted the small yellow station wagon. It had only a driver, no passengers, and at first the fact that it made the same turns they made seemed just a coincidence.

"Let's take some turns," he told the others, and the Marine drivers worked out a quick set of detours along the river, driving through a tourist area. The station wagon stayed with them for a while, then disappeared; a panel truck seemed to take over as they came back onto the main street.

"Maybe that I'm just paranoid," said Ferguson. "But I think we're being followed."

Their backup plan called for them to divert to the embassy, pick up more Marines, then drive out to a military field about seventy-five miles away. Ferg also had the option of driving straight out to the military field and calling for the C-12 to meet them there. He took out his sat phone and called Amanda, who was at the airport waiting for them.

"You really should have showered with me," he told her when she answered the phone.

"Mr. Ferguson, where are you?"

"My girlfriends call me Ferg."

"We were told you were en route."

"I think we have a tail. It's an operation, at least two vehicles, one a panel truck, which doesn't make me feel too good."

"Where are you now?"

Ferguson had to ask the driver for the highway name. Amanda didn't answer when he relayed it.

"You around, Beautiful?" he asked. He saw the panel truck turn off behind them, but couldn't tell what car was following them.

"We think the Russians are watching the airport," said Amanda, returning. "We're checking."

"All right, let's go over to plan B. We'll drive right out to the second pickup," said Ferg. "I think it'd be better if we had the security teams meet us en route."

"I agree," said Amanda.

"I knew you were easy." Ferg glanced at the mirror, trying to make out if there was another car. The Marines were edgy in the back, and even the driver had checked his pistol, snugged into a shoulder holster beneath a sports coat. "Let me think on this a second. Keep the line open."

"What's going on?" asked Guns over the com set.

"People at the airport. Probably pissed that we didn't choose Aeroflot."

"We going over to the field?"

"Maybe. Let's do another loop, what routine are we up to driver—C?"

The driver nodded. They had worked out a series of streets to follow to lose trails without executing high-risk maneuvers.

Assuming those were the Russians behind him, Ferguson realized they'd invested an awful lot of resources into the operation. Given that, they might have staked out the backup airfield as well—it was, after all, the next best choice, and pretty obvious.

Back to the embassy then. Have a helo come in. Too bad they couldn't just land the C-12 on the roof.

"Hey, Beautiful, our airplane ready to go?" Ferguson asked Amanda.

"Yes, of course."

"Tell him to take off."

"Huh?"

"Tell him to take off. He's going to pick us up."

"Where?"

"I don't know yet. I have to talk to the driver and look at a map."

"Ferg—"

"See, I told you I'd grow on you."

———————

nce they were sure the C-12 was in the air, the driver in the lead car pulled a sharp 180 on the highway they were driving on. As the others sped on, he rammed into the panel truck, taking out the only vehicle they'd spotted that could be carrying a sizable force of troops. Veering as he was sideswiped, the driver of the van tipped over his truck, smashing into an oncoming car. Meanwhile, the Mercedes with the prisoner and the van sped off the road back onto city streets, racing through a series of alleys and lots to a stretch of warehouses at the eastern edge of the industrial section.

"You with us?" Ferg asked Amanda back at the airport. She was the only one whose radio could communicate with the pilot of the plane, which had taken off and was spinning back toward the edge of city.

"We're ready."

Ferg saw the plane overhead.

"Do it," he told the driver.

The Marine slammed on the brakes as they turned the corner to Swward Avenue, cutting off the station wagon following them. Ferg jumped from the truck as the Marines piled out in the back, brandishing weapons. The station wagon and a black Russian Lada behind it slammed to a halt; a large truck stopped behind them and men started coming out of the back. Someone got out of the Mercedes—a man in a yellow sports coat.

"Ah, the FSB," yelled Ferg over his com set as the Marines with him in the van piled out, weapons as obvious as they could make them. "Amanda, honey, you guys have a serious security problem at your end of the operation. You have to watch that pillow talk."

At the other end of the long, wide street, Rankin slammed against the prisoner as their car veered across the roadway, blocking off the path of traffic. He pushed to his left as Guns jumped from the car, brandishing his MP-5 at a small vehicle that had stopped twenty yards away, waving at the dazed driver to pull off into the lot on the left. Out of the car, Rankin grabbed the prisoner's side and started pulling him along with Conners.

The C-12 roared down onto the pavement, so close to Ferguson that it knocked him off his feet. It veered slightly to the right, then the left on the long roadway, bouncing in a pothole and nearly tilting too far forward before finally stopping. By the time Ferguson reached the door of the plane, Rankin and Conners were dragging their prisoner around the wing. Guns, taking up the rear, was coming on a dead run.

"Go, just go!" yelled Ferguson as he pushed Kiro into the airplane. "Get this thing up."

Conners crawled over Kiro into the C-12; on his haunches, he pulled the prisoner up and pushed him toward one of the two military crewmen. Belatedly, he realized that the soldier had a gun at his belt. Conners jumped up and pushed his way between the prisoner and the man; even with his prisoner handcuffed, blindfolded, and doped up, Conners knew better than to take a chance he might get the gun.

Rankin jumped in. The plane started to move. The door slapped shut, then flew open. Guns's head appeared in the doorway, followed by Ferguson's.

The plane was already lifting off the ground. As they struggled to close the door, Guns suddenly slipped and for a split second felt as if he were going out head-first.

Ferg grabbed him, hauling him back as the plane lifted, then tilted over on its wing, sending them sprawling inside.

"That's another one you owe me, Marine," the CIA officer told his team member.

The door slammed, then opened, then slammed again as the pilot banked hard over the abandoned factory, narrowly missing a chain-link fence before finally stabilizing and heading southwestward.

Ferguson went over to one of the windows, looking down on the scene they had just left. The Marines had jumped back into the van and were speeding off. There were a dozen troops standing near the truck behind the Mercedes; at the head of the knot was the man in the yellow jacket.

"Doesn't have much taste in clothes," said Ferg. "But otherwise he knows his business."

ACT II

Wise men ne'er sit and wail their woes,
But presently prevent the ways to wail.

—Shakespeare, *Richard II*, 3.2.178–9

1

THE WHITE HOUSE—TWO DAYS LATER

Corrine Alston checked her watch as she finished with the last of her e-mail, trying to decide whether she'd sneak out for a "normal" lunch or just send for a sandwich. Finally, she got up and took her pocketbook, slipped her Blackberry communicator inside, and went to the outer office to tell her secretary, Teri Fleming, she'd be gone for a while. Teri gave her an all-hold wave.

"He wants to see you," said Teri. "Just buzzed."

"All right." Corrine pulled down her suit jacket, then took out her compact to do a quick makeup check. "Anything new with your son?"

"Pitch meeting tomorrow. He's hopeful," said the secretary. Teri's son Billy was in LA trying to make good as a screenwriter, and his various adventures were often the subject of small talk between the two women. Teri probably knew his schedule as well as Corrine's, and she knew Corrine's exceedingly well.

"I'll sneak down for lunch when we're done," said Corrine.

"You have the DEC people at one."

"Hold them if I'm late."

"You will be," said Teri. "It's nearly one now."

"I'll do my best," said Corrine. She stepped out of the office, turned right, then nodded at the Secret Service man in the hallway ahead. Her destination—the president's office—was only two doors from her own. She stopped, rapped perfunctorily on the doorjamb, and pushed in.

In the four months that Jonathon McCarthy had served as president, the faint lines Corrine had noticed on his forehead during the campaign had furrowed deeper.

At times of tension they formed trenches in his forehead and just then they looked like river channels, belying his quick smile.

A Southerner by heritage and inclination—according to his campaign biography his forebears had stepped on Georgian soil as indentured servants in 1710—McCarthy retained the style and grace of the well-to-do family he had been born into and rose as Corrine entered the room.

"Miss Alston, I'm glad you could join us," he said.

He didn't bother introducing the others, as Corrine not only knew them but had helped vet most of them when the president was considering whom to appoint to his administration. Next to the president's desk sat Defense Secretary Larry Stich, his green sweater clashing with his gray suit and red tie. To his right was the national security advisor, Marty Green. The CIA director, Thomas Parnelles, was sitting in a chair at the other side of the room, his hands in a tent over his nose, partially obscuring the jagged scar on his cheek that reminded anyone who met him that he had worked his way up from the field.

"How was the play?" asked the president.

"It was very good," Corrine answered, taken by surprise.

"*Et tu, Brute?*" joked the president, his drawl striking an odd note with Shakespeare's pigeon Latin.

"Actually, it was *Richard II*," said Corrine.

"*When I was a king, my flatterers were but subjects; being now a subject, I have here a king for my flatterer.*"

"Very good," said Corrine. While her father had made his money backing movies, classical theater was his first love, and Corrine had seen or read all of Shakespeare's major plays by the time she was in grade school. Her mother, however, had been an actress, and carefully steered her daughter's interests toward "more useful arts."

"I played Richard in college," McCarthy explained to the others. He laughed. "That doesn't go out of this room now, gentlemen. I can count on Miss Alston's discretion as she's my attorney, but you all are subject to question. If it gets out, there will be lie detectors in your future."

McCarthy used the lie detector line about once a week, but the others laughed anyway.

The president leaned back in his chair, furling his arms in front of his chest as he always did when he changed the subject to something serious.

"We have a bit of a knot I'd like your advice on, Miss Alston. It's somewhat delicate, as of course you appreciate."

Corrine set her jaw, willing all emotion from her face. She called it full lawyer mode, and had learned to do it when, after graduating summa cum laude from an accelerated program, she'd come to congress as a staff lawyer for the House Appropriations Committee. Within a year she had moved over to Defense, and shortly after that went to work with the Intelligence Committee. Still only twenty-six, she no longer needed the set-jaw scowl to get others to take her seriously, but it was by now habit.

Parnelles began speaking, talking in his usual clipped sentences about a combined CIA/Special Forces operation investigating the possible disappearance of nuclear waste in the former Soviet Republic of Kyrgyzstan. The tangled trail of the operation had led to Chechnya, where the operation happened to come across a militant with connections to both al-Qaida and a lesser-known militant organization called Allah's Fist. In the course of their work, the CIA realized that the subject had also caused the murder of several American citizens in an attack on a shopping mall in Syracuse, New York, twelve months before. They had kidnapped him and taken him to Guantanamo.

"Let me suggest that you're using the wrong word," said Corrine sharply. "I don't believe you'd wish to characterize legal actions authorized by the U.S. government as 'kidnapping.' The word you're looking for is 'apprehend.' Such actions have lengthy precedent and are legally recognized. And I'm sure that's what occurred here."

Parnelles gave her the sort of smile a father might give a five-year-old who'd just lectured him on not smoking, then continued. The man was being held at the detention facility on Guantanamo under heavy guard. They suspected he had important information about a plot involving a hazardous waste bomb that might be targeted for the U.S.

Corrine realized what the dilemma was without the CIA director having to spell it out—they wanted to put him on trial for the mall attack, but were afraid of messing up the case by interrogating him improperly.

During his campaign, McCarthy had advocated using the criminal justice system to prosecute terrorists rather than the military tribunal system favored by his predecessors. In McCarthy's view—and Corrine concurred—the entire point of fighting terrorists was to preserve American traditions, freedoms, and institutions. The legal system provided plenty of tools to prosecute such murderers. In Corrine's opinion, terrorists were not enemy combatants—that status implied a certain dignity and righteousness that they clearly did not deserve.

"What do you think, Miss Alston?" McCarthy asked her when Parnelles finished.

"Should I speak as a citizen, or as the president's private counsel?" she asked.

"Both," said the president.

"As a citizen, I think you should tear the bastard's balls off."

The president laughed.

"However, speaking as a lawyer, if you want to try him in federal or state court, you have to consider carefully how you deal with him. I would think it appropriate to consult with the Department of Justice."

"We've followed their guidelines," said Parnelles. "This is new ground."

"If you're going to ask about torture," said Corrine, "that's not my area."

Parnelles glanced at the president.

"Not torture," said McCarthy.

"We have a drug," said Parnelles. "It's a kind of ultimate lie detector test. We would use it in conjunction with the interrogation, so we'd be better able to judge how valid the information is."

"I can't give an opinion on something like that off the top of my head," Corrine told him.

"Is that because you think it's something we wouldn't want to hear?" asked McCarthy.

He'd become adept at reading her hesitations over the past two years; she had joined his campaign as an intelligence advisor and quickly become an all-around confidante, eventually leaving her Senate post to help him full-time. McCarthy had called her in, as he usually did, not simply because he valued her opinion but because it wouldn't be shared with anyone else. And if her opinion was something he had to ultimately disregard, no newspaper would ever start a story: Despite receiving legal advice to the contrary . . .

"There's a possibility of a gray area," Corrine said, still hedging. "A voluntary submission—"

"It wouldn't be voluntary," said Parnelles.

"Few things in life truly are," said the president.

"There are legal theories in both directions," said Corrine.

"Stop speaking as a lawyer, dear," said McCarthy. He could see clearly which way she was leaning, but the others, less familiar with her, couldn't.

"I wouldn't use the procedure, then put him on trial," Corrine said, pausing as she selected the neutral "procedure" rather than a word that might be more accurate but loaded, like "brainwashing." "Anything that violates a defendant's right against self-incrimination is going to be a very big problem. Isolation, stress, and duress—even those techniques can be called into question."

"What if the information isn't used at the trial?" asked Defense Secretary Stich.

"You might not, but the defense will if they find out. I would. Even if it's not directly related to the case, it complicates matters. Even if it didn't provide grounds for an appeal," she added, turning to the president, "the political fallout would be unseemly."

"The information might be vital," said Parnelles.

"Then do it. But forget about prosecuting him in the States. Use a military tribunal if you have to."

"Even that has problems," said Stich. "Or so I'm told."

"There would be a great deal of value in upholding the rule of law," said McCarthy dryly. "But there is a bit of a time limit."

"A statute of limitations?" asked Corrine, not understanding.

"In a way. We have a message predicting that Satan will be struck by May 10. We would be Satan," added the president.

"It's credible?"

"That's what we need to find out," said the CIA director.

"Well, you're best off deciding whether you want to prosecute or not before going ahead," Corrine told him.

They sat silently for a moment. Corrine decided that was a cue for her to leave. "I think I'll go for lunch," she said, rising.

"Set a spell," said the president.

"I don't know if it would be *useful* for me to be present," said Corrine.

"You're always useful, Miss Alston. I believe the gentlemen are finished for now, and you and I have some other matters to discuss. I'll get back to you on this, Thomas."

"Yes, sir."

Corrine nodded to the others warily, aware that McCarthy actually wanted to discuss it further. One of his aides—Jess Northrup, an assistant to the chief of staff who was primarily responsible for keeping him close to schedule—came in and ran down the afternoon's appointments. He had a meeting with the head of the SEC, then a round of phone calls, all designed to push far-reaching business reforms. "Leveling the field for common folk to invest in their future" had been one of the president's important campaign slogans, but doing that in a town tangled with business and political interests was harder than 'rassling daddy gators—another of the president's pet sayings.

"Well?" asked McCarthy, as Northrup retreated.

"That's a deep subject," said Corrine.

"I hate it when my words are used against me," said McCarthy. He leaned back in his chair. "I need a set of ears and eyes I can trust."

"Your problem, Jon, is that you want to have your cake and eat it, too. Either question the prisoner or put him on trial."

"He's been questioned. They're not sure if they can believe what he says," said McCarthy.

They stared at each other, each silently pondering the dilemma. While the president clearly had a duty to prevent the loss of life, he also had to uphold the Constitution and preserve the rule of law. It was the sort of decision that Lincoln had had to make during the Civil War; McCarthy had written a book about Lincoln before leaving academia to go into politics, and the example of the country's greatest president was never far from his mind.

"What has he told you so far?" Corrine asked.

"Let's go back a bit," said McCarthy. "Way back. I want you to understand the perspective better than Thomas explained it. How's your Russian geography?"

"I know where Moscow is."

"Buzuluk mean anything?"

"Haven't a clue."

"Town on the Samara River. Other side of the Urals, a bit middle central. Think of St. Louis, if you could put it in lower Siberia." The president smirked. "The area's supposed to be lovely in the spring, if you can ignore the mosquitoes. During the Cold War, the Russians had an experimental lab there. They worked on reactors, alternate designs for submarines, and a series of nuclear rockets. Not much worked for them, but then that's the nature of experimental labs."

The president leaned back in his seat. "Well now, years go by, the wastes from the operation pile up. Variety of wastes, mind you—spent uranium, they call it U235 or ^{235}U, has the number in front of the letter like an exponential equation."

McCarthy drew out exponential equation in a way that made Corrine smile. He was playing country bumpkin, even though he obviously knew a great deal about the subject. It was a pose he liked to adopt.

"Control rods, contaminated boron-europium, oh a variety of things," continued the president. "A whole briefing paper full of them. Some last a few hours, some centuries. Some of it very nasty, some no more harmful than the glow on a Timex watch. Well now, comes the time and the lab work is done and all of this waste is settin' around—"

"Is this a Defense Threat Reduction Agency project?" Corrine asked. The DTRA was a joint U.S.-Russian effort to contain waste and warheads. It had met with some success containing radioactive material from antiquated bombs and missiles that had been scrapped under disarmament treaties.

"No, for various reasons this isn't under their purview. For a while, the Russian Navy took it over—I guess they weren't satisfied with making a mess up on the Kola Peninsula and thought they'd have a go here."

Despite the president's sarcasm, the situation on Kola was a serious one. Literally tons of waste material—including played-out reactor cores—were stored in deteriorating conditions at Russian naval bases on the Berents Sea. Various efforts were under way to clean them up, but there was a great deal of consternation about security at the sites, as well as safety measures.

"Well, this here project is a bit better contained. French company is working with the Russians, packaging up the worst waste into these containers that are easy to handle. Bit like putting a muzzle and wheels on a daddy alligator and carting him through town. The waste is transported from Buzuluk to Kazakhstan, then down to Kyrgyzstan for burial. Some of it, that is. We have monitoring devices in Kazakhstan, and two months ago, someone noticed a discrepancy. Not a large one, mind you, but one that couldn't be explained easily. So we sent the CIA in to investigate. Which is where Thomas and his people came in."

"What's the connection with Chechnya?" Corrine asked.

McCarthy smiled. "Now you know, dear, these terrorist groups can get more tangled than a pair of rattlers sucked into granny's loom."

That was a new one to her.

"Can they make a nuclear device from the waste?" she asked.

"Scientists say no. The CIA people think they're stealing it to build a dirty bomb," added the president. "But they haven't quite put the pieces together yet. And that's where our guest comes in."

"What did the Russians say?" asked Corrine.

"They were not consulted. That would have complicated things, frankly. They see him as a criminal as well. By the time they're done with him he won't be worth talking to. Their prisoners have an unfortunate habit of passing away in prison."

"You're not going to tell them what's going on?"

"I'm not sure anything is. That's the difficulty. The evidence is less than over-whelming," admitted the president. "The French company has manifests that show nothing is wrong. We have satellite photos that show all of the railcars used to move the waste arrived intact. But the sensors passed their calibration tests. I need to decide if our prisoner has valuable information or not." McCarthy shook his head. "My pref-erence would be to prosecute the son of a bitch in court."

"It's possible you've already lost that opportunity," Corrine told him.

McCarthy did what he always did when someone told him something he didn't want to hear: He smiled.

"How reliable is Mr. Parnelles's interrogation method?" she asked.

"Extremely."

"And the May 10 information?"

"They're not sure whether it's related. It was contained in a message to be deliv-ered at a mosque. The CIA is evaluating it. The interesting thing is that the language referred to a group that hasn't been heard from in years. Whether it's true or not, at this point it's difficult to tell."

There was a knock on the door, but McCarthy ignored it. He leaned forward. "I want you to assess the CIA operation. It's unusual."

"How unusual?"

"Have you heard of Special Demands?"

Corrine shook her head.

"It's a small unit of the CIA that was authorized by executive order on the NSC's recommendation just before we came into office. You were out of the Wash-ington loop by then, helping yours truly win the election. It's not all CIA. As a matter of fact, it seems to rely a great deal on Special Forces, though it uses a CIA officer as a team leader and is under their operation control."

Corrine shrugged. "Special Forces and the CIA have worked together for years."

"On and off, yes. But not precisely like this." McCarthy paused, the practiced politician cuing his audience to pay attention to what he said next. "I'm worried these people are cowboys. I need someone who can sniff around and report back to me without raising a ruckus. Would you do that, dear?"

"Mr. President. Jon—my job description—"

McCarthy's laugh would have shaken the walls of a lesser building. "Give me my pen. Let me fix your job description."

"I'm serious, Mr. President."

"I'm serious, too," he told her.

Corrine sighed. "I'll do whatever you want."

"Very good, dear." McCarthy was instantly serious once more. "We'll arrange for transportation to Guantanamo first thing tomorrow morning. Best watch what you wear. Some of those poor Marines haven't seen a good-looking girl like you in a coon's age."

2

 He was smaller than she expected, stooped over in his orange jumpsuit. His arms and legs were shackled together, and his eyes blinked constantly at the light. With his unkempt hair and beard he looked like a cross between a gnome and a homeless man. He moved meekly, though Corrine had noticed from the tapes she'd reviewed that this was an act; he could inflate his upper body and hold his head erect when he wished. The effect wasn't quite regal, but the difference was noticeable.

Corrine sat at the wooden table, waiting for him to settle into his seat. When he did, she nodded to the interpreter that she was ready to begin. Two soldiers stood near the door, large batons in their hands; two more stood directly behind the prisoner.

"Are you being treated well?" Corrine asked him.

Kiro known here as Muhammad al Aberrchmof, the name he had been given at birth—smiled as the translator repeated the question in Arabic, but said nothing.

"Is there anything that you need?" said Corrine.

"Freedom," said Muhammad al Aberrchmof, in English.

Corrine tried not to look surprised, though the interrogators had told her that he didn't understand English. They had also predicted that he wouldn't speak in her presence—as a woman, she was considered about on a par with an earthworm.

"Are there people who should be notified that you are all right?" she said.

al Aberrchmof said nothing.

"Your wife, your children," she prompted, turning to the translator and repeating the question. "You want them to know that you're well."

"I have only myself," said al Aberrchmof, again in English.

The interrogation team was watching all of this through a closed-circuit television. Though the camera was hidden in the wall, the prisoner probably realized they were watching and intended his performance as a message to them.

But what did it mean?

"It's a shame that you're alone," said Corrine. "Are you willing to cooperate with us?"

"I have cooperated," said al Aberrchmof.

"You speak English very well," she said.

al Aberrchmof didn't respond.

Corrine resisted the impulse to start asking more meaningful questions, fearful that doing so would tip off their importance and complicate the interrogation team's job.

"Is there anything you would like to tell me?" she asked instead.

al Aberrchmof began speaking in Chechen. The translator, who had been chosen because he could handle Chechen as well as Arabic, pushed his glasses back on his nose as he struggled to catch all of the words.

As he spoke, al Aberrchmof's voice gradually faded to a whisper. It was impossible to tell if he was really fatigued or if it was part of his performance.

"The Iranians are working with Allah's Fist to construct a weapon," he translated. "They will be launching it soon."

Corrine waited, as if she were considering this information.

"You are not part of Allah's Fist?"

al Aberrchmof's head had slid down toward his chest. Now it rose slowly, a contemptuous sneer on its face. "They do not understand the struggle of the Chechen people."

"It seems you're only a late convert to that cause," said Corrine.

The prisoner held her gaze for a moment, his eyes large as if he were trying to plumb her consciousness. Then he blinked, and once more his head tilted downward.

"What sort of weapon?"

al Aberrchmof didn't answer.

"A bomb?" she prompted.

Again he said nothing.

"How will they launch it?" she asked.

No answer.

"When will they launch it?"

No answer. She waited for a few seconds, then rose and started to leave.

"A ship," he said in English as she reached the door. "I believe they will use a ship. It is an Iranian plan. We Chechens care nothing for them. Our concerns are with Chechnya."

P eter Wilson, the head of the interrogation team, met her in the hall.

"What'd you think?" he asked, leading the way to the base commander's hut, where they were due for lunch.

"He told me about the Iranian ship," she said. "Pretty much what he said in interview 12."

"You remember the tape?"

"Of course," she said.

"The English is new."

"He was giving you the finger. Were you surprised he talked to a woman?"

Wilson shrugged. "Maybe we've broken him down far enough. Or maybe one devil is the same as another."

"How real is the Chechen rebel stuff?"

"Hard to tell," said Wilson. "It's consistent, but maybe he's just setting up some sort of political line or defense. The Russians didn't consider him important enough to go after, and a lot of these guys set up shop in Chechnya only because they won't be targeted by us. His history of attacks are all against the West."

"Is he telling the truth about the ship?" Corrine asked.

"Maybe."

"I think he's lying," she said. She hadn't made up her mind until then, but she realized she was right. "He's too controlled—he's giving us this information for some reason. Or for a lot of them."

"Obviously he has a reason," said Wilson. He held the door open for her, and they stepped out of the building. A pair of Marines nearby snapped to attention so stiffly they could have served as models for a poster. "But I think he's telling us more or less the truth. Bits of it anyway."

"He's telling us what he wants us to believe, certainly," she said. She stopped short of the waiting Hummer. "I think I'll skip lunch, Mr. Wilson."

"But—"

"I want to go back over the interrogation videos, then I have to get back to Washington."

"You have to eat, too, don't you?"

She smiled at him. "If you send over a sandwich, I'd appreciate it."

3

SUBURBAN VIRGINIA—THE NEXT MORNING

 Ferguson rested his head back on the vinyl cushion of the sofa in the doctor's waiting room, narrowing his eyes to slits and trying to avoid looking at any of the three overweight women sitting across from him. The room had all the charm of a bus depot, though the doctors who ran the practice had taken a stab at adding a personal touch—the beige walls were divided about chest high by a strip of corkboard with patients' photos attached. Most were trying to smile.

A television was mounted in a Formica-clad cabinet at his left, playing an endless loop that alternated segments devoted to cardiovascular distress and the early signs of Alzheimer's disease. Ferg had sat here long enough to be convinced he had both.

The window at the receptionist station slid open.

"Mr. Ferguson?"

"Ah, the condemned man is called for his supper," said Ferguson, unfolding himself from the sofa. He ignored the receptionist's puzzled frown and ambled to the hallway, pushing open the heavily sprung door where a nurse waited to lead him to the examining room.

"You are Dr. Ziest's patient," she said, her voice a question.

"Allegedly."

The nurse gave him an odd look, then led the way to a small room dominated by an examining table and a large medical cabinet. A scale sat opposite the lone chair in the room.

"You reschedule a lot," she said.

"Classic doctor avoidance syndrome," said Ferguson, stepping on the scale and adjusting his weight. He'd lost two pounds since his last visit.

"Dr. Zeist is away," said the nurse, writing down the weight.

"That's what they said. Should we check my height? Maybe I've grown."

"Please disrobe."

"Completely?"

Ferg said it so innocently that the nurse didn't know how to react. He started to undo his belt.

"Dr. Yollum will be in shortly," she said, retreating.

"I'll wait."

Ferguson took off his shirt but left his pants and shoes on; he knew from experience what the exam would entail. There was a large chart on the door about the different types of diabetes, and an article from *Runner's Magazine* plastered to the wall beneath a piece of plastic. The article—which Ferguson had read on his last visit—hailed the possibilities of running as a therapy for insulin-independent diabetes. It was long on feel-good pabulum and short on actual medical science, but had exactly the sort of cheerful tone that most doctors, including Zeist, liked to greet their patients with.

Yollum—Zeist's junior partner—was either too far behind schedule or too inexperienced to offer it. He rapped at the door, then whipped it open, reading Ferg's chart and swirling inside with the ferocity of one of the SF team members on a hostage rescue. He opened the folder and slapped it down on the cabinet, smoothing it over and tapping the top page before even looking for his patient.

"They gave you a hell of a dose of radiation," said Yollum, still looking at the chart. He stood about five-three, and his face was out of proportion to his body—large and square and red, as if he'd washed it with a mild acid before coming to work.

"Yeah. I still don't need a light to read a book," said Ferguson.

"Dr. Zeist is away."

"All I really need is the prescription updated. I'm almost out of the sheets I stole."

"You really shouldn't joke about things like that," said Yollum.

"How do you know it's a joke?"

"It says in your chart. Double funny bones."

"Yuk."

"I do my best." Yollum took his stethoscope and began doing an exam. Ferg flinched as the metal touched his chest—his recent adventures had left him with several large bruises. He was better off than Guns, though—despite his protests, the Marine had been shunted to a Navy hospital ten minutes after a corpsman took a look at him at Guantanamo.

"You have a number of contusions," said Yollum diplomatically. "Scratches on your face."

"Bar fights are my hobby," said Ferguson.

"Cough please."

Ferg choked, proving he didn't have a hernia. Yollum went back to his chart. "You've lost weight."

"Aerobics."

"Mmmm." Yollum started hunting through the papers. "Your lab work doesn't seem to be here."

Ferg stood and reached into his back pocket. "This is a copy," he said. "They sometimes get lost."

Yollum, embarrassed, took the sheet.

"Don't sweat it, Doc. I'm used to the routine. That's why I had a copy sent to me."

Yollum took the lab report, pushing the papers back to see the details of his temporary patient's history. Ferg watched him stop at the pathology report, his nose twitching slightly as he read the size of the tumor removed from his thyroid—4.2 centimeters—and the fact that it had spread beyond the thyroid capsule. He moved on, pushing through the reports from the radiologist on the full body scans he'd already referred to, hunting for the stack of lab results, which tracked the levels of thyroid replacement hormone in Ferguson's bloodstream.

"You're a little low," said Yollum.

"Yeah. Sometimes I forget to take the second pill."

"How often?"

Ferguson shrugged. If he knew how often, he wouldn't miss it. He thought it worked out to about once a week on average, but there were probably times he missed it more often. Once in a while he missed his morning dose as well, which was much higher; there was always hell to pay for that.

"Dr. Zeist has you on an unusual protocol," said Yollum. "T-3 and T-4. We usually just do T-4."

Replacement hormone therapy—necessary for someone like Ferguson who had had his thyroid removed—had the aura of an exact science. It had been done for many, many years; in fact, the replacement hormone drugs were so old they predated key FDA requirements. But the truth was that the exact process of how the different hormones worked in the body was still shrouded in mystery. Though the body converted T-4 into T-3, many patients—including Ferguson—reported that they felt considerably better on a combination. Only a few doctors believed them and were willing to experiment with different dosages; Zeist was one.

"Thing is, Doc, I have a meeting I have to catch. I'd appreciate it if you could write me the prescription. If you want to up the T-3 slightly, I can try it."

"You interpreted the lab numbers."

"Dr. Zeist showed me how," said Ferg. It was a lie—Ferguson had done his own research, and in any event it wasn't rocket science—but Ferguson knew the fib would make Yollum feel better.

"I'm not saying the protocol is bad. But if you're having trouble remembering to take the second pill, it's going to do more harm than good. The replacement drugs are also a kind of chemotherapy for you, and considering the size of the tumor and the scans—"

"I know what the statistics are," said Ferg. He tried smiling, but he was starting to run low on patience.

Yollum clearly had a lecture on the tip of his tongue about how slow-moving his type of thyroid cancer was, how even someone diagnosed with Stage IV had a chance of surviving five years after surgery and even beyond—but he stowed it at the obvious tone of impatience.

"I'll write the prescription."

"I need the lab report back," said Ferguson. "I found it useful to hold on to copies of my stuff."

"Of course. I'll have the office staff make a copy. Bob, you're due for another scan."

"Yup."

"Did you want to set that up now?"

Did he want to? No. The scan itself was a major hassle—you drank a bunch of radioactive iodine and lay in a claustrophobic machine while a special camera climbed over your body and hunted for stray thyroid cells, which by definition would be cancerous. Then you tried not to get close to anyone for the next few days, since you were radioactive. But that was the easy part—in order to do the scan with a high degree of accuracy, you had to go off the thyroid medicine for several weeks. It was like signing up for clinical depression.

"How about the shots?" said Ferguson, suggesting an easier protocol.

"You really have to have a clean scan first, usually two. Maybe next time."

"Uh-huh," said Ferg. He wasn't sure whether to bother with the scan or not; according to all the studies, further treatment didn't affect survival rates, which pretty much meant they were useless.

"You probably want to discuss it with Dr. Zeist. Come into my office, and I'll write the prescriptions for you. Government worker, huh?"

"Oh yeah," said Ferg, pulling on his shirt. "Pay sucks, but you can't beat the health plan."

4

 To get into the Cube, Corrine Alston had to run a gamut of security checks, then stand in a small booth that looked a little like a stainless-steel shower stall that checked for high-tech transmitting devices or bugs. Corrine swore she could feel her skin tingle as she stood in the device, and when she came out her ears were ringing.

Her guide walked her down the hall of the unpretentious building, which was housed in a corner of an industrial complex not far from the Beltway in Virginia. They were on the ground floor, but the elevator they entered went in only one direction—down. When it stopped, they walked down another hall, past several locked doors, then to a stairwell guarded by two Special Forces soldiers in civilian clothes. This stairwell led down to the operations floor, where a secure conference room and a somewhat smaller operations room used to communicate with SF units and officers in the field was located.

Corrine's ID and thumbprint were scanned at the top of the stairs. She was then waved ahead without her guide, who lacked the extremely limited clearance needed to descend the steps.

After such a variety of high-tech precautions, the room itself was remarkably plain. There was a whiteboard at the front, an old-fashioned projector, and a small computer projector. A laptop sat on one of the two tables; the man in charge of the briefing used it to project slides onto the whiteboard. The only person in the room that Corrine recognized was Daniel Slott, the deputy director of operations for the CIA. He sat with his arms folded on his lap at one corner of the first table, his gray-speckled goatee shimmering with the reflected light from the computer slide projector.

Slott introduced Corrine to the others, stating her title and adding that she had just returned from interviewing the prisoner at Guantanamo. He gave no explanation for her presence. Though his tones were politic and soothing, the audience would have had to be deaf, dumb, and blind not to realize he resented her being there.

"Just to give a little background on how serious the matter is," said Slott, turning to Jack Corrigan, "could you please review the slides on reactor waste."

"Sure thing," said Corrigan.

Slott had told him they'd be spoon-feeding a guest from the White House, and so he had dusted off his full set of PowerPoint slides on the waste at Buzuluk. He liked the second slide especially—it showed a pile of reactor rod assemblies on the ground that reminded him of the Tinker Toys he'd had as a youth—except that these were glowing on a clandestinely exposed gamma-ray-sensitive film.

Corrigan quickly went through the background on the experimental reactors built by the Russians and moved on to the waste material stored at the site. A typical reactor fuel load would consist of anywhere from ten to nearly two hundred fuel elements or assemblies; in general these were rods (usually though not always clad in zirconium) that contained uranium oxide pellets. A high percentage of the uranium in these pellets—3 to 4 percent, similar to the amount in Western commercial operations—were ^{235}U. Once inserted in the reactor, they were made to undergo a chain reaction that produced a number of by-products, including weapons-grade plutonium.

Not all of the reactors were configured as the ones indicated in his slides, Corrigan hastened to tell Corrine, but this footnote led to another slide indicating how dangerous plutonium was as waste—ten-millionths of a gram would cause cancer if inhaled.

Corrigan clicked into another series of slides on the waste by-products that had resulted from the experiments and reactor production. He especially liked the strontium-90 slide, since it illustrated how strontium could replace calcium in bones. The slides explained that the fuel assemblies themselves became potent radiation emitters, as the cobalt, iron, manganese, and nickel in the rods as well as the stainless steel interacted and transformed during the process. He touched briefly on the difference between alpha waves, which to be honest Corrigan himself didn't totally understand.

Alpha radiation—actually a helium atom—was easily stopped in the environment, though once in the body it could do very serious damage because it tended to ionize or remove electrons from other elements. Beta radiation in high doses could cause burns; it was emitted during radioactive decay, and, like alpha radiation, was usually a threat once a substance containing it entered the body. Gamma radiation was a problem on a different order—its high-energy, short-wavelength energy penetrated just about anything, even several feet of concrete. Though often compared to X-rays, in general, gamma radiation occupied a different part of the energy spectrum.

The effect of the different radiation-producing materials varied greatly, depending not only on the type of radiation emitted but how the radiation was "re-ceived" by the body. Massive external doses could kill immediately, but effects of smaller doses over time were more complex. Strontium in the body, for example, would replace calcium in the bone. There it could cause bone tumors and leukemia. Irradiated iodine might cause thyroid cancer, and on and on, as the slides indicated, documenting radiation amounts and the damage likely at various distances and expo-sures.

Ferguson had seen these slides several weeks before, and so he turned his atten-tion to *Miss* Alston, the president's personal counsel and unofficial babysitter. Accord-ing to Slott, the secretary of state had gone ballistic when he found out they snatched Kiro without running the notion by him or the Russians, and obviously *Miss* Alston was the result.

Corrine was good-looking—Slott's briefing there hadn't done her much justice—but that only made Ferguson resent her presence even more. She was obviously just another broad who'd slept her way to the top. She came complete with one of those riches-to-riches princess stories the media loved—parents in the movie biz, who dumped their daughter East to GW and then Columbia Law while she was still a teenager, mixing a little righty and lefty influence together. Among the other things the media liked to report on was the marathon she'd run at eighteen.

Ferg lost interest in her as the analysts took over and reviewed the most perti-nent intercepts and satellite data. Using Kiro's information as a lead, the NSA had helped them locate a tanker currently being refitted in Bandar 'Abbās, Iran. The ship was designed to transport ethylene, which meant it had a large tentlike structure cov-ering the main deck—the perfect place to put dirty nuclear waste.

At 89.9 meters long, the ship had held 2960 cubic meters of fuel before entering dry dock for refitting. Drawing from 2.5 to 3.5 meters, it was designed to navigate on inland waterways as well as the ocean—which meant it could sail upriver to its target. Explosives were stored near the ship, another vital ingredient for a dirty bomb, since the material would have to be spread out over a wide area. The analysts were sure this had to be the dirty-bomb ship—if indeed there was one.

"You want to talk to us about the ship, Ferg?" said Slott.

"Straight operation," he said. "We go in, we observe, we blow it up."

Colonel Van Buren, sitting next to him, rolled his eyes. He knew Ferguson was just busting balls—they'd discussed the operation at great length over a scrambled phone as he flew to the States for the briefing. Van Buren had plans for a full-scale assault—two borrowed SEALs units along with his entire Special Forces Army Group, Stealth fighters, and a pair of AC-130 gunships. But he and Ferg had agreed that the initial operation would consist of only a small force. The Team, led by Ferg, would be deposited on shore by the SEALs so they could reconnoiter with the help of local agents. The larger operation would have to wait for hard evidence.

But Van Buren knew Ferguson couldn't resist tweaking noses. He had obviously already taken a dislike to Ms. Alston. The colonel watched her hackles rise; she had no reason to take the CIA officer lightly.

"You can't blow it up if it's loaded with radioactive waste," said Corrine.

Ferguson leaned over to give her a condescending smile. "Why not?"

"Because of the collateral damage," she said. "The whole ship—a tanker—filled with radioactive waste?"

"It wouldn't all be waste," said Corrigan. "There'd be a lot of explosives to spread it around."

"Why should we care?" said Ferg, bothered by the know-it-all tone in her voice. Did she seriously think he hadn't considered the consequences of the operation or his actions?

"It is a legitimate concern," said Slott. "But I don't think Bob is serious about blowing it up. As for the composition of the waste—"

"Hey, shit happens," said Ferguson, sliding back in his seat.

"Ferg and the Team will check the situation out," said Van Buren, realizing he had to save Ferguson from himself. "Very small group, the way we usually operate. We scout it, then we do what's appropriate. We'll have several options. I have a plan already."

"Van's right," said Ferguson.

"According to the analysts, it's possible that they're staging the waste from a different site, or that this is only one part of the operation," said Slott. "If the waste were already at the ship, we think we'd have picked up some readings from different sensors we've had in the waterway. We have got some other targets to look at outside of the port before we look at the ship."

"That's one reason we want the native," said Ferguson. "I know that's a risk," he added, looking at Slott. The DDO had put considerable energy into rebuilding the humint network in Iran, and Ferguson's proposal would jeopardize it.

"It is a risk," agreed Slott. "But then so is the rest of the plan."

Corrine watched Ferguson as he discussed the situation with Slott; it appeared they would jeopardize if not burn at least one native agent, and they were debating whether to take him out with the Team or not.

What a macho bozo, she thought; he probably *would* blow up the ship if he had the chance and call it an accident. The president's fears were on the mark—these idiots *were* cowboys.

And she still hadn't figured out exactly how Special Demands operated. Though it was obviously under the deputy director of operations and therefore part of the operations directorate, it didn't belong to any of the "normal" operation desks or areas and seemed to have unusual access to resources, both within the Agency and the military. Corrine hadn't had a chance yet to look at the executive order or the NSC paperwork explaining it, let alone go over to CIA headquarters and research the files to get some perspective on Special Demands. That would require some time to negotiate the protocols, and would probably require working in a "safe"—an ultrasecure area where she would be literally locked in with material.

She'd get on that as soon as the meeting was over.

"You have a time frame?" Slott asked Ferguson.

"Van needs another day or two to pull the rest of the elements together," Ferg said. "Forty-eight hours from now we can go; we'll have details for you twelve to eighteen beyond that. Swordfish is already in the Gulf. They'll be ready to go by the time we fly in. Yada yada yada."

"I'd like to hear the details if you don't mind," said Corrine. "What's Swordfish?"

A smile spread over Ferguson's face, and he leaned back farther in the chair, his head now draped against the hard back. He waited for Slott—it would have to be Slott—to tell *Miss* Alston that operational details would be restricted to an absolute need-to-know basis, since even an inadvertent comment could put many people in danger.

But instead of telling her to mind her own business, Slott patiently explained that Swordfish was an in-house term for a submarine adapted for Special Operations. Several were prepositioned around the world; they carried a pair of Advanced SEAL Delivery Vehicles, basically minisubs that could be used to deposit Ferguson and his SF squad near the port.

"What happens if there is waste on the ship?" Corrine asked, stubbornly returning to the point that bothered her the most. "Will you blow it up?"

"Should we?" said Ferguson.

"No, absolutely not."

"Well that settles it. We won't."

"What will you do?" Corrine asked Slott.

"That would be an upper-level decision," the DDO told her. "At the moment, our main concern is just figuring out what's going on."

"You can't just blow it up," she insisted.

"Why the hell not?" said Ferguson.

"Because it'll be radioactive."

"And?"

"Civilians will die."

"Better them than us," said Ferg.

"We're not going to just blow it up. It's not our call. Stop egging her on, Ferg," said Van.

"Is there a definite connection between this ship and the May 10 message?" asked Corrine.

"What May 10 message?" asked Ferguson.

"The one predicting an attack. Because if so, this can't be part of the operation. It would take weeks for a ship to get from Iran to an American port."

Ferguson knew about the message, of course, but considered it a red herring; the NSA was always forwarding intercepts, fueling rumors and endless speculation. "It's irrelevant," he said, getting up. "Are we through?"

Slott nodded. The others got up as well.

"She bothers me," Ferguson told Van in the hallway.

"Gee, and here I thought you were in love." He started walking up the steps. "You can't just piss people off. You have to play by the rules."

"I do play by the rules."

"Whose? Yours?"

"Rules are rules." They reached the elevator level. Ferguson nodded at the security people, then punched the button for the elevator. "She's gonna be a pain in the ass."

"They're just concerned about the prisoner. She'll be gone in a week."

"Don't count on it," said Ferguson, getting into the elevator. "Want to have lunch?" he asked Van Buren.

"Can't. Got to go see an old friend."

"I'll talk to you before I fly back." Ferguson saw Corrine approaching as the doors closed. "I'm going to drive out to the shooting range this afternoon," he added loudly. "If I pretend I'm shooting at innocent children, I'm bound to do pretty damn well."

"Jesus, Ferg," said Van Buren, after the doors closed.

5

SUBURBAN VIRGINIA

Though the session had gone longer than he'd expected, Van Buren managed to head out in time to keep his lunch appointment with Dalton. His friend had suggested an out-of-the-way restaurant in suburban Virginia named Mama Mia's, but the place wasn't exactly a pizza parlor. A tuxedoed maître d'met him at the door. The man nearly genuflected when he mentioned Dalton's name, leading the way through the dining room to a table at the far end of the room, obviously selected for privacy. Dalton grinned when he spotted him, amused by his friend's awkwardness in the rather elegant surroundings. The fourth son of a working-class family with eight children, Van Buren still felt considerably more at ease in a McDonald's—or an Army cafeteria, for that matter.

"You dressed," said Dalton, smirking, as the host pulled the seat out for him. "I was afraid you'd show up in combat boots."

"I had a meeting," said Van Buren. He reached across the table. "How the hell are you?"

"I'm just kick ass," said Dalton.

The maître d' dropped the napkin in Van Buren's lap with an expert flick of the wrist, then faded away.

"You have to get used to that," added Dalton.

"Which?"

"Pomp and circumstance."

"Whoo-haw."

"Whoo-haw's good."

A waiter appeared at Van Buren's elbow. "To drink, sir?"

There was a bottle of Pellegrino on the table. "I'll have that," said Van Buren, pointing at the bottle. The waiter nodded, then disappeared.

Dalton stopped Van Buren from reaching for the bottle. "I can't take you anywhere. He's coming back with a bottle."

"What, you're too good to share?"

"Hey, I could have AIDS for all you know."

"I wouldn't doubt it, living in D.C."

"Nah, Reston's a million miles away," said Dalton. They fell into some easy talk about their respective families, both men bragging a bit about their kids. Dalton had a girl who was just entering college. She was heading north to Brown University. A generation ago, her yearly tuition would have paid for a nice house.

"Ridiculous how expensive everything is," said Dalton.

The food was excellent—Van Buren had a tuna that was delicious despite being barely cooked—and the conversation continued at such a leisurely pace that the colonel began to think his old friend had forgotten why he had set up the lunch in the first place. But that was not true at all; Dalton was merely salting the territory.

"Have you heard about Star Trek?" he said after the plates were cleared away. "It's going to be upgraded."

To anyone else in the restaurant, the question would have seemed innocuous, even incoherent. But Van Buren recognized that it was an oblique reference to the Pentagon's advanced warfare operations center, which was sometimes referred to as the Starship Enterprise. Among other things, the center made it possible for real-time strategic information to be supplied to a commander in the field. The Cube was a scaled-down though more up-to-date version.

It was also, of course, highly secret.

"I'm not sure what movie you're talking about," said Van Buren.

Dalton smiled, raising his eyebrows but saying nothing as the waiter stepped over to ask if they'd like dessert. Both men opted only for coffee—decaf for Dalton.

"My company's going to do the upgrade. And there's a lot more business on the horizon," said Dalton. "A lot."

"Movie business must be nice," said Van Buren.

"Is it ever."

The coffee arrived, along with a plate of complimentary cookies. Dalton took one, broke it in half, and nibbled at the edges.

"We need someone who can talk to people, important people, and impress them," said Dalton. "Tell them what life is like in the real world."

"Uh-huh," said Van Buren. He eyed the cookies—they were fancy Italian jobs, the sort his family sometimes got around the holidays—but decided to stick with the coffee.

"You wouldn't believe the salary," said Dalton. "And that would just be the start."

"This a salesman's job?"

"Hardly." Dalton sipped his coffee. He'd expected resistance and wasn't put off. "Congressmen, senators—they need to know they're getting a straight story. No bullshit. And with what's happening in the world—God, the stakes are immense. Every edge we can give the people in the field. Well, you know that yourself."

Van Buren wondered exactly how much Dalton knew about his present assignment. His old friend was obviously well connected—maybe too well connected, he thought to himself.

"We've done other projects you're familiar with," added Dalton, confident that he had set the hook. His strategy wasn't mendacious—everything he said was absolutely true, and he knew that Van Buren would do a great job. He also knew that the job would benefit Van Buren as well. And why not? Van Buren had been wounded twice and earned a bronze star; he was a bona fide, no-bullshit hero. He deserved to have a little downhill time.

"I can't go into the specifics. You could ask around, though. Vealmont Systems does have a reputation in the right circles." Dalton reached in his pocket and took out his business card, sliding it on the table. "The number on the back is the first year's salary. You'd be a vice president."

Van Buren slid over the card, staring at the front quixotically for a moment. He hadn't realized that his friend was president of the firm.

The number on the back was 500k.

"Half a million?"

Dalton just smiled.

"Salary?"

Dalton continued to grin.

"To do what?" asked Van Buren.

"Serve your country," said Dalton, his voice as serious as it got. "Help make sure the right technology gets to the people who need it."

"This is a lot of money," said Van Buren.

"That's true. There's very little overhead. The government already funds most of the R&D." Dalton leaned forward. "Don't let the zeroes throw you off. It's the going rate around here, believe it or not. Everything's more expensive these days. Look at college. The job's an important one."

"Who do I have to kill?"

"No one." Dalton shook his head. "This is Washington, Charles. You'd be surprised at the number of people who consider that a paltry salary. And they haven't done half of what you've done for your country. Nor would their hearts be in the right place."

Van Buren, a little too stunned to really process anything else, simply nodded.

"This is the sort of thing you'll be in line for after you make general anyway," added Dalton, addressing what he expected would be a consideration once Van Buren thought it over. "Here you get a head start. You can bring Sylvia and your son here, have a good life. It's not nine to five, admittedly, but there are opportunities, a lot more opportunities than in the Army. The work is important. It's just that you won't have people shooting at you anymore."

"Mmmm," said Van Buren, draining his coffee.

6

CHECHNYA

 The mosque was a humble one, erected by traders more than a thousand years before. Its walls had seen the rise and fall of many fortunes; the trade route that once passed within sight of the spiraling minaret was long forgotten. Holes pockmarked the walls inside and out; the air within was stale, as if the building were afraid to expel the breath of its ghosts. But for Samman Bin Saqr the mosque was as treasured as any in his native Yemen—all the more so for the fact that it was considerably safer.

The man before him had interrupted his meditation to tell him that it was the Americans who had kidnapped Muhammad al Aberrchmof, known to them by the nom de guerre of Kiro. In some ways this was a relief—Kiro had seen himself as something of a rival, and Samman Bin Saqr had evidence that he was plotting to siphon off some of his material to use on his own.

Kiro, perhaps under the influence of his new Chechen friends, had been interested in cesium 137. Samman Bin Saqr had good stores of this gamma-ray-producing material, amounting to well over fifty pounds more than he actually needed. The waste was one of several used in many medical applications and particularly easy to obtain; had the circumstance been right, Samman Bin Saqr would have given Kiro some for his own use.

But the circumstances were not right; Kiro was not a stable man, as his sudden devotion to the Chechen cause proved without a doubt. His recent inquiries—Bin Saqr had learned that he had gone so far as to send a messenger to speak to a man who had plotted against the Russians with a similar bomb in the 1990s—had alarmed the Russians, who quite properly feared that their capital would be targeted. They had arrested the messenger; surely Kiro had survived only by bribery.

Samman Bin Saqr closed his eyes, trying to guage the effect of Kiro's capture. He had been careful to limit his access to information, but the Americans might yet stumble on something that would lead to him.

No. Allah would not allow it. Still, the timetable must be moved up, even if it meant the mix of waste would not be optimum. Imperfection on this round would give him something to improve for the next.

Bin Saqr's inspiration had been to mix waste containing high-alpha radiation—obtained primarily from radioactive control rods and, in two cases, a very small amount of spent uranium fuel—with gamma-producing materials. The idea was to present the American Satan with a panoply of threats—short- and long-term. When his device exploded, the highly radioactive alpha-producing particles would be pulverized, entering the lungs of all those within a mile or more radius. Some would die immediately; others would linger in their illness.

The gamma waves would do their duty more slowly, seeping into their bodies and causing leukemia and other cancers over five or ten or fifteen years—his legacy to the future.

How many people would die? The scientists he had consulted could not agree. There was no model for such an event. It might only be a few hundred, and most of these by the explosive force needed to shatter and spread the waste material.

Or it might be millions. There was no way of knowing.

What he did know was that the effect would be deep and lasting fear. And Islam would be one step closer to the necessary final confrontation.

There were many things to be done yet, adjustments to be made to assure success. But he was sure that he could accomplish them; so much else had been done in so short a time.

"Honored one?" asked the messenger, waiting to see if there was an answer. Samman Bin Saqr had forgotten him temporarily.

"I will return immediately. Send word to proceed expeditiously," he said. Then he closed his eyes once more, picturing before him the delicious image of the American paradise in ghostly ruins.

7

 Conners felt a brief wave of nausea hit him as he waited in the chamber between the SF section of the USS *Wappingers Falls* and the ASDS, or Advanced Seal Delivery System, a high-tech minisub "parked" against the hull above. The host submarine was a member of the Virginia class of (relatively) low-cost attack boats designed primarily for action in littoral or coastal waters. The boat had pulled to within ten miles of the Iranian coast and waited for darkness; the rest of the trip would be by ASDS.

The SF soldier's stomach problems had nothing to do with seasickness; the submarine was absolutely still in the water, or at least seemed to be. Conners tracked it to do with the volatile reaction of mustard and ham stemming from lunch. His wet suit snugged tightly against his stomach, pressing the two ingredients tightly together.

One of the Navy SEALs charged with "delivering" them ashore asked if he was ready.

"Beyond ready," said Conners.

Ferguson, going over some last-minute details with one of the submarine's officers in the corridor behind him, laughed.

Two ASDS crewmen were already aboard the minisubmarine. Unlike the earlier Seal Delivery Vehicle, the ASDS was a "dry pants" vessels; it kept its passengers warm and dry as it drove through the ocean, conserving their energy for the mission itself. Ferguson and Conners, along with the six SEALs who would make sure they got ashore, would swim the final half mile or so, and were geared up for their excursion in lightweight SCUBA outfits.

From the outside, the ASDS looked like a boxy, oversized torpedo. Powered by batteries, it had tail fins and thrusters allowing it to thread through minefields, along with sophisticated sonar and sensors that could be used for a variety of surveillance tasks as well as self-preservation. Most often, however, the ASDS was little more than an undersea taxi, delivering its cargo to the hostile shoreline undetected. One of the SEAL team members dubbed it the Super Mario, after the pizza deliveryman in the famous video game.

Which made Ferg and Conners the pizza.

Pepperoni and anchovies, the way Conners's stomach felt as he climbed aboard. The ASDS was parked next to a companion in what amounted to a garage on the top of the submarine. With the systems checked and active, the captain gave permission to begin flooding the compartment, opening the garage door for junior to drive off on his date. Door open, the ASDS slipped sideways from its hangar, then pushed silently from the *Wappingers Falls*, its pilot and navigator carefully double-checking their preplotted path against the shifting realities of the ocean.

An hour later, Ferguson and Conners did one last equipment check and pulled their gear next to the hatchway at the stern of the boat. Their CIA-engineered breathing gear was even smaller than the Draeger gear the SEALs used, though like that breathing apparatus minimized telltale expelled air bubbles. Extremely lightweight, the face-formed masks they wore were connected to what looked like an oversized inflatable bib strapped to their chests. Once ashore, the equipment could be rolled up to the size of a portable umbrella. The downside was that it couldn't hold much oxygen; it was intended to get them from the vessel to the surface and back, with about eight minutes to spare.

But then they weren't there to tour coral reefs.

"Gonna be cold," warned one of the SEALs, as Conners got ready to follow Ferg out.

He wasn't kidding. Though they were wearing wet suits and the Gulf water was warm by ocean standards, Conners shuddered as he released himself under the ASDS and began stroking toward the surface. Ferguson bobbed in the water a few yards away. The SEALs—perfect mother hens—swam around them, fussing and fretting, making sure that their two charges and their gear were okay. They were barely a hundred yards from shore, close to the remnants of an abandoned pier once used by an old cement factory on the shore beyond.

The minisub had used a special radar to scan the shore just to make sure no defenses had sprung up overnight; even so, the SEAL swimmers conducted their own survey using night-vision devices adapted to a water environment. They held their hands out, keeping Conners and Ferg back until they were sure it was safe to proceed.

"Gentlemen?" said Ferg. The swimming gear was equipped with com devices.

"Just checking the lay of the land, sir," said the petty officer next to him. "Don't want to deliver you into a machine-gun nest."

"You won't get a tip if you do," said Ferg.

The deliverymen finally gave the okay, and the pizza began swimming toward the shore.

A half hour later, Ferg and Conners unpacked a pair of bicycles from the long plastic cases their SEAL companions had towed behind them to shore. Gear stowed beneath the broken timbers of the pier, they began pedaling toward their rendezvous point with an Iranian who had been recruited a year before by the CIA.

The contact was the most vulnerable point of the mission. Ferguson never completely trusted a foreign agent, no matter who vouched for him or what he'd done in the past. But the native would make it considerably easier to check the onshore sites that might be connected to the waste operation.

The cement factory sat at the far end of what in America would have been a port-area industrial park. There were several other abandoned facilities along the long access road to the highway that went north to the port itself. At the intersection with the highway sat a large area devoted to cargo containers; even though it was three o'clock in the morning, several work crews were unloading and moving containers. The two Americans pedaled past quietly, heading toward a field at the right side of the road where their contact, Keveh Shair, was supposed to be waiting.

A small pin of light flashed in the distance as Ferguson and Conners approached. Stopping immediately, they split up, Conners moving to flank the position in case it was a trap. His stomach felt much better now that he'd gotten out of the wet suit.

Ferguson slung his MP-5A5—a SEAL-issued version of the familiar submachine guns designed to withstand a wet environment—over his back and started walking slowly toward the light. Rubble lay everywhere before him in the lot, and even if he didn't want to give Conners time to find his position, he would have had to move slowly. The two men were connected through their Team communications system.

"Stop," said a voice in Farsi.

A pair of shadows appeared roughly where the light had been. Ferg wasn't wearing a NOD, and had trouble making them out.

"How we doing?" he asked Conners.

"Two guys, guns. Truck back by the road."

"OK," said Ferg quietly. The shadows were moving toward him. He held his hands out, said the password—Ayatollah.

One of the shadows laughed.

"I thought it was funny, too," said Ferg.

"Mr. Ferguson?" said a heavily accented voice in English. "I'm Keveh."

The two shadows materialized into a pair of bears. The one on the left had an early model M-16 in his paws. The one on the right stepped toward Ferguson, extending his hand.

There was a black pistol in it, aimed now at his head.

"Shit," said Conners over the com system.

Ferg stood motionless.

"Where did you go to school?" demanded Keveh.

"Yale."

"Who was your Philosophy Two teacher?"

"Xavier Ryan. Never met a Greek he didn't like," said Ferg. "Which is why he only lasted a year. I had Daniel Frick for conceptual physics. Now that was a kick-ass class. You know, if you run fast enough, you don't weigh anything?"

"Excuse the precaution," said Keveh, lowering the gun.

"Not a problem," said Ferg. "What'd you do, download my course transcript?"

"A friend checked it. You understand here, there are precautions. I understood there would be two of you."

"Yeah. He has you both covered at the moment. Excuse the precaution."

T he *Islam Qaatar*, originally built in India, was one of two ships being worked on at the Al-Haamden Dry Dock. It was impossible to see the ship from the road, but the yard looked as if it were only sparsely guarded.

"Easiest thing for us to do," Ferguson told Keveh as they drove by a second time, "we go in as workmen. We don't have to stay very long; we just plant some automated sensors and split. Maybe I take some pictures."

"I don't think so," said Keveh. "They're bound to have a list of who works there."

"You sure?"

Keveh shrugged.

"How about a government inspector or something?"

"Doesn't happen."

"Then we'll have to figure something else out. Let's go grab some food," said Ferg.

The Iranians took them to the edge of the city in an area that was the equivalent of an American middle-class suburb. The houses were only two or three years old, fairly close together, with identical white facades offset around the circular roadways. It was still dark, but Ferguson and Conners went in through the side door under the carport, stumbling against furniture before Keveh met them with his pin flashlight pointed toward the floor. He led them into a back room that had twin beds, then disappeared to get some food.

"I don't trust him," said Conners.

"Specific reason or general paranoia?" asked Ferg.

Conners shrugged. He didn't have a real reason.

Ferguson took out his sat phone. While he could communicate with the submarine and Rankin by calling a number that connected with a SpecOps/Navy ELF underwater system, there was no need; they'd planned to spend the day reconnoitering. He called Corrigan instead, telling him they were ashore safely and proceeding.

"Anything new?" Ferg asked.

"Corrine Alston is pissing off everybody in sight," said Corrigan. "She's been in the library."

"Good place for her."

"Slott's trying to find out what the hell the story is. I have Lauren babysitting her. I don't trust her with any of the guys. Her legs are too sleek."

"I hadn't noticed. Any new satellite data?"

"Still being studied."

"Jesus—"

"We may have something for you in a couple of hours."

"All right. I'll call you back," said Ferg, as Keveh returned with a bowl and two plates.

Conners and Ferguson sat against the beds to eat, the bowl between them and their plates perched on their knees. The food was a kind of meatless stew. Conners had only a few bites; now that his stomach had settled he didn't want to provoke it again. Ferguson, though, ate two helpings, then eyed what was left on Conners's plate.

"All yours," said Conners.

"Better not," said Ferg. "Might make me fart."

"At least."

Ferg pulled up his shirt and retrieved the plastic envelope containing the satellite photos and diagrams of the dry-dock area. He penciled in the guard post he'd seen, shading the two spots where searchlights covered the perimeter. The security was concentrated around the roadway, probably intended more for its deterrence value than anything else. It was possible that there were cameras or high-tech detectors scattered around the yard; there was no way to tell for sure until they were inside.

He expected there would be more guards. The situation didn't look promising.

"Maybe everybody's so afraid of getting their hands chopped off for stealing that they don't steal," said Conners. "Or maybe this isn't the boat."

"Yeah," said Ferg. He pulled the area diagram to the top of his small stack. The two lots directly across from the dockyard warehoused construction materials, which arrived from an area to the south and were moved via flatcars. One of the photos showed items being taken off by crane in the eastern portion of the yard. There were two long sheds at the extreme western end, and what looked like train rails buried in the pavement running to the fence separating the dock area. If material were being brought down to be placed in the ship, it could come into the warehouse area, be stored in one of those two buildings—or any of the others for that matter—then moved across by flatcar and switcher engine simply by taking the fence section away.

"You're assuming they're not breaking the waste into smaller containers somewhere else," said Conners.

"They may be," said Ferg. "But this would be an obvious place, and since the sat boys haven't seen it anywhere else, looking here makes sense."

"I guess. Didn't move the needle on the rad meter when we drove past."

"Yeah," said Ferg. "But we can't totally rely on that. Maybe it's shielded."

Conners, starting to sense a bust, said nothing.

"Easy to get into the warehouse area," Ferguson told him. He jabbed at the diagram. "We can walk right up this road. Guards are here and here. They have nothing on this side because of the water. So we come around here, look for radiation, check the sheds out, then go over to the shipyard."

"Going to take nearly an hour," said Conners. "That's about a mile and a half you're talking just to get into the site. Hour at least on each of the buildings, then we have to get around that fence. Going to be a long night."

"Yeah." Ferg leaned back against the bed. "You tired, Dad?"

Conners shrugged. "Not really."

Keveh knocked on the door, then came in, holding a small ceramic teapot and three cups. He put the pot down and settled across from them.

"You have milk for that?" Conners asked.

The Iranian looked at him as if milk were the most ridiculous thing you could put in tea.

"Cream or something like that?" Conners asked.

Keveh shook his head.

"Be tough," Ferg joked. He took a sip. The liquid tasted like a cross between Earl Grey and 30w motor oil.

"I was thinking we'd take a drive through the countryside," Ferg told his host. "Couple of things I want to look at."

Keveh nodded. Ferg unfolded his map of the port area and gave him a general idea of where they were going. Keveh nodded.

"When's a good time?" asked Ferg.

The Iranian shrugged. "Now."

"Well, let's go then."

"Scuff your shoes first," said Keveh, pointing down. "Those will stand out if we get out of the car. Nothing's new here."

8

 After hours of staring at the computer screen, the glare from the over-head fluorescents began to feel like sharp fingernails scratching at Corrine's eyes. She hadn't had more than a few hours' sleep for the past four or five days, and between the fatigue, coffee buzz, and all the data she'd been trying to assimilate, she felt like she was back in law school, cramming for a final. She punched the keys to kill the file and stood up, looking at her watch.

It was 6:05 P.M.; she'd missed lunch and dinner. Corrine got up from the desk, remembering that there was a package of Fig Newtons in her pocketbook, which because of security requirements she wasn't allowed to bring into the reference area. She also wasn't allowed to wear her shoes—instead, she had a pair of ill-fitting cardboard slippers that made her feel as if he she were a patient at a hospital with a library.

That's what they called it, with a little sign on the door. They even had a little old lady with bluish hair to help you.

As counsel to the congressional Intelligence Committee, Corrine had been briefed on a number of clandestine operations, including two or three that featured cooperation between Special Forces and the CIA. The history of such operations extended to the Kennedy presidency; while they had been severely curtailed in the wake of the Vietnam War, they had gradually come back into favor and in fact enjoyed some success in Afghanistan during the war on terror. But the Joint Services Special Demands Project Office and "the Team" were unique in several ways:

1. Missions were authorized and conducted without any paperwork whatsoever—no findings, no bureaucratic review, no audit, no log, no mention anywhere in the extensive operations files. Whereas a typical—if there were such a thing—CIA

mission would stem from an NSC finding, Special Demands specifically didn't need such findings, and in fact none were in the records, which meant there had been none. Nor were there any records of direct executive orders from the president authorizing specific Special Demands programs or missions.

2. Missions were not authorized or reviewed at any level below or above DDO; there was apparently no way for anyone outside of the extremely small group of people involved even to know about them.

3. The Team apparently combined collection and paramilitary functions—it collected intelligence, then immediately acted on it. While this, of course, had happened throughout the CIA's history, and in fact started during the OSS days, the line here seemed deliberately fused, with the same mission gathering intelligence, then immediately acting on it.

4. In Corrine's experience, backed up by her review of the Agency's records, most operations involving cooperation between the military and the Agency's clandestine service were of relatively limited duration, ending when a specific goal was achieved. From what she had seen, the Joint Services Special Demands Project Office and its missions weren't tied to specific operations. In this way, the model seemed to be the information side of the Agency, which provided intelligence to the military services on an ongoing basis. Not only could the goals change mid-mission—as they apparently had here—but the unit existed forever.

5. There were no apparent audit controls, and in fact Special Demands seemed to have an almost unlimited budget, with access not only to the extensive resources of a specially created Army Special Forces Group, but a variety of other service assets as well. The man in charge of the military end of the operation—Colonel Van Buren—answered *not* to USSOCOM, but to the head of Special Demands. Unlike other Special Forces groups, his core unit was not assigned a specific geographical area. It appeared to consist of only one battalion—smaller than the normal three combat battalions and nearly another's worth of support people—but even that wasn't clear from the documents Corrine had reviewed. While there were some military constraints on him—for example, he had to draw his men from SF units—from what Corrine could gather he existed entirely in a bubble, with no interference—or guidance—from higher-ups.

There was nothing, absolutely nothing, about the Kiro or current mission in the Agency's own secret files.

Which spoke volumes, in Corrine's opinion. The president's characterization of the unit as "cowboys" brushed the tip of the iceberg.

This was exactly the sort of situation that had led to CIA assassin teams and unchecked, unlawful, and ultimately self-defeating operations in the 1960s. In some ways, the present situation was even worse—not only had technology improved tremendously in the past forty years, but the capabilities of the SF unit was far beyond anything available during the Vietnam War.

If she was reading what she'd heard and seen at the meeting correctly, Special Demands short-circuited the normal CIA chain of command, with the field officer actually running the show. Ferguson was too young to have extensive experience, and the DDO was clearly overwhelmed with his other responsibilities to pay too much attention. The SF colonel seemed to have decent sense, but he was more Ferguson's equal than his boss. Corrigan was just a staff lackey, treated as such.

Not only did this stripped-down structure invite abuse, it encouraged mistakes. The Iranian ship was an international incident waiting to happen.

It was also a mistaken lead. Granted, it was logical; the prisoner had a clear connection to the group thought to have purchased the ship, and there were satellite photos and other data showing that trains did follow a path that would make diversion possible. But the Iranian government had infiltrated the local branch of the Islamic group two months before, and there was no sign at all of their involvement. The ship wasn't guarded by Iranian police or troops, and the funding conduits they normally used for "overseas education" did not include anything related to the ship.

And if the May 10 message was correct, the ship couldn't be the delivery vessel; it wouldn't even be ready to sail by then. Admittedly, the message seemed like a red herring; it did no more than predict "disaster for Satan's paradise." Except that the language was similar to what Allah's Fist had once used, it would seem no different than any dozen predictions the NSA and CIA routinely collected and dismissed.

Corrine had also taken the time to bone up on radiation hazards. The issue was extremely complicated—considerably more tangled than Corrigan's slides had shown. High-alpha waste such as the material believed stolen in transit was extremely dangerous, but only if pulverized and inhaled. That was why Corrigan had mentioned the need for explosives—the waste would have to be spread into the air by a large explosion. Gamma generators, by contrast, were not quite as dire. But they, too, had an effect, usually over time. Overall, the exact health hazard was difficult to estimate, even after exposure, except under very controlled conditions, when the exposure was recorded with the help of a film device worn on the body. A single gray—a dose equal to one joule of energy absorbed by one kilogram—would cause radiation sickness, which meant nausea, vomiting, and dizziness; that level of exposure could lead to death in a few days—or not at all. Much lower doses might not make a person sick immediately, but could cause or perhaps encourage cancer—the exact mechanism wasn't fully understood.

Part of the difficulty in assessing the risk came from the fact that data had to be collected sporadically, largely from accidents and errors. Corrine had read reports on three accidental nuclear-waste releases during the Cold War at the Soviet Union's Chlyabinsk-65 plant. Stripping Soviet propaganda and correlating exposure levels, one of the studies found that 95 percent of the cleanup team at a tank explosion had been exposed to cancer-causing levels of gamma radiation in less than a day. That would be consistent with the effects of an explosion of a tractor trailer's worth of strontium-90, the material mentioned in Corrigan's report. In a less dire accident ten years later, 41,500 people at Lake Karachay were "minimally" and "briefly" exposed to cesium-137 and strontium-90 when the radioactive dust was swept up during a wind storm. According to the study, 4,800 received doses above 1.3 centisieverts, enough to increase cancer risks significantly.

Leukemia, birth defects, lung cancer, stillbirths, sterility—the effects of even a mild exposure measured in curies, perhaps from a few hundred pounds of high-level waste, were definite yet unpredictable, a macabre lottery of death and illness, impossible to predict.

That was the point. You couldn't know exactly how bad it would be, and so you would fear the worst. You would be paralyzed by the ambiguity, terrorized by the possibility of death.

Dirty death.

The threat was real. But it was besides the point. She hadn't been sent to assess it, just check on the Team.

In Corrine's opinion, the only sensible thing to do was to abolish Special Demands. Her case depended largely on this one operation, since it was the only one she knew of. Nonetheless, it made for a good set of exhibits for the prosecution.

"So, Counselor, did you find anything interesting?"

Corrine looked up, surprised to see Daniel Slott, the CIA's deputy director of operations, standing near the door as she retrieved her things from the locker outside the library.

"Always," she said.

Slott scratched the thick five o'clock shadow on his cheek. "Have you had dinner?" he asked.

"Thank you, I'm not hungry," said Corrine, pointedly glancing at Slott's wedding ring.

"I'm not trying to pick you up," he said. "Just, if you need background, I can supply it."

"I don't know that it's necessary, thank you."

"Is there a problem I ought to know about?" said Slott.

"You tell me," said Corrine.

"I don't think there's a problem at all."

"One thing that wasn't clear to me," she said, deciding to do a discovery interview before presenting her brief. "What exactly is the oversight procedure on Joint Services Special Demands Project Office?"

"Usually we refer to it simply as the Team."

"Yes?"

"I review everything."

"How is it that there are no specific findings prior to a mission?"

"Not necessary," he said. "As a matter of fact, the NSC specifically stated that Special Demands is under the direct supervision of an individual appointed by the president, which has been, is, me."

"The streamlined procedure was designed because it wasn't intended to authorize this sort of operation," she said. "Special Demands was intended to be used to develop weapons and other devices that might have applications for your agency and the Special Forces units. Wasn't it?"

"It wasn't limited," said Slott.

Corrine, who had studied the NSC minutes and knew that was the only matter discussed, zipped her pocketbook and started toward the door. Slott followed.

"Listen, we've got an important operation running here—it's proof the system works," he said.

Corrine didn't bother answering.

"It's not like I can go out and start World War III," added Slott.

"Mr. Ferguson can," said Corrine. "There are no holds on him."

"Of course there are."

"Name one."

"Me. Van Buren. The people in the field."

Corrine remained unimpressed.

"Ferguson is one of our best people. I trust him completely."

Slott reached out and grabbed her arm. She jerked back, adrenaline rising; she'd flatten him if she had to.

"We shouldn't be enemies here," Slott said, letting go. "I'm sorry."

"We're not enemies, that I know of," she told him, walking away.

9

The tracks leading to two of the three railroad yards Ferg wanted to look at were ripped up and missing in spots, and when the radiation detector didn't pick up any readings nearby, Ferg decided not to bother with them. The third was located about thirty-five miles northeast of Bandar 'Abbās, in a town that wouldn't have seemed terribly out of place in middle America—once you adjusted for the veils, beards, and minarets.

The rail spur skirted the town; the siding Ferg was interested in sat in a valley at the eastern edge, linking with a large complex of buildings and steel warehouses. Most of the buildings looked dilapidated, but there were two in the center of the complex in good repair.

There were also at least a dozen armed guards.

"What do you think?" Ferg asked Keveh.

The Iranian shook his head. He had no idea what they did inside.

"Why don't we drive in and see what happens?" Ferg asked.

"They may shoot us."

"There is that," said Ferg.

They drove past the road leading to the site, then up around another set of roads that brought them near but not to the train tracks. Ferg and Keveh got out, leaving Conners and the other Iranian with the car. Ferg walked down the siding toward the gated rail entrance to the facility. There were a pair of guards inside the fence about two hundred yards from him; it was impossible to tell whether they were paying attention or not. A boxcar sat on the tracks near one of the dilapidated buildings; there was a tanker car beyond it.

"What if I'm a foreign investor who wants to buy some of the old buildings?" Ferguson suggested to Keveh.

"Very suspicious." Keveh squinted and shielded his eyes from the rising morning sun.

"Yeah, but will it get me in?"

"Better if I say I'm from the Revolutionary Council at Bandar," said the Iranian. "Who am I?"

"A foreign expert on railroads—on steel," said Keveh. "A Russian. Better from Russia—they won't be interested."

"I like that. I always wanted to play with trains."

An hour later, Ferguson and Keveh drove inside the complex, watched but not stopped by the guards. They'd left the others outside, watching as best they could from the road near the town.

As Keveh circled around toward the two train cars, Ferguson slid out his radiation tester. The tester could record sixteen data points or levels for reference in both REM and Rads, and could detect energy levels down to 1 nR/hr, the low end of normal background radiation. Its isotope identification mode tracked a variety of isotopes stored in its memory, and it could record and retain up to thirty-two bits. (Depending on the type of radiation, REMs and Rads were considered essentially the same measure, indicating how much energy was being absorbed and potential biological damage done. At high alpha levels, however, the Rad measurement was more useful. A REM was equal to .01 sievert.) He had a larger device in his pack that could record becquerels and curies for a hundred data points; this used a gas tube and was bulky, and its precision wasn't really necessary. (In fact, the difference in measurements were mostly a matter of math. One becquerel represented the disintegration of one nucleus per second. While standards varied wildly, a waste tank might generate one hundred curies, which was 3,700 billion becquerels. The effects of exposure would vary depending on time and distance as well as the nature of the exposure, but a person working in a uranium mine would be "allowed" a safe exposure to 3.7 becquerels per liter of air a month.)

Ferg took the first level as they got out of the car; it was flat. He walked to the tanker, holding the device on the metal skin. The needle didn't budge, even on its most sensitive setting.

He went to the boxcar—empty—then along the track, stooping at a connection as if he were truly inspecting it. The rail line was very old and not used much, but undoubtedly in good enough shape to handle cars. The building at the left beyond the boxcar had a rail running into it.

"Company," said Keveh. A small Gator-style ATV with two guards had appeared from around the corner of one of the sheds and was heading their way.

"Keep 'em busy," said Ferg.

"What?"

"I have to take a leak," he said, trotting toward the building.

He pretended to check left and right, then stood next to the side and held out his counter.

Nothing. Ferg pretended to concentrate as Keveh called to him. He held up his hand and waved, as if intent on finding a spot to do his business.

A single window stood at the side of the building near the corner. Ferg glanced back, saw that the guards weren't following, and walked toward it. He couldn't see through the dirt on the window, so he walked past, feigning interest in the tracks as he turned the corner of the building.

There were several windows there, the first with a face in it. The face glared at him, its eyes furrowing into its head above a stubby beard. Ferg waved, and held up the radiation meter, as if it were something the face ought to be familiar with. The frown only deepened.

Ferguson moved on to the next window, leaning over and looking through the dirt.

It was some sort of warehouse for DVDs, or maybe a manufacturing operation. There were several piles of boxes near the floor, a woman smiling. He couldn't read the writing. He pushed his head closer, put his hand up to cut off the glare.

There were different covers, but they all had young women on them.

Good work, he thought to himself; I've busted a DVD-pirating operation.

Ferg headed back. As he turned the corner he saw that the guards had become a little more threatening—they had their pistols out. Keveh, his face red, was talking nonstop to one of them, who was shaking his head.

Ferguson shoved his meter in his pocket and walked toward them. He couldn't understand the particulars, but the gist was fairly clear—the guards didn't like the fact that they were nosing around. Ferg gave them a long blast in Russian as he approached, asking if they were filming porn inside and, if so, could they take some walk-ons. Fortunately, neither man had a clue what he was saying.

"Counterfeiting DVDs," he said, in English, to Keveh, encasing the explanation in a sentence of more Russian nonsense.

Keveh gave him a look that didn't need to be translated. Then the guard issued his own command, gesturing with the gun.

"Guess it's time to leave," Ferguson said to Keveh. He took a step back in the direction they had come.

A warning shot in the dirt nearby stopped him.

"Okay," he said, turning around. "*Sprechen sie Deutsch? Parla Italiano?* Speak Englishy?"

The guard's only answer was to raise the barrel of his gun so that the next shot had a reasonable chance of hitting him in the throat.

10

Corrine stopped at a deli on her way back to the office, grabbing a half hero for lunch and dinner; she was so hungry she ate most of it while driving back. Teri had gone home already, leaving three prioritized piles of letters and other matters to review on her desk. Corrine ignored them as well as the full queue of e-mail on her computer, concentrating instead on writing a memo to the president about Special Demands. She pounded the keys in a rapid flow of logic, producing over twenty pages in little more than two hours. She was just about to hit the spellcheck when she heard someone knock on the outer door. Figuring it was one of the Secret Service people discreetly checking to see if the light had been left on accidentally, she yelled out that she was fine and went back to poring over the screen, sorting out contractions and typos.

"I think the electorate would be thrilled at your work ethic," said the president behind her.

Corrine felt her face flush. "You surprised me, Mr. President," she said, turning around from her computer.

"I have that effect on people," he said, peeking at the computer screen. "Addressed to me?"

"I haven't finished it yet."

"How was Cuba? Warm?"

"Yes, sir."

"Our guest?"

"Interesting, but not very talkative," said Corrine. "I already told you the decision should be deferred while they're pursuing his present information."

"E-mail is not the same as a personal report."

"I'm working on my report now." She folded her arms in front of her breasts, feeling almost as if the president had barged into her bathroom as she came from the shower.

"I understand the CIA director and the deputy director of operations are on my agenda for the morning." McCarthy raised his eyebrows just enough to suggest a wink as he continued. "What is it they're going to complain about?"

"They got to you already?"

The president reached for the seat near her desk. He pulled it over and sat down, pulling the pant legs of his gray suit back ever so slightly and exposing his snakeskin boots. "Now just remember, dear, the shoe leather is snake. My legs will hurt if you start to fib."

Corrine had heard the line a million times. "It'll all be in my memo."

"Horse's mouth is always better, not to mention quicker," said McCarthy. "And I am by no means suggesting that you're a horse."

"Yes, Mr. President."

Corrine told him what she had found—an operation with no checks in place and, it seemed to her, ample opportunity for running amuck.

"They're completely outside any oversight," said Corrine. "The fact that they've used a structure intended for something else is, at the very least, a serious red flag."

"You're sure it was intended for something else."

"I've seen the minutes."

"And they would be accurate." The president let just the hint of amusement enter into his skepticism; he knew the past administration extremely well. "They don't have to report to anyone?"

"Just the DDO."

"The person I appoint," said the president. He was drawing an important distinction—the NSC directive did not state that the DDO was in charge of Special Demands.

"Slott's been with the Agency for years; his loyalties aren't to you," said Corrine. "I don't think he has any perspective at all."

McCarthy propped the side of his face against his hand, as relaxed as if he were discussing how they dealt with critters on his Georgia farm. "The problem is that they don't have intelligence findings before proceeding?"

"The problem is they don't have anything. Decisions are being made by the officer in the field and a Special Forces colonel who has enough firepower at his fingertips to start a world war. Slott is a rubber stamp at best. This is exactly what led to catastrophe in the sixties. It took decades to recover from that. Some say they still haven't."

"Well now, they've told me what's going on," said the president. "Shouldn't I trust them?"

"There's no way for us to know for sure what they're doing," she explained.

"The NSC isn't involved, there's no paperwork, no procedures, the director doesn't have to be notified, they don't have to report to the congressional committees—we have to completely trust the people involved."

"And you don't?"

"I don't trust anyone. First rule." Corrine shook her head. "The operation in Iran is a perfect example. What happens if they're captured? Or worse, if they find a dirty bomb on that ship and blow it up? Not to mention that, in my opinion, they're going off on a wild-goose chase."

McCarthy sat back up. "How's that?"

"It's obviously meant to throw them off the trail. The Iranian government took over the Islamic organization months ago. Our guest told them that to throw them off. He's probably hoping we'll give the Iranians trouble."

"And how do you know?"

"I've done a little research. Where do you think I've been the past few days?"

"That didn't occur to them?"

"Probably, but they won't admit it. They get a hot lead, and they pursue it. That's how they operate."

McCarthy put his hand to his chin, rubbing the nubby whiskers of his five o'clock shadow.

"If they really want to find out where the waste is going," Corrine told him, "we should track it from Buzuluk."

"They said they tried," said the President.

"As far as I could find out, they only used satellites and detectors; they weren't actually there. Big difference seeing the bear than hearing about it," she added, using one of his phrases.

McCarthy rose from the chair without saying anything. He walked over to her desk, reaching around her to the computer.

"Here," he said, pointing to the screen. "Insert your recommendation here."

"Which recommendation?"

"The one that recommends that the person in charge of Special Demands be outside the CIA and Special Forces command structure, as permitted by the authorizing directive and executive order. And the law."

"Uh—"

"To be more specific, that the president's counsel be that person."

"But—"

"Then a little lower, down here, plot out your recommendation for following the operation. I think that might be the first thing you do, assuming you're right about the ship."

"But I can't do that."

"Can't do what, dear?"

"I can't get involved in this."

"Whyever not? You have experience working with the Intelligence Committee.

You obviously aren't intimidated by the CIA boys. And I'd bet even those hard-assed Special Operations people'll be eating out of your hand in short order."

"But I'm a lawyer. I'm *your* lawyer."

"I hope you're not bringing up the matter of your job description again." McCarthy straightened, a self-satisfied grin on his face.

"I am."

"I'm beginning to believe you are angling for a raise, Miss Alston."

"You set me up, didn't you?"

"How's that?" asked the president.

"You want to exercise more control over them, but you didn't want to make it look like it was your idea. So you're using me. You sent me—you used me."

"*Nevuh* would I use a woman."

"How much did you know about Special Demands before you called me in? Or this operation?"

"I didn't know everything you've told me," said McCarthy.

"That sounds like an answer a lawyer would give," she said.

"Touché, Counselor. Touché."

11

OFF BANDAR 'ABBĀS, IRAN

 The hardest part was waiting before launching the mission. Rankin busied himself with equipment checks and plans, but eventually all he could do was sweat, the excess energy seeping out from the pores of his skin. He wanted to be onshore, rescuing Ferguson—bailing the asshole out, as usual—but prudence dictated they wait until dark. Conners had the site under surveillance; the situation was pretty stable, given the circumstances.

Though in Rankin's opinion, a bullet in the head might teach Ferguson a lesson.

Rankin had learned to meditate while recovering from a shoulder injury when he was a corporal; he didn't use the full lotus position he'd learned in the yoga class— too goofy in the submarine, with SEALs all around—but he did sit still in the mess area, hands resting on his knees, eyes zoned into a distant space. It helped for a while, settling his muscles and controlling his breath, but inevitably the adrenaline of the people around him pierced through the temporary veil.

When the time finally came to climb into the escape chamber and board the minisub, Rankin moved slowly but deliberately, as if trying to hold his muscles in check. He sat on the bench of the ASDS next to the SEAL team's leader, a large, blond-haired master chief petty officer from Minnesota about Rankin's age. The others called him MC, partly because of his rank and partly because of his name—Mark Carpenter. But he also had the air of an emcee, silently surveying everything and calmly maintaining order.

When the ASDS was ready to slide off the submarine, MC looked at Rankin, lowering his head slightly as if to say, "Are you ready, Soldier Boy?" Rankin nodded. Rather than speaking, MC tapped the navigator, who passed the signal on to the helmsman.

The submarine pushed through the water, a bit unsteady at first. The ride took barely twenty minutes. Rankin wasn't a very strong swimmer, but the watchfulness of the two SEALs assigned to shepherd him to shore irked him; Rankin felt like a recently weaned lamb, crowded by two sheepdogs all the way to shore.

He saw the signal when they were still a good thirty yards from the rocks. The others made him stop and tread water while the coded sequences of signs and countersigns were exchanged and repeated. It was absolutely prudent and necessary, but Rankin felt mostly annoyance, and when the SEALs finally started swimming forward he realized that he had grown somewhat used to working with Ferguson, whose easygoing demeanor infected everything the Team did, even authentication procedures.

It was an odd realization—if anyone had asked, Rankin would have said flatly that Ferg was far, far too ready to cut corners and take chances.

Conners squatted near the rocks with the flashlight when Rankin pulled himself onto the dry land.

"Hey," said Conners. He put his hand out and helped him up.

"Yeah," answered Rankin.

"They're just local security people, as far as I can tell," Conners told him. "I got it all psyched out."

Rankin called over the SEAL team leader and introduced him. Conners filled them both in on the layout and lineup. The other local Iraqi spy was watching the site. They'd gotten close enough to use the boom; the people at the factory had bought the Russian cover story and were torn between demanding a ransom and just letting the two men go.

"I just talked to our guy. No change," said Conners. He had sketched out the facility on a piece of paper. "Pretty straightforward. Two guys at the front gate, a couple of roamers. Pretty light security. No problem with eight guys."

"You sure there's no change?" asked Rankin.

"Fifteen minutes ago, no change. We'll call again once we're close. He doesn't talk English," Conners added. "I used the handheld to get some Farsi and English back and forth."

"Is the waste in there or what?"

"Can't tell for sure," said Conners. "But I don't think so. They're counterfeiting DVDs."

MC took the paper from Rankin.

"Come on," said Conners. "Our bus is over here."

"Bus?" asked Rankin.

"What, you expected a BMW?" said Conners. "The guy who's watching the facility has a brother who owns two buses. He's our driver. It looks like a school bus. Don't worry, he says we won't get stopped."

"Why don't we just get a fuckin' fire truck and go lights and sirens?" said Rankin in a sneer.

"I thought of that," said Conners. "But I couldn't find one."

"You've been hanging around Ferguson too long," said Rankin.

"Ain't that the truth."

Y ou'd think they'd give us some free samples to while away the time," said Ferguson.

Keveh didn't laugh.

Ferg got up slowly from the plastic chair, holding his hands out so that the guard at the door would realize that he was just stretching his legs. The Iranians didn't seem to know what to do with them; Keveh said one of the guards had mentioned that they had to call their "administrator," who apparently wasn't at the factory. They obviously weren't going to call the police—the bootlegging operation was illegal and would either get them into trouble or necessitate a serious round of bribes.

Ferguson had floated hints that they would pay a ransom, but their captors hadn't actually asked how one might be paid. He figured Conners and the cavalry would wait until dark to bail them out; with a little luck this would be merely a burp in their schedule.

The guard stared at him as he stretched. He had a pistol at his belt, easily takeable—obviously the man wasn't too experienced guarding prisoners. Ferg figured it was safe enough to wait; besides, the security office was next door, and there was no telling whether there might actually be someone who knew what he was doing there.

Ferguson began stretching; he felt cramped as well as tired—then pulled over one of the plastic chairs. The guard said something in Farsi. Ferg motioned that he was going to do a push-up against the seat, then did so, hamming the routine up.

"What are you doing?" Keveh asked.

"Limbering up," said Ferg.

"He thinks you're nuts."

"That's good." Ferguson reeled off a few sentences of Russian about the beauty of the white leopard in winter, then added in English "You think they're going to feed us?"

"The guard doesn't know."

"Send him out to ask," said Ferg. "I'm getting hungry."

Keveh asked in Farsi if the guard might get them some food. The man shook his head, then explained that he was not in charge—they would have to wait there until his superior arrived. He, too, was hungry.

As the guard was speaking, Ferguson heard footsteps in the hallway. He rested his left hand on the chair, listening. There was a loud pop in the distance, from near the entrance—with a swift motion Ferguson picked up the chair and tossed it at the guard's face, following underneath with a dive at the man's midsection. Ferguson twisted around and up, pushing his legs underneath him and pinning the hapless guard to the ground. A quick kick to the man's chin ended any possibility of resistance.

"Down," Ferguson yelled at Keveh, grabbing the gun from the holster. "Get over to the side. They're using flash-bangs. Keep your eyes closed and head covered."

He crawled out of the way just as the hinges of the door flew open with the loud report of a shotgun blast. Rankin and a SEAL in battle dress and blackface pushed into the room with a bang; within three seconds a gun barrel pointed at each occupant's head.

"Watch where you point that thing, Skippy," said Ferguson, who'd put the pistol he'd taken under his body.

"You're lucky I don't pull the trigger."

"Then you'll have all those friendly fire reports to fill out," said Ferguson. He held up his hands so it was obvious to the others that he was a good guy, and gestured to Keveh. "He's ours."

"They're all right, they're okay," said Conners, rushing in behind them.

Rankin pushed the Iranian guard to the corner of the room, trussing him with plastic cuffs. Ferguson, meanwhile, went out into the hall.

"Right, turn right," yelled Rankin, following him out.

"Gotta get my hideaway," Ferguson told him. "They took it."

"Fuck that," said Rankin. "Let's go."

"That stinking Glock is my personal weapon," said Ferguson. He trotted down the hall toward the far end of the corridor, where two SEALs were watching the approach from a second hallway. Ferguson signaled to them to follow, then went toward the office where he'd been searched.

He kicked the door in and threw himself back as the two SEALs poked their guns inside. The lone occupant was hunched behind a desk in the corner. One of the SEALs shouted in Farsi for the man to throw down his weapon. He shouted again, and the man raised his hands to show he wasn't armed.

As Ferguson slipped between the SEALs into the room, he spotted a shadow in the corner of his eye. With a quick lunge he pushed on the door and then grabbed his would-be assailant, disabling him with an elbow shot to the solar plexus after pulling him forward. A gun flew to the ground.

"Fucking rent-a-cops," he said, grabbing the Beretta from the floor.

Tears were falling down the other man's face.

"Oh we ain't going to hurt you," Ferg told him. "We ain't even going to tell the mullahs on you. Where's my fuckin' gun?"

As the man babbled in Farsi for his life, Ferguson noticed a metal cabinet against the wall. He went to it, pulled at the door; when he saw it was locked he blew off the handle with a bullet from the Beretta. The thin metal mechanism shattered, and the doors slapped open.

His Glock was on the top shelf, along with his rad counters and the small plastic container with his synthetic thyroid pills, which was what he had really wanted to retrieve.

"Are you fuckin' comin' or what?" demanded Rankin from the hallway.

"On my way," said Ferguson, gulping the pill he had missed.

A bus, Conners?" asked Ferguson.

"The train was busy."

"Kinda feels like we're going home after the big track meet," said Ferguson. "And we lost or something."

"I wouldn't call the mission a smashing success," said Rankin.

"It ain't over till it's over," said Ferguson. No matter what the circumstance was, Ferg thought, Rankin could be counted on to have a stick up his ass.

Generally sideways.

"So, Ferg, you star in any of their movies?" Conners asked.

"I wanted to, but there was a language problem," Ferguson told him.

"What are we going to do now?" Keveh asked.

"Well you and your buddy can either be evacked to the U.S. or just go home."

"People saw us."

"That's what I'm saying," Ferg told him. "Come back with us. The SEALs'll take care of you. Right, MC?"

"Sure," said the SEAL team leader.

"We'll stay," said Keveh.

"You sure, buddy?"

Keveh nodded.

"Good. All right, Skip and I'll go check the ship out."

"What about me, Ferg?" asked Conners.

"You hang back with the bell-bottom boys, Dad. You look tired."

"Fuck you."

"Nah, you do. MC, I'll take two of your guys for backup. That cool?"

"We'll all go with you."

"Too many people," said Ferg. "Dad and I already figured it out. We need you to stay on the perimeter so you can cut off anybody that comes up from that barracks at the north. If we're quiet, we're in and out."

"What if you're not quiet?" asked MC.

"Then we're in and out a little faster, and you guys get some action," said Ferg. "We'll try for quiet. Worst case we go out on the water side."

"What about yourself?" said Conners. "You're not tired?"

"I never get tired."

"You on amphetamines?" asked Rankin.

"I'm high on life, Skippy."

"I just saved your ass," said Rankin.

"And I'm glad you did."

"Show a little respect."

"I respect you, Skip. I just don't want to sleep with you."

"I don't get you, Ferguson. I don't get you at all."

"The day you get me, Rankin," said Ferg, "is the day I hang it up." He smiled at him. "But thanks for saving my ass anyway."

12

 They cut the fence and went in, skirting around a set of floodlights to reach the side of one of the warehouse buildings. Ferg's sensor was clean, and both buildings were empty.

The ship was a little better guarded. Two sentries walked a line that swung across the rail access; they had decent lighting and a clear field of vision beyond a pair of shacks and assorted machinery sheds about fifty feet from the hull. The lights strung around the yard cast a pale yellow haze over everything, but was strong enough that they didn't need their NODs.

"Good place for a crossbow," said Ferg, sizing it up.

"Yeah, well, I don't have one," said Rankin.

"They don't even talk to each other when they pass," said Ferg.

"Maybe they don't like each other."

The men wore berets and couldn't see each other until they were about ten feet apart. In fact, they hardly glanced toward each other. Rankin and Ferguson agreed that if one were eliminated, they could sneak up behind the other and attack as he walked toward the intersection of their rounds.

"You think we have enough time to take one, grab his uniform, then meet his partner in the middle?" Ferg asked.

Rankin studied them, using a small pair of folding binoculars—personal equipment, like the Uzi he favored. "Not the whole uniform. But you'd just need the shirt maybe. Have to be the guy on the left."

"Why?"

"Other guy's too short. Shirt'll never fit." Rankin watched them walk. He guessed that they would be tired and more than a little bored; guard duty sucked no matter where you did it. "When he gets to that rope at the far end there, see by the ship? I could climb up on that scaffold and jump."

"He'd see you."

"Not if I come off the top of the scaffold."

"That's twenty feet," said Ferg.

"Yeah." Rankin said it like it was a dare.

Ferguson called him on it. "Well go ahead. Don't break anything."

"You, with me," Rankin told one of the SEALs. They trotted back toward the fence, then crossed over toward the north side of the yard, crawling forward amid the stacks of equipment and materials. To get to the scaffold, they would have to cross about ten feet of well-lit ground; Rankin wasn't so much worried about being seen as casting a shadow.

As he waited, sizing up the situation, the guard came around to the near side. Rankin saw him clearly—his eyes were focused, wary; he didn't have the bored look most guys would have pulling a late-night shift in the middle of nowhere. It occurred to Rankin that either the Iranian was pretty dedicated or had been tipped off, or maybe both.

The sentry turned, his boots scratching against the concrete. Rankin realized belatedly that he could have rushed him—they were no more than eight feet apart, and it would have taken no more than a second and a half to take him. He'd been so fixated on the idea of climbing the scaffold that he'd missed a far easier chance.

"Next time he comes," he told the SEAL. "When he swings around, I'm up, and I get him."

F erguson checked in with Conners and the rest of the SEALs, who were watching from the perimeter. They had the main guard post covered, along with the approach to the shipyard.

"Somebody's on the ship," Conners told him. He'd climbed atop the bus and could just barely make out the deck. "Up near the bow."

"Just one person?"

"Hard to see, but it looked like one person, moving."

Ferguson watched as the guards returned. "How we looking, Skip?" he asked Rankin over the com system.

When Rankin didn't answer right away, Ferg feared that the SF soldier had already changed places with the guard and was going to do the act solo. But that wasn't like Rankin—a second later he responded.

"I get him this round," said Rankin. "Be patient."

"Alien concept." Ferguson slid forward on his knee as the guard on his side passed, positioning himself to cut the man down if he heard anything.

The sharp steel blade felt warm against Rankin's thumb. He could hear the sentry's footsteps as he approached. They seemed to take forever.

He'd practiced this sort of takedown a million times, but he'd never done it for real; there wasn't much cause in real operations to sneak up on a man with a knife and slit his throat. Getting close enough to do that meant putting yourself at enormous risk, and it was almost always easier and smarter to use a gun and be done with it.

The scraping stopped. Rankin, hunched down in the shadow of a large pump, felt his lungs freeze.

Finally, the scraping resumed. Rankin could hear the feet twisting as the sentry turned and started to retrace his steps. One stride, two strides, three—

The SF man leapt up into the light, pushing air into his lungs, then clamping his mouth closed as he jumped out. The Iranian was farther than he'd thought—a step, another step—the man started to turn.

The knife caught the side of his neck first. Rankin's left arm fished wildly, searching for the gun, his right hand pushing the knife along the sentry's skin.

The gun fell to the ground. Rankin felt something heavy in his hands. He heard the Iranian cough, then gasp for air, whispering a prayer in Farsi as he died.

Quickly he pulled the man's body to the side. He dropped the knife, unbuttoning his shirt—there was no bulletproof vest. Rankin pulled the shirt over his, hunched over—this wasn't going to work. He grabbed the man's beret and pulled it over his head, low, then took the AK-47 he'd been holding and began walking, telling his lungs to breathe now, it was all right.

The guard approached the other warily, either because his timing was off or he'd heard something. Ferguson had anticipated this—he had the SEAL covering him toss a rock in the other direction, and in the half second it took for the sentry to swing around, he sprang. The stock of his MP-5 caught the man in front of the ear; he flew to the ground as if propelled by a cannon.

"Shit," said Ferg, afraid he'd killed the bastard.

He rushed over, kicking the gun away and grabbing one of the plastic restraints from his belt. The sentry was out cold, though he seemed to be breathing. They hauled him over to the side, out of the light, behind a pair of tanks used for welding.

"You should've waited till I was closer," said Rankin.

"Blood on your hands," said Ferguson. "He give you problems?"

"Yeah."

"All right." Ferguson bit his lip; too late to worry about that now. "There's a guy on the ship near the bow, according to Conners."

He went toward the stern, where several lines hung down. They each took a rope, leaving the SEALs to cover the approach below.

Ferg pulled himself over the rail at the top, pausing to get an idea of what was nearby. The superstructure of the ship blocked off the view of the forward area.

A ship this size could hold tons and tons of waste. Blow the sucker up in LA harbor, New York, Boston—pick the symbolic target of your choice.

But his rad counter was still. If they were setting it up as a dirty bomb, either they hadn't gotten very far, or the waste was still heavily shielded.

Rankin met him on the other side of the railing. "This way here is clear," he told Ferguson, pointing to the starboard. "There are some large metal girders or something, like a base for a weapon or a crane or something, beyond the superstructure."

Ferg leaned over the side and waved the SEALs up. One stayed at the rear of the deck near the ropes as the other three men moved forward around the side of the ship. The railing ended abruptly; Rankin took a step too close to the edge and nearly fell off.

Where an oil tanker would have a relatively clear deck forward of the superstructure at the rear of the ship, the Iranian vessel had what looked like a long metal house extending most of its length. While designed to carry ethylene—a colorless, flammable gas—the compartments were being completely renovated, and Ferguson could peer through the open end of the structure and see well into the interior. At the starboard side of the decking area closest to him sat what looked like an oversized rack of bottles, with a rack twisting down toward the hull; some of the mechanism was obscured by tarps.

"You know what that is?" Ferg asked the SEAL.

The SEAL—Petty Officer Sean Reid—studied it for a few seconds.

"Looks like they're making it into a minelayer," said Reid, craning his neck so he could see below. "The roof covers up the mechanism. They'll line the mines up below, right there, they kind of squirt them out over around that spot—I can't see because of the covers, but probably there's like a hatch. Slide open."

"What kind of mines?" asked Ferg.

"Well—mines."

"You're sure?"

"It looks like it, sir."

The SEAL had a way of saying "sir" that implied it meant, "you dumb shit."

Ferguson reached into his shirt pocket for the digital camera. Flipping it to the night-shot setting—it was a near-infrared view—he slid gingerly through the opening of the deck housing and walked forward on a wide piece of wood, apparently something the workmen had placed there, and took some pictures. Below was a large empty compartment with ropes and tools at the bottom.

All this way, just to find a minelayer. Slott was going to love hearing that.

So would Alston. Ah well, thought Ferg, give the folks back home something to gloat about.

He was just starting back when he heard a sound behind him. Before he could even curse, the light burp of AK-47 broke through the night. As he flattened himself against the board, both Rankin and the SEAL nearby opened up on the Iranian watchman, who was firing from the front of the ship.

"So much for the subtle approach," said Ferg, half-crawling and half-jumping to the solid decking near the superstructure.

The three Americans moved swiftly to the stern, where the other SEAL waved them forward. Gunfire erupted near the main entrance to the dry dock; above the crackle of automatic rounds came two sharp snaps, the report of Remington 700 sniper rifles being fired—a pair of SEAL marksmen had found their targets.

"Left, left," shouted Rankin, as more gunfire broke out behind them. Following his own instructions, he pivoted, gun on hip, shooting through the clip as two Iranians ran into the semicircle of light.

"Enough of this shit," said Ferguson, standing and icing the spotlights with his submachine gun.

They were about halfway to the fence when a heavy machine gun opened up from the warehouse yard. Its bullets crashed through the lot, throwing a hail of cement shrapnel before them.

Then another gun picked up the job, its bullets closer.

"Not going that way," said Ferguson.

"Then how are we getting out of here?" said Rankin.

Ferguson looked back at the ship. The other guard posts were on the city side, near the road.

"We swim for it," said Ferguson. "You guys up for it?" he asked the SEALs.

"Uh, we can make it," said Reid.

"Okay. Because I figure that's going to be the easy way out." He pushed up the com system's mike bud as more gunfire flared, this time over near the highway that ran to the east. "Conners, what the hell are you guys doing out there?"

"We just stopped a truck from coming in."

"Good. More reinforcements coming?"

"Maybe. A lot of shit moving north of you," said Conners. "What about those machine guns?"

"They're a pain in the ass. Look, we're going to go out by the water."

"You sure?" asked Conners.

"That way you guys can just slip south rather than trying to hold the fort against the entire Iranian Army, such as it is. Listen, they're working the ship up as a minelayer. Not quite what we were looking for, but they'll want to know back in Washington."

"You're not going to tell them yourself?" asked Conners.

"I'll tell 'em, Dad. Don't fret." The machine guns began firing again—this time considerably closer. "We're outta here, boys."

R ankin took point, running along the dock area toward the water. As he passed a set of large wooden boxes, he saw an Iranian duck behind cover up near the bow. He waited to fire, closing the gap. Rankin was less than five feet from him when the man leaned out from around a portable generator to see what was going on. The bullets from the American's Uzi slapped through his skull, tossing blood and bits of bone away like drops of rain brushing dust from a windowsill. Rankin kicked the body over, frowning when he saw the man hadn't been armed. He swung around quickly, then continued forward. A shadow loomed down from the forecastle of the ship; Rankin threw himself onto his back and emptied his clip in its direction. As he rolled back over and started to reload, the figure reappeared, raising a rifle.

The burst that took down the Iranian sounded like a quick drumroll on a metal garbage can top. Rankin looked up to see Ferguson running forward, the SEALs trailing behind.

"Don't mention it," Ferg yelled through the com set.

A five-foot chain-link fence sat at the end of the cement area; beyond it was a level jetty of rocks. Misjudging his height in the dark, Ferguson tore the seat of his pants on the top of the fence, and the scrape burned like a bullet wound.

Rocks jutted toward the water in a sawed-off W pattern at the base of the fence. The lights of the city to the north shone faintly on the water, making it the color of newspaper that had faded in the sunlight. Ferguson pulled off his boots but left his socks on, waiting at the edge of the jetty as the others caught up.

"That way," said Reid, pointing toward the water. "They'll bring up the raft and meet us. They'll have the gear."

"Shit," said Rankin.

"If you need help, holler," said Reid.

"I can fuckin' swim," said Rankin. "My gun's going to get screwed up."

"Don't be a sissy, Skippy," said Ferguson, slipping into the water. "Pop'll buy us new toys when we get home."

Rankin cursed as he jumped into the water behind the CIA officer. It was shallow—barely reaching his knees. It was also cold; he started to shiver as he waded out behind them, his Uzi strapped to his back.

About fifty yards from shore, Ferguson started to feel tired. He stopped for a moment, treading water, hoping that the burn in his shoulders would dissipate. The current pulled him north, in the opposite direction from where he wanted to go; he started stroking again, kicking harder and putting his head and shoulder against the low run of waves the way a running back might try and wedge himself into a line. Reid stroked about five yards beyond him, guided toward the rendezvous point by his waterproof GPS device. A set of low buoys lay in the distance ahead.

"How we doing?" Ferg asked, as Reid stopped to let the others catch up.

"Got a ways to go," he told him. "You all right?"

"Not a problem for me," said Ferg.

"I'm fine," snapped Rankin on the left.

"Let's go then," said Reid.

"If I wanted to do all this swimming, I would have joined the fuckin' Navy," said Rankin.

The SEAL team leader tried to talk Conners out of going on the raft; he wanted him to go back to the ASDS.

"We may have to swim from the channel up there, and that's a long swim," the leader of the SEAL team said. But Conners refused; he thought he'd be more useful with them. Not only did his com system connect directly with the rest of the team, but he had the sat phone in case they got stranded ashore. Besides, he wasn't about to swim out to the rendezvous alone, and it seemed to him the team couldn't spare even a single man to play shepherd.

MC didn't argue, mostly because there wasn't time. As they set the raft in the water, the team members took up a post and oar without a word passing between them. Conners put his knee on the inflated gunwale, doing his best to copy the man at the port bow ahead of him as they stroked into the black-pearl darkness. There wasn't a special SEAL stroke per se, yet the men had a certain quiet rhythm that propelled the raft forward quickly. Perhaps it came from hours and hours of practice in the cold and dark, or maybe it was injected during BUD/S somehow, the basic underwater demolition/SEALs training camp where recruits to the program were made or, more often, broken. Conners could only admire the teamwork and do his best not to screw it up.

They paddled for a good five minutes, then on some silent signal stopped—a vessel was making its way down the coastline, a pair of searchlights splaying out toward the shore.

"Patrol boat," the master chief told Conners as the craft cut its speed and the lights stopped moving toward them. It cut across their path. "It's a little north of our guys. James, Fu—meet them."

The two SEALs slipped into the water, pulling on masks and fins and taking extra Draeger gear for the others with them. The LAR V Draeger diving gear was a self-contained, "closed-circuit" breathing apparatus. The green oxygen tank held pure oxygen. As the diver exhaled, his breath recirculated through a special filter that took out carbon dioxide. One of the system's major advantages was the lack of telltale oxygen bubbles as the diver swam. It was also extremely lightweight, though its size was one limit on its endurance.

A minute after the SEALs had disembarked, MC raised his hand forward. He and the other SEAL began paddling, pushing the boat toward the open water. The patrol boat, meanwhile, circled north. Its searchlights swung together.

"Tommy," said the team leader.

The man at the starboard bow slid back into the well of the tiny boat, pulling gear from one of the waterproof bags. A heavy machine gun on the Iranian patrol boat began to fire. Tommy rose, and there was a sharp crack—one of the lights went dark. The SEAL steadied his sniper rifle and fired again, but the second light stayed lit. It swung in their direction as the patrol craft's engines revved.

"You owe the team a case," laughed MC.

The gun cracked again, and the second light went out. A half second later, the low, sharp rap and fizz of a grenade canister leaving a launcher filled Conners's ears. A heavy machine gun on the patrol boat began firing.

"You owe a case, too," snickered Tommy from the front, as the grenade exploded well aft of the charging patrol boat. The grenade launcher whapped again, and this time it found its target, exploding on the forward deck of the Iranian vessel, where its shrapnel killed one of the machine gunners.

That didn't stop it. Conners heard a shriek and instinctually ducked; a second later the rubber raft pitched hard to the starboard, nearly throwing him into the water. He knew the shell—fired from a 76 mm cannon—had missed, but there was more gunfire and more explosions, and the thick shadow of the patrol craft kept coming toward them.

"Into the water," said MC. Before Conners could push himself over the side he found himself submerged. He struggled for his breathing gear, lungs starting to burst. He bit water, then something hard; a giant fist grabbed him around the chest and spun him around. Something punched him in his face, and he felt his legs starting to spasm. His age and relative inexperience in the water had caught up with him, and he realized that MC hadn't been overprotective.

Screw that, he thought, pushing back to the surface.

"Breathe," said a voice as he cleared his head. The SEAL team leader was treading water a few inches away. Conners grabbed the Draeger mouthpiece and shoved it between his teeth.

"You swim OK for a soldier," said MC when he gave it back.

"For a geezer, you mean."

MC—who was probably about his age—laughed. "Come on. We got work to do."

"I'm right behind you," said Conners.

When the shooting began, Ferg dived, stroking hard in the direction where Reid had been. Adrenaline sped through his veins; he broke water as a fresh string of bullets crossed just to his right, more like bees dive-bombing an enemy than hard and vicious pieces of lead smacking into the water.

Something floated ahead. He pushed his arms in the water and kicked hard, came to it—Reid, who'd been nailed in the arm and leg.

"I don't think I can swim too fast," said the SEAL.

"I don't think you can swim at all," said Ferg.

Something exploded nearby. The patrol vessel spun around, suddenly interested in something else.

Ferguson grabbed hold of Reid.

"No, turn yourself around," said the sailor, explaining how to properly tow him through the water. Ferguson let go and looped around, his muscles groaning.

Rankin and the other SEAL were a few yards away. Reid checked his GPS; they were only about ten yards from the rendezvous point.

"We may have to go back ashore," said Ferg. "Let's swim south."

"Nah," said Reid. "MC'll be out here in a few minutes."

"Fuckin' patrol boat's going after them," said Rankin.

"You don't know MC," said Reid.

13

Corrine went home to her condo after the president spoke with her, intending to go right to bed though it was still early. She hadn't had much sleep in Cuba or over the last few days, and she knew she was beyond tired.

But she couldn't settle down enough to rest. The idea of being involved in a CIA–Special Forces operation both thrilled and terrified her. As counsel to the Intelligence Committee, she had occasionally daydreamed about what she would have done in different situations that were presented in reports and briefings. That was just a fantasy, though—she didn't have the background or training to be a CIA case officer, let alone get involved in SpecOps warfare.

Then again, the problem here wasn't expertise, it was oversight. And judgment.

She went upstairs and changed into her flannels. Corrine started to pull back the covers on her bed, but as soon as her fingers slid below the fold of the sheet she realized she couldn't settle down. She paced the hallway, went down to her living room, and put an aerobics video into the machine, thinking to work off some energy and put her mind on hold. But rather than soothing her, the workout left her more agitated. She went to the closet and took out some of her dumbbells, starting her regular routine—"regular" being a relative word since she'd started at the White House. After curls and alternating presses she skipped to some lat work, loading up the small metal bars and finally starting to sweat.

Then she realized she was still in her pajamas.

It was too late to change—she worked through the rest of the workout, pushing for a few extra reps on each set, putting her muscles into it, trying to work fast enough so that the rhythm of her breathing kept her from talking out loud.

Not talking—more like ranting. She'd been bamboozled into a no-win job. The president wanted her to be his personal spymaster.

Corrine imagined the congressional hearing when this all hit the fan. There'd be knives in her back from the CIA, the Pentagon, USSOCOM, the Democrats, the Republicans. Hell, even the DAR would find a way to blackball her.

But if she didn't take the job, who would? Because McCarthy would find someone to do it. He was determined to protect America, and that's what Special Demands was designed to do. Not break the law, just skirt around it when necessary.

If the right person kept it on track, it would succeed.

Why not her? Passing a Special Forces Assessment and Selection (SFAS) session and surviving Q Course wasn't what was important—they already had a host of people who could do that. They had hardware, intelligence, muscle—what they needed was conscience.

And actually, she had taken their stinking SFAS, the three-section, twenty-one-day physical and psychological exam that weeded out individuals for Q Course, which all SF soldiers had to pass through before wearing SF tabs. She'd volunteered as part of her first congressional committee job during one of the debates over allowing women in SOF combat units. Corrine had insisted on the full damn thing, and hung in there when they were all smirking behind their face paint.

Not that her showing had done anything for the debate. Nor did she think that she was *really* qualified—just that she could take what the bastards dished out.

She would have liked to try the Q Course, though, just for the hell of it.

If I don't take the job, who will? The idea stung her brain, just as the gradually building acid in her muscles stung her shoulders and arms. Tired at last, Corrine left the weights in the middle of the floor and went upstairs to her bath, filling it with warm water as she stripped off her clothes. She slipped into the water, easing back against the side of the tub.

Who, if not me?

Someone Slott could twirl around his finger. Then things would be even worse—they'd be cowboys with the imprimatur of the White House.

Corrine's agitation began building again.

She'd have to do something right away to get their attention and respect. She wasn't going to be one of the guys—that wasn't possible, and not just because she was a woman. She didn't want to be. They were never going to like her. But she had to show them that she had balls.

Or whatever gender-inappropriate sneer they were using these days.

She'd run the surveillance mission herself. That would prove her bona fides.

More likely, it would make her look like an ass. Corrine put the idea out of her head, then rose, pulling the plug on the drain. She actually felt tired, finally.

Too bad. There were phone calls to make, things to do. Corrine wrapped a towel around her and went to make a pot of coffee.

14

OFF BANDAR ʿABBĀS, IRAN

 Ferg actually found it easier to swim pulling Reid, either because of the adrenaline rush or the other man's powerful kick. The swells from the patrol boat's wake reared across the channel, the water surging up like a pile of dirt plowed by a bulldozer blade. Something had drawn the craft to the south, and as it started to fire its cannon, Ferg realized it had to be the SEAL team.

"Well that was altruistic, but not terribly bright," said Ferg.

"What?" said Reid.

"How close are we to the ASDS?" asked Ferg.

"Mile to the south. Long swim."

"We're going to have to go ashore," said Rankin.

"Hey!" said a voice in the distance. It seemed to come from the wake of the gunboat.

"Hey," said the other SEAL. "James?"

"Where the hell have you guys been?"

"Looking for you."

He handed out swimming gear, including a small inflatable life jacket that they put on Reid. He offered one to Rankin, who refused it at first.

"Don't be macho, Skip," said Ferg, who took one for himself. "We may be in the water a long time."

Rankin finally took the bib, sliding it awkwardly over his neck and trying to square away his gear.

The patrol boat had stopped firing and seemed to have stopped moving. Thin needles of light scanned the water in front of it.

"Our best bet's to get south," said Ferg. "We can head back and make shore where Conners and I landed yesterday, round up Keveh, then look for the others."

"What about the ASDS?" asked the SEAL who'd brought the gear out. "MC wanted us to meet him there."

"Even if we can get past that patrol boat, I don't want to leave the other guys here," said Ferg.

"You think they went ashore?"

"They may be dead," said Ferg.

"Nah," said James.

"It's okay," said Reid. "Head for the ASDS. MC'll be there. Guaranteed."

There were trucks and lights passing on the shore. The patrol boat was a low shadow in the channel, temporarily quiet.

"All right, we're going back south," said Ferguson. "No more debate."

They'd gone only a hundred yards when one of the machine guns on the patrol boat began firing again. Two or three seconds later, an explosion that sounded something like a grenade going off inside a fifty-gallon drum shook the vessel. A whistling shriek like the exhaust of a steam kettle followed.

"Wu knows how to place 'em," said James, increasing his pace.

The other SEAL had taken a limpet mine and attached it to the hull of the patrol boat. The Iranian crew started firing every weapon they had, but it was far too late—the high-explosive mine had blasted a huge hole in the thin hull, and the boat quickly settled at the stern. One of the Iranian's guns either overheated or jammed somehow, and there was another explosion, this one unmuffled by the water; a fire flared, and rounds began cooking off like firecrackers.

"Nice of them to provide a light show," said Ferg, changing direction as the fire died out. "Which way is our sub?"

ACT III

I am armed,
And dangers are to me indifferent.

—Shakespeare, *Julius Caesar*, 1.3.114–5

1

QATAR, PERSIAN GULF—TWO DAYS LATER

Ferguson leaned back in the leather chair, waiting for the secure video screen at the front of the basement room in the embassy building to bleep to life. As secure communications facilities went, this was among the clubbiest—the couch and club chairs were thick leather, and there was a well-stocked bar at the side of the room. He'd watered down his bourbon considerably, but still felt the sting of it in his mouth as he waited for the connection to go through.

"Hey, Ferg," said Corrigan, his face exploding onto the flat plasma screen.

"What's the puss about, Jack?" said Ferg. "It's not payday."

"You're not going to like this."

Without any other explanation, Corrigan's face dissolved into Slott's.

"There's a change in our organizational chart," said Slott.

"Auditors finally caught up with you, huh?"

"One of these days, Ferguson, your wisecracks are going to catch you short. Today may just be the day."

"Gentlemen, if we're through with the fun and games, let's begin." Corrine Alston's face flashed on the screen.

"Well, if it isn't the White House lawyer," said Ferg. "Don't tell me you're DDO now."

"As a matter of fact, Mr. Ferguson, I'm not. But I am in charge of the Joint Services Special Demands Project Office. And by some quirk in the legislation, it appears that while I have to inform the DDO of what I do, I don't actually answer to him."

"Peachy," said Ferg.

"What are you drinking?"

Ferg held the glass up. "Jack Daniel's. Want some?"

"This is government time," she said frostily.

"Yeah. I'm drinking in the line of duty."

"Yuk, yuk," said Corrine. "I understand the oil tanker was a bust."

Ferg raised his hand. "Uh, Madam Lawyer? Actually, it was ethylene. And it was being outfitted as a covert minelayer. That information has been passed along and is of great value to the agencies responsible."

"The information could have been gathered through DRO." The initials stood for the Defense Reconnaissance Office, which was responsible for satellite tasking.

"Sure," said Ferg. "And the Sisters of Charity might have stumbled across it during a fund-raising drive. But they didn't. Now, if we could get timely data from DRO, that would be nice."

"You don't get timely data?" asked Corrine.

"We have trouble getting timely train schedules."

"I thought the entire idea was to do away with the bureaucracy fettering you."

Ferg snorted, and not just because of her somewhat naive notion about bureaucratic prerogatives. He'd never heard the word "fetter" used over a secure com net before.

"The bureaucracy you're referring to," said Slott, rallying to the defense, "is a set of different departments and agencies working together to provide timely support."

"Or not," said Ferg.

"Improvements will be made," said Corrine.

"Hear, hear," said Ferguson.

"In the meantime," said Corrine, "we have a new program."

"I like that. What the fuck is it supposed to mean?"

She frowned slightly at the curse word, which was his intention. She could pretend to be one of the guys, but underneath it she was just another one of those Beltway girls, let into the game because of abstract principles that had nothing to do with reality.

He sipped his drink as she continued, outlining a plan to follow a shipment of waste from Buzuluk in Russia.

"Excuse me, didn't you just suggest we use DRO? The satellites and monitors already keep tabs, and, besides, the Russians guard the trains."

"Maybe they don't guard them very well."

"OK," said Ferguson. "But you're about a week and a half behind the times. Why fool around with the train anymore when we know the waste is going to Chechnya?"

"You don't know that at all."

"Excuse me. Strongly suspect. What's Kiro say?"

Somebody behind Corrine whispered something to her, bowing his head as if he were speaking to the queen. Ferg couldn't believe they were all deferring to her already, waiting for her to speak. Slap the White House label on anything, and all of a sudden it rose to the top of the heap.

"Corrigan," he said, growing impatient. "What's new with Kiro? We're interrogating him, *right*?"

"Nothing new, Ferg."

"Did you guys apply the screws?"

"We're not going to use drugs," said Corrine. "We want to bring him to trial."

"So?" said Ferguson.

"Mr. Ferguson, there are certain legal constraints—"

"Uh-huh." Ferg got up and went over to the bar. His refill wasn't going to be watered down.

"We'll launch our project from Moscow tomorrow evening," said Corrine. "I'll need three members of your team, Mr. Ferguson. I'd like at least one who's already familiar with the operation."

Since he only had two people with him, Ferguson would have been stupid indeed not to realize she was trying to clip his wings. Dealing with her was going to be a serious pain in the ass.

"Not a problem," he said, turning and giving his best smile to the camera. "Give Corrigan the details. I'll work it out."

"Will you be there?"

"No, I'm due some R&R time."

"That's fine," she said sharply. Then her feed went blank.

2

 Slott's reaction to being supplanted was so professionally cold that Corrine couldn't decide whether it hid anger or relief. She saw no sign that he was in on the president's game, though she was starting to realize that was no guarantee he wasn't.

Slott claimed to have no free CIA personnel to assign to the Team; in fact, he told her, the Agency was desperately undermanned in all areas—a hint that perhaps she might use her influence to free up personnel lines. She did so, but all her phone calls succeeded in doing was shaking loose a previously approved but budgetarily frozen slot for a high-level analyst to help the Team. Corrine finally decided that the SF people could undertake the surveillance mission themselves without Ferguson or another Agency minder. The mission was relatively straightforward, with the Team members expected to stay out of harm's way and simply gather intelligence.

Back at her White House office, she tried sorting through some of the other work that was piling up for her. She hadn't gotten very far when the president summoned her by phone; he had left a few hours before for Chicago.

"How is Russia?" he asked when she picked up.

"Russia?"

"Well now, isn't that where you are?"

"Mr. President, you know very well where I am. You called me."

"Generally when I ask to speak to someone, the call is put through without bothering me with minor details such as the location of my callee," he said. "But now that I reflect upon it, the line does not seem to have the usual Russia twang. There's more a kind of static in the background, the sort of electronic fog I associate with Washington, D.C."

"Why do you want me in Russia?"

"I want you running Special Demands. You outlined a project for the Team, and I expected you to see it through. In person."

"But I'm not qualified—"

"I do wish you'd stop putting yourself down, young lady."

"Yes, sir."

McCarthy dropped his playful tone. "They have to respect you, Corrine. Make them see you're a tough ol' gal. As tough as me. I know you are."

"Tough *young* gal."

"Get."

"Yes, sir," she said, hanging up.

3

QATAR, PERSIAN GULF

 "I'll give the nuns one thing," said Conners, slapping the beer mug down on the polished blond wood bar. "They taught you how to do arithmetic, and grammar. They were hell on you, but you learned."

"Yeah?" Rankin reached for the bowl of pretzel nuggets, selecting one and holding it up for examination. He turned it over and over, as if he were looking at a diamond. Both men had had a few shots to go with their two beers. The Foreign Club was an American-style bar, insulated from the Islamic masses by a squadron of security people and a hefty "membership fee." The very expensive foreigners club would have been normally off-limits and out of reach for American soldiers, but Ferg's unlimited connections and moxie had gotten them in. Even Rankin would have had to admit the CIA officer knew the meaning of R&R.

"You're drinking too much," Rankin said, as Conners pushed the shot glasses forward for another round.

"Yup," said Conners. Rankin reminded Conners of a kid he'd known since grammar school, Peter Flynn. Flynn was an only child and a bit of a priss, and when in sixth grade he announced that he was going to be a priest no one was really surprised. Girls—and probably Flynn's father—soon put an end to that, but Flynn always seemed a little angry about it, mad that he couldn't fit into that square hole.

"I'll be but drunk in good company," said Ferguson, slapping them both on the back.

"Hey, it's the devil himself," said Conners.

Ferg pointed at the beer for the bartender, ordering one for himself.

"What was that you said?" Rankin asked Ferguson.

"A quote. From Shakespeare."

"He was an Irishman, you know," said Conners.

"*I'll ne'er be drunk, whilst I live, but in honest, civil, godly company,*" said Rankin, supplying the proper lines from *Merry Wives of Windsor*.

"Whoa, Skip—you know more than you let on."

"Screw you, Ferguson."

"How'd it go?" Conners asked.

"Peachy," said Ferg, taking his beer. It was a Dortmunder export from Germany, "DUB" or Dortmunder Union Brauerei, which had a dryer, slightly stronger taste than the "normal" German lager. Ferguson drained the mug, then pushed it forward for a refill. "Drink up today, boys, for tomorrow we fly. That's not a direct quote."

Conners glanced over his shoulder, making sure that no one was nearby. The crowd was mostly rich businessmen, but a spy might easily mingle, and of course a good portion of the staff would be in the employ of some intelligence agency or another. "Where we going?" he asked Ferguson.

"Hither, thither and yon. Skip, here, is going to Moscow."

"Moscow?" said Rankin.

"Russia, not New York. You're meeting our new boss." Ferguson pulled over the refilled mug. "Guns'll meet you," he said, taking a more sensible sip this time. "I have another SF guy going as well, out of the States. They call him Frenchie—he was on loan to French intelligence for a while and has an accent. Thinks he's a frog."

"What new boss?" said Rankin.

"Long story, Skip. We'll get into it later. Any girls around here?" Ferg asked, turning around to survey the room.

"They don't allow women," said Conners.

"Well, then, we'll just have to go somewhere that they do, eh?"

4

 Rankin's head throbbed as he made his way off the Airbus A330. He turned the wrong way and found himself staring into the stern face of a Russian policeman. He went back and found the route to the baggage area, though he already had all of his luggage, a small carry-on.

The signs were in English as well as Russian, but the glare hurt his eyes, and he squinted until he finally managed to find the proper Customs line. He unfolded his blue passport—it was his "real" passport, not the diplomatic one he could use in an emergency—and after presenting the lengthy Customs form answered a dozen questions about his stay for a twentysomething woman with hair nearly as short as his. Cleared through, he walked around the building, waiting for whoever was supposed to meet him—it hadn't been worked out when he left—to do so.

"Yo," said someone behind him on his third circuit. "What the hell are you doing?"

Guns was standing at the side, shaking his head. He was dressed in a black brushed-leather jacket and jeans and wearing an earring; he looked like a British soccer fan sizing up the country for a round of hooliganism.

"What are you doing?" Rankin said. He'd thought the Marine was in the hospital.

"Looking for you."

"You OK?"

"Good as ever."

"Where'd you get the earring?"

"Car's out this way," said the Marine.

"Where'd you get the earring?" repeated Rankin, following him outside. The light stabbed at his eyes, and he felt a quick wave of nausea, yesterday's whiskey rumbling in his stomach.

"Like it?"

"No."

Guns put his fingers up to it. "It's a transmitter. I'm being tracked as we speak."

"Get out." Rankin grabbed the Marine and looked at his ear. The earring was a simple gold-colored post.

"You kiss me, and I'll slug you," said Guns.

"That's no fucking tracking device."

"Join the twenty-first century," said Guns. "There's our car."

They got into a small Fiat at the far end of the lot. It was a manual; Guns stalled it twice getting out of the spot, grinding the gears when he finally got it into the lane. He managed to work the clutch right at the gate, however, and once they were on the highway he felt comfortable.

"How was Iran?" Guns asked Rankin.

"A fuck-up. Ferg got shitty intelligence and almost got himself wasted in a pirate-DVD operation. They made porn movies."

"Yeah? Right there?"

"No, they just made copies. We gave a bunch to the submarine crew and the SEALs. They had a great time."

"Did we get one?"

"You don't want that shit," said Rankin. He glanced at his watch, already set for Russian time. He still had an hour to go before he could take more acetaminophen for his hangover. "Where we going?"

"Another airport called Domodedovo."

"Why?"

" 'Cause we're flying out to someplace called Orenburg. Or actually near there. I'm starting to lose track."

"Why?"

"Man, you ask a lot of questions."

"How was Paris?" said Rankin, following along.

"Busy. We didn't stay. We drove out to talk to somebody in Reims."

"You see the cathedral?"

"There's a cathedral there?"

"Guns, there are cathedrals in every city in Europe. Yeah. It's pretty famous. Fantastic stained-glass windows."

"How about that."

"What's the new boss like?" Rankin asked, changing the subject.

"New boss is a serious piece of eye candy, but a bit of a bitch," said Guns. "Ferg don't like her."

"Yeah, well, that's one thing in her favor."

Guns laughed. "We're going to track a shipment of waste to Kyrgyzstan."

"We should've done that in the first place."

"Yup. You want to stop and get something to eat?"

"Not really," Rankin told him.

"Well, I have to stop anyway."

"Go for it, Marine."

"I never know how to take you, Rankin," said Guns.

"What do you mean?"

"You making fun or me or what?"

Rankin bent over his seat belt and looked at him. "No."

"You sound like you're trying to bust my chops."

"Jesus, Guns, I got a fuckin' headache, and I feel like I'm being jerked around on yet another wild-goose chase. What the hell you want me to do?"

"Your problem is you need to get laid. I'll tell you, at the infirmary, I met this nurse. First thing I did . . ."

"Oh Christ," said Rankin, leaning his head back against the rest.

5

BAKU, ON THE CASPIAN SEA

 Baku was an oil town, the center of one of the most prolific producing areas in the world outside the Middle East. It was also a place where other things could be had and arranged; the Caspian washed its shores with the rhythmic sound of possibility, and if a foreigner didn't find hospitality there, it was surely because he wasn't trying hard enough.

Ferg and Conners sat at a table overlooking the sea, waiting to meet Ferg's contact, who was running about an hour late. Rahil—Rachel in English—was a raven-haired beauty, the daughter of a smuggler who had inherited the business from his father. Ferguson had had occasion to do business with her once before, and so he wasn't surprised or disappointed by the fact that she hadn't yet shown up at the cafe. He nursed a coffee while Conners sipped at a vodka, staring through the yellowed plastic panel at the edge of the porch.

"My darling, you are here already," said Rahil. She floated to them across the porch, her hand trailing across Ferguson's shoulder. He rose; she kissed him. Four men in black pants and sweaters fanned out across the room behind her—the family business had not thrived for three generations without taking certain precautions.

"Your friend?" Rahil said.

"Dad," said Ferg, pointing to him.

"Your father? But he's so young."

"Just a nickname."

"Ma'am."

"You must watch Mr. Ferguson," Rahil advised him. "He will go light on the paycheck."

"We merely deducted for expenses," said Ferg. She was referring to their last encounter, which had involved smuggling a set of hard drives out of Russia. The disks had been damaged—probably because Rahil had tried to have her people read them—and Ferg's supervisors had insisted on delivering only partial payment.

"You will make it up today?"

"Maybe."

Rahil let a waiter pull over a chair for her, then ordered champagne. She began telling Ferguson about how beautiful the sea was this time of year—how beautiful it was at all times of year.

Conners sipped his vodka, taking in only enough to sting his lips. Rahil looked to be about thirty, though like a lot of women he'd seen there she put her makeup on so thickly it made her look older. She had a thin body, but she moved it the way a dancer would, thrusting it around as she spoke. Her bodyguards eyed them jealously, and Conners guessed that she herself had at least two weapons, including a barely concealed pistol at the belt of her flowing skirt beneath her black blouse, which was not tucked into the waistband.

"I'm going to Groznyy," said Ferg

"Yes?" she said. The waiter arrived with the champagne, a Tattinger brut, 1995.

"I'd like to stay in a convenient place there," said Ferg, who took a glass of the wine.

"There are many hotels," she told him.

"You know my tastes."

"Expensive."

"Not necessarily. Just discreet."

"As I said, expensive. The authorities." She shook her head. "Groznyy is not a nice place these days."

"When was it ever?"

"True. The Chechens are a dirty people. Why go there? Stay here with us. Baku is a very rich place." She turned to Conners. "You are not drinking my champagne?"

"No, ma'am."

"Don't worry, Mr. Ferguson is paying." She laughed.

"Thanks anyway," said Conners.

The waiter reappeared. Rahil called him over and ordered some blintzes, then told him to see to her men. There were three dozen tables on the veranda, more than half of them occupied, but the waiter had no trouble figuring out whom she meant.

"So, a place to stay. That's it?" said Rahil. "The CIA needs my services as a travel agent?"

"I'd like some contact among the rebels."

Rahil shook her head. "No."

"No one who owes you a favor?"

"These sorts of favors would have me dead in a week," she said. "We do not deal with the Islamic madmen."

"They're not all mad, are they?"

"The crazy ones are the sanest. Of course they're mad. They've been mad for centuries. But now they are worse. In the past two years . . ." She waved her hand in the air, as if brushing away smoke. "Drink more champagne, Ferguson. Drink, drink."

"They may have something I want to buy," suggested Ferg.

"Such as?"

"Things," he said.

"Stay away from them. Better to deal with the Russians."

"I deal with them all the time."

"See? I knew you were a wise man. Here, let me write you an address that may come in useful."

nteresting woman," said Conners, as they rode in a taxi toward the dock. Ferguson had hired a boat to take them north to Machachkala, where they'd hire a car to go to Groznyy. They were supposed to be German representatives from an oil company, though it didn't seem as if anyone particularly cared. "Pretty, too."

"Drug smugglers usually are," said Ferg.

"We going to stay in her hotel?"

"Nah."

"You wanted the guerrilla contact?"

"No." Ferguson pointed out the dock and had the driver let them off. When the car had pulled away, he told Conners to grab his bag and follow him.

"Where?"

"There's a ferry we're taking. It leaves from that pier up there."

"I thought you hired a boat."

"I did," said Ferg.

"You sharing information these days?"

"Only on a need-to-know basis."

"What do I do if you get shot?" asked Conners, serious.

"Cash in the plane ticket in your pocket and go home."

"Ferg." Conners grabbed his shoulder. "You've been taking some awful chances lately."

"Name one."

"Walking into that police station, the DVD operation in Iran . . ."

"It's okay, Dad. It'll all make sense eventually." Ferguson adjusted the shoulder strap on his leather duffel bag and started for the ferry.

"That I doubt," said Conners.

erg waited until they were about halfway to Machachkala to call Corrigan. By then the clouds had thickened, and it looked as if they were sailing toward a storm. He stood out on the upper deck, wind whipping against his face as the call went through.

"Where you been?" Corrigan asked.

"Pulling my pud," Ferguson told him. "What do you have for me?"

"The guy Kiro sent a message to is named Jabril Daruyev. You can download the full dossier anytime you want."

"And the FSB investigator?"

"As far as we can tell, he's back in Chechnya. I can't run him down definitively."

"You have him definitely ID'd as Kruknokov?" asked Ferg.

"If you had given us a better picture, I could be definitive," said Corrigan. "But there's a Kruknokov who was in Kyrgyzstan, then went to Chechnya. I have a picture and it looks like your guy. I see a yellow sports coat."

"That's got to seal it," said Ferg.

He was being serious, though Corrigan thought he was making fun of him.

"Don't you bust my chops," said Corrigan.

"I wasn't. How are Guns and Rankin making out with the Dragon Lady?"

"She's not *that* bad. No worse than Slott."

"I'll tell him you said that."

"Please stop busting my balls."

"When I go online, am I going to have all that data on the prisons?"

"It's waiting for you."

"Fair enough, Corrigan. I take back everything I said about you."

"What a guy."

Ferg snapped off the phone.

6

 Rankin reached over the seat, fishing for the bottle of water in the back of the car. He hadn't screwed the top tightly enough when he'd put it on, and the carpet of the Fiat was soaked; worse, he had only a few small gulps left. Even though the train carrying the waste material had parked for the night on a siding, they'd have to stay there watching it, and that meant he wouldn't be able to restock for another six hours, until Conners and Jack Massette took over. His few days in the Middle East had left him dehydrated, maybe permanently; he felt as if he could drink several gallons of water and not quench his thirst. Holding the bottle up in the dim light, Rankin gauged that there were four gulps' worth left. He decided he'd have to parcel them out, a gulp an hour. Postponing the first gulp, he tightened the cap securely and rose in the seat to place the bottle more carefully against the transmission hump. Their gear was on the seat at least, and so remained dry.

A figure approached from the right side of the car. Even though he knew it had to be Corrine, Rankin tensed, caught awkwardly unprepared. He let go of the bottle and pulled his arm back as he saw her face, nodding, then reaching over to unlock the door for her.

"It's cold," she said.

"Everything seems cold to me," he said.

She slid in, adjusting the seat though she'd fiddled with it several times since they parked there two hours before. Corrine had had to relieve herself at the edge of the woods. She hadn't had to squat outdoors since a family camping trip when she nine or ten, but it wasn't exactly the sort of thing she could talk to Rankin about. The Special Forces soldier had hardly said anything since they'd taken the shift together watching the waste train for the night.

"I didn't see anything from the road," she told Rankin. "I walked up and around. There's a gravel road out to the town."

"Yeah," said Rankin. "Listen, I spilled a bunch of water in the back."

"Oh." She twisted around to look.

"It's on the floor," he said. "Nothing really got wet."

"We have another bottle of water," she said.

"That's yours."

"We can share. I don't have cooties."

"Thanks."

A small video screen projected and magnified the view from a set of night glasses positioned on the dashboard. They could see all five cars carrying the waste material from where they sat, though they couldn't see the three diesels that drove the train or the flatcar and four boxcars that had been tagged on to the back, the flatcar for the guards and the others merely cars going south.

Starting from Buzuluk earlier in the day, the train had been escorted by a small detachment of soldiers in a second train, along with a pair of helicopters. Now it had only a small contingent of guards—Russian sailors in civilian dress, according to their backgrounder—and two local policemen. Most of the dozen sailors were asleep in the boxcar nearest the containment cars; the policemen were dozing in a car near the tracks. Four members of the six-man train crew had left earlier, presumably going to the local hotel for the night.

"You get to the point where you almost wish something would happen," said Corrine.

"You got that right." Rankin shifted in the seat. His back muscles were starting to tighten. "Shoulda brought a book or something."

"What book would you read?" she asked.

Rankin shrugged. "Whatever."

"You read thrillers?"

"Nah. Biographies," said Rankin.

"Really?"

Rankin didn't like the surprised tone in her voice. "Brant's history of James Madison," he said, naming the work he'd started the last time he was back in the States. It was a six-volume set of the man who'd been the country's fourth president and principal author of the Constitution.

"Is it interesting?" Corrine asked.

"It's long." He leaned back in the seat, trying to stretch his back. "It explains the War of 1812 a little better than I've seen before."

"How'd you get into that?"

"I just did," said Rankin.

They were silent a minute or so. Rankin decided he didn't want her to think he was mad at her—he wasn't, really. He just didn't like people thinking he was a stupid shit, when he wasn't.

"What do you read?" he asked.

"Depends. If I'm in a mood for a mystery, I'll read something by Lawrence Block maybe, or P. D. James. If I want to laugh, I read Wodehouse."

"Bertie and Jeeves?"

"You know the series?"

"Sure."

"I think the TV shows they did, the BBC shows—they were better than the books."

"Didn't see it. Excuse me. Gotta take a leak." He got out of the car and went into the woods to pee.

Corrine turned her attention back to the small viewer screen, where the large cars sat like unmoving ghosts. She knew she had offended him by being surprised at what he was reading—but she *was* surprised, and whether he was a soldier or not, biographies about James Madison weren't exactly everyday reading.

That was the way it was going to be from now on—no matter what she did or tried to do, everyone from Slott on down would see her as an interloper. She'd just have to deal with it.

Corrine pulled her coat tighter around her, fighting off the chill.

7

THE ROAD TO GROZNYY

 Conners's German was nonexistent, but Ferguson convinced him that if he spoke English with a quasi-German accent, he'd fool most anyone they encountered, since there were rarely German businessmen in Chechnya. Conners began practicing his inflections as they drove along the highway toward the Chechen capital. At some point Ferg found his accent too ridiculous not to laugh aloud, and it became a joke between them. At one point Conners began singing his Irish drinking songs with a German accent, and Ferguson joined in, words and accents morphing together into a new language punctuated by laughter.

The drive might have been interminable otherwise. There were checkpoints every ten or fifteen miles. Usually the two men were waved through with no more than a cursory glance at their papers and car. But several times the Russian soldiers ordered them out and conducted brief searches, which were more like shakedowns than pat-downs.

Carrying weapons was theoretically forbidden, but the realities of travel through the countryside meant that many Russians and even foreigners armed themselves, and in most cases a soldier who saw a rifle in the backseat of an otherwise unsuspicious car—that is, a car that clearly didn't belong to a Chechen—wouldn't blink, as long as the owner agreed to pay a nominal "fine" on the spot. On the other hand, it was also possible that the soldier might "confiscate" a weapon that looked much nicer than his own. They, therefore, carefully hid their Glocks and PKs—they had only pistols—and left a Makarova peeking out from under a blanket in the back to attract attention.

They got off the main highway about six miles from the city, driving north through the ruins of a village that had been burned two or three years before by Russian troops. The land that straddled the village had been farmed for centuries before the rebellions; now the fields were thick with weeds. Here and there the rotted carcass of a shed or a barn, its wood too deteriorated even to be burned for fuel, stood like the starched bones of a horse picked over by buzzards in the desert. They drove north for about five miles, then took a local road to the east. A town appeared off to the side; they found the road for it and drove up the main street, surprised that there were no patrols checking traffic in or out.

"German," Ferguson told Conners as they got out of the car. A small house nearby had a handwritten sign advertising rooms in one of the windows.

"Ya-vole," said Conners in pseudo-German. He started to crack up.

"Don't schpecken ze jokes," replied Ferguson. He knelt and retrieved his small Glock from under the seat. Palming the gun, he slid it into his pocket, then took his battered overnight bag and led Conners into the three-story brick building, which sat about a foot below street level. The structure probably predated the road, but it seemed as if it had slid into the earth, hunkering down to avoid the years of war.

The front hall smelled of fresh paint. A very short older woman with glasses appeared at the far end as they came in, her fingers layered with paint. She introduced herself in Chechen, then switched to Russian, eying them suspiciously. Ferg gave her the cover story—German businessmen who'd come to sell electronic switches for furnaces. They had business in the capital.

"Why aren't you staying there?" she asked.

"Too expensive," he told her. "Besides, this is such a lovely place. Do you speak German?"

She did not, but the promise of payment in euros allayed her suspicions and she showed them to a pair of rooms at the top of the first set of stairs. They decided Conners's was more private, and after searching and scanning for bugs using a small frequency detector, Ferguson took the laptop from the bag, using the sat phone to connect to their encrypted Web site.

"That where we're going?" asked Conners, pointing to the sat photos.

"This one," said Ferg. He double-clicked on the thumbnail and a large .jpg file began filling the screen.

"Looks like an old castle."

"It is. Supposedly built by the Turks about six hundred years ago."

"The Turks were here?"

"Turks have been everywhere," said Ferg. "It's a jail now."

"We're going there?"

"What's the matter? Don't want to leave the Happy Acres Motel?"

"Well it does have TV," said Conners, thumbing toward the set in the corner. It looked like it dated from the 1950s.

"True enough."

"So what's the deal, Ferg? What are we doing?" Ferguson still hadn't explained what they were up to—unusual for him. The SF soldier didn't need long-winded explanations, but he didn't like it when people started acting differently than they had before. In his experience, it wasn't a good sign.

Ferg killed the telephone connection. With the Web browser down, he launched a scrubber program to erase the history files and all traces of what they'd just seen.

"We got a lawyer poking around now, Dad. We have to watch what we do," Ferguson told him.

"She told you not to tell me what was going on?"

Ferguson didn't answer.

"We ain't gonna get you in trouble, are we?" Conners stood against the door, his arms folded. "Ferg?"

"I'm just following my original orders until I'm told not to."

"I'm not arguing with you," said Conners. "I just want to know what the hell's going on, that's all."

"Das is goot." Ferguson took a beat-up black knapsack bag from the suitcase and slid the laptop into it. "Let's go get something to eat."

T he roast beef not only tasted like beef, it seemed to be nearly fresh. The beer the cafe served was thin, but that made it easier to order a second. It was between lunch and dinnertime, and the cafe was nearly deserted; they sat in a booth at the back end of the dimly lit room, speaking mostly in English, though Ferg threw in Russian and a little German every so often.

"I want to get the guy Kiro's guy talked to," he told Conners. "Jabril Daruyev. He'll know what's going on."

"How do you get him to talk?"

"Ve haf our vays," said Ferguson.

Conners frowned.

"Personally, I'd like to just beat the shit out of him," said Ferguson, "but the Russians have probably tried that."

"Even if we grab this guy, Ferg, what makes you think he'll talk?" asked Conners.

Ferg sipped his beer. Grabbing the Chechen was the right thing to do, but he was bound to take shit for it. Ferguson didn't particularly mind; his dad had taught him that lesson long, long ago. The bureaucracy would get its pound of flesh from you no matter what; better to follow your conscience so you could live with yourself when they cut the rope. The old man had lived and died by that creed.

"They have this stuff similar to thiopental sodium," said Ferg. "Only it works."

"That like Sodium Pentothal?"

"Something like that."

"It's OK to use?"

"It works."

"You have some?"

"No. They have it at Guantanamo, though. We'll send him there."

"Why didn't they use it on Kiro?" asked Conners.

"Because the lawyer wants to put him on trial," said Ferg. "If they shoot him up, she figures it'll come out and queer the case."

"That's the only reason?"

Ferg shrugged. Sodium—TFh4—the "street" name of the drug, whose chemical name ran about a paragraph long—would also do fairly serious damage to a person's liver, but no one seemed to worry about that. "Daruyev doesn't have to stand trial for anything he did in America. No objections to using the drugs."

"Lawyer told you that?" asked Conners.

"Not in so many words." Ferg picked up his beer.

"If they're building this thing in Chechnya, maybe they're targeting the Russians," suggested Conners.

"Could be," said Ferg. "But you notice that the Russians weren't all that concerned about Kiro until we blew up the commander's car, right? You think we ought to count on them to stay on top of it?"

Even Ferguson realized that breaking a prisoner out of the Brown Fortress, as the Russians called the prison ten miles away, was impossible. So he had decided to let the Russians do it for him.

The idea had started to form when they were in Chechnya, as a hazy backup plan to the snatch of Kiro. The details remained slightly hazy, because a great deal of it depended on the Russians themselves.

But it was already in motion.

Conners drove into Groznyy early in the evening, wending his way through the streets toward the address Rahil had given Ferguson in Baku. He now had a completely different cover story, one that accounted for his halting Russian—he was back to being an American, sent there as a sewer plant expert by UNESCO. Ferg assured him the cover wouldn't be tested, though he had a folder on the car seat detailing various bacterial tests just in case. Rahil's friend acted as if she had no idea who he was, and even mentioning Rahil—as Ferguson directed—brought no response. A hundred-dollar bill, however, got him a room with working electricity on the second floor of the small hotel.

Inside, he took out his pistol and sat in the armchair opposite the door, waiting.

The store looked more American than Russian, shelves crammed around a cash register at the side close to the door, displays of newspapers and candy in easy sight of the cashier. Ferg walked to the back cooler—it was filled with Coke—opening it as another customer came in. Then he let it snap closed and walked around to the right, where the door to the back room was ajar, a sagging chain lock holding it closed.

"I'm looking for Ruby," he said in Russian. "Ruby?"

A tall, thin man with a black shock of hair hanging over his forehead stuck his face in the crack.

"I'm looking for Ruby," Ferg said, this time in English.

The tall man said something in Chechen that Ferguson couldn't decipher. Instead of answering, Ferg held up his wrist and slid off his watch.

"Where's Ruby?" he repeated.

The tall man reached for the watch. Ferg drew it back. That brought a fresh spree of indecipherable Chechen. When the door did not open, Ferguson slid the watch back on his wrist and walked over to the cooler. He took out a Coke and walked toward the front of the store.

A gnomelike man with a closely cropped beard met him in the aisle. The man wore a long sweater that was so worn it looked like an old woman's housecoat; thick as a brush, his short gray hair stuck up from his scalp as if he'd put his hand in an electrical socket.

"I'm Ruby," he said. The accent was so thick that Ferguson at first wasn't sure it was English. "Come."

The man shuffled to the last cooler at the back of the store. He opened the door and slid the case rack back, passing into the storage area as if he were walking into the secret chamber of a haunted mansion. Ferg followed, waiting as Ruby slid the rack of soda back in place. His steps made a kind of snuffling sound as he went, not unlike the sound rough sandpaper makes as a craftsman finishes off the edge of a piece of furniture. Produce sat in wooden crates beyond the row of soda; behind them were large metal canisters for propane or some similar gas. At the very back of the space was a doorway; as he followed the gnome through it, Ferg slid the Glock down from his jacket sleeve and brought his hand up, and so both he and Ruby faced each other with loaded pistols in the dimly lit room beyond the store.

Ruby started to laugh. Ferg smiled.

Ruby pulled back the hammer on the pistol, a Zavodi Crvena Zastava .357 revolver that looked like a cannon in his tiny hand.

Ferg's Glock, small for an automatic, permitted no such intimidating gesture, though at this range it would do sufficient damage to make the situation a draw.

"I think we can make a deal," ventured Ferguson.

"Your watch is counterfeit."

"No. It's real." Ferguson actually felt insulted.

"Bah."

"Seriously. I got it in New York."

"Now I know it's fake."

"I can arrange other payment."

"Perhaps I will look at it." Ruby held out his hand.

Ferg heard something behind him. His eyes and gun still frozen on Ruby's face, he took a short step to the right, then another.

"I hope he's coming back with a credit approval," said Ferg.

Ruby shouted to the man outside, telling him to go back. The man outside began arguing with him. Ruby shook his head and lowered his gun.

"Children," said the Chechen. He went to the door and leaned into the storage room, his body shaking as he unleashed a string of invective. The man outside—Ferg guessed it was the man he'd seen at the chained door, though he'd looked no more like Ruby than Ferg did—whimpered once or twice, then retreated.

Ruby returned to the room, gesturing wildly and mumbling to the effect that the world was a disappointing place, and there were no greater disappointments than sons. Without glancing at the American or otherwise acknowledging his presence, he walked to the only pieces of furniture in the room—two large four-drawer filing cabinets, legal size, in the corner.

"Chay?" he asked, pulling open one of the drawers and removing a teapot.

"Good," said Ferg. He kept his gun in his hand as Ruby removed the pot and two small cups from the drawer, then went back into the storage room and returned with a card table and an extension cord. Several more trips were needed before the kettle was bubbling with water and metal chairs had been unfolded around the table.

"Strong," said Ferg, when he finally sipped the tea. The dark green liquid tasted as if it had been made of anise and cinnamon as well as tea leaves.

"Yes. There is no more good tea," said Ruby, speaking in Russian. The Chechen had left his gun on the file cabinet and now had the air of a professor down on his luck. There was no hint in his voice whether he thought the liquid an exception to the rule, or proof.

"If anyone were to have good tea, it would be you," said Ferg.

"It would. If anyone did."

"I need weapons," said Ferg.

"Why else would you be here?"

"Why else?"

Six AK-47s—Ruby would sell no fewer than that—and two RPG-18s, single-shot antiarmor missiles with a 64 mm warhead, were available for about three times what they should have fetched, according to the information Ferg had obtained through Corrigan. Which was a pain, not because he couldn't pay it—he had a stack of counterfeit rubles with him—but because to do so would signal him as an easy mark and cause considerable trouble down the line.

A long series of negotiations followed, with Ferg starting at a quarter of the going rate—as much an insult as Ruby's asking price—then working slowly toward one and a half times what Corrigan's data indicated was a fair price. It took nearly twenty minutes for them to reach that point, and it was only the addition of two dozen grenades and six mines that sealed it. They celebrated the agreement by brewing a fresh pot of tea.

"Now a truck," said Ferguson, and the bargaining began all over again. It took another half hour before he finally obtained a pickup with petrol at what he thought was a good price—he could judge that only by how long it took to reach agreement. By then his bladder was overflowing, and he excused himself, positioning some of the necessary cash in his pocket on the way back.

When he returned, Ferguson asked if it might be possible to obtain the services of a few men. The Chechen hesitated sufficiently to let him know it would not be easily done. When he did not protest when Ferguson told him to forget it, the American realized that there would be no way to hire the mercenaries he was hoping for. While that lack complicated his plan, it did not torpedo it, and after one last cup of chay he left a small deposit and went immediately with Ruby's son to round up the truck. Ruby was so pleased with the entire day's work that he gave Ferguson two VOG-25 grenades completely gratis—a thoughtful gesture, even if the grenades were useless without their rifle-mounted launcher.

The son complained about his father as soon as they left the store. When they reached the truck, he hinted that he deserved a tip. When Ferguson scoffed he insisted on one; when Ferg began laughing he started to sulk, almost in tears.

The CIA officer pulled a fifty-euro note from his pocket.

"I need a driver," he said.

And so he obtained the services of Gribak Morkow, who, besides knowing the best roads to Groznyy, spoke surprisingly good English.

The real price of his services was a seemingly unending diatribe against Ruby. Gribak kept making sweeping statements about the sins of fathers in general and asking Ferguson if what he said wasn't true.

Conners had almost fallen asleep in the chair when the rap came at the door.

"Come," he said, his gun aimed at the opening.

Ferg pushed inside. "Still here, huh?"

"Yeah."

"Come on. Get your stuff."

"That's it?"

"Well, if they're not going to arrest you, we'll move on to plan B."

"You didn't want them to arrest me, did you?" asked Conners, taking his small bag.

"Just bustin'," said Ferg.

Gribak had the truck idling down the street. Two AK-47s were beneath the front seat, along with several clips and two of the hand grenades.

"When the police come, make a commotion," Ferg told Conners.

"That's it?"

"Well, that and don't get caught. Meet me back at Happy Acres when you're done. Give Gribak fifty euros when you get there. Don't go more than that; he'll think you're queer."

"OK," said Conners. Ferguson was so deadpan it was hard to tell if he meant it as a joke or not.

T he smoke felt like a saw blade hacking at Ferg's eyes as he entered the bar. He pushed into the crowd nonetheless, sauntering through a crowd of off-duty Russian soldiers and Chechens. The Red Star was not the most notorious bar in Groznyy, but it did rate in the top ten. Ferguson slid forward, pushing his way between two natives and making sure to address the bartender first in English, then in Russian. He took his vodka and walked toward a row of tables at the left side of the room. The tables seemed entirely occupied by soldiers, which would have made things much too obvious. It occurred to him that Gribak might not be as accomplished a source as he pretended to be.

Returning to the bar with his now-empty glass, Ferguson held it out for a refill. When the bartender came back he asked if he knew how one might find Novakich.

The bartender squinted at him as if he'd asked the way to the Statue of Liberty. Ferguson repeated the name. When he got a frown this time, he smiled at the bartender and let a ten-ruble note float to the bar as he disappeared.

The next club seemed more a smuggler's hangout, at least to judge by the efficiency of the pat-down. Ferg once more repeated the routine, adding a visit to a table where he dropped Ruby's name as well.

The third club had an American Western theme, with posters of fifties movies and a saddled horse in the corner. Unfortunately, the horse was stuffed. As Ferg walked to the end of the long bar, he wondered if he ought to ask for a sasaparilla. The bartender's round nose sniffed the air as he approached; Ferg nearly looked at his boots to check if he'd tracked manure in.

"You know a Novakich?" he asked in Russian, holding on to his money.

The bartender looked at him, sniffed again, then shook his head.

"Oh, well," said Ferg in English, letting the money drop before asking for a vodka. The bartender scooped up the money, replacing it with a shot glass and a bottle. Ferg slid around, sizing up the sparse crowd.

Y ou sure that's the police?" Conners asked Gribak as the small car sped down the road. The battered Lada looked like an ordinary passenger vehicle to him, though it did stop in the middle of the road in front of the bar Ferguson was in.

Gribak gave him an exasperated look.

"All right. I guess you'd know," said Conners, pushing open the door. He trotted up the road toward the sewer opening, watching to make sure that the police car stopped. As the two plainclothes officers got out and headed toward the bar, he knelt and dropped the grenade through the grate, returning to the truck at a dead run. When he reached it, Conners pulled open the door and leaned back over the roof, aiming the automatic rifle down the block. He shot off a few rounds, then threw the gun into the street as Gribak cursed angrily and hit the gas. They drove through a maze of alleys and narrow streets, and in a few minutes the Chechen's mood began to improve greatly; he started humming.

"Very good," said Conners when he fell silent. "Do you know 'Finnegan's Wake'?"

The din in the bar was so loud that the grenade could barely be heard, though the muffled crack set off a chain reaction. Weapons appeared instantly; two men started for the rear exit. Ferg followed, only to find his way barred by a large man in a black turtleneck sweater at least two sizes too small for him. More impressive than his haberdashery was his gun, an H&K MP-5.

"Guess I'm going a different way," said Ferguson, stepping back. He saw some men heading toward a door at the right; he followed and found that they were heading out a restroom window that opened onto an alleyway. He followed, turning left away from the street as gunfire erupted in the front of the building. He knew it wasn't Conners—there was too much of it for too long. Someone ahead of him jumped over a fence. Ferg followed, then found himself in the middle of four somewhat angry-looking Chechens.

"Hey—" he started to say as the one nearest him swung a fist at his face. Ferg ducked, but caught a stick from another in the ribs. As the men closed in he swung his fists in every direction, but something hard clipped him on the side of head. As he fell to the ground there was more gunfire in the alley behind him; he lost consciousness for a moment, and by the time he blinked his eyes open his wallet was gone, and so were his tormenters. He also had a thick swag of wet blood on the side of his neck and shirt.

Ferg sat back against the fence, trying to get his bearings. Finally, he pushed his legs under him, rising to his feet. He gripped the top of the fence and pushed upward, peering over into the eyes of a plainclothes policeman.

"Shit," said Ferg, dropping to the ground.

The policeman said something similar in Russian, then began blowing his whistle.

8

CHECHNYA

Before Conners paid off Gribak, he made sure he understood how to work the starter and ignition on the truck, which had been modified to discourage thieves. Then he dropped the Chechen off at his father's store and drove a few blocks to an empty lot where Gribak had said it was safe to leave the truck. He left the rifle under the front seat but took a few of the grenades from the back and walked to the hotel. When he reached the rooms he was a little surprised not to find Ferg there, even though they weren't supposed to meet for another half hour; Ferguson was always showing up places ahead of schedule, the kind of guy who met you at the end of the bar a drink and a half ahead. Conners checked both rooms, then sat in his, waiting. The TV was old, the picture was fuzzy, and the only channel it seemed to receive was some sort of Russian cooking show. He left it on anyway.

Three hours later, Ferg still hadn't appeared. Driving back into Groznyy to look for him was out of the question, but Conners felt as if he had to do something. He walked to the truck and started it up, driving around the town before realizing he was running a good chance of getting lost. It took twenty minutes of left-hand turns for him to find his way back to the lot. Frustrated and needing sleep, he parked and walked back to the hotel, where once again he was surprised that Ferguson wasn't sitting there waiting for him.

"Well God," said Conners, pulling off his shoes. "I'd make you a deal—I'll give up drinking if you take care of the little bugger. He's full of himself but in a good way, the bastard."

He pushed under the covers, his clothes still on, his pistol in his hand. After a while, he fell asleep.

When he woke, Ferguson was sitting in the chair next to the bed.

"Jesus, Ferg," said Conners, opening his eyes. "What happened to your face?"

"Before or after I got the shit knocked out of me?" said Ferguson, rising. His neck hurt like hell, but otherwise the wounds were mostly cosmetic.

As long as he didn't breathe.

"Hey, Ferg, you OK?"

"Yeah." Ferguson took a swig from the vodka bottle in his hand. "First I got robbed, then the police rolled me. Good thing I had a money belt."

" 'Cause they didn't find your cash?"

"Because there was cash for them to find." The police had used some sort of pepper spray on him. Fortunately, the men were either locals or too intent on robbing him to check with the ministry office; they'd even left his fake passport on the dirt next to him.

"It's part of the plan," said Ferg, rising. "Get dressed. They have a strict dress code where we're going—no jammies."

"Where's that?"

"Jail," said Ferg.

9

 Guns's brain flip-flopped as Massette told him a story about watching a group of assassins in Morocco. Though a native of Tennessee, the warrant officer's English had a decided French slant. Even without the odd inflections, the story he told would have been difficult to follow, tracking back and forth between Paris and the narrow streets of North Africa. Jack Massette had been "loaned" to the DGSE-*Direction Generale de la Securité Exterieure*, the French Defense Ministry's General Directorate for External Security—for an investigation into a ring smuggling ricin poison into France, but the assignment had morphed far from its original outline. Massette and the two French agents he was working with discovered that a criminal group was targeting the terrorist ringleader, apparently because of a financial dispute; they'd been told to allow the assassin to kill their target. Their unspoken orders directed the DGSE agents to do the job if the assassins didn't.

"And so I shot him," said Massette, reaching the punch line, "with the police in the next room."

"The Paris police?"

"No, this was in Algiers. We had to pay these guys five hundred bucks so we could leave. I thought it was pretty cheap."

Guns was going to ask how he'd gotten to Algiers when the train started to move again. As he put the Russian Calina in gear, the engine revved like a psychotic lawn clipper. The Vaz-made car looked and drove like a Ford Focus that had gone through one too many rinse cycles, but it had the virtue of going relatively far on a tankful of watered-down Russian petrol.

The road veered sharply to the left, following the rugged line of the hills. The border with Kazakhstan was about five miles to the south; Rankin and Corrine had already gone across. The road gradually became narrower and soon changed from macadam to barely packed gravel. The train tracks ran off to the left, running through a shallow valley to the border crossing. Though they saw that the train was stopping, there was no place for them to pull off; the two men lost sight of the cars as they drove on, looking for a good place to stop.

By the time Guns found a lot in front of a roadside inn, they'd lost sight of the train. Massette got out and walked to the right; Guns took his pocket binoculars and went left, crossing the road and sliding down the hill about twenty yards before reaching a place where he could see the train. It had pulled onto a siding to let another train pass; the soldiers accompanying it milled around, waiting as the approaching passenger train climbed the grade, its single diesel engine spewing black smoke.

Guns began walking back toward the car, angling up the slope. He was just about back to the roadway when an old jeeplike vehicle pulled alongside and stopped. Two men got out; he stopped for half a second before realizing he was undoubtedly staring at members of the Russian Federal Border Service in civilian dress.

As nonchalantly as possible he continued across the slope. The men shouted at him. Guns looked up at them and waved, not sure exactly what to say or do until one of the men reached beneath his jacket and unsnapped the flap on his holster. Guns gestured meekly and began climbing the slope.

The man asked in English what he was doing with the binoculars.

Guns looked at them in his hand, trying to come up with an explanation that would make sense. Before he could find one, a voice on the road above began speaking in a jovial French.

"Permit me to introduce my colleague, Dr. Miles from the University of Paris," said Massette, switching to English as he spoke to the two Russians. He pattered on about ornithology and the presence of a rare wren native only to these hills. Massette's performance was aided by a bird book which he produced from his pocket, and within a few minutes he was quizzing the Russians about possible sightings. They were FSB agents, more dangerous than border guards, but he was so convincing that the conversation continued for more than ten minutes; had the Russians not been en route to an appointment they undoubtedly would have adjourned to the nearby inn, picking up the first round.

"Good thinking," said Guns when they were back in the car.

"I learned with the French that bird-watching is a very valuable hobby," said Massette. "As long as you take it to extremes."

Corrine watched from the hilltop as the train rounded the bend and headed into the long tunnel. She put the glasses down, then checked the map. The train would change engines at a small yard about fifteen miles from here. Guns and Massette were supposed to cover the switch but had been delayed at the border crossing;

Corrine had to decide whether to stay with the train and lose it as it went into the yard, or leave so they could circle northeast to get to the only point where the yard itself would be visible.

Given that the yard was the most likely place for something to happen, she opted to leave. She pulled out her phone as she walked back to the car, telling Massette and Guns what was up. Massette complained that the line to the border wasn't moving.

"Don't sweat it," she told him. "Call me if anything happens." She clicked off the phone. "We'll go to the yard at Kadagac in their place," she told Rankin.

"Your call," he said.

Corrine glanced at him, unsure whether he was questioning her decision or not.

"My call," she said, her voice a little sharper than she intended.

G uns let Massette drive after they got over the border, thinking it might get him to stop complaining about the guards who had held them up for a twenty-dollar bribe before letting them pass. Massette was outraged that anyone would sell out his duty so cheaply.

In fact, the men had been persuaded to *do* their duty for that fee; getting them to do something illegal would have cost a bit more. Since joining the Team and watching Ferguson, Guns had come to understand how money lubricated nearly everything; he tried not to get too cynical or angry about it. Ferg had told him it was simply a fact of life, there to take advantage of.

"You missed the road," said Guns, as Massette blew by the turnoff. "The train line's down there."

"We're so far behind," said Massette. "They're past the tunnel. They should be changing engines in the yard by now."

"Yeah, but we were going to follow the line."

The older man didn't bother answering. He also didn't bother turning back. Guns wondered if he ought to tell him to turn back and what to do if he wouldn't. He decided he was being ridiculous—and as he thought that, he saw the line again through the front corner of the windshield. As Massette had predicted, the train was long gone.

T he train moved slowly into the far corner of the yard, shunted there by an ancient switcher engine. At least two platoons of soldiers were deployed to guard it, ringing off the area.

Rankin and Corrine watched from a hill nearly a mile and a half away as the cars were pushed onto the new line. A row of freight cars as well as two small sheds blocked their view as a pair of American-made SD40s painted bright red began trundling toward the Y-shaped exit the train would take.

"We got a problem," said Rankin. "We're missing a car."

"What? They're all there."

"One of the boxcars they tagged along at the end. It's gone."

"Shit. Are you sure?"

"I can't see too well. Wait."

Rankin pushed forward against the steering wheel, angling the glasses against the windshield. Impatient, Corrine opened the door and ran down the gravel embankment to the train line where they'd parked, standing on the rail and peering into the yard.

The boxcars had been unhooked from the rest of the train and were being towed to another track by the switcher. The cars with the waste remained on their own under heavy guard.

She looked to the left, scanning the yard for the missing car.

Rankin got out and climbed on top of the car to use his binoculars.

"Anywhere?" she asked.

"Can't see it. Why would they take an empty freight car?"

"Maybe it wasn't empty," she said.

And now she realized how they did it—material was loaded surreptitiously at Buzuluk in what was supposed to be an empty car tagged on to the end of the train for transport. That was why the Russians couldn't figure it out—the containment cars all made it. The waste that was being stolen wasn't in the cars.

"We're going to have to find it," she told Rankin.

"We have to stay with the rest of the train," he said. "Otherwise, we can't be sure."

She pulled out her phone, wanting to get the unpleasant task of telling them that she'd screwed up over with quickly.

That was what it was, she knew—they'd missed the decoupling and screwed up.

"They're moving."

"Shit," she said. She was sure she was right—but what if she were wrong? The meter that had recorded the discrepancy was farther south.

What should she do?

Play it safe. She had to.

"Come on," she told Rankin. "They're moving. Let's go. The others will have to look for the car."

10

Ferg and Conners hadn't gone to jail—they were merely staking out the road to it, waiting for the man in the yellow sports coat.

Though it rolled off the tongue easily, Ferguson had not chosen the name "Novakich" to spread around Groznyy simply for its phonetic value. It belonged to one of the people who had worked with Jabril Daruyev on the Moscow dirty bomb plot. Novakich had not been heard of in several years, and according to Corrigan the Russians believed he was dead—which ought to make Ferguson's inquiries all the more interesting to them. If American agents were poking around looking for Novakich here, sooner or later the Russian FSB would want to see what Daruyev knew about him. Ferguson wasn't sure the FSB officer assigned to find out would be Sergiv Kruknokov—the man in the yellow sports coat—but he hoped so; he already admired the agent and would enjoy outsmarting him once more.

If things went the way Ferg wanted them to, the inspector would have the man taken from the jail to be interviewed in the city. At that point, they would ambush the vehicle and take the prisoner themselves. They had taken both the truck and the car they hired earlier, stashing the truck in a wooded copse a short distance away while using the car for surveillance on the hillside dirt road.

"What if they bring a truckload of troops for escorts?" Conners asked, as they watched the road.

"First of all, they never do that," said Ferg. "Troop trucks and convoys are too obvious a target. They move them in cars, with only two guards. The escort runs five minutes ahead and back."

"What if you're wrong?"

"Then I kick Corrigan's ass," said Ferguson. "We position the truck to cut them off and blow it up with one of the rockets. There's a spot on the road where we can do that back by that creek."

"Won't stop them five minutes."

"That's all we need. Five minutes."

"What if they resist?"

"We hope they don't," said Ferg.

"What if they do?"

"Then we deal with them," said Ferg. "You're beginning to sound like Rankin."

"Me? You're the one who's blowing up allies."

"Since when are the Russians our allies."

"The Chechens sure as hell ain't."

Ferguson laid his head back on the seat rest. "Ah, don't worry, Dad. We'll give him back when we're done. I'm betting Yellow Jacket's smart enough to play it cool."

"*Whiskey, you're my darlin'*," sang Conners, changing the subject.

They sat in the car all night and through most of the next day. Finally, around 3:00 P.M. a familiar-looking Lada came out from town. Ferguson was surprised to see that the inspector was alone.

"You sure it's our guy?" asked Conners.

The lone occupant of the car wore a yellow jacket, but of course Ferguson had no way of knowing until he uploaded the plates to Corrigan to check. Still, he cursed; the agent was obviously going to interview Daruyev in prison. The analysts had told Corrigan that the FSB didn't trust the security system at the prison—like most Russian jails, it was essentially run by the prisoners and could best be described as ridiculously lax—and so routinely took people outside to talk to them.

"Fuckin' Corrigan owes me one," said Ferg.

"So now what?"

"Plan B."

"Which is what?"

"I make a few phone calls, then get out the laptop and see if the printer I've used twice in its life will actually work. Then we talk about how safe it is to cut up the explosives in a mine."

Conners whistled.

"And in the meantime," added Ferguson, "you teach me more Irish drinking songs."

The Russian inspector completed his interview around 7:00 P.M. and passed them on the road shortly afterward, alone as Ferguson had guessed he would be. The CIA officer immediately began setting up plan B. Shortly after midnight, he dialed a number Corrigan had set up so that calls from his sat phone would appear to originate from the FSB headquarters in Groznyy. He then dialed the prison, reporting to the half-asleep desk sergeant that Daruyev was wanted for additional questioning first thing in the morning back in the capital; he hung up before the sergeant could reach for his coffee and think of any questions to ask.

At five minutes after six, with the sun poking its nose at the red mist around the hills, a small car carrying a pair of Russian FSB officers turned onto the main road to the Brown Fortress. As it came within sight of the prison, it struck a mine apparently placed during the night.

Fortunately, the guerrillas had not set their ambush very well. Instead of obliterating the car as intended, the explosion managed only to take out the trunk. Still, the explosion compressed the vehicle's gas tank, setting it on fire with an impressive flare of red and orange that could be seen over the nearby hills—and, most importantly, at the fortress itself. The flare and flash were accompanied by several other explosions, as several other nearby mines cooked off. One of the explosions took out the phone line south; while not entirely cutting communications out of the prison, it did complicate them.

The lights inside the fortress blinked on and off several times; before the blinking stopped, the watch commander had ordered a team of soldiers to respond to the disaster, and in the meantime locked down his facility and called all guards to action stations.

When the team of soldiers traveling up the road in an armored car arrived at the site of the rebel ambush, they found the two Russian FSB agents lying near their destroyed vehicle, their clothes singed. One of the men appeared to have had a concussion and spoke incoherently. The other, though his face and body were bruised and his clothes smeared with blood, managed to gain coherence in a few minutes. Some medicinal vodka carried for emergencies by the captain helped clear his senses. Like any good FSB man, he insisted that they must carry out their orders, adamantly cursing the bastard rebels and swearing that they would not keep him from doing his duty.

Which duty he documented with slightly burned and bloodied papers, copied via fax from Moscow, directing that the prisoner known as Jabril Daruyev be taken to Groznyy and reinterviewed by Commander Kruknokov, with a view toward removing him to Moscow for further interrogation.

The two Russian FSB officers—Conners and Ferguson in disguise—were piled into the back of the armored car and taken to the fortress. The nurse on duty at the dispensary marveled at their luck—both men were bruised and scraped, but nonetheless intact.

Officer Androv—Ferguson—said between his swollen lips that this was thanks to his mother's offering prayers for him every day in Izveska. This was supposed to win him points with the nurse, who according to Corrigan's research came from Izveska and was a devout member of the Orthodox Church. Either the information was wrong or Ferg's puffy-mouthed mumbles sounded foreign to her, however; she frowned and started speaking to him quickly about why he had been out on the road when it was still dark. Ferg rubbed his forehead and mumbled again about his orders. The nurse then asked about some of the bruises, which looked a little less than fresh.

He shrugged, and insisted God had saved him so he could squeeze the guerrilla rabble by the short hairs.

When they were taken up to see the watch commander, Ferg dropped the connection to Russia's heartland, instead answering that he had been born in Georgia "before the cataclysm" when the commander asked about his background. Ferguson noticed their orders sitting on the desk and gestured toward them; the commander asked why Kruknokov hadn't taken the prisoner back with him on his own the day before.

Embarrassed silence had no accent, and the inference that his fellow FSB officer had made a mistake was readily believed by the commander, who did not in fact like the FSB nosing around his domain. As far as he was concerned, the sooner the officers were away, the better. A car was found and the prisoner produced, wearing sets of chains on his hands and feet and a dark hood that made it impossible for him to see.

"Very dangerous," said the commander, after checking his identity and entering the proper notes in his log and other paperwork.

Ferguson nodded grimly. Two men were assigned to drive them to town.

They were back in the front reception area when the nurse appeared at the end of the hallway, walking with the sort of grim step that could only foretell trouble. Ferg slid his hand into his coat, fingering his Glock. He kept it there as they entered the gate area, ushering the prisoner and their escorts through as the nurse reached the desk.

The guard at the desk called to them, but by now Ferguson had the door to the car open. He pulled at the prisoner and in the same motion jerked back, as if the man had hit him; he pushed the Chechen inside the car, cursing loudly.

One of the guards pulled down his rifle, ready to fire. Ferguson held his hand up, swearing that he would not let the vermin keep him from doing his duty.

"Slide over," he told the driver, pushing him from behind the wheel. The man started to protest, but Ferguson was well into his act, lathering on anger; the man moved quickly, not wanting to get into trouble with a crazed intelligence officer.

As the guard and the nurse reached the doorway, Ferg turned over the ignition and jabbed the gas pedal. The vehicle stuttered forward through the courtyard, toward the first of the two gates they needed to pass to exit. The guards at the first gate pulled away the metal bars as Ferg approached; he fished into his pocket and waved a piece of paper as he sped through. But the second set of guards were not so easily flummoxed. They made Ferg stop and one took the papers from him, going over to the phone at the station next to the wall.

As he picked up the phone, Ferguson launched into a fresh tirade. It was vintage madman: He was fed up with the bureaucratic bullshit that had nearly cost him his life that morning and was undoubtedly responsible for his two brothers going home in bags three years before. Conners and one of the escorts jumped out of the car to calm him down.

As he did, something exploded beyond the wall of the courtyard. It was a grenade, tossed by Conners as the others stared at Ferguson.

Conners grabbed the rifle from the guard closest to him as the others ducked. He fired a burst at the wall, then ran to the gate, burning the clip at an imaginary group of rebels. Ferguson, yelling all the Russian curses he knew—a considerable collection—pushed the barrier aside.

"Get the bastards! Get the bastards!" yelled Ferguson, as if he'd spotted a pack of them.

The others shouted at him to get down; instead, he turned and vowed that no bearded shithead would ever drive him into the ground. The guerrillas outside answered with another grenade; as the others ducked, Ferguson jumped into the car and whipped forward through the gate.

Yet another grenade went off, this one in the courtyard, though a good distance away. Conners just barely managed to grab on to the car, brandishing the AK-47—which suddenly had a fresh clip in it—as they zipped away.

"That was close," said Conners, as they sped around the first bend. The turnoff for the truck was about a half mile away.

"Nah."

"I thought you were going to shoot the guard with your Glock," said Conners.

"Wasn't even close," said Ferguson, though he had in fact palmed the small gun before getting out of the car. "I thought they were going to find the grenades on you when they picked us up on the road. Good thing you have such a fat belly."

"Smooth, Ferguson, real smooth."

"Would have been a shitload easier if that nurse didn't figure it out. Corrigan's information must have been bad. Fucker couldn't sift through an intelligence report with a shovel."

"He's an officer; what do you expect?" said Conners.

Ferguson slammed on the brakes about a hundred yards before the turnoff. He jumped out and ran to the truck, leaving Conners to take the prisoner. After he started it he climbed up to see if they were being followed. While he couldn't see the fortress because there was a hill in the way, he could see a curl of dust coming from the road.

Conners, meanwhile, had the prisoner by the arm and dragged him to the truck. He put him in the front cab, then backed out of the hiding spot, rumbling toward the road.

The AK-47 Conners had taken from the guards lay on the ground. Ferguson picked it up and fired the last four bullets into the rear fender of the car. Then he took his shirt and draped it on the ground near the driver's side door, which he left ajar. Finally, in an inspired bid for greater authenticity, he took off one of his shoes and threw it on the ground nearby.

There was no sense hopping around on one foot, so he yanked off the other and tossed it in the front seat. His soles were callused, but not nearly enough to take the sting out of the rocks and uneven gravel as he ran in his socks up the road about thirty feet. There he grabbed the Russian bazooka he'd hidden there the night before and fired point-blank at the front of the car. He was actually too close to the target; the missile shot upward and rather than hitting the engine compartment went through the windshield, exploding in the passenger compartment. The fireball blew Ferguson back in a tumble, and he smacked his head against the rocks.

By the time he got to his feet, Conners had the truck moving. Ferg started running, then slowed to a trot, the throb in his skull too fierce to permit anything faster. He made the running board on the second try, pulling himself into the cab as his head spun in a dizzy swirl, the world moving on an odd horizontal axis.

Blinking didn't help; he put his hands to his temples, rubbing as Conners drove.

"Russians are coming," Ferg told him.

"I figured."

"Man, my head hurts."

"Vodka'll do it to you every time," said Conners. "By the way, you have to give those Russian RPGs a little more room. They're not meant for close range."

"Now you tell me," said Ferg.

"You're Americans."

Ferguson turned his head. "And you're not," he told the Chechen, who was trussed and hooded beside him.

"What are you doing with me?" The Chechen's English was very good, and his accent shaded toward American, though it had an obvious foreign ring to it. Though that made it easier for Ferguson to talk to him, it angered him—Corrigan's background data on him had not included any of this information. Once more, their intelligence had failed; the fact that it was in their favor was besides the point.

"We're going to ask you some questions and get some answers," said Ferg.

"Then what?"

"Then we'll see. How do you speak English?"

The Chechen hesitated, suspecting an elaborate Russian trick.

"Last night, you were interviewed by a Russian FSB agent," said Ferguson. "He asked you about a man named Novakich. He may or may not have explained why he was interested in him."

"I've been interviewed many times," said the prisoner.

"Yeah, but not about a dead man."

"How do you know Novakich is dead?"

Ferguson's head hurt too much to play games. The best thing at that point was just to ship the bastard back to Guantanamo and let the intelligence geeks put the drug into him.

"I might be able to help you," said the prisoner after a few minutes. "If you got me away from the Russians."

Ferguson ignored the Chechen—he figured it was just bullshit—and rummaged in his bag for some aspirin.

"How are you going to help us?" said Conners.

"A few weeks ago, someone came to me looking for information about radiological bombs."

"What's a radiological bomb?" asked Conners.

"A bomb built from waste," said the Chechen.

"Who?"

"The Russians call him Kiro. He's not the one you have to worry about," added Daruyev.

"Who's worried?" said Ferguson.

"Allah's Fist is building a weapon. They're taking hospital waste and storing it."

"Yeah?" said Ferguson skeptically. "Where?"

The Chechen said nothing.

"How come you're ratting on your friends?" said Conners.

"They're not my friends."

"Fair enough," said Ferg. He waved at Conners, trying to make him shut up.

"Allah's Fist is not part of the freedom movement," said Daruyev. "And I do not think that Kiro is. He is slime."

"Unlike you," said Conners.

"Eyes on the road, Dad," said Ferguson, exasperated.

Daruyev remained silent as they drove northward. There was a small town about four miles ahead; there were bound to be Russian troops there, and Ferg didn't want to chance being stopped. Instead, they headed toward what looked on the sat photo to be an abandoned farm to the west, figuring they could sit in the ruins until nightfall. By then, he'd have hooked up with Van on an exfiltration plan; no way he was driving all the way to Georgia again.

"My war is against the Russians," said Daruyev. "There was a time when Americans helped me, and because of that, I will help you now."

Ferguson sighed wearily and slid sideways in the seat. "Well, fire away then," he told the Chechen. "We're all ears."

11

 Though he had been with the CIA for more than two decades, Thomas Ciello had never been in the Cube, otherwise known as Building 24-442. In fact, he had never physically been to the "campus" where it was located—campus being a somewhat overblown term for the collection of warehouse buildings on the cul-de-sac just off the Beltway.

While the warehouses and the small administrative building called 24-442 behind them looked like typical industrial architecture, they were anything but. Beneath the outer metal were thick concrete bunkers extending deep into the ground. Each held several floors of disk arrays organized according to an arcane system that even Ciello, an experienced Agency analyst, only partly understood.

Ciello had not been told why he was to report to Building 24-442. He hoped, however, that it had something to do with a memo he had sent to the director three weeks before. The memo detailed his findings on an unofficial research project he had been conducting practically since his first day in the Company's employ: Ciello believed he had found definitive proof in the CIA records that extraterrestrial explorers had visited the earth.

Thomas knew, of course, that the CIA had purposely promulgated UFO reports over the years as part of a disinformation campaign to draw attention from various "black" programs ranging from overflights of the Soviet Union in the 1950s to the development of stealth aircraft and UAVs in the Nevada desert during the 1970s and '80s. But he had meticulously separated chaff from fact, lie from radar contact. His memo had been distilled from a six-hundred-page, single-spaced report; he planned on forwarding the entire report as soon as his memo was officially acknowledged. At that point, he reasoned, the hierarchy would establish a "committee" to investigate, along the lines of the British Ministry of Defense's UFO Team.

Oddly, this had not yet occurred, and in fact he had started to believe the e-mail had somehow been misdirected before the request to appear at Building 24-442 arrived.

He showed his creds at the gate and drove quickly to the assigned parking slot behind the thick berm separating the buildings from the roadway. His pulse started to rise as soon as he locked his car, and by the time he cleared through the elaborate security at the entrance to 24-442, his hands were trembling uncontrollably.

A half hour later, Jack Corrigan entered the room Ciello had been sequestered in on the second subbasement level. Thomas was sweating so profusely that his white shirt was stained front and back. He nodded as Corrigan introduced himself, and unwisely agreed to the offer of coffee.

Corrigan pulled a small radio from his pocket—he used the short-distance device while in the building—and called for an assistant to bring some. Realizing Thomas was nervous, he tried to put him at ease by smiling and making some small talk about baseball. To Corrigan, Thomas's jitters were a good sign; he'd be eager to please, at least at first. While this would have been a horrible trait in a case officer or someone out in the field, for a research dweeb it was just the thing.

"So, I guess you're wondering exactly what the job is," said Corrigan.

"Oh yes," said Thomas, taking a sip of his coffee. The liquid promptly dribbled down his chin.

"We're in great need of someone of your abilities," said Corrigan. "Someone who works for us, but can interface with, you know, the other side."

"Oh yes," said Thomas. "My UFO theory."

Corrigan had not heard of the UFO theory; by "other side" he meant the Directorate of Intelligence, the analytical side of the Agency. He in fact knew little of Thomas except that he was one of only a handful of people with the proper background available to do the work he needed. Thomas had worked with DO as well as DI; he'd been on the Collections Requirements and Evaluation Staff and done some work for the associate director of Central Intelligence for Military Support, who'd been briefly Corrigan's boss. His folder was thick with commendations, and while the occasional supervisor remarked that he could be "eccentric," this was hardly a disqualifier. Filtering information called for a certain amount of creativity, which noncreative supervisor types—Corrigan admitted freely he was one himself—naturally interpreted as eccentricity.

Besides, the other person available had filed a sexual harassment suit against her last two bosses.

"This is a unique job, a unique opportunity," said Corrigan, deciding to sell the slot. "You'll run your own show, providing real-time intelligence for people in the field. Important stuff."

Corrigan described the duties of the position, which functioned like the military support division and could draw on resources from MS as well as DI as needed. They were supposed to have two other staff assistants available to help out soon, but in the meantime Corrigan would lend his own aides as needed. The person handling the position needed a wide range of clearances, which Thomas already had.

"I need someone who can really burrow in and put a picture together from disparate details," added Corrigan. "Our missions are high-profile; everything very, very critical. This is the big leagues. We had someone running the mission support, but then she got pregnant, and you know how that goes."

Thomas nodded, though he hadn't considered pregnancy as a job hazard before.

"We've had nothing but problems ever since. My boss is on my ass about it," said Corrigan. He didn't want to diss the agency's research departments, just the red tape, but it was impossible not to imply at least a small bit of criticism. "What I'm looking for is someone who can interface, who talks their language and can get into the nitty-gritty if they have to. You have that kind of reputation. You know, ferret out information."

"Ferret?"

"Figure things out. I don't mean gather it yourself. Well, if you do gather it, I mean, that's all right. As long as you're feeding us what we need." Corrigan sensed the interview had taken a bad turn. He tried to remember Thomas's résumé. "You were trained as an historian, right?"

Thomas nodded. He was in fact an historian; his Ph.D. dissertation, completed on the day before he officially started work at the Agency, was on the East German Secret Police. He was, for all intents and purposes, the Western world's expert on the East German police. Unfortunately, the day he went to work was the day the Berlin Wall was taken down and the East German police ceased to exist.

"You worked on the Mexico City plot in 2002, right?" prompted Corrigan. A plot to blow up the U.S. embassy had been foiled thanks largely to work by the analysts; it was a major coup.

"I headed the team," said Thomas.

"The Olympics," said Corrigan, mentioning another major accomplishment—Thomas had helped identify an Arab group that had tried to poison the drinking water at the 1996 games. The plot itself had been rather lame, but the work sorting through intercepts to identify the perpetrators was not.

"Oh yeah, I forgot about that."

Corrigan smiled. Eccentric and humble and brilliant: Thomas would be perfect.

"Good," said Corrigan, rising. "I'm going to put you right to work. We're involved in a bit of a ticklish situation—actually, we have two ticklish situations. But I want you to concentrate on Chechnya right now. You've done work on dirty bombs."

"Well of course. But as far—"

"Great," said Corrigan. His radio beeped—they needed him back downstairs. "Debra will be in with you in a second. She'll show to your office, make sure all the clearance work is taken care of—you'll have to take a new lie detector test, but in the meantime we're going to put you right on this."

"What about my UFOs?" asked Thomas.

"UFOs?" Corrigan stopped at the door, looking back at the researcher.

"I, uh, had done a memo. It went to the director."

"Oh, right, right, right," said Corrigan, who had no clue what he was talking about. "Focus on this right now, OK? Jenny'll get you all the backups and the files—don't forget to break for lunch."

12

 In 1996, a group of Chechen rebels—or "freedom fighters" in Daruyev's phrase—planned to blow up a dirty bomb in central Moscow. The operation was doomed from the start—Russian intelligence had infiltrated the guerrilla network. But the project had proceeded to the point of moving approximately one thousand pounds of material into the city. The material had a relatively low alpha value—in other words, it wasn't very radioactive. But no one exposed to the material itself was expected to die immediately; its primary value was as a weapon of terror. And while the bomb itself was never set off, the simple fact that the Chechens were willing to go to such lengths might have played a role in the Russian government's decision to halt the offensive there and begin negotiations, even though the takeover of a hospital in Kizlyar in the province of Dagestan was generally credited with forcing their hands.

Daruyev had been one of the people responsible for planning the bomb. Before the war, he had been involved in research for food irradiation, and had spent considerable time in America as well as France studying the problem. He told Ferguson and Conners that he had originally argued against using such a weapon, though in the end he was as responsible as anyone for its design, as well as for the theft of some of the material used to construct it.

He had also apparently paid a price beyond his arrest and subsequent fifteen-year sentence—he had lung and thyroid cancer.

"The lung cancer, perhaps because I smoke," he allowed. "But the thyroid cancer, a large dose of radioactivity, surely."

"What stage?" asked Ferg.

Daruyev shrugged. "It hasn't been operated on. I can feel the growth with my fingers," he started to pull up his hand to show them, forgetting that they were in irons.

"If you can feel it, you're probably pretty far gone," said Ferguson. The surgeon had shown him how to palpate—the technical term for feel—his own growth before the operation.

"I guess."

Other rebels knew of the plot, and of Daruyev. From time to time they contacted him. Kiro's man was only the latest of a long series. Daruyev claimed that he only listened and never offered true advice.

"A man came to me from Bin Saqr more than a year ago. His questions were dangerous ones," said Daruyev.

"Why?" asked Conners.

"Because he wanted to know if different types of radiation would cancel each other out, as a practical matter."

"What do you mean?" asked Ferguson.

"They were wondering if in arranging the material a certain pattern should be laid out. They were more concerned about alpha radiation—you understand, alpha particles, as opposed to gamma?"

"Yup," said Ferguson.

"They were concerned if there might be a cancellation effect when a bomb was exploded."

"Is there?" asked Ferguson.

"Bah. It was a question designed to see if I would help them, not to elicit a true answer. An imbecile would know there is no such thing."

Ferguson started to laugh—he had, in a roundabout way, just been called an imbecile.

"Did you help?" asked Conners.

"No. But if they are asking about alpha waste—that is a much more dangerous prospect than what we planned. Allah's Fist—they are not against the Russians. They want to destroy all infidels, which means you. I would be wary."

"So why are they in Chechnya?" asked Conners.

"I don't know that they are."

"Someone was to talk to you," said Ferguson. "And what about Kiro?"

Daruyev made a disparaging noise with his mouth, dismissing Kiro. "Chechnya is a perfect place for the misfits of God," he said. "The Russians control the cities, but the mountains and hills—they cannot be everywhere at once. Even where they do control, you are proof that their level of efficiency is not very high."

"You speak like a plant manager, you know that?" said Ferg.

"It was another life."

Conners stopped the truck in the field near the burned-out buildings they had seen on the sat picture. They took the Chechen out and sat him in the back while they looked over the ruins. The cluster of buildings had been burned several years before; there were not only weeds but thick bushes between the ruins.

"Time to call home," said Ferg. "Find him a good place to sit, then you can take off the hood."

"You sure?"

"Yeah. Maybe it'll inspire him."

"Or get him more pissed off at the Russians," said Conners.

"Same thing," said Ferg. He took one of the AK-47s and walked across the dirt road they'd driven in on, climbing a hill that overlooked the ruins.

J ack, next time you give me background on something, get it right," said Ferguson, as soon as Corrigan came on the line.

"What?" said Corrigan.

"That nurse almost got us wasted. I mentioned God, and she dialed up an exorcism."

"Which? In the prison?"

"No, I had a date this morning," said Ferguson.

"It's not like we have unlimited resources," protested Corrigan. "Besides, I told you I wasn't one hundred percent sure of—"

"Then don't give it to me."

"That level of intelligence," said Corrigan, remembering the information now. "Shit, Ferg, that was good stuff. When I was in the Army if we had that level of intelligence—"

"You're not in the Army now, Jack. Intelligence is our middle name, remember?"

"Well, it's going to improve exponentially from now on. I have a replacement for Lauren. A bit, you know, eccentric, but I think he's a real home run hitter."

"Good."

Ferguson saw light glint off a windshield in the distance. He pulled up his binoculars; it was a Russian troop truck, driving on the road they'd taken.

"All right, listen Corrigan, I'd love to stand around and chat, but I've got work to do. Call Van and arrange a pickup for me. I want to get out tonight if we can."

"No can do," said Corrigan.

"Why not?"

"You're in Chechnya."

"Am I? No shit. I thought I was sitting in Disney World. I'm talking to Mickey Mouse, after all."

"Working with you's a barrel of laughs, Ferg."

"Yeah, well listen, I have to go. See what you can figure out for me, Corrigan."

"It may take a few days."

"Pull something together tonight," he said, snapping off the phone and running down the hill.

13

WEST OF KADAGAC, KAZAKHSTAN

 The boxcar seemed to have disintegrated into the air. Guns and Massette drove all the way to the yard and back to the border four times without spotting it on any of the sidings; they sneaked into the yard and searched for it there, going so far as to check several cars to see if they had been painted over. Twice yardmen asked what they were doing, and at one point Guns thought he would have to pull out his gun and shoot a worker who seemed a little too insistent in his questioning.

It wasn't in the yard. Massette thought the tunnel must have something to do with the disappearance; they searched it without finding a siding or even a doorway, Guns's heart pounding the whole time as he worried a train would come and flatten him inside. They used their Geiger counters on the sidings without finding anything, then as a last-ditch effort began walking the tracks with the detectors.

About a half mile north of the tunnel, the tracks ran level with a sandy road on the right. Massette realized there was something odd about it, and began madly kicking around in the dirt; Guns couldn't figure out what the hell he was doing until Massette stopped with a curse, then dropped down and scraped soil from the buried rails.

"That bulldozer," said Massette, pointing toward the woods.

There was a gap between the buried rail spur and the tracks of about four feet, just long enough for a flanged section to be fitted in. They found the pieces—the pair looked like long, curved french fries, with triangular heads—in a pile of rocks near the woods with some blocks and metal bars and chain. A few yards farther on, the rails were no longer buried; they headed through some brush toward a clearing a few hundred yards ahead.

Guns took out his pistol, holding it behind his back as they walked up the rail line. Massette stopped suddenly, catching sight of something in the distance.

"Better flank me," he said.

Guns trotted into the woods to parallel him. The tracks ran in a large semicircle to the east, back in the direction where the tunnel had been. A small clearing sat beyond a set of cement posts; a partially dismantled train car sat in the middle of them.

"And here we are," said Massette loudly, arriving in the clearing. *"Merde alors."*

It looked as if the flat casks from the French processing operation had been stacked on the bottom and sides of the car; at roughly a foot thick, they could have been easily missed by a casual inspection. The rad meters registered only trace amounts of material, bits of contamination that had been picked up inadvertently at the original waste site and left on the car. The casks—assuming of course that they had been there—would have contained high-alpha-producing waste, highly dangerous, but only if the containment vessels were broken and the material pulverized.

"Put it in trucks here," said Massette. "Or one truck. We should probably follow this road," he told Guns. He pulled out his map.

"It's not on the map," said Guns.

"Setting this up must have taken quite a long time."

"Yeah," said Guns.

"The fact that they would then blow up the train and leave the remains, leave the bulldozer, eliminate the possibility of using it again—they're ready to go."

14

The Russian truck drove up the road at a steady speed, not racing but not plodding either. Conners had pulled their vehicle behind the only large hunk of remains and done his best to obscure any tracks leading off the roadway; he hunkered in the ruins with their prisoner, ready with the RPG. Ferguson, crouched in a ruined basement closer to the road, aimed his AK-47 at the truck, even as he willed it to continue on its way.

It did not.

Jabbing off the side, the vehicle came to a shaky halt. A soldier jumped down from the cab, rifle in hand, walking around warily to the back. A minute later the driver got out, stretching his legs and hoisting his own rifle from the cab.

He walked directly toward the ruins where Ferguson was hiding. Ferg slid back into the shadows, aiming his gun, then realized what the driver was up to. He did his best to hold his breath as the Russian's urine splattered on the blackened rocks nearby. The other man came up, making a joke about watering Chechen ashes.

They finished and zipped up, joking loudly as they walked back toward the truck. The driver had a hip flask; as they stopped to share a gulp Ferg pushed his way up through the ruins, trying to avoid the area they'd just wet down.

"Halt," he said loudly in Russian, not more than ten feet behind them as they drank. "Drop your weapons or you're dead."

He gave a quick burst of gunfire as he spoke. The driver, whose gun was hanging at his side, dropped it, but the other man swung the rifle off his shoulder and squared to fire.

"No," said Ferg, but it was already too late. As his finger squeezed the trigger, he caught a blur out of the corner of his eye. He just managed to duck as the rocket shot past, missing the KAMAZ and igniting in the hillside. Dirt and rocks sprayed everywhere.

Ferg's burst had killed the Russian before he could fire. The driver meanwhile flattened himself against the dirt.

Ferguson kicked both guns away and waited for Conners, who ran up with his AK-47.

"I can't believe I missed," said Conners.

"You have to compensate," said Ferguson, mocking Conners's earlier advice. But he was glad his companion hadn't hit the truck, and even more so when he pulled open the plastic tarp covering the back. Two small chests at the side held a cache of AK-74s, automatic rifles chambered for 5.45 mm ammunition. There were also two PKs, 7.62 mm light machine guns, oldish but very dependable squad-level weapons, and an AGS-17, an odd-looking grenade launcher that the Russians liked because it could loft its wares into overhead hills. Besides the ammunition for the guns, there were a dozen jerry cans of diesel.

"What do you say we give them our truck and take theirs?" Ferg asked Conners.

"Sounds like a fair trade."

"Yeah, just about." Ferguson hopped up and examined the AGS-17. Remembering the two small grenades Ruby had presented him with, he dug into the ruck and retrieved one.

"What is that?" Conners asked.

Ferg handed it over.

"This grenade doesn't go in this gun," said Conners, eying the fat slug.

"Figures."

"It's a Russian *mebbe*."

"*Mebbe?*"

"Maybe it goes off, maybe it doesn't," laughed the SF trooper. "They don't have the highest quality control, and this sucker looks corroded to boot."

"Har-har."

"It's a VOG-25L or something," said Conners, his voice more serious. "It's kind of like the 40 mm grenade you shoot from a 203. Russian launcher is shorter. More propellant here, see?" Conners held it up. "Plus this sucker, the nose detonates, and it kicks up again after it lands. It throws shrapnel all over the place. Nasty."

"I'll attend the seminar later," said Ferg, stuffing the small grenade into his pocket. He took the AGS-17 grenade launcher and carried it to a point on the slope where he could see the entire compound. He slapped on the round drum that contained the grenade cartridges, then swiveled it up and down, not entirely sure how the mechanism worked. Russian weapons in general were known for their simplicity of operation, but the boxy gun looked more like something a mad scientist had invented than a weapon. Finally, he settled behind the trigger and fired. The grenade whizzed out across the compound, landing just beyond their truck. It took two more shots before he got the hang of it and scored a direct hit.

Conners meanwhile finished trussing the Russian, leaving him near the road. He took a single swig of the vodka, then thoughtfully offered a swallow to the man before tossing it away.

Daruyev spit in the dirt at them as Conners led him past.

"That's not nice," said Conners, chuckling.

"I have been thinking about what you said before," Daruyev said to Ferguson, as he helped him into the truck.

"Yeah?"

"There are three possible places where they might storehouse material to prepare a bomb," said Daruyev. "I can take you to each one of them."

"Tell us where they are first."

The Chechen shook his head. "Then you won't need me."

"I don't need you now."

"If I lead you to them, and you find a bomb, you will need me to help you neutralize it," said the Chechen.

In truth, he could count on getting all sorts of help to dismantle a bomb. "What do you get?" asked Ferguson, though he suspected he knew the answer.

"If I help you, will you let me go free?" added Daruyev.

"I don't know if I can do that."

"Take me to America then. Put me in prison there."

"America?" said Conners.

"Can you?" asked the Chechen.

Before Corrine Alston had "joined" the Team, Ferguson would have agreed easily—and sincerely. Now, though, with a lawyer looking over his shoulder, he wasn't sure.

"I don't know if I can," said Ferg truthfully. "Help me anyway."

The Chechen stared at him. They had come from entirely different places to the same valley of gray, both living with the ambiguity of the death they inevitably faced. Ferguson's prognosis might be slightly better, and his cause more clear-cut, but the two men walked in the same land of shades and shifting sands.

But Ferg was the one with the gun.

"If you say you will try, that will be enough," said Daruyev.

"I will try," said Ferg. "Take us to the closest spot."

ACT IV

I am one, my liege,
Whom the vile blows and buffets of the world
hath so incensed that I am reckless . . .

—Shakespeare, *Macbeth*, 3.1.107–9

1

 Thomas Ciello sat on the floor of his new office, a viceroy of paper. He had estimates, reports, briefings, hints, and scraps of sheer speculation spread in various piles before him; they covered every square inch of the twelve-by-twelve room, including the desk, the three computer monitors, the bookcases—some pages were on the shelves, which were empty except for a dictionary—and two chairs.

He had started with a system, but the organizing principle now involved several layers of calculus, and Thomas had never been very good at math.

"Oh, my God."

Thomas looked up at the door, where Debra Wu was standing.

"I think I almost understand it," he told her.

Debra glanced down the hall, then bent to her knees and scooped up pages and files so she could get inside. Thomas noticed that her short black skirt rode up high on her thighs.

"You can't do this. These papers—this is such a massive security violation—they'll hang you by your toes."

"I signed everything out, and nothing's left the room," he told her. "A lot of this isn't even classified, I mean, beyond secret. It's just—"

Exasperated, Debra put down the papers she had gathered. "Security is—it's, it's psychotic—"

Indignation welled up in Thomas's chest. The staff assistant was hinting that he was less than professional. He tried to temper his response—it was a *very* short skirt, after all—but it was difficult to remain calm.

"If we're talking about security," he said, "are you allowed to see these reports? Are you even allowed in my office?"

Debra rolled her eyes. "Corrigan wants to see you in ten minutes." She pulled open the door and left, papers fluttering as she went.

Thomas went back to sorting and sifting. Leaving the office was certainly problematic security-wise, but as far as he understood protocol—and if there was anything he prided himself on it was his understanding of protocol—he simply had to cover all of the compartmented material and lock up when he went out. In his desk was a gray blanket, ordinarily used to cover the desktop. There were actually two of them in his desk, which helped him cover a good portion of the floor. A wall map of the world, several empty manila folders, and his jacket took care of all but two small piles near the door; he considered taking off his Oxford shirt and leaving it on them, but it was one of his favorite shirts. Instead, he simply carried the folders with him as he went to see Corrigan.

Downstairs in the Cube's situation room, Corrigan used a video feed to watch Thomas clear a security gate before being allowed down the stairs. Debra Wu had buzzed to say the new staffer was "on another planet," but Thomas seemed perfectly reasonable as he went through the security. He had some documents with him, which he quite properly refused to show the guard at the post. The request was actually a nasty trick; if Thomas had agreed, the man would have written him up for a security violation since he didn't have the proper clearance for the compartmented data.

Cleared, Thomas walked down the corridor and into the stairway, practically hopping as he walked to the sit room. That was just the sort of enthusiasm Corrigan liked, and he awaited Thomas's approach with growing optimism.

"All right," said Thomas as he was buzzed through the glass door. "You wanted to see me?"

"Yes, I did," said Corrigan. "What do you know?"

The question caught Thomas off guard. "About the mission or about anything in general?"

"The mission," said Corrigan. He reached for his coffee cup.

"The mission. Okay. The ship was clearly not related to the plot. See, Kiro—he and the Iranians don't get along. The Iranian defense minister—"

"We're a little past that," said Corrigan. "Tell me about the waste."

"Which waste?"

"The stuff we're tracking."

"Oh that. Nasty. They've scraped uranium—most of it's uranium, but there's strontium, cesium, other by-products—nickel, that's ugly. Now if that were stolen, it'd be important. See, it's being placed in these long containers. They call them casks, but they're actually flat, and you can handle about fifty at a time with a forklift. The French process allows them to get high-level waste in manageable quantities. As long as it doesn't get into the air, you're OK."

"How are they getting it?" asked Corrigan.

"Uh, aren't you working on that?" said Thomas.

"I was just wondering what you had found from your end," said Corrigan, his faith in the new man starting to slip.

"They have bought two forklifts," said Thomas.

"Who?"

"Allah's Fist. They're in Chechnya."

"Are you sure? Bin Saqr is supposed to be dead."

"Ha-ha." Thomas had a quick, tight laugh, as if it were powered by a pneumatic drill. "No. There's absolutely no evidence that he's dead. He just hasn't showed up anywhere. And two companies that were associated with his organization in the past still exist. There are other connections. A Pakistani scientist named Zedian. And the hospitals—there's a real connection there. They've collected and diverted material from cancer-treatment wards. It's gamma-wave generators, mostly low-level, but if there were enough of it—a matrix, see, with all sorts of different wastes together. You explode it in a bomb, there's stuff all over the place, and it's a real bitch to clean up."

"Let's focus on the problem," Corrigan said. "Where is Bin Saqr now?"

"Good question." Thomas scratched his side with his folders. "The evidence points to Chechnya, but that's a big place."

"We need a place where the SF team can make a pickup," said Corrigan. "Colonel Van Buren has a couple of suggestions, but we want to make sure there are no guerrillas there. Or Russians, for that matter."

Corrigan handed him a piece of paper with the names of three villages written phonetically.

"These are in Chechnya?" Thomas asked, looking at the names.

"The spelling may not be correct," said Corrigan. "They were former Russian bases that were abandoned. I think there may be a civilian field in there. Anyway, check them out and see which would be closest to those coordinates at the bottom, where Ferg is. When you're done with that, let's put together a theory on what the delivery system would be. Truck bomb? Ship?"

"UFOs," said Thomas.

"UFOs?" said Corrigan, so incredulous he couldn't say anything else.

"I recognize one of the names, I think, from a UFO sighting," explained Thomas. "I didn't mean they were using a UFO to drop the bomb."

"Oh," said Corrigan, still unsure.

Thomas thought he sounded disappointed.

"If it were UFOs, we'd really have trouble, right?" he said brightly. His suspicions about Corrigan were confirmed—his new boss was a believer. God had finally smiled on him.

"We'll figure it out. I'll be back as soon as I can," said Thomas, snapping the paper in the air. He turned and practically ran out of the room as Corrigan rubbed his forehead, worried that Debra Wu's assessment was too kind by half.

2

 Corrine gave the binoculars to Rankin and got out of the car, stretching her stiff back. She missed her workouts. Who would have thought that this job actually involved more sitting than her old one?

It isn't my *old* one, she told herself. She was *still* the president's counsel.

Rankin got out of the car. "Fresh truck of Russian troops," he told her, gesturing with the binoculars. "We ought to get ready."

Corrine nodded. The train had been met by a contingent of uniformed Russian border guards near Kzyl-Orda. They had added two flatcars at the very end of the train, boarding them and riding along. Obviously, the Russians were worried about something, though they, too, had missed the action.

"I have the next few stops mapped out for us," Rankin told her. "The tracks parallel the road for a ways, and we can use the transceivers to keep tabs. Little town about ten miles from here where we can quick grab something to eat—there's a long stretch with no sidings or any possible stops, so it'll give us some leeway."

"Yeah."

"You down about the missing boxcar?" he asked.

"You could call it 'down.' "

"At least we figured out what they're doing."

"Uh-huh."

"You were right about following the train. We can't expect to pull it all together in one shot. Nobody does that, not even Ferguson."

"Thanks for the pep talk," she said, walking around the back of the car. "You drive."

Guns called her on the sat phone just as they parked at one of the spots Rankin had picked out for a food stop.

"Lost it totally. Massette thinks they took the trucks north, because the road connects in that direction, but anything's possible. What do you want us to do?"

There was no one right answer, Corrine realized—it wasn't like she could pull down a few law books, find some precedents, and present an invincible argument. Whatever she told them to do would be open to second-guessing and interpretation.

As were Ferguson's decisions on the original mission, Corrine realized.

"Damned if you do, damned if you don't," McCarthy would have said—his point being to *do something*.

"All right," Corrine told Guns. She could see the train pulling up an embankment ahead. "Figure out the most likely route to Chechnya. At the moment it's our best bet for a destination. Consider that they probably would prefer to drive at night over decent roads where they're less likely to be stopped. It's a wild-goose chase, I know, but it's better than sitting around with our thumbs in our noses. I'll tell Corrigan what's going on and see if they can supply any information that will be useful. In the meantime we'll see if the survey of the satellite photos has turned up anything."

"You sure you don't want us to come and back you up?"

"No," said Corrine. "I think the theft has already been made. Stay in touch," she said, hitting the kill button.

Rankin pulled open the passenger door and got in, filling the car with a strong odor.

"Some sort of cabbage bilini thing," he told her. "It was the only thing that sounded edible."

Corrine was too busy to argue the point. The train had rounded the curve and was out of sight. She pulled back onto the road ahead of a slow-moving bus, accelerating quickly. It didn't take long to get the train back in view.

"Want some?" asked Rankin.

"It smells hideous."

"It doesn't taste as bad as it smells."

"Gotta make a phone call first." She juggled the phone in her hands, hitting the preset to connect to the Cube sit room. As she did, the wheels slipped off the pavement; she nearly lost the phone regaining control.

"We want to stay in one piece," Rankin said.

"Preferably," she said, glancing at him. She started to laugh.

"What?"

"You have cabbage on your chin."

"Just camouflage," he said, wiping it off.

Corrigan, meanwhile, was asking what was going on.

"I'd like Mr. Ferguson to set up some surveillance at the border areas of Chechnya," Corrine told him after a brief summary of the situation. "I don't know what extra resources we can spare, but at the moment that's the most logical destination."

"Um," said Corrigan.

"Um?"

"Uh, I think you're probably right about that being the likely destination," said Corrigan. "Did Ferg talk to you?"

"No."

"He's already in Chechnya."

"I thought he was waiting for us to find something."

"He had a lead he was working on. I was under the impression he was going to tell you about it himself."

"Mr. Ferguson did not inform me," she told Corrigan. Corrine felt her face flush. "Connect me with him."

"You can probably do that yourself."

"*Now.*"

The line clicked. There was static, then another series of clicks. Finally, a ring. Then another, and another.

"Ferguson," said a voice at last.

"Mr. Ferguson. Where the hell are you?" Corrine asked.

"Yeah, good question," he told her. "According to the map, the town we're near is called Vedona, except that I think there's supposed to be a diphthong in there somewhere. I saw a sign, but the letters were upside down. Whatever its name is, the Russians burned it to shit a year ago, so we're more here than there."

"Why are you in Chechnya?"

"Same reason you're in Kyrgyzstan," he told her.

"I want you to set up some surveillance along the border area."

"Can't," he told her. His voice was so cheerful he could have been talking about a ski holiday. "Following a couple of leads with a promising source."

"What source would that be?"

"You don't really want to know," said Ferg.

"Tell me now."

"Daruyev."

It took her a few moments to remember who he was talking about.

"The Chechen the Russians arrested for the dirty bomb plot? You spoke to him in jail?"

"Kinda."

"You went to a Russian prison? They're cooperating?"

"That would probably be an overstatement," said Ferguson.

"You didn't break him out of jail, did you?"

"You know, Counselor, I'm a little tied up at the moment."

"You were not authorized to do that. You weren't even supposed to be in Chechnya."

"Look, I have a mission," said Ferguson. "The way this works is, I do my job until Slott tells me to stop. How I execute is up to me."

"I'm in charge now, not Slott."

"So?"

"I'm in charge now," she repeated.

"My original orders haven't been rescinded."

"Consider them rescinded," she told him. "You can't just go off on your own."

"Look, there's no way you could have approved this, right? Because you're a lawyer. I just did us a massive favor," Ferguson told her.

"Bullshit, Ferguson. Bullshit."

"I have three possible sites where these bastards may be putting together bombs, and I'm going to check them out. Then Van is going to pick me up and take me home."

"No. I want you to check the border."

"Fine. Then you explain why we didn't check the sites two weeks from now when the bomb's used."

"We'll order satellite photos and survey the sites."

"I don't know where they are yet. Besides, these people aren't stupid. They're checking the overflights. They probably have telescopes watching everything in the sky. Goddamn satellite tracks are posted on the Internet for Christsake. Come on, Alston. Get up to speed. You're in the big leagues now."

She glanced at Rankin. He was frowning, but his eyes were pasted on the road.

"How long will it take you to find out where the sites are?"

"I don't know. My informant's a bit cagey. We should be near the first one soon. It's just about dark. Couple of hours. He says the other two are pretty far west. Couple of days."

"That's too long. I want you watching the roads. They'll take you to the right site."

"OK," said Ferguson. "What am I looking for?"

"We don't know yet."

"Then my way's better, right?"

"Check out the damn sites," said Corrine, realizing it was. She couldn't let a pissing match over who was in charge cloud her judgment.

She'd have to take care of that later on.

"Thanks," said Ferg. The line died.

She hit the end transmit button and threw the phone at her bag on the floor.

"He's an asshole," said Rankin.

"You can say that again."

3

As Ferguson turned up the road toward the mountains, an eight-wheeled Russian armored personnel carrier lumbered across the road, blocking the path ahead. Two Russian soldiers hopped from the back of the vehicle, guns ready.

"Moment of truth, Dad," Ferg said. "Don't talk too much."

"Uh-huh," grunted Conners.

Ferg slowed to a stop. He'd printed himself a set of papers indicating that they were authorized to travel to an outpost at Gora Cobolgo, which was near the border farther south. The papers included a document from the interior ministry, which would suggest to the soldiers that Ferg and Conners were FSB. Daruyev, of course, was clearly Chechen, though the implication would be that he was an informer.

"Ileya," said Ferg, rolling down the window as the soldiers approached. The nearest man aimed his rifle point-blank at Ferg's face.

"What's your business here?" demanded the soldier.

"I have a pass," Ferg told him in Russian, though he made no effort to show it to the soldier.

The turret on the armored personnel carrier swiveled in their direction. The APC was a BTR-70, battered by hard use in the Caucasus. The soldier pointed at Daruyev and sneered, calling him a dirty slime. It was hardly the worst thing he could say, though Ferg could feel Daruyev tensing.

"Let's move," Ferg said. "It's getting dark. I don't want to be on the road too long."

The soldier laughed at him, shaking his head. He brought up the assault rifle quickly, aiming it at Daruyev's head. Ferg smelled vodka on the soldier's breath, and for a split second thought the idiot might actually shoot.

He did, but only after pulling the gun upward. Then the soldier laughed again and waved at the APC, which moved back to let them through.

"Calls himself a soldier," grumbled Conners. "He didn't even look at your papers."

"The soldiers here become quite hardened quickly," said Daruyev. "They quickly become less than soldiers."

"That's no excuse," said Conners.

The road narrowed as they continued upward, until gradually it was just wide enough for the KAMAZ. They started downhill after a sharp turn, and Ferg had to jab at the brakes, barely managing to control the truck on the loose gravel at the side of the road.

"Beyond this curve," said Daruyev, pointing ahead.

The pass was not marked on the map, and at first it looked more like a creek bed than a roadway. But within a few yards it widened slightly, and while not exactly a highway, was easy enough to drive.

Ferg and Conners had agreed that the Chechen might be bringing them into an ambush, and while that seemed less likely with Russians nearby, they'd already decided to stop well short of the village area so they could first scout the access the Chechen had pointed out. Ferguson found a flat area to park about a mile up from the Russian checkpoint; according to the map and Daruyev's directions, the village sat about two miles over the ridge to the southeast.

"OK, partner. You wait for us here," Ferg told the Chechen. "You're going to wait in the back."

"The Russians will kill me if they come," said Daruyev.

"We all take chances," said Ferg. He put the hood on, then led Daruyev into the rocks a short distance from the truck. Conners rigged a crude anchor from some rope, tying it to the leg irons. Then they took a GPS plot and logged it to make sure they could find the spot again.

"I suggest you sleep," Ferg told him. "We'll be back."

"I trust you," said Daruyev. He held his head erect as if he could stare through the hood. Ferg pushed him gently to the ground.

Y ou think you're going to be able to keep him in America after this?" said Conners, as they picked their way quietly up the ridge. They moved parallel to but not on the road, armed with AK-74s. They'd stashed the grenade launcher and the rest of the arms near the KAMAZ and brought along one of the ignition wires to make it more difficult to steal.

"Sure."

"You can't be serious, Ferg. The Russians will throw a fit."

"Who's going to tell them? Our lawyer boss?"

"She may."

"Village is that way," said Ferguson, cutting over the rocks.

According to Daruyev, an abandoned mine sat just below the village. It was in this complex that he thought a dirty-bomb factory might be housed. It was a logical guess; not only would the shafts create a decent hideout, but they would presumably make it difficult to detect radiation.

The southwestern slope they came around had little cover, and while they'd seen no obvious lookout posts in the satellite photo Ferguson downloaded, the Americans moved cautiously toward the village, practically crawling as they tried to make it more difficult for anyone lurking with a nightscope to pick them off.

A deep crevice ran in a jagged line from the top of the hill above the village, as if God had scraped his finger down the mound. The crevice was about fifty yards from the closest foundation; when they reached it, the two men paused to take stock.

"Quiet," said Conners.

"Yeah. Probably a bust," said Ferguson. "We'll leave the village alone, check out the mines."

"Yup."

They followed the crevice, picking their way as carefully as possible. The moonlight gradually grew, as if forcing its way through the clouds. After about a half hour, they came to a shallow crater twenty yards or so from one of the mine entrances.

"Bomb hole," said Conners.

"I guess," said Ferguson.

"That's what it is, Ferg."

"I'm not arguing." The CIA officer knelt at the edge of the crater, staring at the rectangular cut in the mountain nearby.

"All right," he said, getting up and starting toward the hole.

Conners squatted at the edge of the crater, leveling his gun in the direction of the mine entrance. Ferguson stopped about halfway there, then began sidestepping to the right down the incline. A narrow path ran across the slope from the hole, switching back about ten yards on his right. Ferg flexed his fingers on his gun, trying to control his breath so he could hear better. Another shallow bomb crater sat to his right, the indentation so slight he could barely make it out. The mountain gaped at him through hewn-rock jaws, blackness far darker than the night in its throat. Ferg saw something move and jerked right, just barely stopping his finger from squeezing the trigger as he realized he'd seen his own dim shadow thrown by the moon.

Conners, waiting at the lip of the crater, saw Ferguson jerk toward the ground. He waited, knowing nothing was there and yet unsure of his knowledge at the same time. He watched Ferguson continue forward into the opening. Belatedly, he pushed himself out of the crater, trotting to keep his man covered. By the time he reached the mouth of the mine, Ferguson had disappeared.

Conners cursed and went to one knee by the entrance. When the CIA officer didn't reappear after a minute or so, Conners rose and stepped gingerly to his left, then his right, trying to peer inside. He couldn't see anything. Finally, Conners whistled, softly first, then louder.

"OK, Pops," said Ferguson finally.

Conners swung around—the team leader was down the slope behind him.

"Place looks pretty empty."

"What the hell?" said Conners walking in the direction of Ferguson's voice.

"Train tracks down there. Mines are a maze. Looks empty though."

"You walked through them?"

"There's something I've been meaning to tell you," said the CIA officer. "I'm a ghost. I just float right by."

"Always bustin', Ferg. One of these days it's going to come back to haunt you."

"Can't if I'm already a ghost, right?"

They worked their way down the slope. Several other entrances to the mine had been wrecked by explosions. The ruins of a building sat near the largest entrance, which was at the foot of the hill.

"Think Daruyev sent us on a wild-goose chase?" asked Conners, as they climbed back up toward the village.

"I don't know," said Ferg.

"Hope that anchor I rigged up holds him."

"He won't run away," said Ferguson.

The Russians had obliterated six of the seven buildings in the small village, but one house remained. It stood apart from the others, roof shorn off, holes where the windows once were. Wires lay in a tangle across the path leading to it; they looked like snakes in the moonlight.

Ferguson decided to check the house out; he approached quietly, though it was clear the village as well as the mines had been abandoned years before. The interior remained intact, a table and chairs in a room visible through one of the windows. The scene struck him as something out of a bizarre dream.

Conners waited impatiently for Ferguson, suspecting that the Chechen had lied to them to make his escape.

"Have a turnip," said Ferguson, looming from the shadows. He tossed one to Conners.

"What the fuck?"

"Turnips."

"Yeah, I see that," said Conners, turning it over. It was shriveled.

"How long you figure it takes a vegetable to rot?" Ferg asked.

"Jesus, Ferg, how the hell do I know?"

"That's how long ago the Russians burned the village," said Ferguson. "Daruyev didn't know."

"Real test will be if he's still there," said Conners.

"That just means he couldn't escape," said Ferguson.

4

INCIRLIK, TURKEY

 At one point in its venerable career, the Douglas DC-8 had served as an electronic warfare aircraft, mostly for training but in two instances supporting combat operations. Like many an old soldier, however, its days of glory were long gone, and the only hints of its past were a few scars on the gray-painted fuselage where sensors had once hung.

Van Buren—who was just a few years younger than the plane—tried to stretch some of the kinks out of his back as he trotted down the steps to the Incirlik tarmac. Two members of his command team were waiting with the Hummer nearby—Major Corles, who coordinated G-2 or the intelligence aspects of the mission, and Danny Gray, an Air Force major who liaisoned with Air Force Task Group Charlie, a specially constituted command that "owned" and maintained the aircraft Van Buren would draw on for his mission. Like 777th itself, Task Group Charlie was arguably the most versatile in the Air Force, fielding everything from helicopters to Stealth fighters.

"CentCom has some people coming over," said Corles. "We're going to draw on them for some logistics support. Pete's working it out. All we need is a target, and we're good to go."

Van Buren grunted. He'd spoken to Ferg an hour or so earlier; the officer said he had three sites to check out, and one was bound to be golden.

That was Ferg; always the optimist. But if he did find something, they had to be ready to hit it right away. At the same time, they had to plan an exfiltration in case he didn't; he had a valuable source for debriefing back at Guantanamo.

The others updated him on the situation there as the truck sped toward the hangar that had been appropriated to house their unit temporarily. Much of what they said was now routine, and Van Buren's mind drifted back to his lunch with Dalton. The lure of the job—the lure of the money—continued to tease him; he hadn't gotten much sleep on the flight over though the plane had a special bunk for that purpose.

He was thinking of James, and what he might owe his son. A good college education, certainly.

He could get that if he applied to West Point. Van Buren realized on the plane that they'd never discussed that; in fact, he had no idea where his boy wanted to go to school—or even if he did at all. They hadn't discussed much of anything about his future, except for baseball.

The realization that he didn't know what his son wanted shocked him. It was possible, probably even likely, that James didn't know himself. But as his father, Van Buren realized he had a duty to find out. He wanted to pick up the phone and call him, but of course he couldn't; he hadn't even been able to do that while he was in the States.

If he wanted to go to Harvard, what then?

What would keep him from taking Dalton's job? The colonel himself? The thrill of getting shot at?

Van Buren just barely kept himself from laughing out loud—getting shot at was no thrill, though there was a great deal to be said for having survived being shot at. He did love the action, the adrenaline pumping in your chest. But he personally hadn't been under fire for quite some time, and in truth that was the way the Army wanted it. Colonels, even Special Forces colonels, weren't supposed to put their noses on the firing line.

Planning a battle, helping run it—that was an incredibly difficult and important job, the sort of thing only a very few men could do, and even fewer could do well.

But adrenaline *was* part of the reason he was here. If there was an operation, he was going to be in the thick of it, and no one could tell him not to be.

Except maybe his son.

"We should have F-117s available, if needed," Gray was saying. "I'm a little sketchy on when we can get them over here, though."

Van Buren snapped upright. No one who worked for him should be sketchy about anything.

"We'll get everything crystal clear," he told the others. "Everything."

There was a bit more snap in his voice than he'd intended, and the others responded with studied silence.

GURJEV, KAZAKHSTAN

 Guns waited in the front of the basement cafe near the center of town while Massette called Corrine to update her. The server's Russian had an accent Guns wasn't familiar with, but he'd nonetheless managed to order tea and sandwiches. He wasn't exactly sure what was between the bread, but was so hungry it didn't matter. By the time Massette came back Guns had already cleared his own plate and was eying Massette's food.

Gurjev was a large crossroads in western Kazakhstan on the Caspian Sea. They'd driven nearly four hundred miles without finding a trace of their quarry.

"*Mon ami*," said Massette, pulling back the chair.

"They got something?"

"No. But Alston is very stubborn," Massette said. "She wants us to keep looking."

"Yeah. She's almost as bad as Ferg."

"Stubbornness is overrated as a personality trait," said Massette, taking his sandwich.

6

Daruyev hadn't escaped. Ferguson and Conners found him huddled over his chains, snoring loudly.

"Shame to wake him," said Conners.

"Too heavy to carry," said Ferg. He took out his pocketknife and hacked off the rope. "Let's go," Ferg told Daruyev. "Time for door number two."

Daruyev blinked his eyes open. "Nothing?" he asked.

"Not today. Where we going next?"

"A place called Verko. The Russians abandoned it years ago. It's safe."

"Safe for who?" asked Ferguson.

The Chechen smiled, but said nothing, instead tracing out the general direction on the map Ferguson showed him. The base wasn't marked there.

"What was the village like?" Daruyev asked, as they started down the mountain. "Did you talk to people?"

"Russians blew up whatever was there a while ago," Ferguson told him.

"The village?"

"Yup."

"My mother and sister were there two years ago. I got a letter."

They drove down the mountain. The APC was gone. At this time of night, the real danger was from Chechen guerrillas. But they saw no one as they made their way northeastward. Daruyev slept; Conners, too, dozed off. Ferguson stopped before dawn and pumped diesel into the tank.

They'd have to take one of the main roads northward to get to Verko. It would be risky even without a prisoner, and as he stowed the empty jerry can, Ferguson considered whether just to evac him out now. But Ferg decided that for the moment he'd proceed as planned, using the Chechen's help to scout the other two possible sites before taking him home. Assuming they drove during the day, they ought to be able to get to them both by nightfall anyway.

Conners cranked open an eye when he climbed into the truck.

"Long leak," he said.

"I was peeing in the gas tank," Ferguson told him.

"You want me to drive?"

"Nah, sleep a bit. I'm thinking we'll drive into the day."

"That safe?"

"Of course not." He started the truck and put it in gear, winding down the dirt road. Conners rubbed his eyes and stretched as much as he could with Daruyev leaning against him.

"Where are we?"

"Near Noza-Jerk," Ferg said, smiling at the name.

"Noza-Jerk. What a town," said Conners.

"Then there's Gora Krybl," said Ferg.

"I been to Grznyj, Ordzon, Chrebet—I been everywhere, Jack. I been everywhere," sang Conners.

"Sounds like a song," said Ferg.

"It is." He sang a few verses with the names of American cities in Texas. "Old hobo song."

"Not Irish?"

"Came out of New Zealand or Australia or someplace," Conners said. "Changed around a lot. Geoff Mack wrote it, or at least a version of it, that a lot of people did."

"Never heard of him."

"Your loss," said Conners.

"Why do you like those old songs?"

"Why do you?" said Conners. "Remind you of being a kid?"

"The childhood I never had."

"Don't get philosophical on me, Ferg."

"I'm not philosophical."

Bullshit, thought Conners, but he didn't say anything.

"You think I'm philosophical?" asked Ferg.

"That and reckless," said Conners.

"Reckless?"

"I'd call it a death wish."

"That why I hang around with you, huh?" The CIA officer rolled down his window halfway. The blast of cold air stung his eyes, reminding him he was awake.

"You're not an SF type," said Conners. "Not a soldier."

"Not enough discipline, huh?" said Ferg.

"Got that right. You don't like following orders. And you take too many risks."

"Got to."

"You were lucky, Ferg, damn lucky."

"Which time?"

Conners laughed.

"You're telling me no SF soldier is reckless?" said Ferguson.

"Not the ones who are alive."

"Bah."

Conners didn't bother arguing.

"Rankin's not reckless?" suggested Ferg.

"Rankin? No."

"Bull."

"Taking risks and being reckless aren't the same thing, Ferg."

"Oh, I see."

"Rankin's a professional."

"You Army guys like to stick together."

"You don't like him, that's all. Not that I blame you—he hates your guts."

"That doesn't make him *not* reckless," said Ferg. "Let's try that turnoff over there," added Ferguson, spotting the road.

7

BUILDING 24-442, SUBURBAN VIRGINIA

 When Thomas matched Corrigan's scribble with the name on the map—Verko—he felt as if the ceiling had lit up with spotlights. Verko was connected with several UFO sightings during the 1950s and '60s, all reported by villagers in the nearby mountains. The sightings had proven false; at the time Verko was a secret Russian base devoted to a squadron of spy planes.

It looked fairly isolated, a good place to arrange a pickup—but only if he could be sure the Russians weren't using it anymore.

Or the guerrillas. Thomas threw himself into researching it, gathering every slither of information he could. He began with the generic, pulling up SpyNet and working from there. The base had been officially closed in 1992, though it hadn't seen much activity for at least ten years prior to that. Thomas jabbed at the keyboard, calling up a set of satellite photos. He culled through a file, then went over to a collection made by a commercial satellite over the past several years without finding any that showed activity on the runway. He did find shadows undoubtedly related to activity there, though there was no new construction.

A scan of NSA intercepts turned up several hits that contained Verko, but most had not been decrypted. The one that had contained something seemed pure gibberish.

He continued to work, guessing logically and illogically. He lost track of time. He didn't eat. He didn't emerge from his room. At some point he decided he needed a break. Thomas got up and gathered all of the papers that he'd arranged on the floor in a big pile next to his desk, then dropped to the floor and did a hundred push-ups. When that didn't rev him, he tried a hundred more. A third set left him so tired he fell asleep on the floor.

How long he slept there, he couldn't say. He finally woke up because someone was pounding on his door.

"Yes?" he asked, opening it.

Debra Wu stood in the hallway, eying him suspiciously. She was wearing a different skirt, though this one seemed just as short as the other.

"Thomas, the security log says you've been here all night," she said.

"Might be."

Verko wasn't a Russian base, he realized—it was a guerrilla stronghold.

"Corrigan wants to see you. Does he know you were here?" she added.

"I don't know."

"You want some coffee?"

"Why not?" He got up, orienting himself among his papers. "Tell Corrigan I'll be down in a while. I have to put some things together. I need to make a few queries."

"Okey-dokey," said Debra, retreating.

"Don't forget the coffee."

Even though Debra warned him that "the loony slept under his desk," Corrigan wasn't quite prepared for the analyst's disheveled appearance when he entered the secure chamber about an hour later. His hair stuck out in every direction; his shirt was half-out of his pants, and he seemed to have dust and lint pasted all over his body.

"I figured it out," said Thomas.

"What?"

"They're putting the bomb together at this place called Verko. It's in the mountains, and it used to be an airbase."

"Verko—that was one of the pickup possibilities," said Corrigan.

"Verko's the place you're looking for," said Thomas. "Allah's Fist bought ammonia nitrate and had it trucked into a village a few miles away nine months ago. We have two sat photos showing those trucks on the road to the facility."

"When?"

"Six months ago."

"At Verko?"

"No, but that has to be where they're going. And one of the companies that was associated with Bin Saqr rented a house in the village. Medical waste—they've been grabbing all the cesium they can get. Maybe other stuff. The analysts warned about this—I know the man who put the estimate together. Very reliable. I have an inquiry into NSA to see what intercepts may link with this."

Thomas's hair poked out at odd angles, and his eyes nearly bulged from his head. As much as Corrigan wanted to believe that the analyst had solved the problem, the portrait he saw before him did not inspire confidence.

"Take me back to the beginning," he told Thomas.

Thomas explained what he had found a second time. Even laid out in a semilogical manner the shadows and glimpses of trucks near but on the base sounded less than definitive. Corrigan brought up a sat picture of the abandoned base on one of the computers.

"Where exactly would they do the work?" he asked. "The Russians dismantled the hangars they had there in the eighties. These buildings—are they big enough?"

"That is a problem," said Thomas. "I don't know."

Corrigan frowned. "What do they do with the bomb once they put it together?"

Thomas shrugged again. "I haven't figured it out yet. But it would be a perfect site. It hasn't been under Russian control for the past five or six years, exactly when the head of Allah's Fist disappeared."

"That's all you have? No intercepts there, no nothing?"

"Not yet." Thomas peered over Corrigan's shoulder. Maybe the Russians had burrowed into the side of the mountain, putting the planes in a nukeproof shelter. Or maybe there was a ramp elevator along one of the aprons.

Now if it had been an alien base, the transnuclear engines would allow it to slide through a fissure in the mountains without detection.

Probably he could rule that out.

"Maybe you should get some sleep while we work this over," said Corrigan. "I'll put in a request to NRO for every scrap of satellite data they have."

"I have that all under way already," said Thomas. "But I'm sure this is the place."

"Sure sure, or just sure?"

"Sure," said Thomas.

Corrigan debated calling Ferguson. If he was wrong, the officer would bash in his head.

"Get some more backup," said Corrigan finally.

"On it, boss," said Thomas, running from the room.

Corrigan finally realized there might be such a thing as too much enthusiasm, not to mention eccentricity.

Even so, he picked up the phone to call Ferg.

8

 The marshaling yard was less than two years old, and while small by Western standards, it stretched out across the landscape like a city unto itself, with close to a hundred miles worth of track. Freight cars from all over Russia and Europe were scattered along the various spurs, each located and tracked by computer as massive freight trains were put together. Nearly all contained garbage.

The cars carrying the rad waste were in their own section of the yard, heavily guarded. They'd found a spot to watch the yard nearly two miles away from the perimeter of the facility, and though the view was unobstructed, Rankin had to sit on the roof of the car with his binoculars to see.

Corrine slept inside. Rankin had almost had to slug her to get her to take a rest. He was worried that she was going to burn herself out; she was clearly pushing herself because she thought she'd screwed up somehow losing the boxcar.

Rankin reached across the roof for the thermos of tea—coffee had become increasingly difficult to find—and poured himself a cup. He was just taking his first sip when the sat phone rang. To answer, he had to enter a personal ID code, then say his name into the receiver. The computer analyzed his voice pattern; if it didn't match its records, the phone was temporarily locked into transmit mode and Corrigan—or whoever was making the call—alerted. Once the embedded GPS device gave a positive marker on the phone's location—a matter of two seconds—the person on the other side could decide how to proceed.

"This is Corrigan. We have new information," he said. "There's a former Soviet airbase in the southern mountains of Chechnya called Verko. Ferg's en route to check it out, but we think they're gathering their waste there. Van Buren needs Corrine to authorize the SF mission if it pans out."

"She's sleeping right now," said Rankin.

"Well, wake her the fuck up," said Corrigan.

"You sure it's the place?"

"Just wake her up and let me talk to her. Her phone's off-line."

Rankin climbed down and tapped on the window. Corrine opened her left eye slowly, then closed it. He tapped again, then opened the door and gave her his phone.

"Corrigan," he told her.

"Thanks," she said sleepily. She pulled herself upright in the seat. "I'm here."

"We think we know where the waste is headed. Ferguson's on his way to check it out—it jibes with some information he already had. This could be it."

"All right," she said. "Tell Mr. Ferguson to proceed. Inform the assault group and give them whatever preliminary data on the target is appropriate. But no action until my authorization."

"You're sure about that?"

Corrine waited a moment before answering, reminding herself that not everyone was against her—and that even if they were, she wasn't going to help herself by blowing up.

"I'm absolutely sure," she said in an even voice. "I need you to get me on a plane out to Turkey to meet with the strike force ASAP."

"Civilian or military?"

"What's faster?"

Corrigan hit some keys on one of his computers. "I can get you on a flight to Aktau, if you can get to the airport in fifteen minutes."

"Where's Aktau?"

"It's on the Caspian. From there I can get you to Turkey, no sweat. Or Chechnya."

"Turkey will do."

"Someone will be there. It may be a contract; going to be hard to get a military plane in there without drawing attention. I'll round up whatever I can."

"You're a regular travel agent," she said, hanging up.

9

Ten miles east of Verko the highway turned into a minefield. Two burned-out Russian tanks tipped them off; Conners pulled off the road and got out of the truck, scouting it out. They were on a ridge that ran along the side of a mountain maybe twenty-five hundred meters high, with the peak another thousand or so meters above them. Conners felt as if he were being watched, and guessed that the tanks had been mined.

Ferg, who'd been sleeping lightly, climbed down out of the cab and walked over.

"Looks like a bitch," said Conners.

"Yeah, this has got to be the place," said Ferg.

"How we gonna get there? Take us two or three days to drive all the way north and around on the other highway, and we got joker boy in the cab."

Ferguson looked up at the rugged walls. "Got to be paths we can pick our way across."

"Take us two days."

"Maybe."

Ferguson glanced back at the truck. They'd have to take Daruyev's leg chains off to travel by foot.

Corrigan's intelligence jibed with Daruyev's information; they might indeed be closing in on the site. But if they were, terrorists might be all around them. The Chechen was potentially a serious liability—even if he wasn't trying to steer them toward an ambush, he might find the opportunity to escape irresistible. He could easily lead the terrorists back to them, or at least alert them to their presence.

On the other hand, Corrigan's track record on vital data wasn't necessarily impressive. They'd need Daruyev to get to the next site if this one was a bust.

"All right. Let's assume we're being watched," Ferg told Conner. "We back up, go down to that blown-out farm we passed, get the satellite photos, pick our way back over."

"Long way, Ferg."

"Just a day's worth of climbing. Van's going to need time to get everything in gear anyway."

"Daruyev coming?" asked Conners.

"Somebody's gotta carry the gear," said Ferg.

Like most of the other buildings they'd passed, the walls of the main house of the small farm down the road were scorched black, the soot so embedded in the rocks that years of rain had only pushed it deeper. The farm looked like just another abandoned homestead as they parked nearby—until the curtains in the window moved.

"Shit," said Conners. "People are living in there? The roof's gone."

It was too late simply to back out onto the road; the people had seen them and might alert the Russians, or the guerrillas—or both—to their presence. Conners felt angry, illogically blaming them for intruding—they'd have to kill them, he thought.

"Well let's go say hello," said Ferguson, hopping out of the truck. He slung his gun nonchalantly over his shoulder and—once Conners had his own weapon pointing toward the front of the house to cover him—walked toward the front door.

He knocked, though he knew that anyone inside wouldn't answer. After a second knock, he walked around to the window with the curtain. He couldn't see much of the interior, and when no one appeared after two hard raps, he went around to the back.

An old man stood in the doorway, aiming an ancient hunting rifle at him.

"*Zdrátvuitye*," Ferg said to him in Russian. "Hello."

The old man didn't move. Ferguson then tried his Chechen, explaining that they were friends who had to help someone reach his rightful place. When that didn't impress the man—Ferguson wasn't entirely sure that his pronunciation could be deciphered—he switched to English, realizing that while the man wouldn't understand it, it might convince him he wasn't Russian.

"It's all right," he told the man. "We're friends. I need a place to keep my truck."

He switched back into Russian and repeated the sentence. Ferg guessed that the man's sympathies lay with the rebels, and that he would leave them be if he thought they were connected with them. Whether he could be trusted beyond that was a question Ferguson couldn't answer; there were no telephone lines, and no obvious radio antenna, so as far as that went the old man wasn't going to be notifying anyone very soon.

"So can I park my truck?" Ferg asked in Russian.

A voice inside the house said something Ferguson couldn't hear. The old man waved his hand in that direction, as if shushing them.

"That the missus?" asked Ferg.

The man told him something in Chechen that Ferg couldn't understand. He smiled and asked for food in Russian. The Chechen frowned, then started toward the door. Ferguson decided to follow. Inside, he found the old man's wife standing with a long knife by a stove. Behind her were five small children, ranging in age from a few months to two years. The woman was so short and bent over from osteoporosis that her head was just barely above Ferg's knee, but her arms were thick, and her wrists flicked the knife as if she were one of the three musketeers. Ferguson waved at her, then leaned to the side to smile at the children, who were trying to puzzle out exactly who he was.

One of the children started to laugh, and the old woman drew back, still on her guard but no longer menacing. The old man, meanwhile, had hung the rifle on a pair of hooks and taken some paper and matches to the stove, which had a tinderbox for wood directly under the top. Fire started, he moved a kettle toward the front and turned to his wife, haranguing her for not being hospitable. Ferguson reached into his pocket and found some coins; it would have been an insult to give them to the old man, but the children were fair game. The oldest clinked two large coins together, then passed one to the next toddler in line, who promptly tried to taste it. This elicited a tirade from the old woman, who chastised Ferguson as well as the children before confiscating the coins.

Out in the truck, Conners felt his legs falling asleep when Ferg finally appeared. The old people had given him a few hard-boiled eggs, some tea, and bread. Conners fell on them hungrily.

Ferguson had asked for a chisel or saw, but either the old man had neither or just couldn't understand what he was talking about. They got Daruyev out of the cab and brought him around to a broken-down stone wall at the side of the road. Using the tire iron, they managed to break the chains between his legs, but there was no question of getting the manacles off.

"I'm trusting you," Ferguson told him. "But if you move an inch to escape, I'll have to kill you."

"Yes," said Daruyev.

Conners looked up and saw the old man coming out from the house. He took a step back and raised his rifle. The old man ignored him, jabbering to Ferguson that he had a jug of water, and then pointing to a better place to put the truck.

"They'll have that thing apart in a half hour," said Conners as they began walking south across the road, toward what looked like a narrow trail in the satellite photos.

"Nah," said Ferg.

"Sell it then."

"The truck will cause them considerable difficulty if the Russians come," said Daruyev. "They won't be able to explain it."

"Why would they have to?" said Conners.

"If a Russian asks a question, you have to have an answer."

"There aren't too many Russians in the area," said Ferg.

"Good thing for them," said Daruyev.

"Good thing for all of us," said Ferg.

By nightfall, they had reached a narrow plateau in the mountains about seven miles east of Verko. They were making much better time than Conners had predicted, so good in fact that Ferg decided to press on. The night was clear, and according to the sat photos a pass ran to the south which would make it easier to hook around from the southwest, the side opposite the only road into the base. If they could make it, a mountain about a mile from Verko in that direction had an only partially obscured view of the landing strip there, according to the 3-D rendering Corrigan had supplied.

So they kept walking, moving in single file, spread out along the rock-strewn path. Daruyev moved silently; if he was familiar with the way, he didn't let on. Several times Conners, at the tail, lost sight of him and had to hustle to catch up, but the Chechen made no sign of trying to escape.

By midnight, they had reached the other side of the mountain Ferg wanted to use as a vantage point. The cold air clawed at their fingers and legs; their cheeks hollowed out, and their ears began to ring with the wind. They stopped for a rest. Ferg noticed that Daruyev's shoes were stained black; his feet were bleeding.

"I'm thinking one of us stays here, while the other scouts around that ridge there," said Ferguson. "If there's going to be a lookout post, it'll be up over there. You going to fall asleep?"

"You don't have to worry about me," Conners told him.

"Don't sing too loud," Ferg told him, setting out.

It took Ferguson more than three hours to climb up the mountain far enough to cut across to what looked like a lookout post on the 3-D map Corrigan had created and posted on their secure Web site for him. To cross the last hundred yards he had to climb up a crevice and get up and across an overhang. Tired and cold, he sent several loose stones tumbling below. The first time he froze; he was too precariously placed to swing his gun up for defense. When nothing happened after a few minutes, he began climbing again. When more rocks spilled a few seconds later, he barely paused. Either the people in the lookout were sleeping—or the post wasn't manned.

A half hour later, standing behind the ridge, he discovered that the latter was correct—the ridge dropped off sharply, and it wasn't as a good a spot in real life as it appeared on Corrigan's simulation.

But there was a better spot off the side of the road and down about three hundred yards. In the darkness he couldn't tell if there were rocks there or people. Nor was the question academic—the ridge gave him some cover to pass, but anything beyond it would be easily visible, certainly once the sun came up. The only thing to do was to track back down about a quarter mile, where he could pick up a narrow ledge that angled in the opposite direction, skirting around the mountain before rejoining the trail near a V-shaped rift about three miles below.

In the daylight, the climb would have been merely difficult. The combination of nighttime and growing fatigue, not to mention the proximity of the guerrilla guards, lifted it into the interesting category.

There was enough of a moon that Ferguson picked out the start of the ledge easily; he found as he went that he could see the wall fairly well, probably nearly as well as if he'd been wearing his night glasses on a pitch-black night. But after he'd gone about a half mile the ledge began to slope sharply toward the mountain, making it harder to walk on. Clouds had been moving in, making it more and more difficult to see. Still, Ferg was only about fifty feet from the rift when he lost his balance. As his right foot slipped on a loose rock, his left hand reached for a hold that proved to be a shadow. In the next second, he felt himself momentarily defying gravity.

"Oh, shit," he said to himself.

Then he started to fall.

10

 The airport was large by Russian standards, and with decent security. To pass to the main area where her charter to Turkey was supposed to be waiting, Corrine had to show ID and pass through an X-ray gate. The woman guard checking her purse and bags was more interested in her aspirin than the satellite phone; as she held up the bottle to examine it Corrine started to explain that it was for headaches.

"I know what it's for," said the guard frostily in English, tossing it back in the bag and dismissing her.

The terminal had all the charm of a 1970s American bus station, with two rows of plastic-backed seats dividing a scuffed linoleum floor. The seats were empty; the few passengers waiting for planes at that hour milled near the gates at the opposite end of the hall. Corrigan had told Corrine to go to a window with a long name in Cyrillic letters; the word was "special" and when pronounced in Russian sounded almost like it did in English, but with the dots and backward symbols it looked more like a magic spell than a sign. She found the words on a door, not a window, though in roughly the place he'd said; she walked back and forth twice before deciding it had to be the place. But no one answered when she knocked.

She checked her watch; the flight north had taken less time than Corrigan had predicted, and she realized she was probably just a little early. Still, she wanted to call him and see, so she ducked into a restroom nearby. But it was a private facility, with an attendant hovering near the sink. She tipped the woman and went back out without using the facilities or the proffered toilet paper.

Before she could get her bearings in the large room, a man in a long leather jacket stepped in front of her. Corrine took a step around him but he put his hand out to stop her.

"Off," she said sharply in English, brushing his hand away.

"Ms. Alston, I'm your pilot," said the man.

Corrine could tell there was a problem and didn't even bother using the authentication sequence Corrigan had supplied. She started to spin away. But as she did, a short, balding man in a brown polyester coat blocked her way.

"Excuse me, Ms. Alston," he told her in English. "My name is Dolov. I am with the Federal Security Bureau. You will come with me, please."

"Excuse me, I don't understand what you're saying," said Corrine, though the man's English had been excellent.

"You will come with me," he said calmly.

"Are you putting me under arrest?"

"That depends on what comes from our conversation," said Dolov, in a way that suggested jail might be the most desirable of the possible outcomes.

11

SOUTHERN CHECHNYA

 Conners jumped to his feet when he heard what sounded like the faint echo of gunfire.

"Up, up," he told the Chechen. He kicked his shoes when he didn't move.

Daruyev groaned, then turned over and got up slowly.

"Let's go," said Conners. Cursing, he told Daruyev to walk ahead of him. They had to take the trail; there was just no way he could cover his prisoner on the slope, even if Daruyev had been able to climb.

Conners debated whether it would just be easier to kill the Chechen and be done with it.

It took twenty minutes to get to the stop below the ridge where they'd thought the lookout was; by the time they got there the sun was starting to rise. As they came close to the lookout spot Conners grabbed the Chechen by the back, using him as a shield.

"Call them out," Conners said.

"Call who?" said Daruyev.

"Your bastard friends."

"These are not my comrades."

"Call them." Conners nudged his rifle against Daruyev's neck.

The Chechen whistled. There was no answer.

"Again," said Conners. "Use words."

"They wouldn't."

"Call them."

Daruyev called in a calm voice that he had escaped from the Russians and needed help. But there was no response.

The mountain fell off too sharply on the left to give an ambusher a place to hide, and the ridge on the right angled away, but Conner still felt exposed. He pushed his prisoner forward; after twenty yards or so he saw another spot up a hundred yards farther where an outlook post could be hidden. They backtracked; Conners peered over the side and decided they could skirt the position by climbing down to a rift that skirted the rocks northward.

"We go down here," Conners told his prisoner.

"That's going to be hard."

"Tough."

"Take the gun from my back."

"No," Conners told him, pushing him to start. As he started to follow, there was a noise behind him; he whirled, gun ready.

"Relax, Dad, it's only me," said Ferguson, appearing on the slope.

"Ferg, where the fuck have you been?" said Conners.

"Waking sleeping dogs," said Ferguson. "Quiet. There's a pair of guards up the trail that way about a half mile. I fell before, and they started shooting up the place."

"I heard them."

"They didn't bother looking for me," said Ferguson. He'd banged his shins and scratched the side of his face in the fall, but otherwise was in decent shape. "I thought half the mountain was going to come down on top of me."

"Did it?" asked Conners.

Ferguson laughed. "I'm still here, ain't I?" He pointed a finger at Daruyev. "You were going to make him climb down the other side there?"

"I didn't know where the hell you were."

"So you were going down to the bottom?"

"I figured that cutback ahead could be covered. I could get around it down there."

"Sure, if you have a week."

"Don't bust my chops, Ferg. I thought you were dead."

Ferguson smiled at him, then pointed to the way he had come. "There's a ledge here. It's narrow, but if you don't slip, it'll take you across the road. Then we can get up and across and check out the base."

"If it's there," said Conners.

"Don't be such a pessimist." Ferguson checked the grenade launcher on Daruyev's back. He angled it slightly, so the weight would help anchor him to the mountain. "Lean in," he told him. "You walk just behind me. If you get scared, say so."

"I'm not scared."

"No shit?" said Ferguson, starting out. "Come on. If we hurry, we can wave for the satellite when it comes overhead."

12

Corrine sat in the small room, waiting for Dolov to reappear. She had her lawyer face on, assuming that she was being observed, and well aware that anything she said might tell the FSB considerably more than she wished. She sat alone in the room for more than an hour, head up, eyes straight, knowing that Dolov's absence was part of the interrogation process.

Finally, the door swung open. Dolov and the woman who had checked her pocketbook earlier entered. The FSB officer apologized for keeping her waiting, saying that he had to locate a female guard so he could talk to her.

"There's no need for that," said Corrine.

"I have to follow the law," said Dolov. He brushed his hand across his scalp, where he was going prematurely bald. He squinted, then bobbed his head; finally he put his finger to his chin. "The airplane that landed to pick you up—and we do know it's here for you, Ms. Alston—is contracted to a company that works with the American CIA."

Corrine considered what to do. As an attorney, her advice to a client would be to say nothing. But would that help her now?

"Well I'm not with the CIA," she said.

Dolov clearly did not believe her. Corrine realized she needed to find out why he'd stopped her—the fact that they thought she was a CIA officer wouldn't ordinarily be reason to stop her. Were they just sending some sort of message, hassling a suspected agent for passing through the territory? How was the game played? She had no feel for the rules.

She was out of her element. She was a lawyer, not a spy.

Except that she was; her boss had made her one.

"Do you always accuse Americans of working for the CIA?" she said finally.

"Two days ago, a very dangerous man was broken out of prison near Groznyy," said Dolov. "The CIA was involved."

"That's terrible," she said. "But what does that have to do with me?"

Dolov said nothing.

Corrine realized that she had to give him something, a story he could use to justify letting her go. But saying anything meant taking a risk. If she said something that didn't check out, he might jail her for lying. And, of course, she couldn't say anything that would jeopardize the others or the operation.

If you didn't take risks, you didn't succeed. That was what Ferguson was all about. He wasn't a cowboy; he just existed in a system that demanded audacious risks.

"What were you doing in Kyrgyzstan?" asked Dolov. His voice was more aggressive than before; he wanted results, and he would modify his tactics until he got them.

"Mr. Dolov, perhaps we should be honest with each other," she said.

"I would appreciate it," said Dolov.

Corrine turned to the guard. "You'll leave us, please," she told the woman.

The guard looked at Dolov, who nodded.

"There is a train of radioactive waste, heading toward Kyrgyzstan. When it left Buzuluk, there were five boxcars that were not part of the removal operation. Now there are four," she said.

"Boxcars?"

"They must have some way of slipping one or two of the waste casks into the other cars. The regular shipments proceed untouched. They're heavily guarded and all accounted for."

"How do you know?" he said. Only now was it clear to her that he was indeed interested.

"I followed it. You didn't think I turned up in Kyrgyzstan by accident, did you?"

"From Buzuluk?"

"Near there."

"Why would you follow the train if you're not CIA?"

"Certain organizations are interested in what happens to the waste."

"Such as?"

"Greenpeace, among others."

"If I run your name against one of our databases, you won't appear?"

"No."

"And I suppose the aircraft that has come to meet you wasn't hired by the CIA?"

"I have no idea. It may very well be. I daresay that the Russian government has paid for some of our arrangements as well. Radioactive waste is an important problem for all mankind."

Dolov remained convinced that she was lying, but the missing boxcar was nonetheless a matter of great interest.

"Where did the waste go?"

"If I knew, I wouldn't be leaving," she said. "It simply disappeared soon after entering Kyrgyzstan."

"Were Chechens involved?" he asked.

"Chechens?" She shrugged. "I haven't a clue. I just know it's gone."

Dolov began rocking gently on his heels. Radiological waste was an important issue, more so because of the escape of the prisoner. The woman's information was extremely valuable—assuming it checked out.

Corrine had given Dolov the story he needed, but she now had to give him a reason to let her go.

"What prisoner did you lose?" she asked. "And where was he lost?"

She saw the inspector's face flicker with fear for a brief second as he connected the two events. It went from that to a blank officiousness. He was worried that she really was from Greenpeace and that he had told her too much.

And then he smiled.

"Let me make a phone call. Perhaps our misunderstanding can disappear."

13

"Unobstructed runway. Two large buildings, hangar-type, at the north end. I don't see any people, though."

Ferguson shifted around as he spoke. He couldn't see the top of the peak opposite him, so he had no idea what defenses might be hidden there. The mountain also shadowed whatever was directly below him on the western side of the base, and some of the road to the northeast.

"Here's something," he said, as a vehicle emerged from one of the two buildings; it looked like an old-fashioned bread van. Another followed, and another and another. They drove out to three different points surrounding the airfield.

"Maybe they're radar trucks," suggested Van Buren, who was listening along with his intelligence staff to Ferguson's briefing. "The satellites have cleared overhead, so it's possible that they drive out there once they're gone."

"I don't see any antennas or radar dishes," reported Ferguson. "I don't see any missiles either."

Van Buren's G-2 captain began explaining that the vans might contain a short-range, low-power radar, which would give them some early warning of approaching helicopters. Another officer said that it was possible that the rebels were using the mountain itself as the base for tropo-scatter antennas, with the transmission portions relatively short and camouflaged. Such a system would be difficult to see, though it was likely to leave gaps in the coverage.

"I don't know," said Ferguson. "Maybe have somebody look at the satellite photos again. Can you get a U-2 in?"

"Russians'll shoot it down in a heartbeat," said Van Buren.

"Could they hide missiles in the vans?" asked Ferguson.

"Shoulder-launched missiles, sure."

"Hang tight," said Ferguson, as a new set of vehicles appeared from the building. These were tracked ZSU-23-4 Shilka antiair guns, sometimes called "Zoos," old but reliable flak cannons that could fill the air with shells. Their altitude was limited, but they were deadly against helicopters and low-flying planes. Parachuters would be massacred.

The southeastern end of the base dropped off sharply about twenty yards after the end of the runway. The eastern side of the complex south of the buildings was relatively flat, with a dirt road but no aircraft access ramp. Trenches flanked the runway for about three-quarters of its length. The runway itself was rather narrow and pockmarked with small craters at the sides. The Air Force people had already looked at the sat photos and decided they could get a Herky Bird in there and out.

"I have four F-117As," Van Buren said. "We can take out four targets—the vans and one of the antiair emplacements. But every shot has to count."

"Better to take out the guns and jam any radar on the way in," suggested one of his captains. "Then we target the missiles when we're on the ground."

"What if they have heat-seekers in them?"

"We go in with flares and a decoy."

"Still risky."

"Why don't you have the Stealth fighters take out the guns and two of the vans," said Ferg. "Conners and I hit the last van ourselves. We link up near the buildings. We can work it into deek, like we're the real attack. We have a grenade launcher. We have to get down there anyway to confirm this is the place. So we call in, attack starts, we get the van and move on."

"That might work," said Van Buren. "You have readings?"

"Not yet," said Ferguson.

"We're doing a lot of work here, Ferg. It's going nowhere without real data. Even then, we have to get Alston's OK."

"It's got to be the place, Van."

"Fergie?"

"It's all right, Van. You guys just get ready to hit it. I'll get the numbers."

"Don't get so close they induct you into their army."

"I hear they have a hell of a retirement plan," said Ferguson, snapping off the phone.

14

Dolov did not reappear. Instead, a short, frumpy-looking woman in her midthirties came into the room dragging Corrine's bag. The woman said absolutely nothing, staring at Corrine as she checked her things. Apparently she was free to go.

The terminal was by then full of people. Food vendors were hawking wares from boxes and small pushcarts; she bought a bottle of mineral water and a sandwich, which she gulped down while walking back toward the Specials door. As she approached the office, a short man in a leather coat pushed away from the wall and came toward her. Corrine eyed him warily, not sure now who or what to trust.

"Ms. Alston?"

"Yes."

"A friend sent me to get you," said the man. "My name's Tru. I've been waiting."

He was an American, or at least his accent was; it had the brassy tone of the New York area in it.

"What friend?" she asked.

"Jack?" he said, more a question than an answer.

"What's the weather like?" she said, starting the authentication sequence.

"Warm. Visibility at five miles."

"And getting better?"

"Probably not."

"That's good enough."

"I hope so."

She swallowed the last of her water, then threw the bottle in a garbage can as she followed him toward a hall at the side of the airline counters. She hesitated, then tossed her bag, including her sat phone and wallet, in there as well.

Tru continued down the hallway, past a baggage-screening area to a large empty room. Various machinery sat at the far side of the room, piled and bunched up near the wall. To the left was a set of metal garage-style doors. Tru went to one, bent and opened it, waiting for her so he could close it behind them.

Corrine shivered as the outside air hit her. Tru walked to the left, steering around a large yellow tractor used to move aircraft. Jets were lined up along the rear of the terminal building, crews zipping back and forth as they were prepped and loaded. Tru's shoulders rolled back and forth as he ducked past them; the short man strolled past the lineup of aircraft as if he were lord of the place.

Corrine followed as he turned to the left at the end of the building, walking out beyond a large Russian airliner toward a two-engine Airbus, which sat alone in the sea of concrete. The Airbus—an A310, capable of holding over two hundred passengers—had the red livery and insignia of the Turkish National Airline, THY. Corrine expected to find a smaller plane beyond it, but when Tru crossed around to the left side of the aircraft she realized this was the only plane there. A rickety-looking push ramp was at the door directly behind the cockpit; two men in coveralls were standing nearby.

Her contact bounded up the steps to the open cabin door. Corrine hesitated at the bottom of the steps, then clambered up. As she reached the cabin, the men below grabbed the boarding ladder and pulled it away.

"Think you can button up?" Tru asked from the flight deck. "There's a diagram on how to shut it."

Corrine struggled at first, the movement slightly awkward, but once the door was moving toward the side it slapped in easily. She pushed through the curtain to her left, only to find that the rest of the airliner was completely empty.

"No movie today," said Tru behind her. "Come sit up here with me."

"Don't you need a copilot or a navigator or something?"

"Nah. I know where I'm going. But I do get lonely."

Corrine slid into the seat normally reserved for the first officer. The A310 had a glass cockpit, with the latest flight controls and data systems. While normal flight protocol would call for a two-member flight crew, an experienced pilot could fly the aircraft by himself. Tru was already talking in Russian with a member of the ground crew assigned to him, and in a few minutes the airplane's engines spun to life. The pilot turned to her, gave her a smile, then released the brakes and began trundling down the access ramp, taking a place in the lineup to the runway.

"I don't think we're bugged, but you never know," he told her. "I did do a check."

"Thanks," she said, as he turned the plane to the flight line.

15

While Ferguson had been talking with Van Buren, Conners had studied the sat photos and the 3-D simulation, trying to correlate it with what he had seen. The easiest way—"easiest" being a relative term—was up what seemed to be a secondary road through a canyon at the southern end of the base, but the approach was bound to be mined. Conners thought they might be able to get down a ravine on the northeast side of the mountain, since they were already beyond the lookouts who would guard it. The satellite data showed an old dumping ground at the base of the slope; a double fence ran a few yards away from it.

"That's a steep slide," said Ferguson.

"I can make it," said Conners.

"What about Daruyev?"

Their prisoner was sitting a few yards away, hands manacled and a hood covering his face.

Conners didn't say anything. It would be easiest, he thought, to kill him.

"Can't do that," said Ferguson.

"Just leave him here," said Conners.

"Nah." Ferguson looked at the satellite photos again. If they could see where they were going, it might be possible to go down the slope with the prisoner. Even so, they'd also have to worry about at least one and probably two lookout positions that had a view near the bottom.

"There's a Russian satellite that moves overhead just about 1600 hours," said Ferg. "If we figure these lookouts and everybody on the base will make themselves scarce then, maybe we can get through then."

"That gets us at the fence while it's still light," said Conners.

"Yeah?"

"Safer in the dark."

"Not going down the hill. That spot there can be seen from both the base and this lookout here."

"If that's a lookout. Still safer in the dark, Ferg. Even if these guys have night gear, which we haven't seen at all. To get there by 1600 we have to leave now."

"You feeling tired?"

"Why don't we just wait another night?"

"Longer we wait, Dad, the more chance we have of getting nailed. Besides, if we get down there and check out the place as soon as it's dark, we'll have more time to get away if the place is clean."

"You really think it is?"

"No way, or I wouldn't be going down. But it's a possibility."

"What do we do then?"

Ferguson shrugged. "We go back, get the truck, and look behind door number three." He reached into his rucksack for the bread the old woman had given them. "Hungry?"

Conners took the bread. "What I could really use is some coffee."

"What I could really use stands about five-five, and has handles right here," said Ferg.

16

 Thomas stared at the tube, watching as it filled with a list of green letters denoting files of intercepted, deciphered, and translated intercepts tangentially related to Verko. He chose one at random and opened it; it was a Russian interior ministry estimate of how long it would take to clear land mines in the region. Thomas chose another, which referred to the need for firefighting apparatus. A third was filled with gibberish, though whether that was a glitch on the American side wasn't clear.

Thomas got up from his desk. He'd piled up his papers and reports so he could pace from wall to wall; it helped him think.

Why set up a base at an old airport, he thought to himself, unless you have an airplane? And yet there were none there, at least not according to the sat photos or anything else he'd seen.

If it were big enough, Thomas realized, an airplane would be the perfect delivery system. Packed full of explosives and waste, you could crash it into a city, or maybe explode it above—death would rain everywhere.

So where was the plane?

He sat back at the computer and did a search of Interpol and the FBI looking for stolen planes. *Nada*. Then he realized that it wasn't absolutely necessary to steal an entire plane. It might make more sense to take different parts, ship them in by truck, and put the airplane together. He found different sites where plane parts could be purchased. Then he made a few calls for background information and data. A rather cranky FBI intelligence expert told him that it would be next to impossible to put a plane together from parts; not only would it cost much more than the aircraft itself, but finding people with the expertise to assemble everything would be a nightmare.

Besides, there would be records of the purchases anyway, and you'd need a ton of shell companies to obscure what you were doing.

Stubbornly, Thomas clung to the theory. The agent's objections led him to a file listing parts purchases that had been blocked because of Customs concerns, and it was on that list that he found a company whose name matched the gibberish in the NSA intercept he had opened.

Thomas hand-copied the symbols, then went back to the intercept, holding the paper up to the screen. Then he went back to the Customs database and did a general search. There were no hits. But a similar try in one of the Interpol networks led to an Algerian airline company, which Thomas already knew was on a list of possible fronts for Islamic militant groups. The gibberish was actually an acronym for an airline company name in Arabic.

He stood up from his desk, cracked all of his knuckles, then sat back down and began running requests for information on the airline and any company it did business with.

17

By the time Corrine Alston's plane arrived, the mission and its various contingencies had been fairly well mapped out. Colonel Van Buren met her at the foot of the plane, holding out his arm as she stepped somewhat wobbly onto the tarmac. Corrine smiled but didn't take his hand, walking toward the Hummer with a crisp step that belied her fatigue.

The Special Forces command unit was sequestered in a distant hangar at a far corner of the base. A pair of Hummers containing advanced communications gear was parked at one side of the space. Another vehicle—a modified civilian Ford Expedition—sat outside, data from its satellite dishes snaking through the long cable on the floor. A quartet of communications specialists sat in front of flat panels and keyboards at a station behind the Humvees. Besides being able to communicate with troops in the field and the Pentagon at the same time, the specialists could tap a few keys and get real-time information from sources that ranged from the NSA wiretaps to specially launched Predator aircraft.

It was also rumored that they could order McDonald's-to-go around the globe, though the com specialists cited the fifth amendment on the topic.

Near the communications section, a large topographical map of the target area sat in the center of two large folding tables, along with a number of satellite photos and hand-drawn diagrams depicting various phases of the operation. Van Buren's G-2 captain gave the briefing, laying out what they knew and working through the overall game plan. To circumvent detection by the Russian air defenses in the region, radar-evading Stealth fighters and special C-130s equipped to fly below radar level would be used. The attack would begin with four Stealth fighters firing on the air defenses. With the defenses secured, a company of SF troops would jump from an MC-130E, aiming to land along the southeastern end of the airstrip. A second company of SF troopers, along with technical experts and a company of men trained in handling hazardous waste, would be aboard an MC-130E, prepared either to land once the strip was secured or to jump in if necessary. Van Buren would be aboard this aircraft so that he could personally supervise the operation on the ground.

Support would be provided by an AC-130H gunship, which would train its howitzer on any pockets of resistance. Once the base was secured, the dirty-bomb facilities would be examined and secured. Depending on the exact situation—one of the reasons Van Buren wanted to be on the scene himself—it would either be blown up or merely prepared for Russian occupation. Guerrillas considered of value would be exfiltrated along with the assault troops.

The operation would be coordinated with help from the unit's specially equipped MC-17X, a jet-powered aircraft based on the C-17 and outfitted with comprehensive communications gear and a scaled-down side-looking radar adapted from the Joint Surveillance Target Attack Radar System (JSTARS) used by the regular Army to coordinate large-scale ground battles. Dubbed "Command Transport 3" in typical SF disinformation style, the one-of-a-kind MC-17X would remain beyond the border until the Stealth fighters launched their attack. At that point it could move forward and use its sensors to help the attackers.

Once the attack was under way, the Russians would undoubtedly see it. While their reaction was difficult to predict, it was likely they wouldn't be pleased. A flight of F-15 Eagles would accompany the command plane and be prepared to intervene.

The Air Force had also provided two tankers with escorts to cover any contingencies. Two long-range, Special Operations Chinooks would stand by near the border as SAR aircraft; each would have a contingent of paratroopers aboard in addition to Air Force pararescue personnel who were being temporarily plucked from another section for the night.

The planners had debated whether it might be possible to launch the airborne assault before hitting the missile defenses—the attack would tip the ground units off, costing the paratroopers the element of absolute surprise—but in the end decided it was too risky to fly the aircraft overhead without eliminating the antiair. As the intelligence officer began to explain why they were using the Chinooks rather than the Air Force Blackhawks—officially it had to do with the range, though there was a decided prejudice in favor of the massive two-rotor beasts among Van Buren's staff—Corrine held up her hand.

"Colonel, I'm going to accept that you and your people understand the logistical needs here much better than I do," she said. "What you've outlined is fine, and I don't need to cross-examine you on the nitty-gritty. Just make sure we have everything we need."

"We can accomplish the mission," he told her—though he was pleased at the vote of confidence.

"The question is—do we have the right place?" she said.

"We won't know until Ferg is inside," said Van Buren. "It's not a cautious approach, but once we have people in that space, there seemed to be no sense waiting another day or two days before launching the assault."

"Where is Mr. Ferguson now?"

"He called a while ago to tell us he was infiltrating the base," said Van Buren. "He should make his report in four hours. We'll be ready to go; it'll take us a little over two hours to launch the attack from that point. Assuming we have your permission."

"You'll get it if the waste material is there. Where are they building the bombs?"

"We're not sure yet. One of those buildings," said the colonel.

"At what point will the Russians realize something is going on?"

"Hard to say."

Van Buren turned to his Air Force staff officer, who explained that it was likely radar contacts would appear as soon as the F-117s launched their attack. By then, the C-130s would have to come up off the deck anyway. Under ordinary circumstances, the Russians would have from two to four aircraft standing by in the sector; if scrambled, they could reach the base within roughly fifteen minutes, though it was impossible to predict in advance what their readiness status would be.

"What if we're challenged?" Corrine asked.

"Escorts come up from the border as a last resort," said the captain.

Corrine knew from the earlier briefings that alerting the Russians beforehand would almost undoubtedly tip off the terrorists; the military had been penetrated by various resistance groups. She'd contact them once the attack was under way, and hope for some cooperation—though she wouldn't count on it.

They were looking at her, waiting for approval.

She thought back to her meeting with the president, the CIA director, and the others. They'd been worried about the May 10 intercept, unsure whether it was real or not—whether it was a real deadline, or just a day picked from thin air.

It was May 8.

"Proceed as you've planned," she told Van Buren. "Pending word from Mr. Ferguson."

Van Buren smiled, but as he turned from the table he felt pangs of doubt. Questions flooded into his brain: Did he have enough men. Was the timetable too tight? Were the risks too great?

He stepped back and looked at the map. Between the analysis the CIA had provided and Ferguson's scouting, it was clear that there could be no more than two or three dozen fighters at the base itself; he'd outnumber them two or three to one and have twenty times their firepower. It was a good plan.

Assuming the dirty bomb was there.

18

SOUTHERN CHECHNYA

 They'd missed a sentry point, a fact they didn't realize until they were almost on top of it. Fortunately, it was located just below the ledge they were using to skirt down toward the access road, situated to give the men at the post a good view of the north. Ferguson saw it as he cleared a rock jutting from the side; two guerrillas were kneeling forward against the rocks just five feet below him.

He froze, but either Daruyev or Conners kicked some rocks behind him. As one of the guards began to turn his head, Ferguson threw himself forward feetfirst, swinging his rifle up to use as a club. His left boot slammed into one of the sentries' shoulder as he rose, and all three men rolled in a tumble, Ferguson temporarily sandwiched between the guerrillas.

Whether because he had the advantage of surprise or fury, he managed to get to his feet without either man drawing a weapon; the butt end of his AK-74 slammed the nearest back against the rocks senseless. The other guard took a step backward, then slipped and fell down the embankment. Ferguson threw his rifle to the side and started after the man. By the time he reached the road he'd lost his own balance, sliding on his side and butt and landing a few yards behind the enemy guard, who was struggling to his feet.

The man began to run. Ferguson gave chase. After a few steps, he realized with surprise that he wasn't gaining—that in fact, the guerrilla was faster than him. He kept running, in disbelief that he had encountered someone faster than him. Ferguson had won both the hundred- and four-hundred-meter track sectional championships when he was a senior in prep school, and would probably have finished first in the states had he not had the flu the day of the meet—or so he legitimately believed, having finished second and third. He kept sprinting, expecting that the man would soon tire, but it was Ferguson who finally had to slow his pace, and by the time the man left the trail to plunge down another spot in the rugged mountain, Ferguson was so far behind him that he lost him in the wooded copse below. He stood with his hands on his hips, staring at the trees from the trail, repeating the word "fuck" over and over, still not believing that he had lost the race. Finally he retreated back up the road, walking, stretching his legs which were fairly stiff and depleted after the exertion.

Conners—who had no legacy as a track star to uphold—trussed the guerrilla whom Ferguson had knocked cold, made sure he didn't have any weapons, then climbed back up to get Daruyev.

"Let's go," Conners told him, wary that he might be planning a trick. They went back to the lookout spot; Ferguson returned shaking his head.

"Fucker outran me," said Ferguson.

"Shit," said Conners.

"Fucker outran me. Can you fucking believe that?"

"You shot him?" asked Conners, even though he hadn't heard a shot.

"Fucker outran me."

"Ferg—he got away?"

"That's what I'm saying." Ferguson slapped his hands on his hips, cursing again. He looked down at the lookout post. There was no radio, nothing in fact beyond the rifles that the two men had had. He went over to the trussed guard, who was curled over on his stomach and still out of it. Ferguson searched him slowly; the man had nothing but lint in his pockets.

"Probably means they change guards pretty regularly," said Conners.

"Yeah. That and they can count on hearing gunshots."

Neither fact was a real plus.

"Best bet is to try to get inside before our friend reaches the next post," said Ferg. "Doable?"

Conners shook his head.

"Well let's take a shot anyway," said Ferg. They were running behind, and now were at least an hour and a half from the start of the slope, which would take several more hours to descend. It was unlikely they'd make it to the base by sunset, let alone when the satellite would make it easier to approach.

"Going to be a bigger problem for the assault team," said Conners. "We're going to have to tell them."

"I don't disagree," said Ferg. "But let's make sure this is the place anyway. They won't jump if they don't hear from us."

"That supposed to be encouraging?"

Ferg laughed and went over to Daruyev. He tapped him on the shoulder.

"How's it going?" Ferguson asked him.

"If a guard ran from his post," said Daruyev, "he may not turn himself in. It would be a sign of cowardice. He'd be shot."

"Yeah, well, I'm not counting on that," said Ferg.

"He may try to ambush you."

"That'd be easier to deal with," said Ferguson, glancing at Conners. He took the Chechen's elbow and set him in motion, gently nudging him toward the incline and the trail. Conners took the lead, his eyes squinting and his body tightening almost into a squat. He disliked point, not because he was afraid of being shot, and not because he was up front, where any screwup would be obvious, but because it always left his neck buzzing. The muscles along his spinal column inevitably spasmed and pulled against the nerves somehow. There was no way to relax or stretch them, at least in his opinion, without completely dropping his guard.

About ten minutes later, they came to a shallow ridge that ran down across the mountain like an indentation on cardboard to guide a fold. The rift didn't show up too well on the sat photo, but it looked like it would cut off about a third of the hike down. It would also keep them from the view of the first lookout, though not the second. The only problem was a decent drop to the main slope about a hundred feet above the junkyard.

Ferguson studied it, trying to puzzle out if they'd be able to get down from the point where the ridge ended. According to the three-dimensional rendering, the drop-off was twenty feet nearly straight down.

"What do you think, Ferg?" asked Conners.

If they took the shortcut and couldn't figure out a way down, they'd have to come all the way back up. The mission would be scrubbed for at least a day—assuming the terrorists hadn't found them by then.

On the other hand, if they didn't chance it, the man he'd lost would sound the alarm anyway.

"Let's do it," said Ferguson. "Let me take point."

19

OUTSIDE YOPURGA, KYRGYZSTAN

 Rankin took a sip of the bottled water, swishing it through his teeth. The train had been parked on a siding about two miles out of town, waiting for reasons that weren't obvious, at least to him. The guard had been increased and now included two helicopters, which he could hear hovering a short distance away. Kyrgyzstan had supplied two truckloads of soldiers, and the Russians had a helicopter working along the track, checking for sabotage, another new development.

Rankin took another swig of the water, trying to stay awake. The waste receiving station lay about ten miles to the south; his operation was just about done. Obviously, the missing boxcar had contained the smuggled material, but he had to hang in until the bitter end.

Then he could sleep.

He ran his fingers across his scalp, digging in with his fingernails. Scratching was supposed to increase the blood flow, make your brain work better.

He could always take a pill if he had to. Ferg called them "pseudobenz"—though they worked like pep pills, they were chemically different and allegedly nonaddictive. Rankin didn't trust that, and had never actually taken one, not even to familiarize himself with the sensation. As far as he knew, Ferguson hadn't either, nor did he push the pills very much—one of the Team leader's few redeeming characteristics.

Actually, Ferguson had a few positive characteristics, but Rankin didn't like him anyway.

Rankin reached for the door handle, deciding to stretch his legs. He was just getting out of the car as the sat phone beeped.

"Rankin."

"Alston," said Corrine on the other end. "What's it look like there?"

Rankin gave her an update.

"I think we should pull the plug on the surveillance," she said. "We have some action going down."

"OK," he said.

"Corrigan will get you transportation," she said.

The line went dead before he could say anything else.

SOUTHERN CHECHNYA

 The ravine ended in a shallow chimney, almost like the section of a funnel emptying onto the more gentle slope. They had twenty feet of rope with them but no way of securing it above.

"We lower Daruyev, then you climb down," Ferguson told Conners.

"And what the hell are you going to do?"

"I'll just jump," said Ferguson.

"Well one thing's in our favor," said Conners. "It's 1355. The guards'll be hiding from the Russian satellite."

"Try to smile as we go down," Ferguson told him. "Make some Russian photo reader's day.

"Better I give him the finger."

Ferguson took the rope and went to the prisoner, wrapping the end around his chain and making a knot that Daruyev could reach to untie.

Then he took the hood off. "I want you to see where you're going," Ferguson told him.

"Thank you."

"It's going back when you're down."

The Chechen nodded reluctantly.

"You're trusting him?" said Conners, taking the rope.

"He's not going anywhere," said Ferg. "We have a deal."

Daruyev said nothing. Conners mentally calculated how he'd shoot him if the bastard ran.

Once they started to lower the Chechen, there was no way to see where he was.

They kept paying the rope out against the rock at the lip of the drop, straining as it cut into their hands. Finally, they felt a tug. He'd made it.

"You're up, Dad."

"You sure you got me?"

"If I don't, you'll be the first to know."

Conners eased himself downward, putting his legs against the side of the narrow chimney to try and ease the strain on Ferguson. Even so, Ferguson felt himself being pulled forward as he neared the bottom; his feet started to slip, and if Conners hadn't jumped the last yard or so, he might have gone over. He tossed down the rope, slung his pack and guns on his back, and told them to get out of his way.

The sides of the chimney were exposed enough for him to get down about ten feet fairly easily. When they ran out, he began working down the left side, reaching down gingerly to a decent hold and pushing his knees in at one point to maintain his balance. He'd gotten another four feet lower when he felt his grip loosening; Ferg flailed with his foot, and caught something, but then felt his other leg twist around behind him, his muscles too fatigued to follow his brain's command. Fearing he would fall on his back or head, he threw his upper body against the rock, sliding down against the mountain.

Daruyev and Conners, who'd been waiting to help him, both grabbed him as he fell, keeping him from tumbling down the slope.

"Thank you, boys," said Ferguson, spitting the dirt from his mouth.

"You are committed," said Daruyev.

"We call it crazy," said Conners, taking point down the slope.

The Russians had used the bottom of the gully as a junkyard, and the men had to pick their way over piles of wrecked chairs and office furniture as they made their way down the last fifty yards or so. The sun's shadows were starting to darken the bowl between the mountains where the base was, but if anyone happened to come up along the perimeter fence, they'd be seen easily. Ferguson and Conners stopped constantly, aware that they were pushing their luck.

Finally, Ferguson reached the perimeter fence. He could hear the sound of generators humming and some other machinery. The two large hangar buildings were across the field to his left, but the sound seemed to be coming from somewhere closer. As he craned around to get a better view, he saw a vehicle moving on the left just before the start of the runway. He slid down, watching as it moved behind the buildings to the perimeter road.

"What do you think?" Conners asked, sliding down with Daruyev.

"They're working on something," said Ferg. He took out the rad meter; its needle didn't budge. Disappointed, he slid it back into his pocket.

They could hear another vehicle approaching. Ferg and Conners settled back against two large, wrecked filing cabinets, waiting as it passed. The vehicle stopped somewhere to their right, though there was no way to get an angle and see where.

"What's in the mountain?" asked Conners, when the truck didn't appear.

"Good question. We're going to have to go in and find out."

"There's probably a cave or something, with the entrance disguised so you can't see it from above," said Conners.

Ferguson shrugged, though he agreed. "I think it's dark enough to get past that first fence at least. We can go through over there—see where it meets the ground?"

"What about our friend?" asked Conners.

"Let's leave him here and pick him up later," said Ferguson.

"You think that's a good idea?"

"Better than bringing him in, don't you think?"

They used another one of their handcuffs to tie him to a large piece of a desk near the bottom of the pile. Daruyev complained that he couldn't sit comfortably. Ferguson rearranged some of the metal refuse, and the Chechen was able to hunch his legs up under himself into a squat, which for some reason seemed more comfortable to him.

"Will you take off my hood?" he asked.

"Sorry," Ferguson said. "I'm not going to do that. Give him a drink of water," he told Conners.

"No," said Daruyev. "Shoot me."

Ferguson and Conners exchanged a glance.

"Why?" asked Ferguson.

"I'd rather die now than wait," said the Chechen.

"You're not going to get killed," said Ferg. "I told you I was taking you back."

"If the others find me, they'll kill me."

"Don't be such a pessimist."

"Mr. Ferguson, please."

"I'll come back for you, Daruyev. I told you I would."

"Should've killed him, Ferg," Conners said, as they crouched on the other side of the fence ten minutes later. "You coulda used the knife."

Ferguson changed the subject.

"If we get over the fence there, we can walk south along the strip that borders the runway. From there, we can see the other side of the slope, find out if there's a cave or something, then we can cross to the buildings."

"The post at the gate has a clear view of the runway. And God only knows what's in front of the mountain."

"Yeah. What I think we have to do is cross here, that way we can see south around where the truck ought to be. Maybe I move down closer that way, get into the shadows, see if I have to climb over."

The top of the fence had three strands of barbed wire, but he could clip it down and get over fairly easily.

"You get too close to that cave or whatever is over there, there'll be guards," said Conners.

They discussed it for a while longer, Conners in general preaching a more conservative line, Ferguson plotting a considerably bolder course. At the end, Ferg told him he'd go in, cross the runway, and check the buildings. Conners would hang back, covering him at first, and then see what he could find out about the cave. They didn't have their com devices, but they could communicate using the sat phones, which were set to vibrate rather than ring.

"Can you climb over the fence with that grenade launcher on your back?" Ferguson asked.

"If I have to."

"If it's too heavy, leave it. Once you're in, move down the ditch," said Ferguson. "They're not going to be watching the middle of the base. When you find the entrance, let me know. Your meter working?"

"It claims it is," said Conners, who had checked it at the perimeter.

"Take the Prussian blue," he told Conners, referring to the antiradiation sickness pills they carried. Though not a panacea, the drug helped ward off some effects of radiation sickness. "We get in there, we just get a general idea of what's going on. We don't have to collect autographs."

"I ain't arguing with you. What should I do with Daruyev if you get nailed?" asked Conners.

"I ain't fucking getting nailed," said Ferguson, starting away.

Conners thought to himself that he was getting old and tired, confusing caution with wisdom. His body ached, and his eyes were stinging from the lack of sleep. Worse, he could feel the thirst for a beer in his mouth.

He stood up, pushing away the fatigue as Ferg went over the fence.

Ferguson slid down to the ground next to the fence, trying to make his body as compact as possible. Empty, rock-strewn fields dotted by nubs of thick grass lay on either side of the runway. It was several hundred yards across to the buildings. To his right, the mountainside jutted out and cut off whatever was there.

He took out the rad meter, got nothing. The device had an audible alarm; he set it, put the earphone in his ear, then put it back in his pocket. He worked his legs beneath him into a crouch, then sprang across the dirt perimeter roadway, making it in two bounds. Slowly, he began to crawl toward the runway.

After nearly ten minutes, much of it spent on his belly or all fours, he reached a set of runway lights near the edge of the concrete. There were lights in the metal jacket, though one of them had been broken. Ferguson huddled near the structure, listening—he could hear voices riding over the base from the buildings, but couldn't see anyone. Nor did he have a sufficient angle on the cave entrance yet.

Ferguson hunched down and ran to the nearby ditch. He crawled along it about ten yards, looking for a good spot to cross the runway, but of course he would be exposed no matter where he went. Finally, he just thought screw it all, hopped up out of the ditch, and ran for the other side.

It took forever to get there, days out in the bright sun, exposed to the world. Finally, he landed in the other ditch, his heart thumping so loudly he wouldn't have been surprised if the people in the buildings heard it beating.

After catching his breath, he started crawling again, this time angling to his left. A light was on at the side of the building; its circle ended about twenty yards from the fence at a pile of rocks. He thought if he could get into the rocks, he'd be able to get around them, then work his way behind the building, maybe even right up to it.

But to do that, he had to cross the edge of the field, exposed not only to the front of the buildings but the guard post at the gate. He was more worried about the guard post than the buildings, even though he was probably five times as far from it; there were definitely people there. Of course, their job was to look outside the base, not inside, but Ferguson wasn't in a position to hand out demerits if they spotted him.

He continued to crawl, the earth cold against his chest. Twice he stopped to make sure the earbud was still in place, surprised that he'd found no radiation yet.

About ten yards from the flank of the building, he heard voices again. He froze, waiting for them to grow louder. When they didn't, he began inching forward again, finally getting to what he had thought were rocks but turned out to be a collection of cut-up tires. Ferguson pulled himself behind them, caught his breath.

There was another light at the back of the buildings; he'd have to walk through it to see inside.

Ferguson brushed some of the dirt from his shirt and pants, then started out again.

21

 Van Buren decided that rather than waiting on the runway, they would launch the planes and fly to a point just across the border, waiting for word. The increase in risk and logistics problems—tanker time had to be coordinated like a complicated minuet—was well worth the decrease in the time to strike. As far as possible, the flight patterns were arranged to make it appear to anyone watching—which would include the Russians—that the mission was headed toward Iraq.

Van Buren tried to fight off the adrenaline that built as his Herky Bird left the tarmac. Getting too keyed up, too hot for action, would blur his judgment. He had to be just south of the power line—just on the calm edge of the hurricane.

"Ms. Alston for you, sir," his communications specialist told him.

Van Buren nodded, and his headset clicked on. She was aboard the MH-17, which was airborne to the west.

"We're still waiting for word from the ground," she said.

"Yes we are," he said.

"I've been speaking to Corrigan. The NSA has netted two intercepts with the Russians mentioning the base. At the moment they're decrypting more material. They seem to think it's something worth checking into as well. Still not proof," she added.

"That's why we have the Team there," said Van Buren.

"Very good, Colonel. Break a leg."

"Break a leg?"

"It's a theater expression. It means good luck, which is supposed to be bad luck to say."

"Break a leg," said Van Buren.

22

SOUTHERN CHECHNYA

Ferguson leaned against the window, staring inside the large hangarlike building, trying to interpret the different shadows inside. He could see several trucks and a number of crates in the area to the left. Beyond that was a wall that seemed as if it blocked off another section of the building, maybe for use as offices or barracks.

The only way to know what was going on inside was to climb in. The window was the casement kind; it worked by a crank. Ferguson put his knife in and pushed. As the blade threatened to bend, he backed off the pressure. The window squirted open about a quarter inch, just enough for him to put his fingers on the edge and pull.

With the window open, Ferguson got a light click in his earbud: gamma radiation, though at a level barely above background.

The window was so narrow he couldn't fit through with his ruck and rifle, so he placed them against the wall where he could reach back for them and began squeezing through. He had one foot on the floor and was twisting his back to bring the other through the window when the lights went on.

Conners had remained in the shadows by the fence as Ferguson worked his way across the field toward the buildings. He didn't move until Ferguson was on the other side of the runway. Then he ran directly to the trench, his chest heaving as he slid feetfirst into the depression. One of the legs of the grenade launcher's tripod poked him as he got down, but having come that far with the weapon, he wasn't about to give it up.

There was definitely activity at the cave or whatever it was at the mountain flank;

he could hear machinery and people moving and see a whitish glow that had to be coming from floodlights. But the entrance was angled away; to see it he would have to go almost to the end of the runway.

And so he began to crawl on his hands and knees.

Ferguson let his body fall through the window to the floor, as if he were a sack of rice. He thumped loudly—but not quite as loudly as the cough of the truck motor turning over and catching about fifty feet away. He lay on his back for a moment, then turned over. Truck wheels moved on his right; another engine started up, the place smelled like exhaust. Ferguson drew himself to his knees and got up, moving quickly to his right to get behind more vehicles. There were voices, loud—he put his hand over the tailgate of a pickup and rolled over, sliding into the bed as a truck a few yards away started up. He heard the beeping of a backup signal echoing in the empty building.

Then he realized it wasn't a backup warning at all—it was his rad meter.

The door to the pickup opened, and the truck shook as someone got in. Ferguson reached his hand down for his pistol: He could take out the driver, whoever was nearby, call Conners, get the assault started before they wasted him.

Someone shouted something. Ferguson drew his gun up, ready.

The door of the pickup slammed shut. There were footsteps nearby.

Another truck started up. Ferguson leaned against the side of the pickup, waiting.

More trucks, more exhaust. He felt himself starting to gag on the fumes.

Then the terrorists were gone.

Conners had gotten about fifty yards from the spot where he'd gone into the ditch when he heard the first truck back near the building. He stopped, staring in its direction.

Where the hell was Ferguson, he wondered. He brought his gun up and began moving back in the direction he had come. Another truck appeared from the building, then another and another. They stopped in front of the second building; men came out from it and got into the vehicles. Then, with their headlights still off, they drove onto the dirt road that ran around the fence, heading toward the cave area.

Knowing Ferguson, Conners thought, he's in one of the damn trucks.

He had just started to move along the ditch again when the sat phone began vibrating.

"Yeah?" he whispered into it.

"Pay dirt," said Ferguson. His voice was only slightly lower than normal. "Gamma-wave generators around, trace stuff—they stored stuff here. The real shit must be over in the mountain."

"Where are you Ferg?"

"Inside the north building. I'm calling Van in. You at the cave yet?"

"No."

"Wait for me then. Once we have the layout psyched, we have to take out a van for them."

"You OK, Ferg?"

"Never felt better. Well, except after sex."

23

ABOARD SF COMMAND TRANSPORT 3, OVER TURKEY

 Corrine pushed the headset closer to her ear, having trouble hearing despite the fact that the volume was adjusted as loud as it would go.

"Please repeat," she told Van Buren.

"We have material at the base," he repeated. "Cesium in one of the buildings. Looks like medical waste. They're checking out the possible work site now."

"How much material?"

"We're not sure yet."

"They weren't transporting medical waste," she said.

"I understand that. They're still doing the recce. There's a possible cave at one end of the base where most of the waste may be."

Corrine pushed forward, leaning over the console in the jet. She had been looking for it all to tie into a neat bow, but that wasn't going to happen.

She had to make the call. Just her. And it wouldn't be neat, no matter what she did.

Suddenly, she realized why the president had sent her to Russia when she could have run the mission back home. Maybe the thing about proving herself was real, but more importantly, he wanted *her* to make the call on the mission—and not be pressured by the people around her at the CIA or Pentagon. If she were in the White House situation room, or the Tank, or anywhere, generals would be barking at her, cabinet members looking on, their underlings all taking notes.

Here, it was pretty much her, with no one of enough rank to awe her.

"Proceed with the mission, under my authorization." She glanced at her watch to take note of the time for her log.

SOUTHERN CHECHNYA

 Once he'd climbed through the window back outside the building, Ferguson decided that since he'd be exposed to any patrol on the perimeter as well the guard post at the gate, his best bet was to walk with his rifle slung over his shoulder, as if he were one of the terrorists.

Whether doing so fooled anyone or not, he made it to the field near the runway without being stopped or, as far as he could tell, seen. He slid down the shallow embankment, then began working south in Conners's direction, which he had from the GPS reading on the phone. The glow from the mountain bunker had grown; he guessed the trucks had gone there, though he couldn't see them or the opening itself.

Working his way south, he came to a deeper part of the ditch, then found himself walking in half a foot of water. He tried to step to the side but slipped down deeper, falling into a foot of muddy, stagnant water. He crawled up out of the sludge like a primeval salamander. Clambering onto the runway, he decided that was as good a place as any to cross. He rose, and with his first step heard the sound of a pickup truck leaving the building behind him.

With his second step, he saw the truck's headlights come on and arc across the field in his direction.

As Conners caught sight of Ferguson climbing from the ditch about twenty yards north of him, he saw the door to the north building open again and a truck emerge. But this time, the vehicle threw its lights on. Soldiers ran near the gate. Conners realized the man they'd lost earlier had finally reached the base and sounded the alarm.

The lights swung across the field as Ferguson started to run. A moment later, a machine gun began barking, a PK of some sort mounted on the back of the truck.

Conners threw the Russian grenade launcher off his back, setting it up to fire. As he did, Ferguson sprawled across the runway to his left, rolled back, and began firing his AK-74. The headlights on the pickup died, but the heavy machine continued to fire, chewing up the concrete just short of them.

Before Conners could sight the weapon, Ferguson had managed to reach the ditch. He ran to the north, away from Conners, and fired again, this time raking the side and catching one of the spare jerry cans of fuel in the back of the vehicle. The can exploded, and flames shot up, cooking off machine gun ammo in a thunderous orgy.

Conners let go of his weapon and took out the sat phone.

"We have a hot LZ," he said, warning the assault team to expect gunfire.

Automatic fire stoked up again, this time from closer to the runway.

Corrigan was on the line, and Van Buren. Conners told them they were taking fire, described the arms he'd seen, and gave the basic layout of the firefight.

"We'll be there as quickly as we can," said Van Buren calmly.

25

BUILDING 24-442, SUBURBAN VIRGINIA

 Thomas found it at the bottom of a small slip of blue paper that held a summary of a translated message dating back nearly a year.

Manila.

One of Bin Saqr's companies had rented a hangar at Manila airport. They had also bought fuel there.

He secured his room and hurried down to tell Corrigan what he had discovered. His adrenaline was flowing and he felt light-headed as he waited to be cleared through the security and in to see Corrigan. But as he walked down the hall Debra intercepted him.

"I got it, I got it, I got it," he told her, waving the small blue paper madly.

"Calm down, Thomas. Calm down," she told him. "He's really busy right now. The operation is under way."

"I have to tell him," said Thomas, and he pushed her aside, overcome by his conviction that he was right. He marched into the situation room.

As soon as he saw the analyst, Corrigan threw his hands up, trying to flag him to stop and be quiet. He was in the middle of a four-way conversation with Colonel Van Buren, Corrine Alston, and Conners. The Team had been discovered at the Chechen base.

"Manila," Thomas hissed. "They're going to Manila, and then LA."

Corrine must have heard him, for she asked what was going on.

"We're working up new intelligence," said Corrigan, trying to sort everything out. His brain felt like it had taken some of the rounds exploding near Conners.

"We'll be at the target inside forty minutes," said Van Buren. "We'll get them out."

"Good," said Corrine.

Thomas stood on the balls of his feet, bobbing slightly. Debra stood behind him, shaking her head.

"All right. What do we have?" Corrigan asked.

Thomas smoothed out the paper and explained. Corrigan's brain was suffering from the effects of far too much coffee and far too little sleep; he couldn't quite follow the logic.

"You were supposed to look for an airplane," said Corrigan.

"Yes, but here—they have a hangar in Manila. They've purchased jet fuel," said Thomas.

"What do they need fuel for if they don't have an airplane?" said Corrigan.

"*That's my point!*"

Corrigan put up his hand. "Okay," he told Thomas. "See if you can flesh this out with more information. And Thomas, you can use the phone, right? You can call me, rather than running down here."

"Is there one in my office?" asked Thomas, honestly not remembering seeing it.

26

 As soon as the truck blew, Ferguson turned and began running down the ditch toward Conners. As he reached him, a flare ignited above; the night went crimson, then bluish white, then quickly black.

"Cheap Russian flares," he said, spotting Conners coming toward him.

"Stay down, Ferg. There's another truck heading toward the top of the runway."

"You call in Van Buren?"

Before Conners could answer, one of the guerrillas in the back of the truck began firing a machine gun. It took a few moments for the Americans to realize they weren't being targeted.

"The assault group's on their way. Forty minutes, give or take."

The machine gun stopped. The truck raced by, not fifty yards away, speeding toward the southern end of the runway.

"Can we get the missile van from here?" asked Ferguson.

"If I knew where it was, I could tell you," said Conners.

"In that general direction," said Ferg.

"You sound more and more like an officer every day, Ferg."

"It ought to be near the gate," said Ferguson, starting in that direction.

Conners took the launcher and bumped behind him, trying to keep up. The Chechens, meanwhile, seemed to have convinced themselves that their enemy was at the southern side of the base and were concentrating there. Every so often, someone fired an automatic weapon at the shadows.

Ferg and Conners were just about at the end of the ditch when the Chechens lofted another flare. They hunkered down, but several rounds of automatic fire showed they'd been spotted.

"Let's go, let's go," said Ferguson, jumping up and running. Conners fired about half his clip, then hustled after Ferguson, who crossed the paved area and threw himself into the weeds and rocks beyond the start of the runway. Something green lit up the area to the right, and the ground to the right of them churned into dust and rocks.

Conners slapped the grenade launcher down and fired into the burbling stream of tracers. He got off two rounds before the maelstrom swung lower. Conners found himself in a sea of dust and debris. He couldn't breathe. Coughing, he fell on his back, struggling to get away.

A large rock splintered from one of the shells hit him in the leg, smacking him so hard he flew back from the launcher. Pelted by fresh dirt, he had started to get up when a piece of metal hit his chest. He screamed with the pain, even as it pushed him over into the ground. Then something began dragging him away.

Ferguson had grabbed him and started to retreat back toward the ditch, only to find his path swirling with the 23 mm slugs spit out by the gun. He changed direction, pulling Conners back near the fence where they'd come in as the ZSU-23 churned up the field near the runway.

"I couldn't nail it," said Conners.

"Yeah," said Ferguson. "F-117s'll have to get it on their own. You all right?"

"Beat to shit."

"Bleeding?"

"That or I pissed in my pants."

Automatic fire stoked up again. Headlights circled the field, and a searchlight, apparently on a vehicle, appeared at the far end of the base, near the entrance.

"Think you can make it over the fence where we came in?" Ferguson asked. "I think it's probably quieter for us there."

"My leg's fucked up," said Conners.

"How fucked up?" Ferguson took out his phone, pushed out the antenna arm, and hit power. But the phone didn't come on.

"I can walk." Conners pushed it under him and rocked a bit. The pain increased, but they couldn't stay there, and he thought he might be able to hobble away.

Ferguson rapped the phone against the ground, trying to get it to work.

"I can tell you're Irish," said Conners.

"Give me your phone."

Conners reached for it, but it was gone; he'd lost it somewhere in the confusion.

They ducked as lights swung toward them. Ferguson shoved the phone back into his pocket, then belatedly slipped a fresh clip into his gun.

"Patrol," warned Conners. "They're going to the ditch."

"Let's get some distance between us and them," said Ferguson. He grabbed the back of Conners's jacket and pulled him upright, getting Conners to lean on him as they ran along the fence toward a spot he'd seen earlier where they could crawl under. Ferguson found it, then held it up for Conners as he squeezed through. The trooper's pant leg had been torn to shreds, and Ferg guessed his leg had been mangled as well. Ferguson grabbed his side, working his body against Conners's to push him through, then sliding under himself. He got under the soldier and levered him upward, tottering forward to the outer fence.

"Gonna be mines around here," Conners groaned.

"You think?"

"Ferg."

"We're clear. Come on," said Ferguson, pushing him to the fence. The ravine they'd come down earlier was somewhere nearby, but he couldn't find it. His head raced. Something seemed to move above him; Ferguson pushed up, raising his rifle, but there was nothing there.

The ZSU-23 started firing again, its four barrels spitting great bolts of lightning across the field and runway.

"*If moonshine don't kill me, I'll live 'til I die*," mumbled Conners, singing the words to the song.

"Stay with me, Dad."

"It's there. The hole is there," said Conners, pounding on the fence. He surprised himself by lifting his body up on the fence. Suddenly he realized his leg didn't hurt anymore—he pulled himself upright, then rather than sliding below he climbed up and over, holding himself carefully before starting back down.

Ferguson crawled through and met him below. The waste area where they'd left Daruyev was up about ten yards on his left. Conners started along the fence, leaning against it for support. As he went, he took out his pistol.

"Daruyev, we're back," yelled Ferguson.

"No!" yelled the Chechen.

A hail of bullets followed. Ferguson and Conners threw themselves to the ground as the fusillade tore through the fence.

"You fucks," shouted Ferg. He jumped up, finger nailing the trigger on his gun. Fire burned his brain—he was the gun, spitting bullets, ferocious fury thunder mangling the twisted metal and rocks before. The magazine clicked empty—he changed it without thinking, still the bullets smashing through the guerrillas who'd ambushed his prisoner.

Conners had left the grenade launcher and its charges, but he still had his hand grenades. He took one from his jacket, set it, and yelled to Ferguson to duck as he heaved it as far as he could.

Ferguson didn't hear the warning. The blast slapped him onto his back.

By the time he got up, a fresh flare shot up from the base behind them. In the grayish white shadowlight, Ferguson saw Daruyev twenty yards away, slumped over his bound hands. There were bodies all around him. Ferguson watched in the fitful light of the flare, expecting Daruyev to move. When he didn't, the CIA officer began clambering up the pile of debris, making his way toward Daruyev.

Three figures started down the slope, maybe seventy yards away, silhouetted by the light of the flare. Ferguson hunched down, carefully took aim, then burned his clip on them, folding the three guerrillas in half.

Daruyev remained slumped over. Ferguson reached to push his head up, to see if he was breathing, but as he did his fingers felt wet and mushy, and he realized two or three bullets had gone into the back of the Chechen's skull, fired from so close that they had come clean through. He let go and began making his way back down.

Conners rested against the fence, waiting, a grenade in his hand. A new song played in his head, but he couldn't place the words; they were tangled somehow, confused. His leg didn't hurt, but his head pounded from the inside out, as if he had a ticking bomb there.

"Dad, let's go," said Ferguson, reaching him.

"Yeah," said Conners.

Somehow, Ferguson had kept his knapsack through all of the confusion. He pulled it off his back, sorting through the contents as he searched for more clips for his rifle. He had the laptop and the roll-printer, another shirt, a second pistol with ammo, first-aid kit—

"Ferg!" insisted Conners, reaching for him. "We're sitting ducks here."

"All right, let's move," said Ferguson, finally finding a pair of clips at the bottom. He cinched the bag. He reached for the fence, then lost his balance and fell through—the Chechen gunfire had ripped through one of the posts, and the metal swung open like a rusty screen door.

Ferguson helped Conners through, then found the hole in the second fence. The SF soldier's cheek was wet; he'd been hit somewhere in the face and was bleeding. Conners felt an overwhelming urge simply to lie down and sleep, but he knew he couldn't, knew in his head that he had to watch out for Ferguson. They began working their way toward the cave area, their goal now not recce, but survival. Meanwhile, the Chechens gathered for a sweep across the base, starting from the top of the runway.

The fence ended with a roll of barbed wire and a large cement column that had been set into the rocks. They moved into the tumble of rocks slowly, looking for a place they might hide until the assault began. Ferguson's boot kicked a low cement curb in the darkness, and he tripped, just barely getting his hands out in front of him as he fell. He pushed up, grunted at Conners to warn him, then realized there was a door directly ahead of him on the side of the mountain, camouflaged by an overhang and a boulder at the side.

Something moved on his right. A voice asked in Chechen who he was.

Ferguson froze, then slipped his right hand back to his belt, grabbing his knife. The Chechen said something again; it sounded like a name, and Ferguson—the rifle now in his left hand pointed at the shadow—took a chance and repeated part of it, clipping it off as if he were annoyed.

This elicited more words from the guard, enough so that Ferguson finally got a good idea where he was, ten feet away. The man's legs started to crunch the gravel of the narrow path.

Ferguson slipped down, waiting. The man walked forward, cursing his companion for running off and leaving his post.

In the darkness, Ferguson's aim was off, and rather than pulling the knife around the front of the man's neck and cutting him cleanly, he jabbed it on the side, pulling down to the left as he did. But his momentum as he leapt was so great the blade severed the external carotid artery as well as the jugular and sliced the man's windpipe. Ferguson heard him gurgle, felt the convulsions as the man tried desperately to grab back his life.

Conners waited a few yards away, clutching his pistol. His head had begun to feel light, and when Ferguson rose and called to him, he thought he said it was time to grab a beer. Conners stumbled on the path, nearly tripping over the dead guard before he reached Ferguson by the doorway.

"Let's see what's inside," said Ferg, nudging it open. He could hear machinery humming somewhere ahead of them. Ferguson took a few steps forward, his eyes adjusting to the dim light. He was on a narrow ramp leading to a well-constructed bunker. There was light beyond, and a much larger hangar area. The facility had been built by the Soviets, not to house their spy planes, but rather a small squadron of planes equipped with hydrogen bombs. It had been camouflaged to avoid detection from the air, or space for that matter.

"Dad, you with me?" he asked Conners, who was still back by the door.

Conners grunted. "My head's fucked up," he told the CIA officer when he came back to him. "Something smacked it."

"Let's find a place for you to stay while I reconnoiter," Ferguson told him as he tossed the first-aid pack to him. "Our friends'll be landing soon."

"I'm OK, Ferg," Conners insisted.

"Don't be a crybaby," said Ferguson. They moved down the ramp, toward the light.

Samman Bin Saqr yelled at the team that was supposed to be readying the plane. The men were in the way, fumbling at their duties rather than moving expeditiously. Time was of the essence; from the alarms that had been sent, he thought the infidel Russians had discovered the operation and sent soldiers to infiltrate it. Soon they would call in bombers for the attack.

In his fury he considered changing his target and flying to Moscow rather than striking the American paradise as he planned. But that was vanity, jealousy at being found—it was not what God had directed.

Bin Saqr mastered himself, calmly listening while Jehid, who was in charge of preparing the aircraft for flight, reported what needed to be done to finish placing the casks of high-alpha material along the outer skin, where the explosives would shatter them and produce a radiological cloud. At the same time, more work remained to set the fail-safe charges in the airplane's freight compartment.

There was too much to be done. The flight preparation alone stretched a half hour, and it could not be done safely in the hangar.

And then Allah whispered the solution to Bin Saqr, as he had many times in the past.

"Get the work teams outside," Bin Saqr told Jehid. "Do everything at once. As soon as we are sure we can take off, we will."

"Some of the material may not be in place."

"That is immaterial now."

"But it means working in the darkness. It may take longer—"

"We will leave in fifteen minutes," snapped Samman Bin Saqr.

Jehid turned quickly and sprinted to his work teams.

Sound echoed oddly against the concrete of the hangar. There were people and machines somewhere beyond where they were, but Ferguson couldn't quite figure out exactly where. He walked up the ramp into a long open area, where he saw a set of metal railings blocking off a section below. Light shone up through the space. Ferguson slid on his belly to get a look, pushing along the floor like a swimmer gliding across an Olympic-sized pool.

An airplane sat in the massive space below. He craned his head, trying to get a view of the aircraft, a large 747 that was being worked on. Men were running around it frantically. There were two large lifts near the rear of the plane and a ladder up to the flight deck. A welder was working on something near the wingroot on the right side.

"Fuck," said Ferg, backing away.

"What'd you see?" asked Conners, back by the ramp. The side of his head was caked with blood. His leg looked worse.

"They have a plane," said Ferguson. "I bet it's packed with waste."

Ferguson took off his backpack and pulled out the rad meter. He registered enough gamma and alpha radiation to sound the alert; the isotope ID flashed: Cesium.

And uranium. They were taking both gamma and alpha radiation, with a bit of beta thrown in for good measure.

"Don't breathe," he told Conners. The REM equivalent was pushing over a sievert.

"Very funny."

"I want to look at that plane," said Ferguson. "There's only a bit of uranium— some sort of spill. I bet there's more on the plane, or in it."

"Come on—don't be crazy. There'll be guards all over," said Conners.

Ferguson slid back to the front, adjusting the meter's sensitivity as he tried to work out where the waste was. The workers were moving—there was a loud cranking sound, and a rush of air.

The bastards were going to take off.

Ferguson began moving along the railing, looking for a way down. Conners, meanwhile, had gotten down on his hands and belly—his knees wouldn't hold him—and pushed himself out to see what was going on. He saw Ferguson reach a stairwell at the end of the room.

"Ferg," he croaked, trying to stop him.

Ferguson didn't hear him, and wouldn't have stopped if he had. He slid over the rail onto the steps, not daring to jump. A ramp ran alongside them. At the foot there were barrels and crates, most empty, which had once contained waste.

The large jet just barely fit in the space; its tail towered over two rows of large crates at the back of the hangar. There were toolboxes and other gear scattered along the floor at the left.

Ferguson dropped behind the crates at the back as two men approached. He pointed his gun in their direction, but the men stopped at a tool case, picking it up by the handles at the side and walking toward the front. He could see as he peered around the side that the door to the hangar was open.

Ferguson thought he might be able to shoot out the tires of the plane, but he'd have to get under it to do so. He took a step out from the crate, then saw feet walking toward him. He took a step and jumped onto the side of a mobile ramp, flattening himself against it. Conners crawled around above, reaching the ramp next to the stairs. He pulled himself up on the railing, hugging it as he slid down.

Ferguson climbed up the scissor apparatus that lifted the mobile ramp, then pulled himself onto the platform, above the Chechen workers who'd come for more tools. He aimed his rifle at them, no more than six feet away, but once more the workers were too absorbed to notice him. When they turned around and walked toward the front, Ferguson went to the machine to climb down and saw Conners at the end of the ramp next to the stairs.

Ferguson angrily waved at him to stay down, but the sergeant didn't seem to notice. He started hissing at him. When that didn't work, Ferguson started to climb over the rail. But he put his hand on the joystick controlling the platform, inadvertently telling it to descend. He jerked his hand back but the machine continued downward, the lever locked. Conners saw him finally, scanned the nearby area, then limped toward him, reaching the platform as it hit its stop.

Both men waited, guns ready. No one appeared—the noise of the platform was just one more background sound of people doing their jobs to get the plane ready.

"Hey," said Ferg. "You think we can shoot out the tires?"

"Why don't we toss a couple of grenades inside?" suggested Conners. He bent over the platform.

"Now you're talking," said Ferguson, pulling him onto the scaffold and standing up to hit the lever. The machine began to rise.

Conners reached to his vest for his grenade, patting his chest before realizing he wasn't wearing his combat webbing; he wasn't in his SF gear, of course. He reached down to his pocket for the grenade he'd had back at the fence, but it was gone. He'd already used it.

"Get the grenades ready," said Ferguson, as the ramp hit its stop.

"I only have a pair of flash-bangs," said Conners.

"All right," said Ferguson. "We'll get the tires and maybe the engines once the action gets close. In the meantime, let me check out what's going on inside here." They were just below the rear cargo door of the plane—a door that had been added as part of the operation to turn the large jet into a flying dirty bomb. Ferguson turned and looked inside the jet. The space was narrow, lined with metal containers—actually carefully packed radioactive materials and explosives arranged in a precise pattern to maximize the spread of the material at detonation. Ferguson climbed inside, scaling a row of boxes that had been bolted to the floor; he felt as if he were inside a kid's giant Erector set.

Conners heard someone yelling, then saw a strobe light flashing against the walls. The plane started to move.

Not wanting to leave Ferguson behind, Conners screwed up his strength and got to both feet, the pain pounding every muscle and nerve and fat cell in his body. He threw his pistol into the hold and lurched across the open space onto the plane platform.

Ferguson ducked as the gun flew in, then fell with the shifting momentum of the aircraft. He got up, grabbed Conners, and started to push him toward the open door space, ready to jump back, but it was already too late—the platforms were a good ten feet away.

27

OVER CHECHNYA

Fifteen miles from the airfield, Major Greg Jenkins put his hand on the control for his F-117A's IRADS system, jacking up the contrast on the target. During the Gulf War, the Stealth fighters had had to rely on laser-guided bombs, which robbed the pilot of some flexibility during the attack as the system had to lase its target. But Jenkins and his flightmates were firing GPS-guided munitions. Their targets had been preprogrammed before takeoff, and while the pilot could override them, his gear showed him there was no reason to. He got a steering cue on his HUD, the computer compensating for the wind.

As he swung to the proper position, Jenkins hit the red button on his stick, which gave the computerized bombing system authority to drop the bomb. The bay doors behind him opened with a clunk—air buffeted the plane, and warning lights blinked on the dash, reminding him he was a sitting duck, an easy and very visible radar target as long as the plane's symmetry was broken.

This was the longest part of the flight. Even though it took the automated systems only a few seconds to eject the bombs, in these few seconds Jenkins was the most mortal of men, obvious to the radars and a slow, barely maneuverable black target in a light sky.

And then the buffeting stopped with a loud clunk, and the warning lights were gone, and though he was too busy to glance over his shoulder—and the view too obstructed to see—Major Jenkins knew he had just nailed his prize and would live to celebrate it.

Van Buren listened as the F-117A pilots checked in, announcing that their missiles had been launched. The Hercules with the first drop team was late, about three minutes behind schedule. But they were into it now, no turning back; the gunship was just coming on station, its first task the van that Ferguson was supposed to hit.

His hope that Ferg had somehow made it disintegrated a few seconds later as the gunship pilot reported a direct hit on the van, with "shitloads of secondaries."

As the gunship began mopping up the two ZSU-23s left at the north end of the field, Van Buren said a silent prayer for his friend and Conners, then made himself get up and check on his men.

SOUTHERN CHECHNYA

The plane had already gotten outside the hangar when Ferguson heard the first rumble. There were shouts from below and explosions in the distance.

"Let's get to the cockpit," he told Conners. "We'll stop the bastards from taking off."

Conners grunted and started after him. As Ferguson began to run, he heard a sound similar to a vacuum cleaner and felt the aircraft starting to shake. The dim light narrowed. The engines whined to life.

"The door," yelled Conners.

Ferguson tripped as he ran. He grabbed his rifle, but then stopped himself from firing as the mechanism slapped shut. They were in the dark.

"There's got to be some sort of switch if it's powered," Ferguson told Conners. "We'll get it later if we have to. Let's try to get in the cockpit. Come on."

Ferguson reached the wall at the front of the plane and slapped at it with his hands, trying to feel for a ladder or something that would take him up to the flight deck, which on a 747 sat at the top of the plane, almost like the second story of a two-story building. There was no ladder, and he couldn't find a handhold. He went to the side, found a place to climb up, but lost his balance and tumbled to the floor of the plane, smacking his head so hard as he landed that he temporarily lost consciousness.

Conners, unable to climb, felt around with his hands for a ladder or steps. As he did, he smelled metal burning. A loud secondary explosion sounded in the distance, rocking the jet.

"Get down here, you guys," he called to the assault team, as if they might hear him over the engines on the plane. He stepped back, pulled his rifle up, and aimed it at the door. But as he started to press the trigger, the plane jerked forward. Conners lost his balance, and the three slugs buried themselves harmlessly in the material wedged along the roof of the fuselage.

OVER CHECHNYA

The AC-130 located not one but two different active antiaircraft batteries. The first shot from its howitzer nailed one of the ZSU-23s in the center of its chassis, causing the four barrels to fold in on themselves midshot. Flames crescendoed in every direction, red and yellow streamers that unfolded like the petals of a flower.

The pilot of the AC-130 U "U-boat" had to come hard south to get a shot on the second battery, which had been located to the east of the camp proper. As he pulled the big Herk on to her mark, he saw that the Chechens had moved an airplane onto the end of the runway.

They were committed to the flak dealer, which began spraying lead in their direction. The pilot got a cue on his target screen and hit the trigger, but the shot trailed off as the Herk hit a sudden updraft current. He worked the stick and the rudder as if he were piloting a World War II dive bomber, homing in on its prey. Sparks flew across his bow, but he had the shot. The large aircraft shuddered, then seemed to push forward and simultaneously dip her right wing. They'd been hit—but they'd also nailed the ZSU-23-4.

30

Samman Bin Saqr realized with the first explosion that he had miscalculated badly—it was not the Russians who had found him, but the Americans. As calmly as he could, he worked the plane, starting the engines, securing the hatches, moving forward on the runway.

His flight engineer had not come aboard, but that was a minor matter. He began to turn as he reached the northern end of the runway, his right wing nearly scraping the side of the building as he turned. He hesitated for a second, fearful that in his ineptitude he had failed Allah. But then God smiled at him—he cleared the building and had the nose of the plane pointing into the wind, directly down the runway.

"Let us proceed," he told his copilot, Vesh Ahmamoody. Vesh reached for the thrusters, propelling the flying bomb into the sky.

ACT V

Mischief, thou art afoot,
Take thou what course thou wilt.

—Shakespeare, *Julius Caesar*, 3.2.260–1

Rankin settled into the seat on the upper deck of the Antonov An-22, trying to compensate for the thin padding by adding one of the blankets he'd found in the overhead compartment. He hoped to start catching up on his sleep, though between the seat and the loud snores of Guns and Massette behind him—somehow managing to pierce the drone of the four turboprops on the wings—his prospects were rather dim.

The An-22 the three SF soldiers were flying in had been designed in the 1960s as a long-distance freight hauler for the Soviet military; this particular version had ferried T-62 tanks around the country for nearly two decades before being surplused and then sold—illegally, though its papers demonstrated otherwise—to a small airfreight company based in Germany. The company had gone bankrupt, and one of its creditors ended up with the plane; the creditor had in turn sold it at auction, and within a few months the aircraft belonged to a private company partly owned by a man known to have connections with the Egyptian secret service. These connections were actually a cover for his true relationship with the American CIA, a connection that had allowed Corrigan to arrange for the Team's transport to Japan relatively quickly.

Though in Rankin's opinion, delays that would have meant a more comfortable flight and something to eat would have been well worth the time. He hoped they'd be able to grab something in Tokyo before going back to the States. His end of the mission had been pretty much a wipeout. Worse, he knew from Corrigan that Ferguson and Conners had hit pay dirt and was pissed that he had missed it.

The plane hit a run of turbulence and began skittering up and down like a kite.

When it finally settled down, Rankin bunched the blanket up behind his head to take another go at trying to sleep. As he closed his eyes, his sat phone buzzed.

"Rankin, we need you in Manila, right away," said Corrigan. "We're getting a flight for you into Tokyo."

"Yeah?"

"We're still pulling the details together. The assault's under way, but we have information on a hangar in Manila. It fits with the LA theory. Things are fluid."

"I'm hungry," Rankin told him.

Corrigan couldn't quite compute what the comment meant. He took a shallow breath, then stuttered. "What are you talking about?"

"I want to get some food in Japan," Rankin told him. "I'm starving."

"Shit, Rankin, I don't have time for your crap," said Corrigan, killing the line.

2

Van Buren didn't understand what they were telling him at first. There was so much happening around him and on the ground that it was difficult to keep everything in place.

"There's a plane—it's taking off," repeated the Air Force lieutenant. "It's in the air."

"What kind of plane?" asked the colonel. The first assault team had just reached the ground. Resistance appeared unorganized.

"A big jet—747. It's off—they're getting away."

"Tell the escort flight," said the colonel. "Get someone on him. Tell Ms. Alston."

Corrine sat at the edge of her seat in the MC-17, listening to Air Force Major Daniel Gray explain what the AWACS data meant. Gray was tasked with coordinating the SF group's actions with any and all Air Force units that were part of the operation; much of his job involved acting as a translator for the different parts of the mission.

Russian fighters had been alerted to the activity and were now within ten minutes of the Chechen base. They were not answering radio hails. Meanwhile, the aircraft that had taken off from the base was a 747 and seemed to be heading for Iran. More than likely it was an Iranian aircraft being used as an escape plane by the Islamist terrorists.

Or, wondered Corrine, was it loaded with radioactive material?

"Where do you want our warplanes?" Gray asked.

Corrine could send the F-15s to protect her people, or attempt to shoot down the plane; she couldn't do both.

Doubts and guesses crowded into her mind—what if the 747 crashed in a populated area? She pushed the questions away but hesitated a split second longer.

What would the president do, she asked herself. That's why she was there—to make the decision he would and take the heat for it.

"I want to talk to the Russian commander," said Corrine.

"There's no guarantee he'll listen," replied the major.

"I understand that. In the meantime put enough F-15s between the MiGs and our ground force to protect them," she said. "Tell the flight leader he has my permission to use whatever force he needs to protect our people. He can shoot the bastards down if he has to."

"Yes, ma'am. But I'll have to commit all four fighters to that intercept," said the major. "The 747 is going to get away."

"Send our escort to pursue the plane," she said.

"We're pretty far off, and that'll leave us defenseless. If the Russians decide to come and get us—"

"*Go!*"

"They're on their way."

Scorpion flight leader Major Cliff Salerno put his hand to the throttle and selected afterburner, goosing his F-15C onto the new coordinates. Scorpion One's Pratt & Whitney F100s punched out roughly twenty-four thousand pounds of thrust, rocketing the plane over the speed of sound. The fierce acceleration slammed Salerno back against his ejection seat, the laws of motion desperate to remind him that he was still under their domain.

The Eagle pilot checked his radar, sorting out what was going on in the air ahead. He was crossing over Armenia headed southeast; the assault team was striking a base to his left. The AWACS controller gave him an intercept vector for a 747-type aircraft, which ought to be roughly 150 miles off his right wing.

"Your instructions are to terminate its flight," added the controller.

Salerno repeated the instructions, then double-checked with his wingmate, Captain Jed "Patsy" Klein, commanding Scorpion Two. Among the many calculations the two men now began was an assessment of their fuel status—they had to make sure they'd have enough to get back to a tanker or risk turning their multimillion-dollar interceptors into gliders. The 747, which was still too far ahead to be picked up by the Eagles' APG-70 radars, was over the east coast of Lake Sevan.

Armenia, which had been part of the Soviet Union before the downfall of the Communists, had no air force to speak of and provided very little threat to the American planes. The Russians, meanwhile, were concentrating on the Chechen base; the 747 was theirs—if they could catch it.

The controller gave them fresh data for their intercept, adding that the 747 was flying exceptionally low in the mountains. At present course and speed they should have it on their screens within five minutes.

The two aircraft were at twenty-six thousand feet above sea level, pushing toward a mountain that rose roughly thirteen thousand feet. Both planes were carrying four AMRAAM AIM-120 medium-range air-to-air missiles and two shorter-range ATM-9 Sidewinders. The Eagles were also equipped with 20 mm cannons. Any of those weapons would suffice to take down the airliner.

"Be advised also we have a flight of Iranian MiG-29s operating on the northern border of Iran," said the controller. "They haven't reacted, but they're there."

"Scorpion One," acknowledged Salerno.

Ferguson and Conners were tossed around the back of the plane like golf balls in a tumbling footlocker as the 747 zigged and zagged southward. Conners took his pistol out and fired wildly, but if the bullets made it through the heavy canisters of waste material strapped around the interior portion of the fuselage, they had no effect on the plane. Ferguson shouted at him to stop, but Conners kept firing until the clip ran out.

"Stop!" Ferguson yelled, crawling toward him in the pitch-black darkness. "Stop!"

"Ferg? What?"

Ferguson reached Conners and touched his arm. It was wet with blood from his head wound.

"Conners, stop shooting," Ferg told him. "Let's figure this out."

"Where are you?"

"This is me holding your arm," Ferguson told him. "What, you think I'm a ghost?"

The aircraft jerked hard left and descended sharply, then twisted on its wing back to the right. Ferguson fished in the pack and retrieved the flashlight. He shined the beam on Conners's face; the SF sergeant was pale and disoriented.

"Fuckin' cold, Ferg," said Conners.

"Yeah. Let's figure this out," Ferguson told him. "We'll have to find a way to climb up to the flight deck at the front. There ought to be a door there."

Salerno acknowledged the fresh vector from the AWACS, then took a long, steady breath, reminding himself to stay calm. His wingmate, offset a few thousand feet in altitude and about a mile to his right, reported that he had a contact on his radar.

It was too soon to be their target, Salerno knew, but he told him to query it anyway. Like all interceptors, the Eagles carried identification friend-or-foe gear that electronically "asked" another airplane who it was. Friendly aircraft and commercial flights were programmed to respond with a code that would tell the fighter pilot who they were. In this case, the IFF signal came back indicating that the plane was a civilian flight, which was confirmed by the AWACS controller. The aircraft was an innocent 767 en route to Iran from Russia; they let it go.

A minute later, the controller's voice came back, now two octaves higher. "They're asking for help—the Iranians are scrambling—their defenses—the MiGs are on an intercept. We have more planes coming off Tabriz."

The controller took a breath of air, then resumed more calmly, updating the position of the 747. It had changed course and was now flying directly south.

"Very low," added the controller. "He's going to hit the mountains."

"I think I have him," said Salerno, the image flashing in his brain as well as the radar. He took another long breath. The big plane was a little over sixty miles away, too far to launch the AMRAAMS.

Salerno put his pedal to the metal. The Iranian MiGs were coming north, SAM radars were switching on, and the Russians were sending something south—he pushed his head forward, his fist locked around the stick, willing the fat 747 into the targeting reticule on his HUD. He needed more closure—he had to build momentum for the missile and get closer to the target to fire. He had the damn thing; it was a question of taking his time, hanging in long enough to fire.

His radar warning receiver picked up one of the approaching MiGs trying to target him. Salerno's consciousness flicked away the threat, considering it irrelevant.

"I'm spiked, shit," said Klein. He began defensive maneuvers.

The 747 moved into the box on the HUD, the aircraft's avionics closing its fist on the fat target.

"Yes," said Salerno, and he pushed the trigger on the stick, launching the AMRAAM toward the plane. He dished a second and punched the mike button to tell his wingmate that the missiles were away, but the transmission was overrun by a new warning.

"Missiles in the air!" said the AWACS controller. "Break ninety."

"I'm spiked!" said Klein again.

Everything ran together in Salerno's head. Two Hawk missiles had been launched from a ground station near the border; the MiGs were firing Russian-made homers, long-range radar missiles. Klein turned to engage them. The 747, meanwhile, had disappeared from the screens. Salerno started to press toward the mountains where the aircraft had been flying, then heard Klein call for help.

"I'm coming," he told his wingman, tucking hard in his direction.

s it down?" Corrine asked Major Gray.

"The AWACS thinks so; the missile was launched before the 747 disappeared from its screen. But we can't confirm the kill; there's too much else going on."

"We need to know," she said.

"Our Eagles have to get back, or they'll run out of fuel over Iran. One of them is being targeted by the Iranians already. Believe me, that's the last place we want a pilot," said Gray.

"All right," Corrine told him. "Alert CentCom to what's going on. The *Nimitz*'s planes should extend their patrols around Iran just in case."

Corrine leaned back in the seat. Things were actually going fairly well. The Russians were not happy about the appearance of the American assault team at the Chechen base, but were grudgingly holding off from firing at them. Van Buren's people had secured the airstrip and all but one of the buildings; he was about to land and supervise the rest of the operation.

At that point, they could sort out exactly what they had. Hopefully, they'd find Ferguson and Conners hiding with broken telephones.

Corrine took a deep breath, trying to relax.

Samman Bin Saqr struggled to hold the nose of the big aircraft level as the missile exploded a hundred yards away, sucked just off course by his defensive chaff and ECMs.

His decision to call on the Iranians for assistance was not without consequences, for the now the Iranians were hailing him with orders of their own—he was to change course and fly to their main airport near Tehran.

Samman Bin Saqr did not acknowledge. He was gambling that they would not shoot him down in the next ten minutes, and that was all the time his calculations showed he needed to fly out of their range. At that point, if his radar showed that he had no contacts following him, he would press the button on the altered Ident or identifier module. The black box would tell anyone who cared to ask—electronically, of course—that the plane was a duly registered Sri Lankan aircraft.

Bin Saqr would then swing onto the course that the plane which corresponded to that identifier routinely took. Assuming that his operatives had followed their orders—and at this point, he could only assume that—he would be free of pursuers.

A warning blared in the cockpit—he was precariously low. A mountain loomed ahead, its peak a hundred feet above his nose. Samman Bin Saqr touched the yoke, trying to squeeze through the pass on the right. He saw the rocks and closed his eyes, trusting that Allah would not let him die before his mission was complete.

Salerno pulled the big F-15 through a hard turn, sending nearly seven gees slamming against his body. His pressurized suit compensated quickly, fighting to equalize the forces on his body and keep his brain swimming in just the right amount of blood. As the pressure began to ease, Salerno found himself twenty miles from one of the Iranian MiGs, and closing fast. His wingmate was ahead of the MiG, trying to shake it off before it could fire.

"Firing," said Salerno calmly, pulling the trigger on the MiG.

An AMRAAM clunked off the rail, its engine igniting with a fiery flash. The missile's onboard radar asked for an update from the Eagle as it closed in on its quarry at just over Mach 4. It made a slight correction, then sent the Iranian pilot to meet his maker.

In the meantime, Klein had turned the tables on a second Iranian, knifing downward, then using his superior engines to thrust himself onto the MiG's tail before the other pilot could quite figure out where he was going. Klein closed the gap, his Sidewinder ready to launch. The MiG-29 jinked left, then rolled hard back the other way, the airplane cutting an almost-perfect Z in the sky. Klein hesitated, not quite in a good firing position but aware that juicing the throttle too much might send him flying in front of the Iranian. Finally, as the indicator on the Sidewinder growled at him to fire already, he realized he had the MiG nailed and goosed the Sidewinder into the air.

The Iranian tried jinking right, but the American air-to-air missile was nearly in his tailpipe when he started to turn. The explosion ripped the backbone out of the plane; the enemy pilot did well to bail out and escape the fireball.

"We have two more planes to get by," Salerno told his wingman. "Hang with me."

"Two," acknowledged Klein. He felt his heart pounding in his throat and tried to force the elation of his first kill away—they were a long way from home, with a gauntlet yet to run.

Salerno checked his fuel matrix once more. If they drove straight on through to the tanker, they'd get there with perhaps five minutes of airtime to spare—more than a little close for comfort. But flying on a direct path to the tanker meant flying right through the two Iranian MiGs, which were just turning to meet them about fifty miles ahead.

"Let's take it to them," Salerno told his wingman. "I'm going to ask the tanker to come south."

"Roger that," acknowledged Klein, his voice an octave higher than normal.

3

 Van Buren trotted off the ramp of the MC-130, an A-4 carbine under his arm. A captain in charge of the initial assault team was waiting for him a short distance away, ready to lay out the situation.

"Talk to me," yelled Van Buren as soon as he saw the officer.

"Some sort of fabrication facility there," said the captain, jerking his hand back toward the mountain. "Plane must've been in there. We have the two buildings on the north side of the base. Guerrillas in the southern one, holed up at the far end. First building is empty; we're checking it out now. Looks like trace radiation only. Defensive position on the south was taken out by the Stealth fighters; same with the other SAM site at the north. We think there are a couple of people in the hills farther out," he added, gesturing in the direction of the base's external guard posts. "At the moment, we have the road secured, and we're gathering prisoners. There's one area I want you to see."

"Conners and Ferguson," said Van Buren. "You find them?"

"No, but that has to do with what I want to show you," said the captain. "Prisoner of theirs, I think."

The SF troops had brought two small ATV-like vehicles in the Hercules to use as utility rovers and help with transporting captured material. One of the trucks—usually called a "Gator"—was just coming down the ramp of the aircraft. Van Buren commandeered it and rode with the captain toward the perimeter area where Conners and Ferguson had infiltrated. The fence had been flattened by the paratroopers, and the entire area, now secure, was lit by a searchlight confiscated from the Chechens. Several bodies were up in the rocks, mangled by large, bloody wounds. One of the men was handcuffed to a large piece of metal in the ravine.

"The manacle on their hands, I think it's a Russian manacle," said the captain. "That's one of our plastic jobs, holding him to the girder there."

"He must be their informer," said Van Buren. "The guerrillas must have ambushed them here."

"Captain!" shouted one of the troopers. Van Buren turned and walked toward the soldier, who was trotting from the area of the runway. "Sat telephone, sir. Found it back over there by the runway."

Van Buren picked up the phone and slid open the antenna.

"They might have gotten away," said the captain. "Could be anywhere in those hills. Or they could be with the guerrillas in that other building."

Van Buren nodded. Knowing Ferguson, he was sitting back in the Hercules, smirking while Van and his men searched the area.

God, he hoped that was the case.

"Let's secure the building and find out," said Van Buren, closing the antenna on the phone and heading back for the Gator.

4

The two American F-15s thundered over the mountains, nearly nose-on for the two MiGs and closing at a rate of roughly twenty-five miles a minute, which gave Jenkins about thirty seconds to decide on a strategy.

The encyclopedic brief Jenkins had received before his mission had covered Iranian aircraft capabilities and declared that the MiGs would most likely be equipped with heat-seeking Russian-made R-73 missiles, known in the West as "AA-11 Archer." These were potent weapons, and in theory they could be fired from any aspect in a dogfight. As a practical matter, however, the Iranians would probably choose between one of two strategies—either breaking and turning as the F-15s came close, spinning and trying to gain momentum for a close-quarters attack from the rear; or taking head-on shots as the Americans drove by.

The MiGs were roughly three thousand feet below them and had to anticipate an attack as well as line up their own. The Iranians couldn't carry a lot of fuel, which was likely to limit their ability to pursue at high speed. They would have to play for a single shot and make the most of it.

Though flying superior planes with better weapons systems, the Americans had one disadvantage—they were very low on fuel. Their powerful radars and easily detected airfoils left no doubt about where they were. And by the time they reached firing range for the AMRAAMS, the enemy fighters would also be able to attack.

"I have the one on the right," Jenkins told his wingman. "If they break, just fire your AMRAAM and go on through—we don't have the fuel to fuck with them."

"Two."

Technically, Jenkins's ROE or rules of engagement allowed him to fire only if directly threatened; that clearly covered the first engagement, where he had been tracked by hostile fire-control radar. He might be open to second-guessing, as neither MiG had yet made an unambiguous move to shoot him down. But there was no way—no way in the world—that he was going to allow himself to be a sitting duck, much less paraded through the streets of Tehran as an American imperialist.

As the planes closed to within forty miles of each other, the Eagle's RWR blared. The two MiGs were carrying radar-guided R-77 series missiles, supported by an upgraded radar; known to NATA as the AA-10 Adder, the Russian-made air-to-air weapon was roughly the equivalent of an American AMRAAM—a little surprise for the intelligence folks back home, who had claimed the Iranians didn't possess such missiles.

Jenkins took it in stride. The next few seconds passed like a rap riff—the lead MiG launched two missiles; the other began to cut right; Klein fired an AMRAAM, then another; Jenkins fired his; the radio went crazy with static; Jenkins watched his MiG tack downward into a turn, trying to get behind him; Jenkins's RWR whined; Jenkins dished chaff and flares but held to his course; the AWACS operator belatedly warned that they were being targeted; Jenkins leaned on the throttle for half a second; something exploded in the far corner of his canopy behind him; the air in his face mask suddenly felt heavy, reminding him of a summer afternoon before a storm.

And then they were past the MiGs, Klein yelling that there were missiles in the air, Jenkins calmly unleashing the last of his decoy flares. Something exploded behind him; he heard a light pop, the sort of sound a cap gun might make. His plane stayed true, the emergency lights off.

The AWACS controller scored two more MiGs down.

Not a good day for the enemy. Just a routine ho-hummer for the U.S. Air Force.

Even before he realized he hadn't been hit, Jenkins worried about his wingman. He clicked the mike button twice, fear suddenly overwhelming him.

"Patsy?" he asked, feeling his voice starting to edge toward a tremble.

"I'm here. You?"

"Looks like it."

"I fired a second missile," said the wingman. "I got all juiced up and fired without even a lock. Shit."

"Yeah, roger that. We'll take it out of your pay, cowboy. You got one."

"I got one," said the wingman, not really believing it. Typically, Klein was focused on what he had done *wrong* rather than what he had done *right*.

"I've had enough of this shit. Let's go tank and go home," said Jenkins.

5

BUILDING 24-442

 He knew it didn't fit, though Thomas couldn't quite decide why. The distance from Chechnya to Manila to LA was perfect, and yet, it just didn't fit.

He picked up a report a DI analyst had prepared a year before on possible terrorism targets in Los Angeles and the impact a 747 loaded with high explosives would have. It was horrible, of course, truly horrendous—but it didn't fit. It had been assumed to be the target because of the photographs found on Kiro when he was apprehended.

But Kiro wasn't connected with this operation at all; they'd proven that in Iran.

Thomas sat back from his computer, rubbing his eyes. It reminded him of the UFO sightings off Brazil in 1968—two totally different sightings believed to be connected, and only upon further analysis proven to be separate incidents altogether.

Manila was right, but not LA, he decided. But the Philippines wouldn't be the target if they were buying fuel there. And now that he looked again at the receipts, he saw that the amount of fuel purchased was extremely small—not nearly enough to fill a jumbo jet.

Still searching for clues, he retrieved his folded world map from the floor, spreading it over his desk, then using a pencil to estimate radiuses the plane could fly to. Looking for UFOs, he decided, was a heck of a lot easier than this.

6

ABOARD SRI LANKAN FLIGHT 112, BOUND FOR KANKESATURAI

The coldness came clandestinely, sneaking up on Ferguson like a warrior infiltrating a frontier settlement. By the time he noticed it his hands were frozen; he had trouble moving not just his fingers but his wrists. Conners huddled in the front corner of the craft, shivering and passing in and out of consciousness. Ferguson dressed his wounds as best he could; the sergeant wasn't bleeding anymore, though he'd obviously lost a good deal of blood. Not only were his clothes soaked, but Ferguson's were as well.

When the plane finally stopped jerking up and down and back and forth, Ferguson returned to his search of the interior, sliding the flashlight's beam around the interior. He saw what he thought had to be the door to the flight deck at the front of the space, a full level above his head. The ladder that would have been on the bulkhead in a standard cargo version of the plane had been removed, but the metal cladding of the explosives and radioactive cargo formed a ledge on either side. He started to climb up the space by pushing against the narrow walls directly below the door—they formed a kind of artificial chimney—but the space was a little too wide and shallow to make ascending easy, and as the aircraft hit turbulence, Ferguson lost his balance and dropped a few feet to the floor.

Looking for an easier climb, he found a section of the metalwork nearby that had pieces welded on like a ladder; he went up and found an irregular, roughly eight-inch ledge about nine feet off the floor on the left side of the hold. He worked his way toward the front of the plane, alternately using the flashlight and rubbing his cold knuckles across the surface, trying to decipher the indentations. The terrorists had packed roughly five feet of explosives and material on each side of the hold, arranging them in a patchwork pattern to maximize the plane's destructive power; they were not very concerned with rounding off edges or filling gaps, and Ferguson cut his fingers several times as he worked around. Finally, he reached the doorway.

Ferguson steadied himself, then reached to his belt and took his pistol out. His plan was simple—he'd yank open the door, swing with it, and get onto the flight deck, where he'd shoot out the pilot and the rest of the crew. He didn't bother thinking beyond that; it was superfluous.

But as he reached for the handle, the plane jerked upward. For a second Ferguson felt weightless, suspended against gravity. Then the floor of the plane seemed to reach up and snatch him down, and besides feeling cold he felt the incredible shock of pain hit him in the back of his head.

The thump of Ferguson's body slamming to the floor a few yards away shook Conners awake. He stared as the flashlight spun wildly toward the rear of the plane, its beacon illuminating the metal grids lining the interior. The lids of his eyes felt like ice-cold daggers poking at his eyeballs. Conners started to get up but felt a heavy hand press against him; he crawled instead, making his way toward the light. When he finally got it, he pushed back to find Ferguson, who was lying on his back, arms and legs straight out.

"Jesus, Ferg, let's go now," Conners told him.

It was hard to tell if the CIA officer was even breathing. Conners put his ear to his chest, trying to listen.

The plane dipped forward, and Conners tumbled over his comrade. He tried to push himself off, and the plane jerked hard to the right. His stomach suddenly felt queasy—he leaned over and began to throw up.

7

Corrine listened as Gray explained the abilities of the reconnaissance satellites, veering from the overly simplistic to the overly technical and back again. The bottom line itself was simple—it could take days to actually find the wreckage of the downed 747.

Assuming they had gotten it.

"Let's assume we didn't get it," Corrine told Gray. "Where can it go?"

"Well, 747 range would be something over seven thousand miles," said Major Gray. "Maybe even a bit more, depending on the version, how it was loaded, flight conditions."

"We'll have to search every airport or field that a 747 could land on within that range," said Corrine.

"That has to be well over a thousand. I doubt it's still in the air. The Navy would have found it by now," said the expert. "They have the Gulf completely covered, and they're in the Indian Ocean. Nothing without a civil registration—no plane is going to get past them. I'm sure we got it," added Gray.

"Just in case," said Corrine. "I'd like to talk to the *Nimitz* battle group as well. In the meantime, we'll raise the alert level at Manila."

"Your call," he said.

"It is," she agreed, clicking into the com circuit to get an update from Van Buren.

8

ON THE GROUND IN CHECHNYA

 Based on her preliminary readings, Van Buren's radiation expert, Captain Renya Peterson, declared the hangar area in the mountain completely off-limits until the robot probes could survey it. Tests at the mouth of the cave showed there were weak- and midlevel gamma generators and traces of alpha material inside; while the levels were not serious outside the cave, they were bound to be considerably higher inside. In contrast, only the building Ferguson had explored earlier had any level of material, and this was relatively low, generating the sort of readings one might find in a medical radiation department where procedures were lax.

A knot of radiation-containment specialists and support troopers huddled in space suits near the cave, waiting for an hour until the last of the guerrillas in the second building surrendered. Van Buren had fourteen prisoners, all severely wounded. He decided to evac them right away, which would avoid any conflict with the Russians, who were reported en route. That necessitated more off-loading of equipment and more delays, and so, by the time they were ready to send the little rover into the mountain, the sky had faint hints of the approaching dawn ripening its edges.

Larger than the PackBot Explorers made by iRobot and used for exploring caves and minefields in Afghanistan, the lower chassis of the Atomic Rover looked like a squashed shoe box with two sets of tank tracks at each side. The main set ran the length of the vehicle; at the front, another set of treads rose like arms, helping the critter climb over obstructions. On top of the robot was a small disk not unlike that used to pick up satellite transmissions; in this case it fed and received a stream of data to and from the base station, which was contained in a pair of large suitcases and a laptop about fifty yards from the mouth of the cave. In front of the disk were two very small video cameras, which fed high-definition optical and near-infrared images back to the station. A pair of radiation counters and isotope analyzers, along with a chemical warfare "sniffer," were mounted near the nose of the tiny vehicle. A fuel cell propelled AR and could do so for roughly twelve hours.

As Van Buren watched, the device rolled across the gravel where they were standing and rambled onto the hardened apron the 747 had used to get out; it popped up on the lip of the cement near the entrance and moved inside. Two men controlled AR, one handling the driving and the other the sensors. Each lieutenant had been thoroughly cross-trained in his companion's job and, if circumstances required, could handle the entire show himself.

The small vehicle stopped in the middle of the hangar-sized area and began scanning around. Since Ferguson and Conners hadn't been found yet, Van Buren assumed they were somewhere inside, though he was starting to fear that the two men would not be found alive.

The radiation suits the team wore provided protection against alpha and beta waves, where the real danger was contamination by breathing or swallowing particles, or infection in open wounds. They could not, however, shield out gamma waves; safety there depended largely on limiting time and proximity to the source. Each man on the team carried several film sensors, badges similar to those worn by medical personnel in X-ray departments to record their exposure to potentially harmful radiation. Each suit had a sensor that would sound if the exposure levels exceeded the preset limits. Before disembarking, the gear would be shed and left at the site. Upon returning to Incirlik a strict decontamination and isolation procedure—VB's experts jokingly referred to it as twenty Saturdays' worth of baths—would be followed.

Captain Peterson peered over Van Buren's shoulder. "Crazy fucks," Peterson said, holding a small Palm-like computer device that analyzed the radiation data fed from the robot. "Crazy fucks."

Coming from the mouth of any other member of the SF team, the words would have seemed normal. But Peterson wasn't just a woman—she was short, weighed maybe a hundred pounds, and had the complexion of a porcelain doll. Van Buren could not have been more surprised if her head began spinning around on her body, and he stared at her, waiting either for an explanation or a ventriloquist to appear.

"How bad is it in there?" he asked.

"Layman's terms?"

"Please."

"If you stayed inside for four hours, you'd have about twice the lifetime dosage you would give a patient with Stage IV thyroid cancer," she said. "Won't kill you right off, but eventually it'll catch up with you. They've got all sorts of different material. There's a lot of low-level gamma rays, but they were working with some nastier stuff as well. They must've had an accident at one point, a small spill that they had to contain."

The specialist began talking about radiation levels and probability curves, and Van Buren started to get lost in the details.

"Layman's language," he asked.

"There are a couple of hot spots that we have to watch for inside," she said.

"What about our guys?"

"We can go in, but we stay away from the hot spots and limit exposure. Nobody more than an hour, and no one inside without a suit."

"I meant Ferguson and Conners."

"If they haven't been inside too long—well, it depends on where they are and what else we find. We're talking about long-term effects, how close they are, how susceptible to cancer they may be. It's complicated."

"Bottom line is, sooner they're out the better," said Van Buren.

"Amen."

A large storage area at the left of the hangar had fifty-gallon drums packed with middle-level waste, mostly cesium 137 and cobalt 60 from medical applications. These generated gamma radiation partly shielded by a low, thick wall separating the space from the main hangar area. Almost directly opposite it at the right side of the building, microscopic amounts of uranium filled several cement cracks, the remnants of the accident Peterson had speculated about. Besides presenting a danger, these traces suggested that the terrorists had had greater quantities and taken them away in the plane.

"This is what's really scary," said Captain Peterson, pointing to a chart display on one of the laptops. "That's nitrate."

"A bomb?" asked Van Buren.

"Has to be," said Peterson.

"Uh-oh," said one of the lieutenants driving AR.

A loud crack sounded through the speaker on the console. There was a flash in the screen, and the feed died. Cursing, the lieutenant's fingers danced over the keyboard. Backup wire controls allowed the Rover to reverse its course, though the driver could not see where he was going and had to rely on the unit's grid map.

"At least two guerrillas, maybe more, inside," yelled the lieutenant on the monitor.

Van Buren pulled on his hood and ran toward the men crouched near the entrance to the hangar.

"Kalman's in there," said Lieutenant Yeger, who was in charge of AR's four-man escort detail.

"Where?" said Van Buren.

"On the left."

"Why did he go in?"

"He and Jacko went in to set up a backup relay antenna. The area where he was had been cleared. Jacko had started out, and Kalman was just about to. They were like, five yards apart, max."

"Tell him to stay where he is."

"I can't. Radio's out. Either he's behind something that's messing up the line-of-sight transmission, or the hangar shielding is killing it. I lost him on the com set."

Peterson and two men dressed in the protective gear and carrying M4s ran up behind Van Buren as the guerrillas inside the mountain began firing at AR again. The rover stopped dead about a hundred feet from the entrance, its top blasted to pieces.

"We have to go in and get our people," said the colonel. The hoods of the protective suits were equipped with voice-activated communications devices.

"Here," said Peterson. "Come here and let me draw it out for you. There's a few spots to avoid."

She knelt and drew a diagram in the dirt, a kid working out a play in a pickup football game.

"This spot, you stay away from," she said, showing where the worst of the radiation was. "Avoid these cracks. And keep your suit intact."

The guerrillas were on a second level of the cave near the rear, above the hangar level. A team was waiting at the rear entrance to the facility, which Ferguson and Conners had used earlier. Yeger suggested that they make a feint at the entrance, drawing the attention of the people inside, while a team went in from the back. Van Buren agreed, after making sure they had their protective gear on.

The rear deck of the hangar where the gunmen were angled away, limiting their line of fire to the left side of the cave. This gave Van Buren's men access to the interior—though it would bring them perilously close to the area contaminated by the uranium dust.

Of course, if the guerrillas came down to the main level, anyone going in could be easily cut down. The colonel decided to send a second rover—this one had no nickname, but looked almost identical to AR—inside to survey the area first. As they got ready to go, Peterson suggested they put a flash grenade on the robot to draw attention away if they needed to rescue Kalman or move under fire.

"No way to set it off," said one of the rover controllers.

"Fuck hell there is," said the diminutive woman. "Attach it to the front and pull the pin with the claw."

Even Van Buren laughed at her eloquence.

Five minutes later, the robot ambled inside, not one but two grenades attached to the chassis by a thick band of duct tape. Peterson told them through the headset what she was seeing on the video. Her voice sounded almost seductive.

"You're clean at the lip of the cave. One man, two on the ledge. There's Kalman—he's alive, I can see him moving. He's on the left side, behind the lip of that wall," she said.

"Team two ready at the back door?" Van Buren asked.

There was a slight delay while the message was relayed.

"Good to go," said Peterson.

"Go," said Van Buren.

9

HOKKAIDO, JAPAN

 Rankin, Guns, and Massette unfolded themselves from the seats and walked toward the hatchway as the aircraft stopped rolling near the hangar area. Massette popped the door open, then jumped back—they were a good distance from the ground, with no ramp in sight.

A gray, four-engine DC-8 sat across the tarmac waiting for them, engines idling; the old aircraft had been leased by the American military and been commandeered to take them to Manila.

"Yo! Let's go!" shouted a short, squat man, who stood on the ground about halfway between the two aircraft. "Let's go!" he shouted again, his voice somehow loud enough to be heard over the idling engines. He was wearing civilian clothes, but his haircut and demeanor gave him away as military.

"Jump," Rankin told Guns.

"Fuck," said Massette, who could feel the pain in his leg already.

Rankin started to push him aside. Guns dropped to the floor and lowered himself, pulling his gear out with him as he hopped—literally, since he lost his balance and nearly toppled over—to the ground. Rankin just stepped off, though when he landed he wished he hadn't, the sting punching his ankles. Massette finally decided to play it halfway, easing down to his butt and hanging his feet over before plopping to the ground.

"I'm Murphy," said the man. "Where's Rankin?"

"Yo," said Rankin.

"You gotta get to Manila. This is your plane. Your boss has been trying to reach you."

"Yeah, no shit. So who the hell are you?" said Rankin.

"I just told you."

"You got to be a SEAL," said Guns. "And I'm going to guess master chief, right?"

"And you're a fuckin' Marine," sneered Murphy, who said nothing else as he walked back to the DC-8.

"How did they know that?" asked Massette.

"By smell," said Rankin, pulling out his sat phone to call Corrine.

10

ON THE GROUND IN CHECHNYA

 One by one, Van Buren's team slipped into the cave while the rover moved forward to catch the guerrillas' attention. The terrorists aimed their weapons at it, but did not fire; the audio feed picked up muffled conversation as the guerrillas discussed what to do about the miniature beast.

"Couple of people behind them," whispered Peterson.

Van Buren was the next-to-last person inside. The team moved along the wall, crouching behind a low row of machines and broken crates. The point man stopped behind a pair of molded plastic chairs and aimed his M-4 toward the balcony.

"I can get one," he whispered.

"Just hold," said Van Buren. "Let the other team move into position."

He nudged to the side, trying to locate Kalman. He thought he saw something moving in the dim light filtering in from the outside but couldn't be sure. He resisted the temptation to run across and find him.

The rover stopped just before the wall beneath the guerrillas' position, then backed slowly and began making a circle, primarily to draw their attention but also to check through an area of crates at the back to see if anyone was there. The second team, meanwhile, had entered from the back door and made its way to the edge of the ramp, using a simple scope device to observe the interior.

The seconds ticked off like the long hours of an interminable schoolday. Van Buren took a slow, controlled breath, vision narrowed to the dim viewer of the night-gear monocle. He fought off distractions—the thought of what he might tell his son about the mission tickled him a moment, then disappeared.

"Ready," whispered Peterson.

"We go on the bang," said Van Buren. "Shield your eyes."

The rover slid to a stop. One of the guerrillas stood and started to get down, climbing over the rail so he could go to it and examine it. The arm on the unit clicked, but nothing happened, the lieutenant having trouble manipulating it correctly.

Just pull the damn thing, Van Buren thought to himself. Then bam—the grenade flashed and exploded, a big Fourth of July firecracker going off at the back of the cave. The point man took out the terrorist on the balcony, while Yeger blasted the one who'd jumped down to examine the rover. A second flash-bang, tossed by the team at the ramp, exploded, followed by a pair of short bursts from MP-5s.

Van Buren ran across the open floor, looking for Kalman. Something hard bounced off his back—a ricochet that caught just the right angle—and he felt a stinging numbness in his arm. But he pushed up to his feet and found his man hunkered behind a row of long crates.

In the forty seconds or so that it took for the others to finish securing the hangar, the numbness in Van Buren's arm spread to his neck, then up and around his face. His legs stiffened and he felt as if he were being choked. He grabbed Kalman by the arm, pulling him toward the mouth of the cave.

What would he tell James?

Van Buren reached the mouth of the cave, where men in space suits fell on Kalman, who was already protesting that he was fine. Someone shouted in Van Buren's ear:

"Colonel, we're advised that a convoy of Russian armored vehicles is on the highway roughly one hour away."

"All right," said Van Buren. His jaw hurt to move. "We're wrapping up. Prepare the aircraft. Get the demolitions people in—blow the roof down."

"Make it quick in there," warned Peterson.

"Go, let's go," said Van Buren. "Where are Ferg and Conners?"

"They're not here," said Yeger. "We have two prisoners, two dead men."

"Outside, get everyone outside." He turned to go back in but someone stopped him—Peterson.

"Your suit," she said, pointing. "It's torn."

"I'm OK."

"Over here!" she yelled. There was a strict protocol, and not even Van Buren could avoid it. Medics swarmed around.

"No blood," said someone.

"Thank God," said someone else.

"I'm OK," said Van Buren.

"Hit the back of the vest," said a medic. "Concrete."

"I'm all right," he said.

"Make sure it didn't get into his skin."

"No blood."

"I'm OK," insisted Van Buren. Dizziness and nausea swirled in his head; he pulled his hood off, breathing the crisp night air, hoping it would revive him.

"I want a board," said the medic next to him. "Piece of concrete ricocheted and hit your back. Your spine may be bruised."

"No, that's not necessary," said Van Buren, his head clearing. "Did we get Ferguson and Conners?" he asked. "Where's Ferg? Where the fuck is he?"

"They're not here," said one of the sergeants whose team had secured the buildings, then conducted a search. "AC-130 is using its infrared to locate guerrillas. There's two groups moving out down the road, and all those guys have guns. Ferguson and Conners aren't here. They must've gone out on the plane."

"Typical Ferg, always looking for another party." Van Buren walked with one of the medics to a second area, where he was to shed his gear and take a cocktail of anti-radiation drugs as a precaution. "Where's communications? Somebody get me hooked up to Ms. Alston. Everybody else—let's go, saddle up. Come on, you know the drill. Go. Go."

11

The ground crew Samman Bin Saqr had chosen was waiting at the hangar when he landed, alerted by his message. Two fuel trucks met him in the apron area; he permitted himself a short respite, climbing down from the plane as it was "hot pitted," refueled, and prepped so it could leave without hesitation.

The terrorist leader made his way down to the tarmac where his men were working feverishly. The replacement crew met him as planned, fully expecting to fly the plane to its target. Samman Bin Saqr studied both men, then tapped the pilot on the shoulder.

"You will take the first officer's seat," he told him. He turned to the other man, who had been trained as the copilot. "Go with the others. Your time will come."

Both men nodded, without commenting, and moved to their respective tasks. One of the maintenance people walked toward the rear of the aircraft.

"Where are you going?" said Samman Bin Saqr sharply. He had handpicked the maintenance people, just as he had chosen all of the people involved in the project. But now he feared that the Americans had somehow managed to infiltrate his team.

The man pointed toward the side-loading cargo door. The door had been welded shut early in its overhaul; only the specially built opening at the rear had been used to load the aircraft.

"Leave it," said Samman Bin Saqr. "Leave the plane as it is."

The man started to object. Samman Bin Saqr turned to the head of the ground team, who was just trotting up to see what the problem was. "Shoot him," he said.

He heard the shot as he walked back toward the cockpit. Samman Bin Saqr permitted himself a short pause on the steps, waiting as the fuel trucks finished. He was taking off several hours too soon, but it couldn't be helped. It wouldn't do to wait. He had an appointment with destiny.

By the end of the day, America's island paradise would be a hell of unimaginable proportions. His legacy would be known for decades, perhaps even centuries, to come.

F erguson knew they were on the ground, but nothing else made sense to him. He could hear the engines humming at idle. He wondered if they had been forced down, unsure whether that would mean the rear door would be opened or if the plane would simply be blown up.

He fished in the darkness for his rifle. He found his rucksack, then crawled over it, still searching for the AK-74. Conners lay half on it, breathing unevenly. He'd thrown up all over himself.

The first sign of radiation poisoning? Or was it simply motion sickness?

Ferguson pulled the rifle out from under the sergeant's body. As he retrieved it, the 747 began to roll. He began firing wildly at the floor of the plane, thinking he might strike the landing gear or otherwise disable it. The plane's engines were so loud he could barely even hear the gun as it fired. He burned the clip, slapped it away, grabbed the last one from his ruck and fired again, even more wildly, peppering the back of the plane.

Ferguson lost his balance as the jet pushed its nose up into the air. He tumbled against the metal, landing near the cargo bay door that he had come in through. Desperate, he pulled out his pistol and fired wildly at what he thought was the door's locking mechanism; two bullets ricocheted off to his right, and if any of the others hit, they had no effect on the lock.

"Shit," he said. He gave in to his frustration, slamming the heel of his gun against the metal-grate floor, pounding it down and screaming, venting his fury at the plane, cursing himself for stupidly boarding it, cursing the bastard terrorists, cursing his inability to think clearly and come up with a plan. He punched and kicked the floor until not just his hands but his shoulders and thighs were numb.

When finally he had purged his rage, he sat back up in the darkness and tried to figure out what to do next.

12

Corrine listened to Van Buren finish his summary of what they had found at the base. He had three additional prisoners aboard his aircraft, which was about fifteen minutes from the Turkish border. Two of his men had sustained small wounds. The radiation exposure to the team was within acceptable limits.

The facility had been temporarily sealed off by exploding several large charges near the entrances. The damage would not preclude the facility from being repaired and reused; presumably the Russians would have to see to that themselves. They were already en route.

Of more immediate concern: A smorgasbord of waste material had been stored in the cave. The plane that had taken off was a flying radiation bomb.

And Ferguson and Conners were undoubtedly on it.

"Thank you, Colonel. Job well done," she told him. Then she looked up at the communications specialist. "Put the president through now," she told him.

The young man nodded, doing his best to hide his anxiety at channeling a transmission from the commander in chief. One of the president's aides came on the line, and the specialist pointed at Corrine as the White House connection went through.

"Well, dear, you are making a considerable amount of noise in Moscow, so I cannot imagine what is going on in the Caucasus," said the president.

"We've secured a terrorist facility in pursuance of U.S. and international law," she told him.

"I understand the Russian ambassador has a slightly different interpretation of the affair," said the president. "As a matter of fact, the secretary of state is standing outside my door as we speak, and I hear that his white hair is clumping on my rug."

"Then perhaps someone from his legal team can dredge up Memo 13-2002, relating to the antiterrorist letter signed during the second Bush administration," said Corrine.

"You're thinking like a lawyer," said the president.

"You don't want me to?"

"I'm not complaining, Counselor. Just offering commentary."

The president paused, distracted by one of his aides in his office. When he came back on the line, Corrine tried to seem more conciliatory and less tired.

"Notifying the Russian government of the situation as it developed would have meant jeopardizing our people," she told the president.

"Now, now, I didn't put you out there to be offering excuses. I'm expecting that you did the right thing and that the chips will fall where they may. As I understand the memo you cited," the president added, his voice making it seem as an aside, "the letter covers the pursuit of terrorists, and there seems to be some concern that it means 'hot pursuit.'"

"I'm not sure I understand the difference between hot and cold," said Corrine.

McCarthy laughed, though she hadn't meant it as a joke.

"Mr. President, we think some of the terrorists managed to escape in an aircraft with considerable nuclear material on board. The aircraft was pursued and fired on by fighters that were part of our attack group, but it's not clear that it was shot down; there's heavy cloud cover in the area obscuring the crash site. I've authorized a team to survey the area, which will undoubtedly lead to more protests."

"Understood."

"The aircraft that escaped was a 747 that may have been set up as a bomb; we're simply not sure. There's also a good possibility that two of our people are aboard that aircraft."

The president remained silent.

"If we didn't get it, and it crashes somewhere," said Corrine, "it'll be a hell of a mess. I have a net set out, but if I just shoot it down, it may explode. The fallout is bound to be a problem. People may die."

"Am I speaking to my private counsel?" said McCarthy.

"Yes," she said, realizing that he wanted the communication to be confidential.

"Shoot it down, girl."

"We're working on it."

"That's what I want to hear. Keep me informed."

13

The flashlight batteries had gone out, but Ferguson realized he could use the light cast from the laptop's screen to see, at least for short distances. He took it with him as he moved around the plane.

The floor and ceiling panels were screwed in; it occurred to him that it might be possible to unscrew them and reach the control cable for the rudder and elevator in the tail. Ferguson knew nothing about how the controls worked, let alone whether they were hydraulic or electric. But he was so desperate to do something that he instantly became consumed by the idea, focusing on it as the one solution to the situation, the one real thing he could do. If he could find them, he might get through the cables somehow—hack them if they were wires, or use the bullets remaining in his pistol if they were metal to puncture them.

He started looking along the floor first, mostly because it was the easier place to look. On his hands and knees, Ferg took his knife and began working at the screws, which had Phillips head crosses. He got three off and was working on a fourth when the laptop's power conservation program kicked in, turning it off; he decided that was a good idea, and continued in darkness, feeling his way to each screw on the eight-foot-long panel. He found there was a trick to it—he set the knife tip in at a slight angle, then slapped at the handle with the palm of his hand, using as much force as he could to get the screw started. Once it moved, he could turn it a few times with the blade at a slightly different angle, and then use his fingers to finish it off. The screws were only an inch long, and with one exception came free fairly easily.

Ferguson knew that if his plan succeeded, he would die in the plane. He saw no alternative; he realized that the metal jacket around the cargo bay contained waste material and explosives, and didn't even bother getting the rad meter to see how bad it was. From the day that he had been told he had thyroid cancer he had faced the possibility of death, and the fact that it was closing in now did not bother him. He worried instead that the terrorists might succeed in flying the plane into some American landmark, or even crash it into a Third World city. He wanted to stop them, and would use all of his energy to do so.

One of the screws refused to come off. Ferguson slapped at it, punching the end of the knife hard. He tried prying underneath it, and finally wedged the blade in. But then as he poked the dagger in the slit again, the tip of the knife broke off.

He lay with his head down on the deck for a full minute. Then he stabbed at the screw, playfully at first, then more seriously, managing to use the sheared edge as a chisel and pushing off the head. That broke the blade more, but not so badly that he couldn't use it to help pry up the floor panel. He slid it down toward the back and brought over the laptop, turning it on so he could see.

There was a solid layer of metal below him. When Ferguson climbed down to examine it, he found soldered seams. The thin cover took two blows from his knife and gave way.

Instead of wires, the space was filled by a low-grade radioactive sludge, processed from medical waste. He reached in and began to scoop, pulling out what looked and felt like dry, lumpy clay. Finally he reached metal. He felt all around with his hand, but found no cable. He took his knife and pounded again; this time it didn't give way.

All right, he thought to himself, the roof is next.

Ferguson took off his shirt and cleaned his hand, tossing the shirt back down. Then he pulled over the floor panel, worried that Conners or even he might roll around and fall through if the plane hit violent turbulence.

Lying near the front of the cargo bay, Conners alternated between sleep and a vague, light consciousness, his mind dipping back and forth between black darkness and gray twilight. A dozen songs played at the back of his head, and at times he saw the face of a friend of his, a kid he'd known in high school, real party animal, always ready with a smoke or beer. Other sensations slipped through his mind, colors and sounds and smells, but he didn't focus on any one thing until Ferguson came over to him, sitting him up to search for his knife. Conners groaned, his stomach rumbling again.

"Just want your knife, Dad," Ferguson told him. "You rest."

Ferg's voice salted his clouded consciousness—Conners snapped fully awake.

"We have to stop these fucks," he told Ferguson.

"Yeah, Dad, no shit," said Ferguson. "I need your knife."

"Force the door," said Dad.

"They welded it or something," said Ferguson. "I couldn't get it open."

"Blast it."

"I need your knife."

"OK."

Ferguson didn't bother explaining. He took the knife and the laptop and began looking for an easy area to scale.

"We got to get them, Ferg," Conners called to him, yelling over the high hum of the engines. He pulled off his vomit-soaked shirt, pushing it toward the pile of puke on the floor.

Ferguson examined the panel over the center of the plane. He thought he could get all but the last three screws relatively easily. With the others gone, he could put his weight on the panel and pull it down. He propped the laptop up nearby and went to work.

Conners pushed to get up, thinking he would help Ferguson. Ferg heard him groan as he settled back down.

"Listen, Dad, you just hang out down there, OK?" Ferguson squinted at him. "I have this under control."

"We have to stop the plane, Ferg."

"I'm with you. You just relax."

The laptop flew off the narrow ledge where Ferguson had wedged it as the airplane bucked with a strong eddy of wind. It smacked into pieces on the floor back near the door. Ferguson cursed, then continued to work, managing to get four screws off in the darkness. He tried to shortcut the process by wedging the knife in and hanging off the panel; when that didn't work, he went back to working at the screws, his weight shifting precariously as he leaned across from the built-up panel at the side. It was almost impossible to move the screws that were tight, but he found that he could push the heads down a little by prying and hanging on the panel. He began to snap them off, one by one.

"How's it going?" Conners asked.

"We're getting there. Three more years, and we'll be done."

Conners moved his legs, trying to warm them somewhat. He started humming to himself without really thinking about it, falling into "Jug of Punch."

"Glad you're feeling better," said Ferguson.

"How's that?"

"You're singing."

"Just humming. Trying to boost your morale."

"Go for it." Ferguson grabbed hold of the side of the panel and put his legs against the edge of the small shelf he'd been perched on. Then he sprang forward, pushing with all his might. The last screws snapped. He tumbled to the floor, the aluminum grate clanging on top of him.

"*Finnegan lived in Walken Street, a gentle Irishman, mighty odd,*" sang Ferguson, starting to look for his knife. By the time he had found the knife, Conners had joined in. Ferguson walked back toward him to climb up; Conners sensed him coming in the dark and reached out his hand.

"When you take out the controls, we'll be goners," he said. His voice was matter-of-fact.

"Yeah," said Ferguson. "We got to do it, Dad."

"I just want to say, you're all right for a CIA spook."

"Yeah, we're not all dicks," said Ferg, reaching in the blackness for his handholds. "Though we try."

14

Thomas stared at the screen, which had all of the information he had been able to compile on assets connected to the companies he now saw must be related to bin Saqr. Those assets included a 747—but it wasn't the right airplane.

He knew it wasn't the right airplane because he had tracked through the ID registries and—after an assist by the Boeing people to make sure there was no possibility of a mistake—had found the aircraft in operation just a few days before in India. It was registered to a legitimate Sri Lankan firm, and had made a flight into that country's airport at Kankesaturai.

But of course that couldn't be, since the plane was in Chechnya.

Thomas at first resisted the obvious conclusion: that the terrorists were using the Sri Lankan company and owned two aircraft. He searched for more information about the Sri Lankan company and its other holdings: several very old 707s. He thought that the listing of the aircraft with the other firm must therefore be a mistake, since unlike the one believed to have flown from Chechnya this one made legitimate flights.

The company had to be involved, and there had to be at least two planes. But the firm was not on any of the hot lists and had no connection to bin Saqr or any of the terrorist groups associated with Allah's Fist, al-Qaida, or any other group. Thomas dismissed it once more as a mistake. But as he prepared to ask for a fresh affiliate search from the DCI Counterterrorist Center, it occurred to him that he was merely avoiding the obvious. He was, after all, doing what countless disbelievers in UFOs did—going through contortions to disprove what was right in front of their noses.

Two planes. Bin Saqr had two planes, and access to legitimate identifiers belonging to the Sri Lankan company.

Thomas jumped from his chair. His energy grew as he covered his materials; by the time he hit the corridor he was in a frenzy of conviction. He raced downstairs, impatiently submitted to the security checks, then walked so quickly to the sit room that he was short of breath.

"You need a shave, Thomas," said Corrigan, looking up from the desk.

"Sri Lanka," Thomas told him. "And I think they may have two planes."

"Two?"

Thomas started to push his papers toward Corrigan. "Look at these registries."

"It's all right, I trust you," said Corrigan. "We'll put Sri Lanka on the search list."

"Kankesaturai," said Thomas. "The airport there—I have satellite photos of their facilities, and I've asked for information on flights out."

"What about Manila?"

"It doesn't fit yet."

Corrigan had taken a shower and a twenty-minute power nap, but he was still bogged down by fatigue. He struggled to focus on Thomas's data and compute what it meant.

"Would they bomb Sri Lanka?"

"They're not," said Thomas. "They're just refueling."

"Refueling?"

"It must be. They could fly from there to Manila."

But they hadn't bought enough fuel to refuel there. Did the Sri Lankan airline have a terminal at the airport?

Thomas thought it didn't, but he'd have to check.

"Thomas?" said Corrigan. "What about LA? Is it the target?"

"I don't know," said Thomas. "To get to LA they'd have to refuel, so it could be. But they didn't buy enough fuel for that."

"What did they buy fuel for?"

"A little water taxi, probably just a cover, a phony company."

"You sure?" asked Corrigan.

"No. We should check it out," said Thomas. He was back to his map—Hawaii had been just outside the range of targets from Sri Lanka. "We have to protect Honolulu," he said.

"Hawaii?"

"Paradise!" Thomas practically shouted the word, realizing now the significance of the NSA intercepts he'd seen the first day he started.

"You sure?"

"Do it," he said. "And Sri Lanka. We have to check there. And Manila."

"All right. Take a breath," said Corrigan, picking up his headset. "Give me the names one at a time."

15

 When Rankin arrived, the airport had been locked down. No aircraft was allowed to land without escort, and none could take off except after a thorough search. U.S. and Philippine military authorities controlled the airspace around the islands, and security was so tight that Rankin and the others had to prove their identities even after an F-16 escorted them to the base.

A temporary joint command task force had been established in an empty hangar, and they went immediately to find the commander. He turned out to be a lieutenant general from the Marines, who took one look at the unkempt men in front of him and demanded to know what the hell they were doing in a military command post.

"We're Special Forces, part of Special Demands and the operation that found the terrorists," Rankin explained.

Before he could get to his request for a helicopter and troops to check out the boating operation, the general waved over one of his aides, a major whose shoulders were wider than some small cars.

"Debrief these men," said the general. "See what useful information they have for us."

"With all due respect, sir, the briefing should come from uh, the Team desk," said Rankin. "We have our own orders—"

"I'm countermanding your orders. You're under my command now."

"Well, no, that's not the way it works," said Rankin.

"What? Who the hell do you think you're talking to, soldier?" asked the general.

"With respect, sir," said Rankin. "We already have a job to do. We want to find these fucks."

The major looked like he was ready to grab Rankin by the neck and wrestle him outside.

"You're not addressing me, are you?" said the general.

"Well, sir—uh, with respect," said Rankin, his tone suggesting anything but. "Our orders come through a different pipeline."

"Have them debriefed, Major."

"Let's go, soldier," said the major, putting his hand on Rankin's chest.

Guns tugged at Rankin's arm, and the two men followed the major outside, trailed by Massette. Had the Marine officer simply grilled them on what type of aircraft they were looking for, Rankin might have calmed down and simply called Corrine and asked her to talk to the thickheaded officer. But instead he started bawling Rankin out for disrespect; when the words "court-martial" left his lips, Rankin turned in disgust.

"I don't have time for this horseshit," said Rankin, furious. He started to walk away.

"Soldier, you get your butt back here until you're dismissed," said the major.

Rankin's graphic description of what the Marine officer could do with that particular instruction was deflected by Guns, who suggested that all parties concerned would benefit from a phone call to the Cube. He pulled out his sat phone—the major's eyes grew a bit wide as he saw it—and dialed into Corrigan.

Massette took advantage of the momentary diversion to pull Rankin away, and the two men walked away from the hangar.

"Fucking asshole," said Rankin.

"He's an officer; what do you expect?" said Massette.

"Exactly," said Rankin.

Guns in the meantime managed to calm the major by handing the phone to him; Corrigan applied some of his PsyOp training, assuring the major that it was due to his unit's efforts that the Philippines were considered secure—and by the way, the hippies who'd just arrived there were CIA employees, not familiar with the chain of command. Temporarily mollified if misinformed, the major handed the phone back to Guns. Corrigan told him to run down the water taxi service Thomas had found and stay the hell away from the lieutenant general until Corrine talked to him. The service had an office at Polillo, an island in the bay on the other side of Luzon.

"How we supposed to get there?" Rankin asked Guns when he came back.

"Corrigan suggested we rent a car."

"Screw that. We're at a fucking airport." Rankin craned his head around. There were several Marine Sea Stallion helos nearby, but it was a good bet the Marines wouldn't be lending them out anytime soon. Nor would the Navy give up any of its aircraft if it had to check with the lieutenant general for clearance.

On the other hand, there were four Philippine Air Force MD 500MG Defenders parked by an auxiliary building near an American Airlines flight that had been parked for a search.

"Beats driving," said Massette.

They made their way over to the helicopters, and after checking with their guards were directed to the colonel in charge of the unit. The colonel had indeed been shunted away from the action by the Marines and was none too pleased about it. The MD 500s were older versions of the A-6 Little Bird scouts, which were used by SOAR and other SF units; though no longer on the cutting edge, they were still potent scouts and capable gunships. Rankin explained who they were and that they had a lead out on Polillo.

"Why would the terrorists want a water taxi?" asked the colonel.

Rankin could only shrug. "We won't know until we get there," he said.

"Well, let us go then, all of us," said the colonel, turning and snapping orders to one of his aides.

"You're beginning to sound like Ferg," said Guns, as they climbed into one of the choppers.

"Fuck you, too," said Rankin.

16

Ferguson stabbed the knife at the thick wire cable, unable to see in the dark what he was hitting.

The blade deflected off something hard. He pounded again, felt it slap through something softer. Ferg pulled it out and stabbed once more. The knife found the plastic covering of the cable, cut through—he hacked at it, confidence beginning to build. But with his next blow he felt the knife tip break. Stopping, he leaned back and put the knife into his belt, then reached up to feel the spot with his fingers. A thick collar ran beneath the plastic; beneath that was a piece of pipe. He took the knife out and hacked more carefully, prying away material until he had about six inches' worth of it exposed about the thickness of a fist.

"I'm going to try shooting through it," he told Conners. "You with me, Dad?"

"I'm here, Ferg."

Ferguson adjusted his feet, then leaned on his left arm, trying to get into position so he could brace his arm as he fired. He shifted around twice, leaning back and forth.

"Yeah, here we go," he said. Ferguson pushed his forehead against his arm to help steady it, then pressed the trigger.

17

As soon as Corrigan described the Sri Lanka connection, one of the operators at a nearby console put up his hand and started waving at Corrine. "There's a Sri Lankan aircraft approaching grid space F-32," he said. "It's a 747."

"Get planes on it."

"They're already approaching."

The aircraft in question was a cargo version 747 just entering air space over Malaysia. It took about three minutes to arrange for a radio feed directly into the pilots' circuit. Slammer One-Four and Slammer One-Six were about sixty seconds from having the plane in visual distance. It had already been checked electronically, and Corrine's own information confirmed that the plane was on a scheduled flight to Brunei.

"We want them to land at Subang," Corrine told the pilots. Subang Air Base was part of Kuala International Airport. Two American Special Forces soldiers were assigned as advisors to an army unit there, and the Malaysian military had been contacted to stand by and secure any diverted aircraft. "They're to land there immediately."

"Understood," said the lead pilot, Commander Daniel "Wolf" Clarke. Wolf and his wingman were coming toward the 747 at about thirty-eight thousand feet, at roughly a thirty-degree angle from its nose. The Sri Lankan pilot had not yet answered their hails.

"Four MiGs from Malaysian Number 17 squadron preparing to take off," relayed one of the controllers.

"I don't think the Navy needs their help," said Major Gray.

Corrine's aircraft was several thousand miles away, helping coordinate the search over Iran for the supposedly downed jet, which more and more looked as if it hadn't been downed at all. The interplay between the two Tomcat pilots made her feel as if they were just a few miles away—as if she might go to one of the windows at the front of the aircraft and spot them up ahead.

"Slam Six, you getting a response?" Wolf asked his wingman.

"Negative, Four. You sure these guys speak English?"

"Yeah all right, I see him, correcting—stay with me six. Definitely a 747."

"SF Command Transport 3 copies," said Gray. "You have a 747 in sight. Does it have markings?"

"Negative. No markings. No markings at all," said Wolf. "They're holding course. We're coming around."

The two F-14s banked, circling around so they could come at the 747 from the rear. Though as far as they knew it was incapable of offensive actions, they nonetheless approached it gingerly, their adrenaline level steadily climbing. The Sri Lankan plane still had not answered their calls on any frequency, nor had it acknowledged the order to land. The Tomcat crews were close enough to see in the cockpit, but the Sri Lankan pilots steadfastly refused to look in their direction. It was five minutes from landfall.

"There's no way they don't they see them," Gray told Corrine.

"Get their attention," Corrine told the Navy flight. "Make sure they know you're there."

The Navy aviator hesitated for just a moment, then requested permission to fire a few rounds "across the bow."

"Yes," said Corrine. "Do it."

The bursts lasted no longer than a second and a half. The big plane lurched off its flight path, seemingly in the direction of Slammer One-Four. Wolf tucked his wing and cleared away from the Boeing's path. It took a few seconds for the two Tomcat pilots to sort out the situation and make sure they weren't in each other's way.

The Boeing pilot, meanwhile, began accelerating, his nose pointing downward.

"He's descending," Wolf radioed. "But he's still not answering our hails."

"He's not heading for the airfield," said Gray. "He's going south. He's on a direct path for Singapore. He'll make landfall in two minutes. We have to get him over the water. Now."

Singapore sat more than two hundred miles to the south of Kuala Lumpur, a fat and inviting target. And in fact while the cities and towns along the coastline were considerably smaller and much, much poorer, they were all potential targets, once the aircraft was over land.

"Slammer One-Four, fire more warning shots," said Corrine. "Advise him that we will shoot him down if he does not immediately respond to your commands."

"I've done that."

"Do it again," said Corrine. She pushed her sweater away from her wrist, noting the exact time on her watch.

Samman Bin Saqr felt something in the aircraft giving way or breaking behind him; there was noise deep in the cargo bay, something like a muffled explosion, though the engines themselves seemed in order.

The explosives had been packed and arranged to prevent accidental ignition; his engineers bragged that neither lightning nor fifty rounds from an American 20 mm cannon would set them off until the proper moment. But there had definitely been a sharp crack in the back, a noise that to him sounded like an explosion.

With no way to check the problem, he checked his position on the GPS device, making sure that it coincided with the internal navigation equipment. There was no deviance; the plane would fly itself perfectly to the target once he left.

Basher One-Four to Command Transport Three. No response."

Corrine watched the seconds adding themselves one by one to the window on her watch. There was no question in her mind now that she was going to order the plane shot down; she wanted merely to wait until the last possible second—the lawyer in her forming the opening argument.

The seconds clicked off until there were forty left.

"Basher One-Four, has the aircraft responded?"

"Negative," said Wolf, surprised that she asked again.

"Shoot it down. Now," said Corrine. "Do not let that aircraft go over land."

"Basher One-Four, confirming order to shoot down Sri Lankan cargo aircraft registry 5SK."

"Confirmed. Shoot it down immediately," said Corrine.

The Navy pilots traded terse commands, then Wolf took the shot, opening up with his cannon from point-blank range from behind the airliner.

"He's going in," said Basher One-Six."

"Watch yourself! Watch!"

The two aircraft had to pull off as debris flew from the stricken 747. The terrorist plane turned into a fireball, spinning toward the ocean just short of the coastline.

18

 Ferguson squeezed off another shot. He'd cleared right through the pipe, but as far as he could tell, nothing had changed. He put the gun next to the edge and fired again. This time his weight wasn't quite balanced, and he slid; unable to catch himself, he tumbled down to the deck.

"Ferg. Ferg!" yelled Conners.

"Yeah, I'm all right. I shot clean through the motherfucker."

"Maybe they have a backup. Or maybe that's not the control cable."

Ferguson climbed back up, taking the knife. He felt thin wires in the hole, and described them to Conners.

"If we weren't in an airplane, I'd say they were for detonators," said Conners when he finished. "Or something thin."

"Lights maybe?"

"I guess."

"I think it's a backup explosive system," said Ferguson. "Maybe we can find the bombs and blow up the plane."

Conners didn't say anything. He sat back against the side, pulling up his shattered leg. It wouldn't bend. The blood and vomit had dried, but his head still pounded. "How fucked are we, Ferg, with this radiation?" he asked.

It was about the last question Ferguson was expecting, and he started to laugh. "Oh, pretty fucked," he said.

"How much? We going to get cancer?"

"You think we're going to get out of this without getting blown up?" Ferguson asked.

"Shit, yeah."

"Well, on that scale, cancer's not that bad."

"Fuck you."

"Yeah." Conners needed some sort of reassurance, and Ferg decided to try and offer it. Even so, he had a hard time; it was one thing to make fun or be sarcastic, and another to sugarcoat reality. There was no way they were walking away from this.

But if they did walk away, he thought, what would it be like?

"Remember those slides we saw that Corrigan made? Worst effect is the alpha stuff, but that has to be ingested, which probably won't happen here until the particles are blown up, right? Because they didn't spread uranium dust in the plane—they probably have it in those containment wafers scattered in these boxes here. As long as we don't breathe it, we're cool."

Ferguson paused. His stomach was feeling queasy, but that might just be because he was hungry and tired. It somehow felt reassuring to talk about the effects of the radiation as if he were writing a science report; it had been that way with his cancer, too, explaining it to his sister.

"What we're getting mostly is gamma, and some of that it probably shielded, too," continued Ferg. "I mean, we're sick dogs, Dad, don't get me wrong—even if we get out of here pretty soon, a lot of interesting medical stuff in our future."

"Leukemia?"

"Oh, sure. Think of it this way—smoking cigarettes probably isn't going to make things any worse."

"What's cancer like, Ferg?"

"How's that?"

"You got it, right?"

Ferguson felt something prick at him, as if the question were a physical thing. No one in Joint Demands, not even Van or Slott, knew.

"That's compartmented need-to-know, Dad," he said, pushing past the surprise by turning it into a joke.

"We heard rumors, but no proof. Now I can tell."

"It sucks, Dad. But at the moment, it beats the alternative. Come on, let's get to work."

"I'm sorry you got it."

"Me too. Come on, let me see what happens if I strip those wires down and cross them."

"I got a better idea, Ferg. Since we're going to kill ourselves anyway."

"Fire away, Dad."

"We got two grenades. Throw 'em up near that door, see if they blow through the panel."

"They're only flash-bangs, Dad," said Ferg. "They're just going to make very loud booms."

The aircraft seemed to tremble, then Ferguson and Conners felt it tilting forward and starting to descend.

"Let's go for it," said Ferguson. "Let's do it."

"Yeah," said Conners. He handed over the grenades, then slid down to the floor. Ferguson reached down for him, but got the shirt he'd discarded earlier instead. It had something in the pocket.

"What about the Russian grenade Ruby gave me?" Ferguson asked. "The VOG thing. Any way to set it off?"

"We don't have a launcher. It works like one of our 40 mm grenades in a 203. The pins inside hold the trigger off until there's centrifugal force. It has to spin fast."

"Can we take it apart?"

Conners tried to focus. The grenades came in two basic models, one with an impact fuse in the nose, the other—this one—slightly different, designed more specifically as an antipersonnel shrapnel weapon, throwing metal over a wide area. It hopped up when it landed, then exploded.

If they could set off the cap at the back, the propellant might explode.

Or not.

Hit the charge in the front. Something would go off.

"Spit it out, Dad," said Conners.

"There's a fuse in the nose, an explosive charge—if you hit it point-blank, I think it would explode. It might be enough to set off the propellant then."

"You think I could throw hard enough to set it off?"

"Not even you could do that, Ferg," said Conners.

"So if I shoot it, what happens?" said Ferg.

"Yeah," said Conners, as if Ferguson had given the answer rather than the question.

"I don't know if the shrapnel will go through all the shit they have inside the plane," said Ferguson. "But it will go through us."

"Yeah."

"All right," said Ferg. He took the grenade and his gun. "I'll do it near the cockpit. Take those bastards with us maybe."

"Go for it."

Neither man moved. Both were willing to die—both realized they were *going* to die—but neither wanted to cause the other's death.

Then Conners had another idea. "The flash-bang might set it off, if you wedged them together right. It's not much of a killing force, but it could set off the percussion cap at the back, or maybe the fuse in the front, because it has to be pretty loose to begin with."

"Which one?"

Conners thought. "The back. It's like a bullet being fired."

"I could shoot the back point-blank, like a striker."

"Yeah."

"What the hell," said Ferguson. He grabbed hold of Connors and dragged him toward the front of the plane.

"What are you doing, Ferg?"

"We'll use the grenade to blow open the door. We'll huddle under the ledge, the explosion misses us, we go get the bastards. The flash-bang will be the striker. It'll work."

Conners said nothing as Ferguson dragged him forward, convinced belief was better than despair. Finnegan's saga floated into his brain. Oh, for a good slug of whiskey right now, he thought to himself.

"Shoot me before we crash," said Conners, as Ferguson let go of him.

It was dark, so Conners couldn't see Ferguson wince. The CIA officer patted the SF soldier on the arm, then started to climb up toward the door he'd found earlier.

"I'm going to stick the grenades in the door and jump," Ferguson told him. "If it works, it'll either blow a hole in the fuselage, or the door to the cockpit, or ignite the whole plane."

"Or it won't work," muttered Conners.

"Always a possibility," said Ferg.

Conners curled himself against the metal, hunkering his head down. The pain of his wounds hadn't disappeared, but his mind seemed to have pushed itself away from it. He felt as if he could think at least; he was conscious, awake, and knew he'd be awake when he died. That wasn't necessarily a good thing.

It took Ferguson two tries to get back on the ledge near the door. The small metal bar that had acted as a handle for the door was about a half inch too tight to hold them together; Ferguson squeezed it back but still didn't have enough room. He fit the Russian grenade in place and forced the stun grenade down, wedging it with his knife between the two devices. He tried to position the tip of the blade at the center of the Russian grenade, like a striker against a detonating cap, but he couldn't really see what he was doing. The flash-bang squeezed only about a third of the way down.

It wasn't going to work, Ferguson thought as he gripped the top of the M84 grenade.

Better to do *something*, Ferg's father always said, even if it's futile. You're going to pee your pants one way or another.

Maybe the sound of the damn flash-bang going off would scare the piss out of the terrorists, and they'd lose control of the airplane. Or maybe it would ignite the Russian grenade, shoot it through the cockpit, and put a hole in the back of the pilot.

And maybe they'd all just go boom. There certainly were enough explosives packed into the 747.

"So this is the way I go out, Dad," he said. He was speaking to his own father, not Conners, though maybe in a way he'd always been talking to his dad when he talked to the older SF man.

"See ya in heaven, boys," said Ferguson. He pulled the pin on the grenade, heard—or thought he heard—a click, then jumped off the ledge.

19

OVER THE PHILIPPINES

Rankin leaned out of the helicopter as it whipped over the compound. There was a docking area with a pair of small boats, but no helo in the flat helipad area at the side.

"Can we get down for a look?" he asked his pilot, pointing.

"Not a problem," replied the pilot, who like most Filipinos had spoken English all his life. The four choppers tucked downward, buzzing the shoreline and small building in formation. They turned back to land, slowing to a hover over a dirt road at the back of the facility. Rankin covered his face as he jumped off the skids, ducking and coughing as he ran toward the buildings. Six Filipino soldiers came off the helicopters behind him, and by the time Rankin rapped on the door to the small shack they were lined up at the corner of the building, ready for a takedown. Guns and Massette had their MP-5s out directly behind Rankin.

The soldier knocked several times, Uzi ready. He eyed the door and lock; it was flimsy, easy to kick down, but he was wary of booby traps.

"I'm going in," he told the others. He blew off the lock, tensing, expecting a booby trap. Nothing happened. He kicked in the door, hesitating as it flew against its hinges. But there were no explosives, no trip wires; it looked like the sleepy office of the sleepy, one- or two-man operation Corrigan said it claimed to be.

They went inside. There was a desk with two computers, some folders and old newspapers. Nautical memorabilia—a miniature ship's wheel, a decorative clock—were scattered around the room gathering dust.

"Looks like a water taxi office," said Guns. "Except that there's no dispatcher here to take calls."

"Maybe they're out," said Rankin. "Where do you figure the helicopter is?"

"I don't know. They're missing their boat as well," said Guns. "Neither of those little skiffs out there rates as a water taxi."

"You sure they have one?" Rankin asked.

"Either that or the picture's a fake," said the Marine, picking up a framed photo from the front desk.

"Maybe we should go look for them," suggested Rankin. They left Massette with the Filipinos to search and secure the building, with orders to seize the computers and papers as part of the terrorist investigation. Guns and Rankin climbed aboard one of the Defenders and pulled back out over the ocean.

"What are we looking for?" asked the pilot.

"This boat," said Rankin, showing him the picture.

"I can check with the Navy patrol," added the pilot.

"Go for it," said Rankin.

20

 Corrine felt as if her body deflated as the Navy pilots reported seeing the 747 disintegrating as it hit the water.

"Down, it's down," said Wolf.

"Good," she told him.

She turned to the others, giving them a thumbs-up. Then she punched back into Corrigan's line, relaying the information.

"I'm afraid Ferguson and Conners haven't been located yet," he said.

"Yes, I know."

Neither one stated the obvious—the two men were probably aboard the plane that had just been shot down.

"Navy is challenging an Indian flight over the northern Philippines," one of the communications specialists said to Corrine. "Data says it's a 707. They're off their filed flight plan, but they're a regular flight for Hawaii. Carry flowers, that sort of thing."

Corrine started to say that they could let it go, but then she remembered the bulletin Corrigan had issued earlier—the terrorists had two planes.

"Do they have it in sight?"

"Negative. It's responded properly to the civilian controllers, however. Looks like it's OK."

They all wanted to knock off. They deserved to. And this plane was a 707, not a 747—and Indian besides.

Corrine reached for the mike switch. Her job was to be the president's conscience, and she'd done it well, ordering the shootdown of the terrorist plane at the very last second—a tough decision that had to be made. Now it was time to go home.

Or was it? Nothing could be overlooked—that was the lesson of the boxcars, wasn't it?

"Tell them to get it in sight," she told the Navy controller. "Tell them to make sure it's a 707, not a 747. And don't just settle for a radar contact either."

She hit the switch and keyed back into Corrigan. "Mr. Corrigan, what was the information regarding the planes the Sri Lankan company owns?"

"Which ones?" asked Corrigan.

"They have 707s?"

"They have three, all being refurbished. Bought them surplus," Corrigan stopped, checking through his papers. "They got them from an Indian airline—I don't have the exact information in front of me. Is it important?"

Corrine turned back to the com specialist. "Set up a direct line to the Navy patrol, just like you did for Basher. I want that plane stopped."

21

 As the time to leave the plane sped toward him, Samman Bin Saqr thought more and more of staying in the plane, guiding it the next several thousand miles and ending in a blaze of glory in downtown Honolulu. After such a long struggle, paradise would be a welcome reward.

He reminded himself that there were many other battles to wage—the Americans would have to be taught again and again the reality of their sins. His next operation would be even greater. It was selfish to leave the fight so soon.

And so, as they cleared the last of the American patrols and adjusted course to skirt the Philippines as he had planned, Samman Bin Saqr undid his restraints and turned to his copilot.

"We are doing well, Vesh," he said over the intercom.

The copilot turned and smiled. As he did, Samman Bin Saqr reached to his outer thigh and drew the pistol from the pocket in his flight suit. He fired three bullets point-blank into Vesh's chest.

"You will still see heaven," he told his follower. "But this way it is guaranteed, with no opportunity for cowardice."

Samman Bin Saqr checked the autopilot unit, which had been customized to ensure it would reach its target. Once set, the aircraft would be locked on its path. Radio queries would be analyzed by a special computer section, with recorded answers played back to soothe inquiring minds.

Bin Saqr pressed the buttons in sequence. The yoke moved slightly, away from his hands. The Americans' fate was now set.

He smiled, permitting himself a moment of satisfaction, then rose from his seat. As he did, the rear of the flight deck exploded.

In the cargo hold, Ferguson threw himself over Conners as the flash bang detonated the Russian grenade. Rather than launching forward, the grenade's propellant exploded and set off the charge in the fuse as well. The shock wave rumbled through the plane, shaking its ribs like the water in a shallow bowl. Ferguson looked up and saw a shaft of light streaming above him from the flight deck. He jumped up, slamming his fingers into the metal and scrambling upward, gun in hand. He couldn't hear anything, not even the jet engines—the blast had temporarily deafened him.

The plane dipped forward. The door had remained intact, but the blast had punched a jagged, eighteen-inch hole through the middle. Ferguson scrambled on the ledge and saw that the welded bar at the side had been shattered. He put his hand on it to steady himself and felt it move as the plane began to dip sharply on its left wing. Ferguson started to fall backward but managed to grab the end of the bar, suspended for a moment in midair.

Inside the cabin, Samman Bin Saqr struggled to get up. He knew the devils had somehow managed to board his plane, and knew also that he would stop them. He pushed away from the captain's seat, his face wet with blood. He reached back to his thigh for his pistol, then wiped his eyes with his sleeve, trying to see.

As Ferguson struggled to hold his balance, he put his hand back on the doorframe. Before he could steady himself, however, the door began to slide down like a sled on a slippery slope; he pulled back as it shot to the floor, the aircraft still reeling in the sky. He threw himself into the empty white hole, falling onto the carpeted deck and losing his pistol.

Ferguson pushed upright as the plane tilted to the right. Something rose in front of him, more shadow than human, more devil than anything that breathed. Every ounce of energy in his worn and battered body boiled into rage, and Ferguson threw himself forward, forgetting everything but rage.

He grabbed Samman Bin Saqr by the neck. The terrorist swung his pistol wildly, firing and at the same time trying to hit his assailant with the barrel. Ferguson swung his right fist down into Samman Bin Saqr's temple, pounding and pounding.

The airplane, its automated pilot damaged by the shrapnel of the grenade, nosed into a dive, accelerating as the two men struggled. As its speed multiplied, the aerodynamic design of its airframe took over, stopping it from its plunge and making it rise. The two men tumbled backward, their fates intertwined with unfathomable hate and fury. Samman Bin Saqr managed to pull Ferguson over his side and pin him against the side control panel.

"I'll kill you, American," said Samman Bin Saqr, choosing English so his assailant could understand his last words.

Ferguson felt the barrel of the pistol against his head but heard nothing, still deaf. His gun was behind him somewhere, but he remembered the second flash-bang in his pocket. He reached desperately, hooking it with his thumb and trying to grab the pin, but the plane shifted downward again, rocking left and right with the windy turbulence outside. Ferguson slid the grenade around to get at the pin but then lost the grenade as Bin Saqr pressed against his hand.

The Muslim fanatic cursed as the American slid away from the barrel just as he fired the gun. Bin Saqr struggled to get the gun back and fire again. He would kill the devil, kill him, then fly the plane himself to his reward.

As he pulled the barrel close to Ferguson's head, he realized someone else was on the flight deck behind him. He turned, expecting somehow that Vesh had come back from the dead. But it wasn't—it was Conners, on his knees, a pistol in his hands. The SF sergeant squeezed off a shot; the nine-millimeter bullet caught Samman Bin Saqr square in the forehead as he turned.

The second bullet took off the top part of his skull and splattered a good portion of his brains against the side windscreen.

22

ABOARD SF COMMAND TRANSPORT 3

 As soon as Corrine heard the report from the Navy patrol, she knew that somehow, some way, Ferguson and Conners had managed to take over the aircraft.

"Can you raise it on the radio?" she asked.

"We're trying. Looks like it's out of control. It's flying south but very erratically."

Corrine looked over at Gray, who was tracking the position. "If they fly south another ten minutes, they'll be in a sea-lane," said the Air Force major. "Beyond that, they'll be over land."

She nodded, then clicked her mike to talk. "Close your distance so you can shoot them down," she told the Navy pilot. "I want you close enough to read any markings on that plane. If they don't respond to you and change their course, I want you to shoot them down."

"Understood. I'll get close enough for a cannon shot. I'll be right on top of him," replied the pilot.

"I don't care if you use an ax to take that plane down, as long as it's not over land."

23

Rankin spotted the speedboat fifty miles offshore. It was sitting in the middle of nowhere, a large radar revolving on a platform near the stern.

"Guns, why would a boat be way the hell out here?" Rankin asked.

"That a trick question?" the Marine asked, leaning forward from the rear bench.

"Let's take a look," Rankin told the pilot.

"Wait," said the pilot. "We're being hailed—the Navy fighters are warning off aircraft."

"Holy shit, look at that," said Guns, pointing out the right-side window. A 747 tucked out of the sky, weaving drunkenly.

Aboard the terrorist airplane, Ferguson squirmed around to get out of Samman Bin Saqr's death grip. His head pounded and he had trouble breathing; his mouth tasted blood.

Conners, worn-out by the exertion it had taken to get up to the cabin, remained on the floor, just barely conscious. Ferguson made his way over to him as the plane began to level off. He shook him; Conners looked up and smiled.

"Finnegan rises again," muttered the soldier. "Now what the hell do we do?"

Ferguson saw his mouth moving, but heard nothing.

"They got my ears fucked up, Dad. I can't hear—you can sing all you want."

Conners slumped back down. Ferguson shook him—they'd have to figure out how the radio worked so they could get instructions on how to fly the plane and maybe ditch it in the water. Since he couldn't hear, he needed Conners awake.

Ferguson saw a door at the rear quarter of the flight deck. Realizing it must be a bathroom and thinking he could use the water to revive Conners, he pushed into the small space. A man he only vaguely recognized as himself gaped at him from the mirror. Ferguson started to laugh. He lost his balance, falling onto the toilet, whose lid fortunately was closed. He looked down at his shoes. Between his feet was a ring lock; the bottom of the floor was a hatchway.

Ferguson reached down and pulled at the latch; it moved, but to open the panel he'd have to go back outside.

"I think I found out how they set the bomb," he told Conners. He saw the sergeant's mouth move in response—Conners only grunted—then told him to get his rest; he'd figure out how to defuse it himself.

"Or I may blow us up," he added. For some reason, the idea struck him as the funniest thing he had ever thought of, and he was still laughing as he pulled the panel upward.

Instead of the bomb controls, he found a parachute rig. As he took it out, he saw there was a hatchway below it, with a large locking wheel in the middle.

"Some fuckin' martyrs," he said, examining the bag and webbing.

Jumping from an airliner was difficult under the best circumstances; Ferguson had gone out of C-141s and done both high-altitude, high-opening (HAHO) and high-altitude, low-opening (HALO) jumps, but always with the help of a special baffle that allowed for an easy—relatively speaking—egress from the airplane.

On the other hand, he figured, if these fucks could do it, he could.

But there was only one rig.

Ferguson sat Conners up against the side of the cockpit and got him to hold the thick webbing of the chute straps in his hands. He climbed into the pilot's seat, wondering what the odds were of flying the aircraft to some sort of landing. As he pulled against the unresponsive yoke—the autopilot had been rigged to completely override the cockpit controls once locked—a yellow streak flashed across the bow of the plane. Ferguson, unsure at first what he was seeing, stared as the streak turned black, then disappeared. He turned to his left, looking out the window.

A Navy jet flashed below. Ferguson pounded on the glass and cursed. Something crashed into the plane hard from behind; he felt a low rumble, and realized they were shooting at the plane. He reached to grab the headset from the dead copilot, then remembered that he still couldn't hear. Cursing, he jumped back up.

"Dad, let's get the fuck out of here," said Ferguson.

Conners saw his companion's face as he picked him up. He had no idea where they were—a bar back in Jersey? He wondered.

Then he remembered they were in the terrorist airplane.

"We gotta get the bastards," he told Ferguson, who for some reason was turning him around.

The straps would only fit around one of them. Ferguson put the rig on Conners so that the chute was on his stomach, then managed to work his own leg through the left strap and tied himself to his companion with his belt. The arrangement wouldn't exactly pass muster with the U.S. Parachute Association, but it was going to have to do—the aircraft waddled and shook with a fresh round of cannon shots at the rear.

Ferguson pulled Conners with him to the air lock. It turned easily, and as soon as it hit its stop, began to descend. Unsure what was happening, Ferguson hesitated a moment, then saw a side brace inset into the opening, which looked as if it were a manhole opening for a sewer. He grabbed for it, pushing over, then felt a rush of air. The plane's nose kicked toward the earth—Ferguson and Conners fell into the opening, which extended like a laundry chute through the bottom of the aircraft and below the fuselage and its murderous jet stream. As soon as they were inside the wind howled; Ferguson tried to instinctively grab on to the side to stop his fall but a jet of air forced him and Conners downward and away from the plane, literally spitting them toward the ground, temporarily overcoming the fierce counterforces near the airfoil. In an instant they were tumbling free, in about as uncontrolled a free fall as possible, projectiles tossed from the underside of the aircraft.

They'd gone out around twelve thousand feet, which under other circumstances might have been considered an easy jump. It allowed for about a minute of free fall before it would be necessary to pull the rip cord, which ideally Ferguson would do around three thousand feet. But as he spread his arms to try to arch, he felt Conners lurching away from him. Ferguson grabbed at him, shouting for him to arch and trying to pull his upper body back in a way that, to his confused mind, would perfectly stabilize them. As he did, the parachute exploded out of the pack, preset by an automatic altimeter. Caught unprepared, Ferg jerked back, hanging off Conners as they spun wildly in the air. He saw the nylon of the canopy rising and spreading above him, and pushed over the trooper to grab at the togs, which would control their descent.

The chute had been designed and packed for a high-altitude opening, and it unfolded in slow motion, which made it somewhat easier for Ferguson to react and get control. But he was working practically upside down, and even if he'd been completely upright, the weight of the two men would have knocked off the custom-designed rig. Ferg couldn't even reach the left tog. The cells of the chute filled, slowing them, but then the uneven tilt pushed the left side of the canopy in. The rear flagged out, catching the wind but pitching Ferguson around awkwardly as he struggled to grab the other controls. The blood drained from his arms and head. He felt dizzy, and his stomach flipped over.

The chute stalled, and Ferg's hand slipped off the toggle; the two men sailed forward, stopped in the air, sailed forward again, rocking crookedly as they descended.

The boat jerked to life as the parachute opened. Rankin realized what was going on—it had been sent to retrieve the pilot of the 747.

Rankin pulled up his Uzi, checking it to make sure it was ready, while Guns did the same with his MP-5 in the back.

Above and to the west, the terrorists' flying dirty bomb veered toward the empty ocean, arcing on its left wing. Black smoke trailed from the belly of the plane. Blackness enveloped the underside. Something flew off the plane—its right wing, shattered by cannon fire from the F/A-18 and sheared off by the violent aerodynamic forces as it plunged. The plane put down its nose like an otter, diving into a lake; then it plunged into the water, breaking up as it hit and disappearing in a cloud of steam.

"The chute," Rankin told the chopper pilot. "They're almost in the water. Go. We want to take the boat out before it gets there. Go!"

When they hit the water, Ferguson felt his stomach explode, ice and vomit crashing together in his mouth. In the next second he was underwater. His fingers fumbled to release the belt and strap, tearing at the metal locks impotently. Desperate to breathe, he pulled his right hand free, then tore at the harness. Caught by the wind, the chute pulled away, bringing him to the surface, then dying back down as it filled. Ferguson managed to undo it from Conners first, then kicked and got his leg out as the chute pulled away. He fell below into the darkness of the cold water, still attached to Conners by his belt. He pushed upward, feeling Conners kick as well. Fresh air hit his eyes; he gulped and got only a little water in his mouth.

There was a boat nearby, a hull or something—Ferguson started to push toward it but a swell caught him from behind and smashed him back down.

Rankin and Guns stood in the helicopter, emptying their guns at the occupants of the boat. One of the men brought up a shoulder-launched SAM just as Rankin started to reload. The American slammed home the fresh clip, and in the same motion pressed the trigger of the gun; the Uzi hiccuped, then splattered into the terrorist, who had raised the missile, sending both flying backward into the ocean.

"They're there, they're there!" yelled Guns, and in the next second he'd whipped off his boots and jumped from the helo, the spray strong in his face as he left the bird. He took two powerful strokes after he surfaced, grabbed Conners by the chest, and pulled. The sergeant felt heavier than he'd thought, but two strong kicks brought them to the stern of the boat, which was slowly taking on water from the bottom.

Rankin, not as a strong a swimmer, was just pulling himself up the other side. Ferguson pushed Conners up on deck and found himself being dragged there as well. The Filipino helicopter swung in an orbit around them as an F/A-18 whipped overhead.

Released from the belt, Ferguson flopped on his back in the open speedboat, not sure whether he was alive or dead or dreaming. Guns and Rankin pulled Conners to the back, propping his head on a cushion as they worked to revive him.

For all four men, time had ceased to exist. The past and the present and the future swelled in the spray of the waves, churning in an endless moment that had no boundaries. And then one by one they fell from it, coming back to human time, human hurt, human triumph and fear—all except Conners.

Ferg didn't understand at first. His hearing had come back in his left ear, though not his right, and when Guns told him, he shook his head, thinking he didn't quite get it.

"Dad's gone, Ferg. He was too shot up," said the soldier.

"He was alive on the plane," said Ferguson, who wanted that to make a difference.

Guns shook his head and shrugged. Tears were slipping from his eyes.

"He was fucking alive," said Ferg.

EPILOGUE

For some must watch while some must sleep,
Thus runs the world away.

—Shakespeare, *Hamlet*, 3.2.273–4

![1]

 Corrine felt the tears starting to come even before the monsignor approached the lectern at the side of the altar. Like many of those crowded into the large church, the monsignor had known the Conners family for decades, and when he talked of the sergeant, still remembered him as a young man. The priest's words weren't elegant, but they came from the heart; he spoke of sacrifice and duty, and he illustrated those qualities with things he had seen Conners do himself. Even Van Buren, sitting next to Corrine, felt tears forming in his eyes.

As Rankin and Ferguson got up to join Conners's relatives and friends bearing their comrade from the church, Corrine noticed that Ferguson had an odd smile on his face. She thought to herself that he was a cold creature, a man so out of touch with his emotions that he couldn't cry. His eyes met hers. She shook her head; he smiled and seemed to wink at her.

Rankin had found a real trumpeter to play taps at the cemetery, but there was a surprise waiting next to the tarped pile of dirt when they reached the graveyard—a bagpiper, who played two songs, one a dirge, the other closer to a jig. And then one by one the mourners went to the grave, tossing their flowers.

Ferguson was the last to go to the grave. He knelt and slipped a bottle from his pocket.

"For you, Dad," he said, sliding the whiskey gently down to lie at Conners's head. He looked back as he walked away, part of him truly expecting that Conners would pull a real-life Finnegan and rise from the grave.

In the car, Corrine took out her sat phone and checked for messages. One had come from Corrigan—the Team was needed for a briefing ASAP. The war against terror knew no days off.

"My car's at the airport," she told Rankin and Guns. "I can drive you over."

"Sounds good," said Rankin. Van Buren had already offered him a lift, but he preferred riding with her.

"Hey, what about Ferg?" said Guns.

"What about him?" said Rankin. "He was with one of the cousins. They gave him a lift."

"He know where we're going?" asked Guns.

"Call him," Corrine said.

Rankin made a face, but took out his phone. Ferg's voice mail answered, and he left the message.

An hour after he left the cemetery, Ferguson strode into the bar that Conners had told him about while they were on their mission in Chechnya. Its wood-lined walls were thick with the accumulation of nearly a century's worth of tobacco smoke, and the polished surface of the bar had heard a million tales of glory and misery. It was only one o'clock in the afternoon, but the place already had a decent crowd. There was a lively buzz in the air, the sort of sound that made Ferg glad his hearing had come back.

"Two shots whiskey, neat, both of 'em," Ferg said, pulling his wallet. "Beer chasers—make it Guinny," he said, pointing at the Guinness tap.

As the bartender poured the drinks, Ferguson took a tape out of his pocket.

"I wonder if you'd play this for a friend of mine," Ferg told him.

The bartender took the tape and looked at it quizzically. He was an older man, and he'd heard much stranger requests than this, so he shrugged and went over to the tape deck, putting in.

Liam Clancy's voice filled the bar, off an old album Ferguson's sister had tracked down for him. Ferg raised his shot glass and turned to the room, adding his own to Clancy's as he came to the final verse of "Parting Glass":

> All the comrades that ever I had,
> They're sorry for my going away
> And all the sweethearts that ever I had
> They wish me one more day to stay.
> But since it falls unto my lot
> That I should rise and you should not
> I'll gently go and softly call,
> 'Goodnight and joy be with you all.'

As the song faded, Ferguson tossed the whiskey down his throat and turned back to the bar. Standing, he reached into his pocket and pulled out a thick wad of hundred-dollar bills, withdrawn from his personal account that morning. He spread them out on the bar near the untouched shot glass.

"No one pays for their own drink today," he said. "All for the honor of Sergeant Hugh Conners, a braver man you'll never see."

And then he took a last sip from his beer, leaving the glass half-full as he walked out into the cold New Jersey afternoon, alone.